Heavenly's Child

By Brenda Reid

The House of Dust and Dreams

Heavenly's Child

BRENDA REID

First published in Great Britain in 2012 by Orion Books,
an imprint of The Orion Publishing Group Ltd
Orion House, 5 Upper Saint Martin's Lane
London WC2H 9EA

An Hachette UK Company

1 3 5 7 9 10 8 6 4 2

A CIP catalogue record for this book is
available from the British Library.

ISBN (Hardback) 978 1 4091 1473 4
ISBN (Trade Paperback) 978 1 4091 1474 1
ISBN (ebook) 978 1 4091 1475 8

Typeset at The Spartan Press Ltd,
Lymington, Hants

Printed and bound by CPI Group (UK) Ltd,
Croydon, CR0 4YY

The Orion Publishing Group's policy is to use papers
that are natural, renewable and recyclable products and
made from wood grown in sustainable forests. The logging
and manufacturing processes are expected to conform to
the environmental regulations of the country of origin.

www.orionbooks.co.uk

For Daisy, Trixie, Cora, Calum, Sophy,
Margot, Theo, Bailey, Sasha and Jessie
with very much love

ACKNOWLEDGEMENTS

I owe so much to Fanis Eikosipendakis and his mother, Eutoxia. They selflessly relived fast-fading memories with me as did many of the villagers in Pefki, Crete, along with their friendship.

Many thanks are due to my agent Zoe Waldie and her assistant Mohsen Shah at Rogers, Coleridge and White. Also to my inspired editor Kate Mills who, along with Susan Lamb, Juliet Ewers and Jemima Forrester at Orion, help with all the mysterious mechanics of turning my words into a published book.

Thank you, Constantinos Pappadopoulos and your team at Dioptra, especially Glykeria Dimitropoulou who dealt with all my research questions with warmth and knowledge. Also Daphne Djaferis, an old friend who took me to the gates of the Athens polytechnic and showed me her city, and Vasso who drove me around it on her motorbike. A special thank you to Mikis Theodorakis who provided musical inspiration with his Anthem for November 18th 1973.

Zafeirenia Proestaki helped me with the Greek language, and thanks to C.M. Woodhouse whose knowledge of modern Greek history is unsurpassed.

And for David, always. His generosity and love makes me believe I can do anything.

AUTHOR'S NOTE

After the Second World War in Europe, Greece, like many other countries, struggled to come to terms with the peace. Competing factions sprang up everywhere. Brother was set against brother; father against son. There are as many definitive histories of those bitter years of civil war as those who claim them to be false.

The only certain thing is that on 21st April 1967 a group of high-ranking military officers seized power and ruled, often ruthlessly, for the next ten years. Throughout the reign of 'The Junta', through good times and bad ordinary Greeks tried their best to carry on with their lives while, all the time, resentment and loathing of the unelected 'colonels' grew like a contagion until, on the night of 17th November 1973, it exploded with a ferocity that touched the lives of every man woman and child and still reverberates through Greece to this day.

ANGEL

It was in the heat of a midsummer day that I came home. I smiled all the way from Heraklion, simply because I was here, and I ran up the steps from the little square to our house, still known all these years later as the old Orfanoudakis house.

There was the vine springing through the cracked stones of the threshold, the dusty red geranium still clinging on with very little dignity, looking as though the slightest breeze would bowl it over.

It was the afternoon, so most of the village was sleeping after a morning spent in the fields; taking goats to pasture, collecting honey from the hives on the hillsides or, if you were a woman, cooking, sweeping and cleaning the house as well.

My brother Will was coming up the steps behind me, carrying my trunk; a battered old leather one my parents had used travelling around the world. Will is so strong that he swung it along as if it were a bag of feathers.

As she heard us, Will's girlfriend Lucy came running out, her face rich with a lovely smile, pink from the sun and probably the heat of the kitchen. That's what Lucy does; she cooks. I was happy to see her. I love her and I'm so glad for Will that he found her. But as she hugged me, still I wished it were my mother here to greet me.

I ran around the house from room to room checking that nothing had changed.

The pile of many-coloured cushions in one corner of the long living room was the same as ever. I knelt down, my hand brushing across the soft, aging silk, the brilliance of the scarlets, lavenders, greens faded long ago but there was a faint perfume rising from them releasing a million memories for me. All of them happy.

My scaggy nails caught on a delicate thread and pulled a magenta strand free.

In the other corner, ranged around the stone circle of the old winepress, were the dried fruits – apples, plums, grapes, pomegranates and the prickly browning leaves of artichokes – that my mother and I had collected walking on the hillside last year and the years before. They gave off musty sweet scents, filling that great room with the hunger for fresh-picked versions of the same.

Everywhere reminded me of my mother. I longed to see her, have her hug me to her. I needed her to help me understand and explain to my father the things that had gone wrong for me recently.

This house, this village, Panagia Sta Perivolia, in the far south-east of Crete, is where Will and I grew up, and everything then seemed to be perfect. My father was in Athens, a diplomat at the embassy there, and visited us only for the odd weekend or holiday. I'm afraid I always felt a great sense of relief when he left each time. He's a stickler for good behaviour, brushed hair, neat clothes and all the other things I struggle to get right.

I knew it was him who made me go away to a boarding school in England and I remember dear Will trying to make it better for me; telling me of his time in our father's old school.

Lucy cooked us a wonderful dinner. All my favourite things: a mix of tiny dishes of olives, anchovies, crispy rings of squid – a *meze* it's called here – and then lamb roasted in the oven with lemons and herbs. Lucy has a column in one of those glossy women's magazines you see in dentists' waiting rooms. She's a little bit famous.

The mothers of girls in my school read her recipes and their daughters told me. It didn't do much for my popularity even so. I always felt I was a misfit. There is the problem of my name for a start, Angel. I gave up ages ago trying to persuade

English people to call me Angeliki (Ann-gell-ee-kee), my real name. They always just laugh.

'It's Greek,' I say and off they go again, as though I had told some great joke.

Actually, I was supposed to be named after my mother's best friend, Anthi, but my father never liked this friend much so Angel it is. I'm very tall and clumsy. Mother says she was too but it doesn't help, because she's certainly very graceful now. Worst of all, I think, is that my hair is curly and frizzy and sticks out all over the place and it's sort of brown with red bits, conker coloured. Will says I look like our mother, who's got rather wild reddish hair but he's got to be joking, *she's* beautiful.

And of course I was totally hopeless at all those English games; lacrosse, hockey, netball, tennis. I'm a whizz at back-gammon though – I can beat Will and my father.

After I helped Will clear away I said, 'Can I go to see Chrissi now?'

Chrissi was my very best friend in the world and I had missed her more than anyone except my mother and Will.

There was a sudden silence and Will said, 'Of course, but I'll have to come with you.'

'Lovely, but why? I do know the way.'

'There's a curfew now in the villages. No child to be out at night without a parent.'

'What? Why? It's 1971 not 1871! And anyway, I'm sixteen. Not exactly a child.'

'No one really knows why,' Will said. 'It's a new govern-ment rule.'

'Girls get married here at fourteen – are *they* allowed out alone?'

Lucy said, 'Stay here with us just this evening, why not? Will has missed you so much and he's off again in a week or so and won't be back for ages.'

I stayed; of course I did. Will is my super-hero. He's ten years older than me but he's always looked out for me. When I was little, here in the village everyone was mostly really nice to me, I think because of Will. That was then, now he's this brilliant filmmaker. He makes documentaries. Last year a film he'd made about the Amazon River was on the BBC and he was interviewed on the Greek television news. He was so young to have spent months making the film alone. Here in the village there is a television set at the Piperia and everyone crowded in to watch and cheered when he came on; I know it's true, because Chrissi wrote and told me.

Will's really handsome. He's tall too, of course, taller than me, but he moves like a lion – smooth and easy. He has the same hair as me, but all black, and on him it looks great, like Mick Jagger. He's better looking than Mick, even Chrissi says so and she says she's saving her virginity for Mick – as if!

I remember when that television set was put in. It was 1965 and Greece was trying to qualify to get into the World Cup the next year. They didn't; they only came third in their group, so we were all fed up. Lots of people here were supporters of Panathanaikos, and eight of them were in the Greek side, but even so, no luck. I remember it well; probably because it was the following year, 1966, that my whole life changed.

Father was sent off to a different embassy; this time in Thailand, a million miles away, and he absolutely insisted my mother went with him. She told me as gently as she could, but it meant I was going to be sent to a school in England, a girls' school at that. The village school here is mixed, of course, and although I know we are English underneath, in my opinion I'm really mostly Greek. Actually Cretan, that's what I am.

The only good thing about it was that my mother took me to England herself, just the two of us. And she made it into a treat. We went a bit early and had two whole days in London. We stayed in a really grand hotel, one that Father's secretary arranged for us and we had a whole suite of rooms just to ourselves. Even two bathrooms – one each!

You could stand on the silk couch in front of the window and see all the buses going down Piccadilly – hundreds of them; one after another, after another.

First we did all the boring bits like getting my uniform.

It was grey, grey and more grey, with just the occasional tiny bit of miserable burgundy red. Even a grey hat.

We went to several museums, but only the really interesting ones. We looked at the Elgin Marbles in the British Museum. What a cheek they have, calling them that! Years ago, this old Englishman, Lord Elgin, hacked them out of the Acropolis in Athens, broke lots of bits off and shipped them any old how over to England. Most people in Greece – and Mother and me – think they should come back and be the Parthenon Marbles again.

For the rest of that day we just walked around London looking at people and what they were wearing.

It was like stepping into a different world! No, another planet. All my entire life I had lived in a place where nothing changed for hundreds of years. There were no shops, because nobody needed them. Everyone grew what they ate and ate what they grew. All the scrappy bits went to the chickens or the goats. But in London you can buy baked potatoes and roast chestnuts on the street. Or ice cream; all different flavours.

Not much grey there. There were girls with skirts that stopped just below their bums. I said, 'Imagine Chrissi and me walking around Panagia wearing those?'

'Would you like to?' And this was my mother!

We went to somewhere in Chelsea she said she had lived in for a while when she was young. And there the girls were not just wearing these weeny skirts; they had long white boots as well. White! What would happen if they walked through rain or mud? I said, 'Maybe we should take a pair back for Yorgo to wear instead of his black mountain boots.'

And we both found the thought of Chrissi's father in white boots so hilarious that we almost fell over giggling.

'They are for women,' Mother said, 'so we should get a pair for Aphrodite.'

That was Chrissi's mother; she is sixty and as wide as a London taxi, so we giggled even more.

The second day we went to Liberty's where my mother bought some clothes for very hot weather – embassy-lady frocks, swirly and floaty and silky with lots of flowers on them. Then round the back of Liberty was the most amazing place of all – Carnaby Street. There were boys singing Beatles' songs in the street and people dancing and everyone wore brilliant colours and had hair rather like mine, sort of wavy, and long ponytails – even the men.

'This is where the Beatles come shopping.'

After that I was looking for them everywhere, even just one. John especially – he's my favourite. There was suddenly a noise like goat bells on the Panagia hillside and I spun round to see a little group of people, I think they were men, walking down the middle of the road. They were all wearing orange togas and chanting.

'What are they saying?' Mother asked a man.

He laughed. 'Harry Krishna,' he said.

I caught her eye and we shrugged at each other, no wiser.

There were girls in long cotton frocks with their hair in plaits – hundreds of plaits, and necklaces, beads. They handed out flowers to people and smiled. There was a lovely smell in the air, sort of musky and sweet. Like cigarettes but not cigarettes; something else. We went into a restaurant in a basement nearby, called Jimmy's, and we had Greek food! The walls were all curved over into the ceiling and tiled like a bathroom.

In the afternoon we went to a cinema called the Academy and saw a French film with English subtitles and the girl in that was wearing a black polo neck sweater. I loved that. And when we came out into the light of the afternoon we went to a shop near Piccadilly, a French shop called Galeries Lafayette, and Mother bought me one just like it. It's my favourite thing, and even though I've now almost grown out of it, I still wear it a lot.

Then suddenly it was Friday morning and our last lovely breakfast in the hotel and even the delicious frilly scrambled eggs couldn't make me smile. The waiter bent towards me and whispered, 'Cheer up. It may never happen!' But I knew it would.

Then it was time to get the train to Surrey to this school. I was almost counting the minutes, our last time together.

My mother was smiling as we walked around the streets of Greenbridge. She kept pointing to places and telling me stories of when she'd been a nurse in the hospital there. That was where she had met my father.

And then she was gone and I was there in that school on my own. And I was so absolutely determined that I wasn't going to cry that I could only walk about with my face all screwed up so that girls, hundreds of them, looked at me and giggled and moved away. And that night was probably the worst night of my entire life so far. It was the first time I had been away from my mother for all night. When she hugged me and said goodbye, I thought her face looked all screwed up too and I wondered if she was crying that night. And if she was and she was miserable without me and I was miserable without her, then why the bloody were we not together?

After that I knew that nothing would ever be the same again. It felt to be a time of nothingness; an endless trail of days, not to be remembered, all filled with meaningless hours with people I scarcely even knew. Some were teachers, some were pupils. Everyone seemed to look the same. Everyone was grey. There was a lot of laughter around me, but I never understood, never learnt how to join in.

And I did try, I really did but every single thing was different to the village school in Panagia. There, there were just three classrooms: one for the babies, one for the middling ones and then a small one for the seniors. Chrissi and I were just about to go into that one when I had to leave and I'd looked forward to it so much. The Greenbridge school was called The Oaks; but I never saw one oak tree anywhere near and there were fifteen classrooms – fifteen! Everyone looked the same in those horrible uniforms and it took me months to learn all the names.

Anyway, now I've been thrown out of that school, expelled, and my father is going to be completely outraged.

Will jumped up. It was twilight already and we were sitting on the terrace, and the stars here, even though they are the same all over the world, are brighter and shine more glowingly than anywhere else. Certainly more than in England. Lucy was yawning, and trying to cover it up. Will stood up and said, 'You go to bed, and Angel and I will go for a walk.' I was not at all tired, just happy to have a chance to be with Will on my own.

We followed the path around and up and past the Piperia where some of the village elders were sitting under the great branches of the pepper tree playing cards. They paused as we passed and waved a greeting. I couldn't help but smile. We crept past; disturb the game at your peril. They are here every night playing a complicated game called *prefa*, which seems to have no ending. Chrissi and I play it sometimes but we're rubbish. It seems mostly to consist of banging the cards down hard on the table and anyone who didn't know would think they had stumbled upon World War Three, so passionate did it sound.

We joined the mountain path winding up and up and passed some villagers coming home with their goats and they all shouted '*Ya*' to us, 'hello'.

There was the cluster of houses forming Pano Panagia – the upper village. Below there was Mesa, the middle part with our house at the edge and further down is Kato, the lowest part tucked snugly in at the bottom.

The air was heavy with the animal scent of warm fur and that curious goaty smell that echoes the taste of goats' milk or cheese, which is one of the main parts of their food. I sniffed it in. It's one of the things I've missed, being in England, that smell.

The whole of Panagia sits near the top of a mountain, all the houses seeming to cling to the side of it. If you shut your eyes and listened you could mostly hear just silence and then slowly a bird will start to sing, cicadas will clatter and the bells of the goats will ting ting. With every step I saw the dying rays of the sun sinking in the still warm sky. I felt such a surge of happiness to be back. Looking around me I saw the two great arcs of mountains enclosing and seeming to protect this little heaven. The slopes fell gently away beneath. Every curl in the land is like a caress, and every turn seemed framed like a painting in the cypress trees.

We left the last houses behind us, even those crumbling into the hillside with their tiny windows. In front of one of them, fresh washing told of the life inside. Darned white sheets, denim overalls, two head kerchiefs, under-drawers (extra large size) and a pink brassiere so big you could swing a pair of fat twins in it.

The old couple that lived inside ran out to call to us.

We waved and smiled and Will said, 'Did you hear that? She called you Heavenly.'

We stopped to pick some of the herbs that fill the air with perfume up here; sage, thyme, wild garlic and lavender and the pungent *rigani* that seems to be in every Greek thing I've ever eaten. I know all the names – Lucy taught me.

Will sat, his back against a rock. The sky was turning rapidly into night. That's how it is here. We were sitting on one of the goat tracks that pepper these hills and I could no longer see Will's face.

'I guess that couple remember Mother when she first came here. You and Heavenly they called them. Couldn't quite manage Hugh and Evadne.'

'He never liked her being called that, did he? Everyone calls her Heavenly now.'

'Probably not in Thailand, though.'

'Oh I do wish she didn't have to be there. I miss her so much. You're all right, you've got Lucy.'

'Father said after the war, when she lived here in the village on her own for years, he'd never go through that again. "A wife is a wife," he said to me once, "not someone who does up an old ruin five hundred miles away."'

'She told me about that. She worked on it, didn't she? With Chrissi's father and his nephew who came from over Sitia way. That was brave for a woman in those days.'

A slight breeze riffled through lavender, brought the sweet scent in our direction.

Will took out a cigarette. As he lit it, I said, 'Can I have a drag?'

He passed it to me and said, 'Are you telling me you're smoking now, is that it?'

'The odd puff; it was the only thing to look forward to – a ciggie at the weekend.'

'Nothing else? '

'Well, sometimes a glass of sherry as well.'

'Sherry? No one under sixty drinks sherry, do they?'

'I drank it here, with Chrissi, last year. It was in the drinks cupboard. I think Mother bought it to try to wean Father off the *raki*.'

'About the school, being expelled, and the barn,' I started. 'I was just doing an experiment.'

'And?'

'And, well, it is true. It was only a little bit of straw, and it was a sunny day and I just happened to have a magnifying glass with me. What I didn't know was how fast it would work. And it spread to the barn and well, it was sort of burning a bit.'

'A bit? How much is a bit?'

'I didn't know it would go up like that. Honestly.'

'You're going to have to tell the parents, you know that, don't you?'

'Do we have to do it straight away? Can't we just—'

'No, Angel, we can't just anything. I promised Dame Rachel, whatever-her-name-is, your headmistress, we would do it when we left. That's already two days ago. You never know, Hugh might just decide to ring you up there. Then what?'

'He's never rung me up, not once. Anyway, I thought it would be good to have a plan when you tell him.'

'Did you? What plan is that, and since when do I have to tell him for you?'

'I thought it would sound better coming from you.'

'There's only one way it's going to sound.'

'I know, I know. But the plan is: I thought I could go to the *gymnasio* in Tres Petromas. Finish there.'

He laughed, 'It's not exactly known for its excellence academically. Father won't accept that. You've obviously worked hard at The Oaks; all your exam results are top grade.'

'There was nothing there to do except work.'

'Well, Father is going to be very impressed with that; he's going to insist you finish at a similar school: if they'll take you. You'd better come up with one that doesn't have any barns.'

'You mean if I hadn't worked hard, if I hadn't done well, he'd probably let me go to school here?'

'I know it's tough, but in a way, yes.'

'That is so unfair.'

'I'm sorry, Pickle, but where would you live?'

The moon was out again and lit up his face, he was smiling. He hasn't called me that since I was a baby.

'With Lucy.'

'She may stay on for a bit, but then she will have to get back to London.'

'I could stay with Aphrodite and Yorgo. I'm sure they would have me.'

He jumped up. 'You can ask Father, but don't get your hopes up. Come on,' he said, 'you must be tired; it's been a long day.'

Slowly we walked back through the dark. Will was slightly ahead of me.

I said, 'What will happen to me now? Where will I go?'

But he was busy pushing aside gorse and brambles and I don't think he heard me.

I caught up with him.

'Where are you going next? Lucy said you are only here until next week.'

'Afghanistan; I'm making a film about the lapis lazuli

13

mountains there. Not many people know that there are great caves in the mountains lined with that brilliant blue stone. Almost a wonder of the world, I think.'

Again I was stumbling along the path downwards, following in his giant strides.

'Do you have to go so soon? I feel I've only had you for such a short time.'

'I must. I have to go to Athens and sort out my visa. Things like that.'

Lucy was asleep on the terrace in one of the big steamer chairs there. Will crouched down and stroked her forehead where little tendrils of hair clung. She smiled without opening her eyes. I felt a pang of jealousy. I walked to the edge of the terrace and looked at the lower village where the houses were clinging to the mountain. I could smell the deep lavender scent of the dark. Some windows glittered with light; bright and sharp. Of course, that was what was different. Some of the houses now have electric light. We do, in the Orfanoudakis house but my mother always preferred the soft glow of the oil lamps and Lucy had lit them. Mother would be pleased by that.

The air was hot and still. Only the call of a lone falcon broke the silence around me. A moment and then the high shrill screech of some small rodent told me that his hunt had been successful this night.

It was our neighbour Irini's cockerel that woke me the next morning. I was about to stuff my head under the pillow and ignore the world for a bit longer, but then, within moments the church bell started to call for some worshippers. Bong bong bong, bong bong bong – the triple chimes of a Greek service, so much simpler than the great clangs of English ones.

And then I thought of Chrissi, probably already up. It was June, so school was out, and this was the time to see her. I was up and away, leaving Will and Lucy still sleeping. They'd know where I would be.

But I didn't get even to the path leading down to her house

14

when she appeared, running along towards me. We shrieked as we collided and grabbed each other in a hug and a dance.

'I knew you'd be here now. I couldn't wait. Aphrodite wants me to go and dig in the *gypo* but I had to see you first; it's been ages and ages.'

'I know; so much to tell you!'

We could hardly stop hugging each other. I just wanted to laugh and shout and dance up and down. It's a year since I've seen her.

'You've grown,' I said and she looked at me and said,

'Guess what? So have you.'

We walked back along the path, arm in arm, matching our steps together.

I do seem to tower over her a bit. I wouldn't say it to her, but Chrissi is stocky and she has definitely got bulges under her top – breasts.

We practically spent our entire childhoods together on the floor in Aphrodite's kitchen or ours. Hers always smelled gorgeous. Aphrodite was a wonderful cook and there were usually big pots of mysterious and delicious things bubbling in there.

'Do you want to tell me about your school?'

I shook my head violently.

'No I absolutely do not. I've been chucked out so I never have to go back there.'

'We heard that.'

'Tell me what's going on here? Have you been over to Aghios Demetrious much?'

'A bit.'

'Any trouble?'

She shrugged. 'You might have to help me out with a bit of a problem I've got from there.'

Aghios Demetrious was three kilometres away around the mountain. Everyone in Panagia reckons they are really descended from Turks round there. We are sworn enemies and there have always been a few fights on Saturday nights. Usually it's all blown over in a couple of days.

'Why? What do you mean?'

'I got myself into a game of truth or dare.'

'And?'

'Thing is, I've got to . . . I can hardly tell you, it's too awful.'

'What, Chrissi, what?'

She turned her back to me and said over her shoulder, 'I've been dared to hang my knickers on the flagpole in the square.'

I collapsed, helpless with giggles.

'I'm not going to tell you any more than that, so don't even ask.' She was bright pink now. I've never seen Chrissi blush before.

I hugged her. 'We'll do it together. When's it supposed to happen?'

'Saturday night.'

I counted quickly on my fingers – 'That's tomorrow!'

'I just prayed you'd be back in time to do it with me.'

'Of course I will.'

'Do you know about the curfew?' I nodded. 'That makes it even more difficult.'

'Oh pouf, it's nothing. You've climbed up there before haven't you?' She nodded. 'Well, we'll do it together, don't worry. It'll be a laugh.'

We ran on to her house and there was Aphrodite, and she gave me a great hug. She smelt like she always did, faintly of cinnamon mixed with a flowery hint of mimosa and honey. Whatever happened in the wider world, Aphrodite seemed never to change. Chrissi had inherited her mother's build: round but not fat, just comfortable in every way. And nothing seemed ever to surprise her; world wars, drought, hunger and poverty passed around her and her smile was always ready; her kitchen full of comforting food, her arms wide with welcome.

I wouldn't swap all this for anything. This feeling of being in the right place, being back where I belong, being home.

APHRODITE

It is five days since the last inspection of my house. For sure I know they will come today or tomorrow and nothing is ready, nothing changed.

Ah! *Panagia mou.* What a way to live your life. Always waiting for the voice over your shoulder. The sharp, barked question as if I am a dog in training.

My old neighbour, Anthi, writes me from her farm in Zealand, it's where she lives now. She tells me people knock on your door there, if they want to come in. Imagine the Papa coming here: 'Knock knock, oh Aphrodite, oh Yorgo, may we come in please? Can we see your walls are clean with new *asvesti*? May we just have a little look to see if your children have clean shoes and underwear? Thank you so much.'

Easier to imagine my bees giving us fruit jam or the olives giving us wine. Pah! Now I sound like my Yorgo – foolish.

Only two of our children are at home now; Manoli who works side by side in Yorgo's shadow, and our youngest, my baby, Chrissi.

Manoli is just a little slow, that's the truth. Not quite right in his head. He can't read any words. If he writes his own name, he writes it backwards – Ilonam – or with the letters all mixed up. Sometimes Limona, even. They laughed at him in the school so he doesn't go. But when he works with Yorgo with a chisel perhaps, or a wood plane, he is a master. No laughing at him then. And if Yorgo sends him to the *apotheke* for wood, he knows all the names: olive, pine, cypress. And Yorgo only has to show him the length between his hands, like so and he brings the right size, every time. That's not stupid, that's clever. His own way of being clever, that's all.

And he has a heart as big as our house. He's always smiling and he is kind to everyone, even animals. Even insects. Everyone in Panagia loves him. Well, nearly everyone.

And then there is my Chrissi, just seventeen. She should have been a boy, I tell her. All she wants to do is play football or men's card games. She wouldn't rest until Yorgo taught her the rules of *prefa,* and even I know that is the most difficult and complicated game that the men play in the *kafenion.* But he says she is good and some nights he sits with her and they play together. Not *prefa,* you need more than two for that, but backgammon or dominoes. She is so quick. Beside her Manoli seems even slower. But she is kind to him, loves him, protects him. He is her devoted one. He will follow her wherever she goes and she never seems to mind, but his father will try to distract him with some task, and he will turn straight away with a smile so sweet as to break your heart.

Chrissi was my last-born, and I was already forty-three years old. We have two others, all away now.

My oldest, the first-born, is Aristos, named of course, for Yorgo's father. He is a doctor, a heart surgeon in Athens. He is married to Irina. She is nice enough, but too busy with her own life, her own work, for me.

My Zambia now, she is a different person entirely. She is a teacher married to a good man, Adonis. He is a teacher also, but they have three children already and another on the way. I wish they lived closer, but he is the head of a school in Chania. A good job of course, so what with their work and their children we rarely see them in Panagia.

Zambia tells me his mother is very good to them and lives next door. Well, almost. In their pocket, I think to myself. Her husband is dead. I try to smile, to be polite, when we see her. Last Easter when they came for the celebrations his mother came too, like always. He is the only son. Nothing more to say. And their children? My grandchildren? They call us by our names. I said, 'No, I am your *Yaya*, that is what you call me.'

And Yorgo the eldest boy, eight now, laughed. He did, he laughed and said, 'Our Yaya is there,' and he pointed to her!

I tried with Zambia too, but she laughed as well, 'Oh, Mama, Yaya is with us all the time nearly and you are far away.'

I said to my Yorgo, 'Does she think we should pack everything up and move to Chania? Is that it?'

But all he said was, 'Be glad they see us at all!'

Huh. No problem for him, they call him *Pappous*. They follow him around every moment they are here – and he encourages them; chipping away at wood with them in his workshop, happy as sunshine.

Another hot day. A cloudless sky and no shade, not out in the *gypo* where I have weeded, dug and watered for hours.

Some have gardens nearer their houses, small patches of earth. I am proud of ours out on the hillside. But it is twenty minutes to walk there and twenty minutes back again. I rise with the sun mostly and work in the cool air of dawn. But coming home I am as wet as a river rat with the sweat that never seems to cool me. Tell the truth, I love that time alone each day. The great strength in those mountains fills the earth too and for sure, my vegetables are the envy of the village.

And now, I'm supposed to *asvesti* the walls of our house before another inspection. Marina, at the spring this morning, said she thought the inspectors were coming back to check today or tomorrow.

I asked Yorgo to do the *asvesti* with Manoli but he has two coffins to make for tomorrow's burials and we need the money for sure.

So, no rest for me today. I hate this, this regime telling us how to live in our village; 'clean, clean, clean; order, order, order'. Where once the priest, the schoolteacher and the village president were, well, if not exactly close friends, we lived together in a tolerable kind of way. Now they are our inspectors. We are simple people here, we live by the rules, that's what we are used to. So when these men are told by the military generals in Athens how to run the village, that's what they do and we have no choice in doing anything except obey.

I saw the woman again this morning. Outside the house, just standing watching.

Yorgo says it is nonsense, but I think she comes here from Kato Panagia and Eleftheria said at the spring that she was the one who spied on us for the inspectors. Certainly, when I have seen her before something bad has happened. She is small, squat, wrinkled not unlike a toad. I think there are three of them in her family; all women, a toad family.

I am sure it was her who put the evil eye on me when I was carrying Manoli. His birth was long, lasting two full days and a night and when he was born I knew straight away he was not like other children. He was too quiet, too placid. Yorgo said I should be glad he did not cry for his food like his brother and sister had done, but I said it was not normal. I vowed not to carry any more children after Manoli, but on the night of my brother's wedding, Yorgo plied me with so much of his wine that when he came in our bed that night I was too silly in the head to push him away. And it's true I enjoy our closeness. We laugh together. At our age! He is a good husband; kind and caring for my pleasure as much as his own, and nine months to the day after the wedding, on the fifteenth of May, I gave birth to my lovely Chrissi. The toad woman was nowhere to be seen when I was carrying her. No need to spit three times to ward off her evil.

And now she is back and I want to know why.

After I left the *gypo*, I went home and sat for five minutes before getting the rags and the *asvesti* ready. But I was only through two of the walls outside and here they were; the three clowns. I call them the *malakas*.

Crude, I know, but so are they.

You could see their noses in the air as they came in. Sniffing, I thought, for any signs of decay or neglect. Well not here, not in my house.

Stelios was first, the president of the village. After him, Vangelis, the teacher and last, the fat hugeness of the priest, Papa Michaelis.

'*Kalimera, Kyria,*' said the Papa. And he held his hand out for me to kiss his ring.

Of course I did so, but I couldn't help flinching back a little. His hand smelt of a foul mix of old onions and chicken shit. They come to inspect me for cleanliness and stink of the farmyard themselves.

'*Kalimera,* Kyria,' said Vangelis and almost in the same breath, Stelios muttered a swift 'good morning'.

'*Kalimera,* Stelios, Vangelis,' I said and with some delight watched them raise their eyebrows. I said nothing. Since we were children together and played the same games I have known them and their families. They can wait for cows to fly to the sun more likely than I will bend to their so-called superiority in my own home.

If Yorgo were here now, I know that he would be on his knees to them. He has told me so many times, I must play the same game. Well, civil I will be, but no more than that.

'*Café daki?*' I ask. Only the Papa nods yes.

I fill the *briki* and put it on to boil.

I indicate the chairs around the table and as I move in the other side of the kitchen they sit themselves down and wait.

Once, twice, the *briki* comes gently to the boil, and then I pour it in one of my everyday cups. I will serve only my family with my grandmother's best china, when they visit.

How did they get all this power? One day Vangelis was a skinny little runt, hiding in dark corners, never picked for a team – no friends. Greedy, fat, sweaty Michaelis who pissed his *vrakes* if a teacher so much as spoke to him. And Stelios? Now there was a little weasel of a child. His nose was running every day in winter, leaving a silvery trail on his sleeve where he constantly wiped it. These three are now the fascists in our village. At least with the Germans we knew they were the enemy – they had never been one of us.

'Warm day,' said Stelios unnecessarily. He is as thin as a

stick insect (and about as attractive) so what does he know about feeling warm?

He has noticed the dark sweat patches under my arms and probably down my back as well. Serve him right for looking.

'You have some water, perhaps, Kyria? Cold water?'

I fill three glasses from the jug in the refrigerator Aristos has bought for us. I add lemon slices for good measure.

'You enjoy your new appliance, Kyria?' This is from Papa Michaelis.

I'm glad to see he is sweating as much as me, and drops like olive oil dribble to his chin. He is so fat! Could it be the greed with which he gobbles up everything offered? I starve myself every day and I am as fat as the Papa too. Hormones, it said in Chrissi's magazine, whatever *they* are. But of course, only women have them.

'Yes, Papa. My husband works very hard as you know, to make sure we are as up to date as it is possible to be.'

'Hah!' chipped in the president, Stelios, and I could bite my tongue off. I know what is coming. 'Hard work is all very well. And necessary of course, but without the generosity of the Colonels, there would be no power in the villages so ordinary people can have the appliances of the well to do. Electricity is something to be thankful for, I'm sure you will agree?'

The others nodded like a group of gulls sitting on an olive tree together; waiting to spot the snails below. In fact they were so busy congratulating themselves that they didn't notice I had ignored the comment.

Of course it is good to have electricity here. They try to claim triumph for the provision of water as well, but only some of us are stupid and we know we have the spring of the purest mountain water on the island. Always have had, always will have.

Yorgo says always praise the Panagia for our natural spring. And oh, yes, yes I know, children now have injections so they will not get the sicknesses or whatever; too late for my children. And there is one that I know of in Kato Panagia, who had the needle, who is a cripple now. So much for the new medicine!

'Is Kyrios Yorgo here, today?' This from the teacher, Vangelis. He has known Yorgo all his life and he knows where his workshop is, beside the house, so why waste his breath? And he knows he will work there with Manoli all day.

'Yes, Vangelis, as always.'

'His turn for the village work, I must give him his duties.'

I know they are baiting me now, want to raise my temper. Well I'm not so easily fooled and I don't answer, just go to the door and call, 'Yorgo! YORGO!'

And Manoli comes running. Oh bless him, *Panagia mou*, he has not buttoned his *vrakes* and if he is not careful they will be down around his ankles.

Flakes of sawdust fall around him but I will not chide him, not in front of this lot.

'Mama, Papa says tell me what you want.' His deep brown eyes glow with curiosity. He stands tall, my lad, and is well formed and fit. But, sweet boy, I must cut his hair tonight; the dark curls are down past his neck at the back and fall into his eyes at the front. The clowns will not like this, and sure enough Papa Michaelis says:

'His appearance needs a little attention I think, Kyria.'

'His appearance will get it,' I answer and I give him a loving stroke as he stands there.

He smiles. 'What shall I tell Papa? Shall I tell him we have visitors?'

'Tell him we need to see him. Er, what's your name, boy?'

'Manoli, just as it's always been, Vangelis.' I answer for him, furious at the attempt to humiliate my son. 'Go, Manoli *mou*, and tell Papa to come for a minute only.'

He runs off and we can all hear him call to Yorgo, 'Come, Papa, Mama has men here.'

And Yorgo is with us in a moment. He is a good-looking man, and his blue eyes twinkle, I think, just as they have always done. He was considered a good catch in the village and there are many who think I was lucky to get him. Well, lucky or not, I am proud to be his wife and to mother his children.

He bows his head when he sees who is here in our house, and mutters into his moustache what I take to be greetings. Behind him is his shadow Manoli, of course.

'Come to my house tonight, Yorgo,' says President Stelios. 'We have roads that need to be dug.'

Yorgo, of course, just nods assent. Not for him to argue or give cheek to these men.

Every year now it is the same. Every man in the village between the ages of sixteen and sixty-five must work for the supposed betterment of the village for ten days each year.

'I can't remember what your son did last year, Kyria?' says Papa Michaelis.

Stelios answered for me. 'Manoli was supposed to be unwell and was excused, Papa.'

'Perhaps he should do double this year then? Everyone must take their turn.' This from the teacher, Vangelis. He has never liked Manoli, or Chrissi.

Manoli was just a thorn in his side when he attended the school. Vangelis swore he was deliberately getting his words wrong, to avoid the work. And no matter how many times Yorgo or I went to the school, he refused to understand and I think he did little or nothing when Manoli was beaten. A blind eye was shown and Manoli came home day after day with his clothes ripped, his legs bruised and bleeding, and never – not once – would he name the instigator.

And Chrissi? Well, I know she can be cheeky, give the lip to anyone who crosses her, but oh, *Panagia*, she is so bright, and can do any of the reading, or arithmetic, no matter how complicated. But Vangelis had not one good word for her, ever.

Yorgo was arguing now, unlike him. 'I will keep Manoli with me when I dig your roads, Kyrios.'

Oh Yorgo! How many times have I told him? We grew up with these men we saw them fall down drunk with too much raki, time after time, when they were young; why should we now call them Kyrios and treat them as gods?

And even his grovelling means nothing to them as Stelios says, looking to his fellows for support, 'Oh, I think Manoli can undertake work of his own, Yorgo, Aphrodite? I'm sure we are all agreed that your son is a grown man now. He can't hide behind his parents forever, can he? I am sure you won't wish to treat him as a baby? How about that, Manoli, you are a man now, aren't you? Why,' and he sniggered, 'I expect you even have a girlfriend? Or perhaps two?' And they all laugh as though it were the funniest thing just heard on one of the radio comic shows. But all I can see is my son trembling, and his face turning pink, and his hands twitching together. He looks bewildered and turns from me to Yorgo and back again.

'Don't worry, *Manolaki mou*. We shall sort this out for you. Go now, back to Papa's workshop.'

'You can finish planing that piece of olive wood you started this morning,' Yorgo says.

And Manoli is off at a run, clearly relieved to be away from this situation that he cannot begin to understand.

For the first time I see that Vangelis has a little notebook in his hand, and a pencil. What is this? His black list?

'So,' he says now, 'Manoli Babyottis, man or boy?'

Panagia mou!

'You know, as do I, that our son here is not quite as others are. It is best he works beside his father, just as he does here. Maybe when he is older he can be treated as a man, but for now . . .'

I can say no more, the words are sticking in my throat. I am betraying Manoli with my pleas. I loathe myself for accepting these tyrants.

As I turn and begin to cut up some fruit, I whisper for forgiveness to the Panagia and cross myself three times.

The truth is we are being punished, Yorgo and I, and there is nothing we can do about it. The memories of a past life here in this village will haunt us for the rest of our lives.

And now I need to deal with the problem of Manoli and the

hard labour he will be given. We cannot refuse; some other punishment will be found, I know it.

Our friends Marina and Matheos tried last year, when Matheos had a broken leg and they were punished daily for this lapse. Their honey was lost, the bees all fled from overturned hives. Their vines were stripped mysteriously over three nights when they were attending the burial of Matheos's uncle in Aghios Demetrious.

No, Manoli will do as he is told and if I have to I will go and help him dig or otherwise work at his side. Chrissi will also help. I know she will.

She has suffered enough for tiny faults. One year she lost the 21st April badge every child has to wear. She was given extra work in school for weeks for that little offence.

Once Yannis Peridakis refused to fly the national flag over his house on 28th October. No special reason; he was as happy as anyone that we should celebrate the day of freedom from the German occupation. But he told Yorgo one night in the Piperia he was simply tired of doing as he was told like a child or an animal by a bunch of army men.

So he flies his flag on every day of the year except 28th October. Then the flagpole on his roof is empty.

Some here, our friends, feel the same. It is impossible nowadays to live your life just governed by the seasons, the weather and the rotation of our crops.

We have to be so careful, of course, because many of those we thought of as friends in the village have welcomed these colonels, these changes they have made.

Tired of wars and fighting, weary from the threat of violence we lived with for years, they think all these rules are a good thing. Yorgo tells me every night in the Piperia there are as many voices raised in anger as during the civil war.

Grown men squabble like children among themselves.

The Papa has finished noisily slurping his coffee. The water sits untouched, the ice long melted, the fruit I prepared for their refreshment, dried on the plate. They rise and like the royal family they clearly think themselves to be, they bow their heads and depart.

Yorgo shuffles to the door after them, his hands twitching together. I am horrified to hear him call after them, 'Thank you, Kyrios, thank you, Papa.' As if they are guests here!

'Speak for yourself only, Yorgo,' I say furiously. 'They are not welcome in *my* house.'

He doesn't answer. Shaking his head sadly he goes back to his son and his coffins in the workshop. And I am alone, contemplating the time I will have to give up watching Manoli break his back in two as he works on their damned roads; coming home to rest only after a hard day's living another day.

Outside, an old man, Fanis's grandfather, creaks carefully down the street; his stick tapping his steps along. A falcon wheels overhead, stalking an unseen creature. The sun is hidden behind a cloud but only for a moment or two and then it is beating down as strongly as ever. Sighing, I pick up the rags and the bucket of *asvesti*. I must finish the walls, inside and out. I smile for a second: at least the three *malakas* forgot to check on that! But the smile fades fast – they will be back another day.

And now it is another day, and Chrissi has vanished. She was to help me this morning, but no sign of her.

If Angel is in the village already, that's where she will be for sure.

I finished the *asvesti* on all the walls outside and almost all the walls in, two to finish. Two coats each time, I am not mean with either my time or Yorgo's money.

'Mama! Mama!' It is Chrissi calling from the top of the hill.

I turn to look and shield my eyes from the strong light that is filling the sky. It's her – who else would shout like that around here? Yes, it's her. Her head kerchief missing again but before I can call to chide her, I see she is waving it in her hand. I can see from here she is laughing – but when is she not? Where did this mad spirit she has come from? I was never like

27

this as a girl, and her father was a working man by the time he was twelve and already serious about the living he would make, the craft he would learn. She is pounding down the hill now and, breathless and sweating, she lands almost at my feet. Anything more like a whirlwind or a tornado I have never seen in my life.

Such energy! I feel sweat beading my face at the very thought of moving that fast. I must lose some weight. But every time I try Yorgo says, 'No! Don't be thin. Nothing to get hold of!'

And here is Angel with her! Oh, *Panagia mou*, how that child has grown. And what a beauty she is becoming.

'You look just like your mother,' I tell her, hugging her to me.

'How I wish that was true.'

'You will come and eat with us tonight, I hope? And Lucy and Will, of course.'

'Yes please. If only you knew how I have missed your cooking.'

'How's that school of yours?'

'Don't ask.'

'Go and say hello to Yorgo and Manoli. And behave yourselves.'

But I might as well have saved my words. When those two are together it is as though they have the electric light in them. They are wired up, jumping, giggling.

I suppose, in truth, I rather like it. It's how girls should be. At least their spirit, their laughter, is not restricted by this regime. The inspectors cannot still them or take away their sense of fun.

Now Chrissi is hugging me too.

'Enough! It's too hot for all this nonsense.'

'Mama, please, please can we go down to Tres Petromas and swim?'

They can see I am wavering so Angel says, 'Aunt, if you let us, I absolutely promise I will help Chrissi and you in the *gypo* later. When it's cooler.'

'It's cleaning the walls I have to do, the *gypo* can wait.'

'We'll do it, won't we, Angel?'

'Yes. I'm good at that.'

It's impossible not to laugh.

'Is that what you did at that English school? Paint the walls?'

They can't think of another argument, I can see, so I wave them away.

'Go on, be off with you, go and swim.' As they are vanishing, I call, 'And Angel?'

'Yes?'

'Go and see your Uncle Yorgo and Manoli. They won't be too hot for hugging.'

I'm happy she's back. Chrissi too. Truth is, I like being called 'Aunt' just as if I were really a member of the family.

Oh, *Panagia*, I must sit for a minute. This is all too much for one day and it's not even noon yet.

ANGEL

It's so good to be back here! All I want to do is run around the lanes and the goat tracks, roll down the hill; smell the wild garlic, the bitter tang of the dill. I love the movement of a breeze through the gorse and the wild thyme filling the air with the scent of summer.

The seaside in Tres Petromas is wonderful and there is never anyone there. The beach stretches for miles; just miles of white sand. Paradise! We flung our clothes off and Chrissi made her breasts jiggle about and that made us laugh until we fell over and over and got covered in sand. Then we rushed into the sea to swim.

She swam on her back so that you couldn't see any of her body or her face, just these two mounds floating with raspberries on the top. She said if anyone came and saw them they'd think that they were a new breed of jellyfish.

But my troubles weren't washed away in the sea, and when we went back to Aphrodite she shooed me home. Lucy was trying to find me to speak to my parents.

I walked slowly back. Chrissi wasn't allowed to come.

Even the vine with its early grapes or the red geranium, dustier than ever, couldn't cheer me as I dragged my feet up the steps. Will was up on the roof with a bucket and brush. It seems everyone is doing their *asvesti* today. He waved cheerily, his old denim shirt splattered with white. I hope he leaves that shirt here when he goes away.

Lucy was talking on the phone. She even laughed. She made the whole barn business sound so much more of an accident, and I knew my mother was sweet and kind and I was sure she would understand. Then Lucy passed me the phone and I had to speak to her myself. And, just hearing her voice, I burst into tears.

'My darling girl,' she started, in that gentle, loving way. I could tell she was finding it hard to be angry with me. 'What are we going to do with you, Angel?' she said, and I knew she was trying to be stern.

'I didn't mean it to happen,' I said through my tears. Oh bloody! Then my nose started to run but Lucy passed me one of Will's giant handkerchiefs and I sort of propped the phone up on my shoulder and blew.

'Angel, are you ill? Have you got a cold?'

'No, no. Mama, do you have to tell Father?'

'You know I do. Of course I must.'

'He will be so angry with me.'

'Well, just at first I suppose, because he worries about you, you know that, just as I do. I'll find a good moment— Oh, He's here right now.'

And he *was* angry.

'You are an idiotic child,' he began, and he went on from there. After a minute or so I realised there was a silence and I was about to say something – sorry, even and he started again.

'Put Lucy on will you? Let me talk to her.'

Mutely I handed her the phone.

'You know she got straight A's in all her exams?'

But I don't think he even listened as I heard him say something.

Lucy said, 'I suppose I could stay for a while.'

Oh hoorah!

Then, 'Yes, could you spell that?' And she was waving at me, 'pencil'.

I found one, and then he'd gone and she said he wanted her to track down some organisation called Gabbitas-Thring. They find places in school for people, presumably difficult people – i.e. me. And she had to send him a list of schools.

'Oh no, please! I don't want to go away to some other old school in England.'

Then Will came in and they opened a bottle of wine and I probably looked really fed up so they offered me a glass, and I said was there sherry in the cupboard? And there was, so we all went and sat on the terrace with our glasses.

Will said (oh he's so wise), 'There's no point in us all getting miserable about this. Lucy will stay here for a while when I've gone and we'll just take it one day at a time. And tonight,' and he leapt to his feet, waving his glass in the air, 'we are all going to Aphrodite and Yorgo's and we will have a *feast*!'

And that's what we did. Aphrodite had made a huge dish of *pastitsio*. Lucy frantically scribbled things in her notebook. She said there were many different versions of this macaroni pie, but Aphrodite's was the best she'd ever tasted and she wanted to know every single little thing about the making of it. I can see Aphrodite found this quite strange – *pastitsio* is *pastitsio*, isn't it? We were all completely stuffed when it was finished – well, I was. And then Aphrodite disappeared into the kitchen and brought out a dish of roasted goat and a huge bowl of potatoes cooked in olive oil and lemon and a big village salad. We all had some – well, quite a lot actually, it was so good.

Aphrodite's sister, Georgia, who is married to the baker, came in with her children and a couple of neighbours and somehow there was room around the table for them – Will was right, it *was* a feast! We all found ourselves eating special wedding bread – Vassili, the baker brother-in-law, had made some for a wedding and said, 'I always make a little extra – it's so good!'

And then Papa Diamedes came in his swirling black robes and his wife and her friend Titi, who had brought her needlework with her, a dress she was making for Chrissi, and the room was full to bursting. Everyone was talking around the table about the inspections there are these days in the village.

Aphrodite had the most to say – she loathes the inspectors, *malakas* she calls them.

I sat beside Lucy so that I could keep her up with what everyone was saying.

Papa Diamedes said he had been friends with Papa Michaelis before, but now he feels only watched by him.

'If I put one finger wrong, get one phrase out in the incantation, I know he will be making a note of it to use against me somehow.' He shook his head sorrowfully. 'I know we must take the good things along with all this, but it's hard, it's hard.'

I felt a little kick under the table and looking up saw that Chrissi was trying to get my attention. She nodded to the door. She meant, 'come on let's get out of here'. Lucy had seen too; she winked and gave a tiny nod. But as Chrissi stood up, Titi the dressmaker jumped to her feet waving her fabric at us.

'Come here, Chrissi, this is a dress for you. Let me see how this looks.'

Chrissi didn't need to tell me what she thought – it was hideous and she would hate to wear it. Nobody would wear it, I thought. It's disgusting! All shiny bright yellow – like a puddle of mustard.

But Aphrodite had other ideas for her daughter.

'I bought that for you specially from the merchant who came with all the beads, remember?' There were murmurs round the table: everybody remembered. Obviously that was a big day for the village. 'It's time for you to have one good dress, now, not just these old rags you seem to want to run around in.'

'Oh, Mama, I don't want a dress. I want some new jeans like Angel's.'

Will and Lucy, knowing I would have outgrown all my clothes here, had brilliantly bought me some great jeans and stuff; I should have begged a pair for Chrissi.

Titi looked flummoxed. She was a thin woman and all her features were bony and beaky, a sad face with a rather long nose in the middle. Poor woman, the Panagia had not been in a good mood when she was born.

'The stitching is the finest I've ever done, look!'

And all the women craned round to see and there were murmurs of delight.

'Fancy that. It's like lacework, so delicate,' said Georgia.

'I'm sorry, Titi, but I think I am the wrong person to wear that colour,' said Chrissi.

Aphrodite looked like thunder.

'You will look like a ray of sunshine, won't she?'

And everyone murmured assent. Aphrodite was not a person to be disagreed with.

It didn't look as though Chrissi and I were going to be allowed out of here easily.

'You could wear it to church, couldn't you?' I thought I had to try and help my friend.

'Will you make it very plain and simple, Titi?' said Chrissi. She knew she couldn't win this. 'Only with such a colour, it shouldn't be too frilly, should it?'

'The dress will be straight up and straight down.'

Chrissi brightened. 'Well then . . .'

'With just the sleeves being like golden trumpets.'

The murmurs round the table all agreed now.

'Lovely, Chrissi, special sleeves. You will look like a flower.'

I knew if I caught Chrissi's eye now we would both be in disgrace. I saw her mouth was twitching in the effort not to laugh. And I knew I was on the brink myself.

Lucy could see exactly what was going on and came to the rescue.

'Why don't you two go and get a little air outside, and see if there is a new moon?' and we were gone before she had finished the sentence.

We fell into each other's arms outside the door.

'Straight up and down,' I spluttered.

Chrissi said, 'With sleeves like golden trumpets.'

'How I envy you,' I said wickedly. 'You will look like a

35

flower and all I've got are these awful new jeans. How I long to have a dress with "sleeves like golden trumpets"!'

'I'll cut them off.'

We ran round the corner of her house and outside the door of Yorgo's workshop we crumpled down to the ground.

'Here,' said Chrissi, pulling a pack of cigarettes out of the pocket of her old jeans. 'Have one.'

'Where did you get them from?' I was astonished.

'Manoli gives them to me.'

I opened my eyes even wider. 'Why?'

'Aphrodite doesn't mind if he smokes – he's a boy. And they make him cough, so he gives them to me.'

We sat in happy silence for a while, puffing on our cigs and trying hard not to cough ourselves.

'They do make you feel a bit nice don't they?'

'Oh yes,' I said. I could feel a headache coming on. I wasn't going to admit to that, though.

'We should make a plan for tomorrow night. You will come with me, won't you?'

'Try and stop me! I've been perfectly behaved for a whole year, time for a bit of a fling.'

'Have you? Truly?'

'Well, apart from a bit of an accident, mostly.'

'What time do you think?'

'Well, it doesn't get dark until late, so not before midnight.'

'The later it is, the easier to get out. Everyone will be sleeping then.'

'So I'll meet you in the square at midnight, then.'

'Don't forget to bring a spare pair of pants. Tell you what, I will as well; let's give them a real surprise – two pairs flying high.'

We finished our cigs down to the last little stubs and scratched them out on the ground, and just at that moment there came the sweetest sound from the house. Where before all we could hear was the gentle hum of distant voices, a little laughter, now there came something so beautiful we both sat totally still, entranced.

36

'It's Manoli,' Chrissi whispered. 'He taught himself to play the accordion. Years ago my brother Aristos bought it, but he was hopeless and gave up. It's been sitting in a cupboard ever since. Papa bought Manoli a book and he's been practising for ages. Isn't he clever? He can't read an ordinary book and yet he can understand music.'

We crept back closer to the house and sank to the ground under the window.

The murmur of voices had stilled now and when the tune was finished, everyone clapped and called for more. I heard Yorgo say '*Perimeno, perimeno*', 'wait for me', and then the music started again but this time there was a lyre playing alongside the accordion.

'That's Papa,' whispered Chrissi.

That wonderful haunting sound must have drifted over the village as more neighbours were coming in now. Luckily, Yorgo and Aphrodite had a big room and as we got closer the music changed. Now it was a dancing song, and inside we heard the banging and shuffling of furniture, and laughter, lots of laughter. They were dancing! Inside, the table and all the chairs were stacked against the wall and the wonderful sight of the dipping and swirling and stamping of the dance had taken its place.

Papa Diamedes was in the centre and I remembered that he was a wonderful dancer. His black skirts swirled around and around and underneath he was wearing the traditional high boots of the mountain men. Stamp, stamp! he went, and the others followed his steps in rhythm. All the men were wearing their *vrakes* tucked into boots. Their backs were straight, and as they swirled, their heads – with their fine black moustaches twirling – looked first over one shoulder and then the other.

Chrissi grabbed my hand and in we went. I had had lessons in Tres Petromas with her when I was at school here so I knew some of the dances, the easier ones. It was a wonderful feeling – so free; like mountain water we glided.

It is beautiful. A bit like a mix of Irish and Indian music; it's lively, repetitive. Papa Diamedes was alone in the centre now, a magical sight. This man became a youth again before our eyes. I watched the Papa, enchanted. One hand was folded around his waist, the other holding his amber *komboloi*, his string of beads. His head was bent over and he moved slowly with heavy strong steps. He swayed and leaned from side to side as if about to fall. Then he suddenly made a fast turn-around himself and bowed low so as to hit the floor with his hand. Slap! And then he was upright again. His movements became stronger and he lifted his foot and stamped down with his heel. Bang!

And then everyone was up again and a couple of the men danced as the Papa had done.

I felt so full of happiness just to be here, to be part of this; this was what I had missed with all my heart. I was clapping now with all of the women, watching the men who felt no oddness in dancing together.

I don't care that my parents are both English; all this feeling makes me know I am a true Cretan. This is who I am.

Like all gatherings here the men all sit in one place around the raki and the women cluster like hens together in corners, passing food around, urging everyone to eat more and then more.

I sat beside Lucy; she's Irish and good at the chat, but she has very little Greek, even though Will tries to teach her, so she usually ends up slightly apart, on her own.

'Oh I wish I could do this stuff. I can manage a jig to the uillean pipes, but not this complicated foot twisting.'

'I used to be hopeless, but I had lessons. You could do too if you like, or Chrissi and I could teach you an easy dance.'

'The priest, Papa Diamedes, he's a cool one. Look at him! He looks like Fred Astaire in a sexy black robe.' Her voice dropped to a whisper. 'Look at the women's faces as they watch him, lust if ever I saw it!'

'Lust? For the priest?'

'Oh you bet. See his wife is smiling, of course she is. She knows who he's going home with tonight.'

We left soon after that, just Lucy and I. Will stayed.

'Leave him,' said Lucy, 'he's enjoying the craic.' I looked puzzled. 'The stories, the chat.'

We linked arms all the way home and Lucy stumbled a bit here and there, I think she'd had a raki or two.

The soft strains of the music followed us along the paths as we walked.

There was a breeze flickering through the branches of the olives and their leaves glinted like silver pieces in the moonlight.

The distant music lingered; a timeless, forever sound, gently blowing through these hills and mountains as if for a thousand years. And when it had faded into nothing we sang ourselves; 'Shenandoah' and 'Danny Boy' until we were both in tears when we got home.

We pushed the heavy door open and I showed her the tiny carved flowers in the portal done by Yorgo Babyottis when he mended this house for my mother all those long years ago.

I made some tea; thick, brown, milky for Lucy, and dictamus, mountain herb, for me and we sat for a while on the terrace in silence, the warmth of the night like a cloak around us. Stars like I've never seen winked on and off as if some magic electrician was testing them up there. And then the moon tonight, smothering the stars with its brilliance as the thin cloud dissolved.

'All my best memories of Will are on this terrace.'

I nodded. 'It's my favourite place in the whole world. I won't go to England, you know, to another school. I couldn't bear it.'

Poor Lucy, she didn't know what to say to me. 'Don't let those thoughts spoil this lovely evening.'

I sat back and tried to think about tomorrow night's adventure instead.

The next day Will and Lucy slept in, recovering. Will had crept in noisily at about two. I was still awake; too excited to sleep.

I was a model child all day. I helped Lucy in the kitchen

when she finally got up and together we went and talked to Irini and Eftoxia about mountain greens, and how to cook them. I translated for her. None of the village women have any English.

After supper Will and Lucy were both yawning their heads off and I think it was me persuading them to have an early night that did the trick. Certainly the house was totally silent by eleven thirty. It was a hot night again and I tiptoed out of the house and keeping my back to the wall slowly moved down the big steps to the square below. The moon was low and full, mostly breaking through the curtain of the dark.

Inching past Irini's house, almost toe by toe, I wasn't quiet enough; beside me her chickens suddenly screeched. And a dark flash ran over my foot and I bit back a yell as another followed and yet another.

Sweat broke out all over me as my eyes took in the path down. It was alive with moving shadows. I bent down, peering and then I stumbled with a cry. I'd hit my head on a spade, propped against the wall and it fell with a clatter. Tiny pip-like squeals came up to me: baby rats, squirming, naked all over the steps. Somehow I must have kicked their nest. The mother rat would be somewhere about. She would feel threatened, fly at my throat. I leapt forward and saw at the end of the line a larger silhouette and a soft purr – a cat.

Another few steps and I thought I was safe. There ahead was the square, the flagpole and a moving flicker – Chrissi there before me.

'*Pou enai?*' Oh bloody, someone on the last balcony, a wisp of smoke, the smell of tobacco and again, 'Who's there?'

Looking up I saw hanging over the balcony a white face, a scrawn of scraped-back hair and the glint of silvery metal curlers. Maria, feeling the heat of the summer night, was sleeping like many others, outside.

Too late, she had seen me and cackled with laughter. 'Angel!'

I waved in what I hope was a jaunty, uncaring way, said, '*Kali nichta.*'

She started a chat about the weather, and I muttered only, 'Yes, hot night, tonight.' And again, desperately, '*Kali nichta*!'

'Your friend, Aphrodite's daughter, is in the square already. Party tonight, is there?' But the effort of speaking was too much and she was racked with a coughing fit and moved back into the shadows.

I ran the last few steps and pulled Chrissi with me into the bushes lining the square.

'I heard that,' she said. 'Couldn't you have been a bit quieter?'

I didn't dignify that with an answer, I said, 'Now she knows it's us, we can't do it.'

'Of course we can. We must! We have to hope she thinks it was a dream in the morning. She's a bit batty anyway; no one will listen to her.'

She pulled a pair of grubby grey knickers out of her pocket. 'Did you bring yours?'

I handed them over and glanced down. 'What have you got on your feet?'

'Manoli's trainers. They're a bit big but they grip better than mine. Come on, let's do it.' And she clambered on to the wall around the square, but she was still too low to catch the end of the rope dangling loosely from the pole. 'You'll have to give me a bunk up.'

'No, I'm taller than you. Hold me steady, I'll do it.'

It seemed to take hours but was probably less than five minutes, ten at most. I was puffed but triumphant. At first I thought the rope wasn't going to move and then, after a few strong tugs, it creaked slowly up and, at last, there from the pole hung not the blue and white of the Greek flag, but two pairs of panties. There was barely a ripple of breeze so they didn't billow out which was probably a good thing.

'We had to do it tonight. The Saint Demetrious lot are coming here in the morning for a thirty-day service.'

'Who died?'

'Oh someone's grandfather, I expect.' And with that she jumped back up on the wall and flinging her arms wide whispered, 'Hoorah. A triumph again for Panagia!' but at that moment she slipped, lost her footing on the wall and, legs in the air, slid gracelessly down the thin grass and weeds that eventually led to the goat path down to Tres Petromas.

I peered over the wall in a panic. Suppose she . . . ? But she was already scrambling back up. Yes, her hair was all over the place and her T-shirt was ripped across the back but she was safe. It was only when she flopped, breathless, beside me that I saw the real damage. She had on only one of Manoli's trainers. I think she spotted it at the same moment; we jumped up together and peered over the edge. The moon was behind a cloud now and it was dark, too dark. The path was steep, especially here at the top. You could hunt for a muddy shoe for days and never find it.

We sat side by side on that wall smoking Manoli's cigarettes, desperate.

'Manoli loves those trainers. He'll never forgive me.'

'Perhaps you don't need . . .'

But looking at each other we knew it was hopeless. Whatever had happened, Manoli's shoe was halfway to Tres Petromas by now.

There was worse to come.

Not surprisingly I slept late the next morning. I had stirred briefly as the church bells rang out for the thirty-day service, turned over and gone straight back to sleep.

It was Will, standing at the end of my bed that woke me properly.

'Get up now please, Angel.'

I burrowed my head in the pillow.

'Whassa time?'

His voice didn't sound too friendly. 'Time for you to come up and do a little explaining.'

I didn't have a dressing gown, so I staggered out to the terrace in my pyjamas. The sun was bright, too bright. Will and Lucy sat side by side and Lucy didn't even turn to smile and say 'Good morning' like other mornings. They were like a pair of statues there, neither moving.

Then I saw what Will had in his hand. My knickers. My mind started to race with questions.

'Care to look over the edge of the terrace?'

So I did. If you look down to the right, a way away, you could see the square, and the flagpole. Nothing on it. No Greek flag like usual. No knickers. Just what seemed like everyone who lived in Panagia staring up at our terrace. Staring up at me. It was all a bit quiet and that was a big crowd.

'Anything to say?' This was Will.

'Erm, I'm not sure . . .'

'No, it's all right, no need to say a word. Maria has already told anyone who will listen, and believe me, that is the whole village, what happened in the square at midnight.'

'Oh bloody, I'm sorry.'

Will carried on as though he hadn't heard me. 'But even if she hadn't, Flixo's goat boy brought Manoli Babyottis's trainer back up from the hillside.'

'Well . . .'

Will held his hand up to silence me.

'And even if that had lain hidden for weeks, which we agree could have happened, Lucy and I think if you are going to try and be anonymous, it's probably better if you . . .' and he paused, holding up my knickers, and then I saw what he could see, and Lucy and indeed most of Panagia probably had looked at: the Cash's name tape sewn into the waistband of my panties – A. TIMBERLAKE.

APHRODITE

We knew nothing. Nothing. There was the thirty-day service at the church for Emanoli Gerolakis. They all came from Saint Demitrious, all the villains and rogues who live there. Dark and swarthy they are. You can tell them from the end of our village. I swear the air changes, it's thicker. Even the donkeys look straggled and poor.

What we none of us needed was for my daughter, mine and Yorgo's youngest child, to make us the joke of the mountains.

Underwear, Chrissi's underwear and Angel's too, blowing in the fresh breeze of early morning in the square. The square where we honour our heroes.

There are no words. She, of course, had plenty to say.

'I'm sorry, sorry,' she said, again and again. 'It would have been worse, Mama, if they had come for me. And they would!'

'I think not,' I said. 'Nothing could be worse than that humiliation. And the *malakas*, for sure they will be here. There will be punishments. And so there should be. Deserved, well deserved.'

And almost worst of all – she wore Manoli's shoes (they cost very dear from the shoe truck that came last year just twice. Yorgo offered a brace of rabbits but they laughed, opened the doors of the truck, the back doors, and there were rabbits hanging everywhere. So it was good money we paid). So when Andreas, who looks after Flixo's goats, came up this morning with the shoe in his hand, well, everyone thought it was Manoli who had done this thing; stolen his sister's underwear and the rest. Angel came, with Will. What could I say? Yorgo, of course, was useless.

'Just a joke,' he said, 'we did the same – and worse. Remember when—' but I stopped him right there. This is now. Will understood.

'I'm not sure where this idea came from,' he said, 'but we will go along with any punishment you think is fit.'

Chrissi had run down the stairs when she heard his voice.

'It was me. Angel just came to keep me company. She had nothing to do with it, nothing.'

'Nice of you to say that, but I doubt her knickers flew out of the window and up the pole all by themselves.'

Will took Angel home and we waited. And waited. At four o'clock in the afternoon, just as Yorgo fell asleep in his chair, Stelios the village president came, his moustache twitching excitedly in his face.

He didn't take long. Long enough to tell us that Chrissi was denied all privileges at the school: no outings, no playground time, no games – just work, work and more work for one month. This was to start when the new term began in October.

When we told her this, she tried to look upset, but we could see it meant little.

'You are lucky it's not more,' I said.

Girls, I thought, so much more trouble than boys. All the business of what is suitable to wear. Why, boys and men are straight into *vrakes* and a shirt, maybe a scarf at the neck and that's it. Girls, it's all looking at each other and skirts, how short is too short? And trousers, like men wear. I remember in the war how shocked everyone was when Marina wore her husband's trousers in the fields one day to protect her legs from thorns. She never did again. In my day it was a head kerchief and long dark frocks.

And all this make-up stuff – painting lips and eyes. What is the point of all that on a sweaty day on the hillside?

We used to pinch our cheeks with fingers to make them glow and that was it. Now, when the trucks come up the mountain as they do every day with food and fish and the like, they even bring up private things for women and girls of a certain age.

Hard to believe I know, but there, between the bags of sugar and rice, I caught sight of some of those things for those days of the month! We used to make our own rags. When I was a girl there were no trucks to blare up the hills and disturb our peace, we used to trade at the only shop. I would take in tobacco from our field and come away with some maize flour already fine ground.

I tried to keep Chrissi busy with me. That way I knew where she was and what she was up to. Angel came by most mornings and, good for her, helped me as well. An hour or three at the *gypo* did no harm and even some afternoons I could sit on the chair for a little and close my eyes. And then when I thought it had all settled and life could go on with no worries – that's when the trouble happened to Manoli.

Thinking back, it seems important that I must get everything straight in my head about that terrible time. It hurts to think of it. I could weep.

Wait, I am running my thinking ahead. Before that, yes the fairground and the gypsies came, that's right.

It all started on the day Titi came to bring Chrissi's dress for her to try. Manoli came in with a cut hand and, as I cleaned it, Titi asked if he ever thought to play the accordion for other people's parties. He blushed red and looked at the floor. Chrissi came in and almost ran out the door when she saw Titi was there with an armful of bright yellow. But I grabbed her and told her to get out of her things and try this on for size.

Manoli was trying to inch away out of the door but I stopped him.

'Come back here, Manoli.' And he shuffled in again, still bright red and gazing at the floor. 'Titi is asking you something.'

Chrissi paused in wriggling out of her jeans and looked up with interest.

47

'Is she going to make you a shirt? You'll look very fine in yellow, won't he, Mama?'

'Enough from you, miss. Go with Titi into the good room and come back and show me when you have the dress on.'

When they'd gone, I turned to Manoli.

'You could play for Titi, if she asks you, couldn't you, Manoli?' He looked stricken. 'Maybe you could make some money that way.'

'I don't need money,' he said.

'Of course you do. Everyone needs money, and think of the things we could buy if you brought some money into the house.'

He looked astonished now, as if to say, 'Things, what things?'

Titi was back with us again and said she was asking because her niece was having a baptism celebration over in Aghios Demetrious – her late husband's family were from there.

I always thought there was a dark side to Titi and I sometimes forget she married from outside our village. I never have totally trusted her, if I am honest. She hangs around too much with the warty woman and I certainly know *she* is evil.

But she has an idea for Manoli and that could be good for him. Get him out more. She thought it would be fine to have some music at this baptism party.

'I'm sure they would pay him something.'

'And Papa too?' Manoli asked. 'He could play?'

'Yes, if that gets you over there.'

Titi has so little money. Most of the women here do their own dressmaking and have no need of her. Her husband died two years ago now and she hardly scrapes a living together. To be honest, I had only got her on to this dress for Chrissi for a kindness. Though I can barely afford to be so charitable myself. Especially to her.

Chrissi was back, hanging inside this unfinished sack of a dress. Oh, *Panagia mou*, she was right, it looked terrible on her. And I thought even poor Titi could surely see what we all

48

saw. I tried to think of something to say, anything. But Chrissi was waving some magazine in her hand, foreign with a brassy-looking girl on the front.

'Could you change it, Titi? Could you make it look like this?'

'What's this?' I started but Titi had taken the open magazine and was looking inside.

'Show me here.'

The picture was of a blonde girl, grinning like six cats and jumping in the air with yards of skirt flying around.

'You can see her underclothes!'

'Yes, Mama – but that doesn't mean you would see mine. It's really great fashion. Please, Titi, Mama, I would love this.'

'Can you do this, Titi? If it means I could get this girl into a dress?'

For a moment or two Titi looked dubious, and then, 'I think, maybe I could try.'

'There is spare material,' I said, 'isn't that right, Titi? I bought so much.'

She looked anywhere but at me. Had she thought to keep the stuff for herself?

Chrissi was jumping with excitement.

'I'm going to find Angel and show her. She can keep her new jeans.' And she was out the door and away.

Manoli was shuffling after her when Titi said, 'If Manoli will play for my niece – part of that payment would be for the extra work I must do to change the style.'

Manoli looked from Titi to me and back again; not quite sure where he stood in these dealings but before he could speak I said, 'Of course he will. How nice to be able to help your sister for a change, Manoli. She does so many things for you.'

He looked puzzled, and then brightened.

'She reads me stories,' he said, 'I like her reading me stories.'

'There you are then, Titi, done.'

She sat on. There was my little rest going.

'Some coffee, Titi?'

'No, no. But if you have some cold water from your machine, and one of your cinnamon biscuits . . . ?'

She was fumbling in her skirts now and pulled out a sheet of paper.

'Did you see this? There are some pinned to trees in the square. The fair is coming.'

I haven't been to the square since our trouble, so I took the paper from her. It was printed bright red and green, and the ink was messy and came off on my fingers. It said that the travelling fair was coming.

'Not here,' I said, 'to Tres Petromas. And only for one day, before it goes to Aghios Nicholaos for three nights.'

'Oh yes, of course,' she said. 'I saw that.'

This was not the truth. I know, everyone knows, she cannot read. Mind, she is not alone in that. Women especially are in the fields and working from the age of eleven and fast forget any school learning.

'Not for the likes of us,' I said.

Chrissi was back with Angel. So fast they must have run all the way – in this heat!

I don't know how to describe what Angel was wearing. Some old stuff of Will's, I think. Like jeans but with the legs cut off. Not sewn up even, all hanging raggedy down.

I saw Titi's eyes go straight to see; sometimes Will and Lucy seem to have no idea of how Angel should look and behave in the village.

The girls grabbed some water and cookies and ran out of the door, laughing. I yawned and Titi took the hint and saying goodbye left soon after.

The leaflet for the fair must have gone with her; it wasn't lying on the table any more.

ANGEL

Chrissi was so excited she was almost jumping up and down, and laughing too.

'All right,' I said, 'it will be a wonderful dress; you will look terrific. Now calm down!'

'No, no,' she said. 'Read this!' And she thrust this garish, creased paper into my hand.

It was saying there was to be a fair and a circus for one night at Tres Petromas.

'Wow, but we won't be allowed to go, will we? Unless we can persuade Will and Lucy to come with us.'

'We'll go on our own then – much more fun. I'll think of something.'

I knew she would, my wonderful wild friend. It's one of the things I really love about her. She is game for anything.

'I bet Petros and Andreas will be going. They wouldn't miss this.'

Petros and Andreas are at school with Chrissi and until I left the village we were all a group together, the four of us. Their families have them working in the fields or with the goats, during the summer. They are strong, so I bet they are sent to the pine trees to collect the resin. It's men's work. It was as if Chrissi could read my mind.

'They pick the tobacco, as well,' she said. 'But not at night. Look, Angel, read this,' and she thrust the paper under my nose. Her fingers were already coloured from the cheap inks.

I read aloud, 'Papa Polydefkis is touring the south and east

51

coasts of Crete with his one and only, the very best, original, electric powered funfair.'

She grabbed it back from me and read out the starred attractions.

'Listen. Fire-eaters, Varvara the best high-wire walker in the Aegean. That's his daughter, I know that. A shooting range with magnificent prizes to be won each night. Petros would go for that, he's a great rabbit hunter. Never misses. Kyria Eftoxia, the internationally famous fortune-teller.'

'Ha!' I said. 'For international read Crete and Rhodes.'

'But even so, it will be a wonderful night of fun down on the beach. We *have* to go.'

'I'll find out whether Will and Lucy would go.'

'Well, just find out what they plan for Saturday, that's the night. Don't tell them why yet.'

And that's what I thought to do. But when I got home there was no sign of Will and Lucy was crying quietly on the terrace. The moon was like a blazing torch tonight and it turned her cheeks to a shine where her tears ran down. I crept across to her.

'Dearest Lucy, what's the matter? Why are you sad? What's happened?'

She lifted the edge of her flowery cotton skirt and wiped her face with it.

'Oh, I'm just being stupid. I knew this day was coming. I know it has to happen. But suddenly it's here and I'm trying to look happy and not doing very well.'

'Is it Will? Is he leaving?'

She nodded and tears welled up again.

'When?'

'Saturday afternoon. I'll take the hired car he got and drive him to Sitia. He'll take the bus to Heraklion from there. I'll keep the car for a few more days until I have to leave as well.'

'Don't talk about that. I can't bear it!'

And the thought of a night at the fair with my friends didn't seem nearly as wonderful if it meant losing my family.

'We will ask if you can stay with Aphrodite.'

'Will said Father would never allow it.'

'I'll use a little Irish charm on him. He'll see reason, I bet. What else are you supposed to do?' She paused. 'Well, come back to London with me for a while until . . . ?'

'Exactly, until what? And I don't want to be rude, or ungrateful, but I want to be here. In the village, my own home.'

'Quick quick! Wake up!'

This was Chrissi the next morning, very first thing. As I opened my eyes she was standing at the end of my bed.

'We're meeting Petros and Andreas this afternoon – to make a plan.' She jumped on top of me, laughing as I groaned. 'They're going, of course, and so must we!'

Lucy had made us chicken in the oven with wine and olives for dinner last night and she had cheered up loads. I think that's what cooking does for her. I wish I had something I could lose myself in just like that. I told Chrissi what was going on, about Lucy taking Will to Sitia on Saturday. Instead of being fed up for me being left with no proper home, no family, she grinned all over her face.

'That's brilliant,' she said. 'We'll go with Lucy as far as Tres Petromas and say we're going for a swim or something and we'll tell Yorgo and Aphrodite we are going to see Will off on the bus – all of us together. How about that?'

I could see it was a solution so I felt a bit better, but still I kept thinking of Will's face as he waved goodbye and I got all choked up about it.

That afternoon was hot and still and Aphrodite's *gypo* offered barely any shade.

I loved going there; it smelt so richly of all the things growing. There were oranges, lemons, nectarines that tumble around your shoulders as you stumble through the suntouched trees. We picked some up and bit into the sweetness. So different to the stuff at The Oaks they called fruit.

'A manky old apple, all wrinkled and pruney,' I told Chrissi, and, laughing, she threw a small unripe pomegranate at me.

'Bite up on this,' she said, 'if you think they are all so wonderful.'

We had climbed over the wall when Chrissi tugged on my arm and said, 'I want to tell you something.' I looked at her. 'Before we see the boys.'

She pulled out a cigarette and sat on the springy grass.

'You know Petros?' I nodded. 'Swear not to tell anyone?'

I nodded. 'Swear.'

'He kissed me and had a feel of my top, last week.'

I nearly dropped my cigarette. 'He what?'

'You heard me. It was nice actually, I quite liked it.'

'Under your T-shirt, or over?'

'Over to start with and then I let him get under.'

'What kind of kiss?'

'Oh, tongues, of course. We're not babies.'

'Had you done it before?'

'What, with him, or with anyone?'

This was astonishing. I'd never ever had this kind of conversation before. Even with Chrissi.

'Anyone, I suppose. Or him. Oh, I don't know.'

'Well, Takis kissed me and tried to do tongues and get under my T-shirt once, but I didn't let him, so no, I suppose not, really.'

'You sound so cool about it, like you're talking about the harvest or what you had for dinner.'

'Well, I'm seventeen, you know.'

'I know, but so am I . . . well, nearly, and *I've* never done that.'

'Well, you were at a girls' school, weren't you, so I don't expect you had much chance.'

This was all a bit sudden and surprising.

'I need to take it in, think about it,' I said, getting to my feet rather clumsily because my foot had gone to sleep. Chrissi jumped up too.

'Oh don't be off with me. I'll wish I hadn't told you.'

'I'm not off with you. I'm just a bit surprised, is all: you and boys and that. Last time we had a chat you weren't like this. It

54

was about jeans and music and stuff. I thought you were like me.'

She threw her arms around me suddenly and hugged me really tightly.

'Oh Angel, dear Angel, I'm sorry. I didn't mean it to sound like that. I just wanted to tell you. You're my best friend, my only friend, really, and as soon as I'd done it I thought, Oh I must tell Angel about this. And I thought we'd laugh about it.'

She looked so fed up and sorry for herself, I had to laugh anyway, and I felt better and arm in arm we went to join the others.

The cicadas were noisy, but over them and all the little things that were crooning and buzzing in the rich undergrowth I heard laughter.

I was really pleased to see everyone. Even though I had been back for what felt like ages now it seemed, the days had all been so full with doing I don't know what, that I hadn't thought to see anyone except Chrissi. Andreas slowly came up to me first and for a moment I thought he was going to kiss me. He did once, when we were both ten, but that was really only because we were playing kiss-chase in the playground. He's miles shorter than me, he always has been and now, I reckon, always will be.

He stopped right in front of me, looked me up and down and, turning a bit pink, banged me on the arm instead. He was sort of smiling and I saw he'd managed to lose one of his front teeth. He also, and this was really amazing to me, had a moustache. Sure, it was only a thin one so far but there were definitely black hairs along his upper lip. He's always been part of our gang, with Chrissi and me. Petros was right behind him and also banged me on the arm. I guess this is some form of greeting, not a handshake or a hug or a kiss, but a sort of general, physical way of saying hello.

He's quite good looking, Petros, just like his father the ironworker, who has a terrible reputation as a flirt with any woman in the village. Even the old ones like Athena. He makes them laugh, twitching his great moustache, and they blush pinkly. Petros is a bit like that himself; he's a giggler, too. But he's fun and I like him. I tried to look at him normally, but I kept thinking of him and Chrissi – it was weird.

He was wearing what looked like a new pair of jeans; Levi's, it said on the label. But the fact that I could read that and they were shiny and stiff told me they had come from one of the travelling markets. He reached up to grab some oranges from the tree we were under and I saw the label actually said Lewis.

The orange tree was catching rays of sunlight and dappling the fruit-laden ground. I rubbed a leaf in my fingers and the dark oily citrus smell tickled in my nose.

The others had fags, but they shared them. They wanted to know about my school and why I had been chucked out.

'She only set fire to it!' Chrissi said.

'I didn't! Not all of it anyway, just a barn.'

'Funny schools they have in England – in barns.'

But although we all laughed together and it was good to be back with them, there was an awkwardness.

I told myself I imagined it. But neither of the boys could look in my eyes. They shuffled about on their bums and looked far away.

I thought I belonged here, with these, my real friends, but they've moved on, away to a world I'm no longer a part of. They joshed and nudged and teased each other and I felt that although they gave me a fag or two, I was now in a different place. Not one they were comfortable to be in.

Then when Chrissi talked about the dare, about the flag-pole, it was a little bit better.

'That was really something.'

'You lot were no help.'

Petros looked at me then, properly.

'We never thought Angel would do it. Come back from her posh school and hang her drawers out to dry!'

And Chrissi said, 'You should know better. Nothing scares her. She even had Irini's rats running all over her feet that night, didn't you?'

Andreas said gruffly, 'Rats is nothing.' But he'd gone white and looked queasy.

Petros said, 'OK, my friend, I'll remember that one day – you're a rat lover.'

Andreas kicked his foot. 'Shut up!'

'Good for you, Angel,' Petros said.

Of course they were going to the fair. They laughed when I asked about the curfew and how they would break it.

'We're not afraid of them, those people you call inspectors.'

'And Aphrodite calls the *malakas*!'

'They don't bother us so much. It's only the old reds, the communists, they give trouble to.'

'Like my father,' said Chrissi, 'just my luck.'

Lucy made a special supper for Will on Friday night. I know they tried to include me and were terrifically kind and talked to me, but I could see their eyes could barely leave each other for a moment and from time to time I saw Will's hand stroking Lucy's on the table.

We went over to Aphrodite's afterwards and the special fruit raki came out of the cupboard and we all had a glass. It was delicious, made with wild berries Aphrodite had gathered on the hillside last autumn. She had cut up lots of fruit and her own cheese and arranged them all on a huge old china plate with butterflies painted all around the rim. The fruit sat on a bed of those shiny green orange tree leaves. It looked nearly as good as it tasted.

Will and Yorgo talked in the corner and Papa Diamedes came by to say goodbye and wish him a safe journey, *Kalo taxidi!*

It was late when we all went up the hill and home and when Will and Lucy went out on to the terrace I went to my bed. But how could I sleep while I was such a great jumble of mixed feelings? I was happy to be here, sad at the thought of Will leaving; excited about the fair, but secretly worried that I was letting him down by sneaking off to it.

My friends no longer seemed to care whether I was here or not. They thought I was a posh girl from a posh school, not a village friend, part of that easy group we used to be.

I longed to talk to my mother. I just wanted each day to begin and end in the same way, in the same place. A rhythm, of hours, days, weeks that would be familiar, comforting in that sameness. And I wanted everything to go back to being just as it had been when I was a child. I had come back here for holidays from The Oaks, of course I had. But she was here then, Heavenly, my mother, and because of that I didn't notice that they thought I was different.

Outside, those old bullfrogs croaked, a scops owl hooted, and under that there was the low murmur of my brother's voice, as he spoke sweet words of love to Lucy. Oh how I wish, I wish . . .

But I don't know what for. And banging my head down under my pillow, and curling my body around itself I eventually grumbled into sleep.

Driving down the hillside with all the windows open it was the noise we heard first; clashes of cymbals, bells, accordions, pipes and whistles; and under all, the thomp, thomp, thompity thomp of drums. The long beach seemed, for the first time in my life, crowded. It felt like hundreds of people were there, wandering around the different stalls and their offerings. They must have come here from every village in the mountains. There were villagers from Panagia, small groups of them, kids with their parents. There were smells, all of them good; sweet pink candy sugar flossing in cones; sausages and *gyros*, barbecuing chicken with fragrant herbs; nuts, all kinds, soft green pistachios and sugared almonds galore. All to be bought in little fancy paper cornets.

Overall, the smells: excitement, energy, perfume and a musty sweet smoky aroma that was filling my hair with forbidden scents. The night sky was changed by deep yellow swirls rising up from the engines, turning the night back into a wicked twilight. It seemed a night where anything could happen.

There were swings and roundabouts, their motors grinding unknown tunes that somehow faintly echoed sounds from my childhood.

People wandered slowly, their eyes feasting on the sights, their noses twitching with anticipation. There were competitions too: who could run furthest with a pig in their arms, for instance, and we watched as a giant of a man with no hair and a long beard ran around the site holding a wriggling squealing animal. His friends called the lengths, '. . . nineteen, twenty, twenty-one . . .'

Andreas said, 'No one is going to beat that.'

A woman, I think it was a woman, in jeans and a long shirt was calling through a megaphone for volunteers for a tug of war. She had collected about six men so far.

'Shall we?' said Andreas with a longing in his eyes.

'Nah,' said Petros. 'Maybe later.'

We had left Will and Lucy, rather sheepishly abandoning the pretence that we had decided to stay behind for a quiet late swim.

'Forget it, Angel,' said Will as he stepped out of the car to give me a last hug. 'I don't know about Chrissi, but we know perfectly well what you are up to.' But he laughed and even gave me some money as he curled his longs legs back into the driving seat.

'This is all on the condition that you meet Lucy here on her way back and ride with her home to the village. OK?'

We nodded. 'Absolutely!'

'Two hours,' she said. 'And if I'm delayed wait there by the sea wall, right there, yes?'

'And run a mile if you see any of the *malakas*,' said Will.

'Yes! Yes! We will be there.'

And suddenly they were gone and I wanted to run after the car and stop it and jump in and hug Will hard and even harder. Chrissi saw and pulled my hand under her arm saying, 'Come on, the boys will be on the shooting range, let's go.'

59

And we did and they were. Chrissi had not been wrong; Petros had already shot several of the moving ducks set as targets and beside him Andreas held a collection of dolls, straw hats, plastic trumpets and, of all things, a teapot.

There were some girls hanging round him, and he knew it and liked it. He was playing to his audience.

'Take your pick,' he shouted over the din. 'Look, a lovely knitted bear for your mother, Chrissi. She'll like that.'

'What shall I tell her? That I found it as I walked along the beach collecting shells?'

And the girls nudged each other and giggled.

Petros said, 'I'm hungry, starving. Get us a *gyros*, will you?' And he pulled some drachmas out of his pocket.

I took them and said, 'I'll go. You wait here.'

I jostled my way through the crowds to the man selling *souvlaki* from the barbecue. I bought enough for the four of us and when I got back Petros was still holding a rifle but there was no sign of the others.

He took the sweet-smelling packets of food and placed them up with his still-growing pile of prizes. He called over his shoulder, 'They've gone to find the tattooist, over there,' and pointed vaguely to the other end of the long beach where some painted caravans stood separate from the crowd.

I wandered over, gazing at all the magic as I went. Everything so brightly coloured, everything smelling different, sounding strange. Like music, but not like any tune I knew. I passed a child riding on the back of a mule, the battered old saddle sliding back and forth as the child, a girl I think, clung on, and beside it, a woman in spangled sequins with glossy black hair riding bareback on a black horse. She must have been part of the circus. Further along there were a couple of camels lazily nuzzling the sand and I paused beside them, but they didn't even look at me, just rootled on.

There were the caravans and in curly gold lettering on the side of one it said, 'Kyria Eftoxia – world-renowned clairvoyant and mystic'.

60

Beside it was another caravan, this one painted green and gold, and coming down the steps, giggling, was Andreas.

'Look, Angel,' he called and pulling his sleeve back I saw he had an anchor there now, blue.

I felt a sudden thrill; the gardening boy at school had tattoos; he had shown me. There was one on his back of an angel. I remembered the head gardener coming over and yelling at him to put his clothes on.

'Did it hurt?' I asked Andreas, trying to peer closely at his arm.

'Oh yes, terribly,' he said, but he laughed.

And from behind I heard, 'Wait for me!'

Chrissi emerged from the gloomy interior of the caravan with her arm waving.

'See! See Angel.'

I looked and in red ink it said MANOLI. I bit back a laugh. Whoever has a tattoo of their brother's name? I wanted one myself now, desperately.

'Wait for me,' I said, 'I'm going in.'

Andreas said, 'Posh kids don't get tattooed,' and they laughed.

That was it. I'd show them.

'You can wait for me or not, just as you like, but I'm going to do it.' And I marched up those steps as if I was going to join the army.

Inside, although dark, the walls were brilliantly coloured and on them, painted huge, were dragons, thunderclouds, lightning flashes, musical notes and lots of names all with curly flourishes. There were flowers, all sorts, trees and anchors: large ones and small. A man was sitting on a high stool. He was young, I guess, well, older than me. And Will. He seemed about to smile but it was just a twitch that went nowhere. He had piercing eyes, as if he could see through me.

'Come for a little souvenir?' His voice was high, squeaky and the effort of speaking made him cough, a wet, loose sound.

'I think so.'

He chuckled. 'No good thinking about it in here. It's either yes or no. Transfer is it, or the proper job?'

'Oh proper job, of course. Well, I think so.'

'Know what you want, do you? Something along the lines of your friend outside, is it?'

'I don't want my brother's name, if that's what you mean.'

'Only we can't rub it out afterwards.' And he laughed and coughed some more.

'Can you do an angel?'

'If that's what you want.'

And he reached for a huge book on the shelf behind him, laid it open in front of me and turned the pages. I could see it was crammed full of pictures of butterflies, flowers, hearts and curlicued names. Then he pointed at one and turned the book to me; there it was on the page, a couple of angels. Just like the gardener's boy's.

'That one.' I pointed at the smaller of the two.

'And where do you want it?'

I was already pulling up my sleeve. 'Here, just here, near my shoulder.'

'Money first.'

I pulled Will's money out of my pocket and tried not to let him see the notes.

'How much?'

He named a price which seemed a lot. I handed it over; it was almost all I had and I wondered how Chrissi had enough to pay for hers.

'Nervous are you?' I shook my head. 'Only you're a bit sweaty, see, and you've got to keep your arm still.'

I held my arm out rigidly and breathed deeply. I watched while he took down a big box and rifled through it. Holding a paper out to me, he said, 'This the one?'

It was an angel. A rather over-sweet cherubim, with fat puffy cheeks and curly hair. It was blowing a trumpet and it was on shiny tissue paper, just like Titi used for patterns for dresses.

'Can I have it without the horn, please?'

'Pay your money, you have what you like.'

'And without the curls.'

'A bald angel, then, and certainly not one of the heavenly choir.'

He was actually quite twinkly. I liked him.

I watched as he wet the paper and then placed it on my arm, holding it there, very still for minutes, rubbing his hand up and down, side to side, over and over. As he gently peeled it back, the image was left behind on my arm.

'Is that it?'

He laughed and coughed again, scrabbled around on his table, took out some tobacco papers and carefully rolled a cigarette. He must have been smoking since he was a baby to have a cough like that.

'Want one?' He slid his pink oily-looking tongue along the length and squeezed it.

'No, thank you.'

'So, going on are we? The full business?'

'Of course.'

He pulled from behind him things that looked like spikes on a striped ragged electric cord and a wobbly stained metal tray, splashed with colours. I shut my eyes tight as he gripped my arm straight. The first thing I felt was like whizzling on my skin; a bit like a sausage sizzling in a frying pan. Then a burning sort of tickle that went on and on, around and up and down. It did hurt, a lot. But I wasn't going to let him see that. It seemed to go on for hours and I bit hard on my lip. Every few moments he stopped and I opened an eye a crack and saw him dip the needle into one of the colour pots on the tray. The ash fell off his cigarette, and splattered down on to his grubby jumper. I don't know how long the whole thing lasted, but I do know the minute he said 'All done' was the moment it began to hurt like mad. It was like hundreds of bees stinging on my arm together and I bit my lips harder to stop myself squealing. I dared to look around and my arm was pink and lumpy but there, through the droplets of blood and the beginnings of a magnificent bruise, was the angel, my angel, right where she belonged.

He was staring at me. I thought, He thinks I'm going to cry, so instead I laughed and said, 'Easy-peasy, thank you.'

He stood up and so did I and was about to roll my sleeve down when his hand shot out and grabbed my wrist.

'No no, wait till it's dried. And no water on it for a week.'

I saw then that when his mouth opened he had a flashing gold tooth inside. I thought, Rich business, tattooing.

'You're a brave one, I'll say that. More than your little friend.'

What did he mean? But I didn't stop to find out. I wanted to get out of there as fast as I could, show the others what I'd done.

I stood at the top of his steps and peered around. I heard a whoop from out of the dark and there was Chrissi running towards me.

'You've been ages, what did you get? Let me see.'

'Does your arm hurt?' I asked her.

She looked at me for a moment, laughed. 'Erm, no.'

'Oh come on, Chrissi, you're not that brave. I've seen you yell at a stinging nettle. Admit it. Bloody, it's painful.'

There was a moment of silence; she didn't move. Then, 'Angel, tell me you're joking?'

Before I could answer, the tattooist had appeared at the top of his steps behind me. And he was laughing.

'Show her, go on, show her.'

And I slowly lifted my arm which by now was throbbing and burning enough to bring tears to my eyes and twisted it round so that the image was clearly visible. Ugly it was, still swelling and bruised, but my very own angel. Behind me the gold tooth was still laughing but when I turned to look, furious at his mockery, he disappeared behind his door and click, bang, a lock clearly slid into place.

'*Panagia mou!*' And for a moment she sounded just like her mother. Her face was pale, her mouth open.

'What's going on? Why do you look like that?'

She didn't move or speak at first, then slowly, 'Andreas was sure you wouldn't go all the way.'

'Did you have a dare on me?'

'I really didn't think you'd do it.'

'You had one, didn't you? And Andreas?'

She took my hand and pulled me from the steps.

'We had the ink ones, the pretend ones. It was just a tease. We didn't think you'd really do that.' As she said 'that' she looked at my arm as though it was some terrible wound, a scar, which I suppose is exactly what it was.

Before I could say anything, Petros was there, Andreas lumbering along behind, carrying all the prizes.

'Come and see what Angel's done.'

They crowded round, peering at my arm, real surprise on their faces.

Petros spoke first.

'You are so brave, girl.' And shaking his head he rolled his sleeve up and I saw there, on his shoulder in red and green, ELVIS.

'I had that done last summer. Good, isn't it? It hurt like hell, but it was worth it. My dad's got loads.'

Andreas was looking at me as though I'd dropped in from another planet. I supposed it was going to be all right, in one way at least. I was back at the centre of my friends again, one of them, and that was a good feeling. And I really did like having my own tattoo, my angel.

'What about your parents?'

'They're not here, are they?'

'Your brother?'

'On his way to Afghanistan.' It was as I spoke that I realised properly; I was completely on my own. Yes, there was Lucy. But she wasn't family. 'That'll teach them to desert me, won't it?' I laughed, but it was a hollow sound and only served to cover what otherwise would be tears.

'Come on,' Chrissi said and pulled my hand.

Andreas said, 'We're going to get more *gyros*, they were really good. You coming?'

'No, Angel and I are going to see what's in the other caravans.'

And she was away already and peering at the open doorway to the fortune-teller. She pulled me up the steps to the dimness inside and I could just see what was probably the Kyria Eftoxia herself, and she was smoking a fag.

When she saw us, she leaned forward and in a rather scary, crackly voice said, 'Come on, don't be afraid. I can see you've got a lucky face. I'll see what the cards tell for you. It'll be bound to be good news with a face like that.'

One final shove from Chrissi and I stumbled into the dingy caravan.

'I'm going to see what else there is,' Chrissi called cheerfully and as I turned, unsure suddenly, not wanting to be alone here, she had already vanished into the crowd.

The woman's hands were like claws, the nails painted bright green. They scrabbled at my sleeve, pinching my arm, and I felt trapped.

It smelt strange in there; musty, scented like old ladies' face powder, tobacco smoke. She pulled me to a tiny gold chair that I thought would collapse under my weight, but I clung on to the edge of a little table as she sat in a rather more substantial metal chair on the other side.

I got my hands back to myself for a moment, and rubbed them together, sniffing them quickly, trying to make sure I didn't carry any of her smell with me. My sleeve had got pulled down now and my arm hurt like anything. I suddenly longed for a glass of sherry or a cigarette.

There was a tablecloth in shiny blue satin with dragons on it and a fat candle in the centre of the table. With a scrabble under her skirts she produced first a box of matches and then a pack of cards. She lit the candle and a strong waxy smoky smell rose up.

She took hold of my hands again and peered into my eyes.

'Hmm,' she said and stared down at the palms. 'Hmm,' she said again and shook her head. 'I don't think the Tarot for you. I think the crystal would be truer, luckier. Let's hope so anyway.'

What did she mean? I wished she'd let go of my hands. It felt like I was being scratched on my palms with pincers, like a crab, but worse, cold and dead – ugh!

I didn't want to be on my own; I wanted Chrissi to come back to me. I wanted Lucy here with that car to take us home, safely home.

The fortune-teller had pushed the candle to one side and the hot melted wax dripped on to the blue cloth as she did so. Still clutching one hand she reached under the table with the other and a round glass ball banged down on the tabletop. Was there a light inside it? I couldn't tell but it glowed in the dimness of that place in an eerie way.

She peered into the ball now and pulled my hands open palm side up on the table. She was tracing a line on my hand with one of those green talons. It was sharp enough, I thought, to draw blood.

'Well, dear. You certainly have a long life ahead of you. But I'm not so sure any more that it's going to be an entirely happy one.'

Why did she say that? She looked up and caught my eye in her glance and her mouth curved into a rictus. I had a sudden memory of a biology class at The Oaks. The skeleton in the laboratory had a skull that was just like this. I pulled back as far as I could, which wasn't far. I was already hard against the wall.

'I don't think you will be very lucky in love, dear. Some are, some aren't.' She shrugged and leaned forward. Her breath smelled bad, rotten. 'You've got nice eyes, nice hands, but that doesn't always mean what we'd like it to mean. Do you have a little coin for me, darling? A few drachma, perhaps, and I can tell you some things about yourself that I think will surprise you.'

'No, my friend has our money.' I shook my head frantically side to side.

I wanted to run away from her and her unhappy pre-dictions. How could she know anything about me? She was a fraud, making it up. And summoning a strength from some-where inside me I pulled away, freed myself, and as I turned to bolt the few steps to the door, the table toppled over, my chair turned on its back and as the cloth swished languidly to the floor I saw that the wooden top was part of a box ad-vertising some sort of meat. That would account for some of the lingering smell.

She called after me, 'I'll make sure you'll be sorry! Hasn't anyone told you never ever to cross the luck of a gypsy?'

And reaching the doorstep of the caravan I glanced back and she was right there, behind me. I shuddered and she spat, hard and fast on to my shoulder and it clung there like a quivering blemish.

Petros was outside and I almost collided with him as I leapt down the steps.

'I waited for you,' he said. 'You've been ages, are you all right? Your arm, OK is it?'

I nodded. At least I was away, out of there, dripping with the sweat of a hot night, a cramped room. As Petros grabbed my good arm, I heard behind me Kyria Eftoxia call, 'Bad luck to you, girl with your foreign ways.'

What did she mean? What could she see?

'Where's Chrissi?'

'Over here, listen, you can hear them.'

Over the shrieks and whines and jangle of the fair, through the thickened saffron air from the oil lamps and machines, there was a faint sweet music drifting upwards.

'Come on, they're these musicians. You'll like them.'

I did. More than that, I loved them. There were two girls and a man and a couple of the sweetest-looking children. I looked at them and felt a curious and marvellous feeling of safety, but also excitement. I knew I was smiling and I didn't know where it had come from or why.

They were sitting on the ground around one of the thousand-year-old olive trees that fringe this beach. They wore clothes of scarlet, emerald, sapphire – all like jewels.

Even the man; he was dressed in a sarong and a T-shirt and

it didn't look odd at all. I looked down at my jeans and grubby top: how dull! I felt Chrissi looking at me and there was a longing in her eyes; so she could feel it too.

They had lots of hair. One girl had little plaits all over her head with beads threaded through. The man's hair, crinkly and a bit grey, was all swept back in a fat ponytail.

I had seen people like this before, years ago in London.

They told us their names, and even they were exotic somehow, different.

The man was Raggeh and the woman who sat with her head on his shoulder, the one with the plaits and beads and the little girl sleeping on her lap, was Anya. The other woman, who had long silky red hair that picked up the moonglow as she swung her head, was Libby. The boy was her son, Rufus. As we sat down with them, this boy, with a mop of thick black curly hair, jumped across the circle and sat with Chrissi. He smiled up at her and snuggled into her side like she was his best friend. She was smiling and put her arm around him, as if protecting him, but from what?

They were playing music, delicious, lyrical sounds. Raggeh had a guitar. I don't know much about this but I think it was a good one – the wood gleamed richly with glittering lights sparkling off the silver bits. Anya and the girl played penny whistles and Libby sang. I wanted to stay here with them. I wanted to thank them for being here. This was another world that I had crept into and this is where I want to be.

The words of the song were sad, plaintive; but I knew it. I even knew some of the words, but although Libby looked encouragingly at me, and took my hand, I wouldn't spoil the delicacy of this moment with my scratchy voice.

She looked at the man and said, 'Shall we?' He didn't answer but strummed a few chords and then it was, 'In Dublin's fair city, where the girls . . .' and, 'Come on,' she said, 'this one is for you.' So I did sing, and I thought of Lucy who came from Ireland and loved this song. I thought I must be nice to her now. She is going to be alone like me.

They told us they lived in caves the far side of Kato Zakros.

But they said they came to visit the fair every time it was in the neighbourhood. They had come, some time or another, from all over the world. They weren't Greek or English. Anya was from San Francisco, Libby from Australia and the man, Raggeh, said that although he was born in England, he had lived in Mexico for most of his life. They looked so happy, peaceful.

Anya said, 'Why not come and join us? You would enjoy our life.'

And I almost jumped up and said, 'Yes! I'll come.'

I wanted to be part of this group. Let *this* be where I belong.

I looked at Chrissi with the little boy cuddled up to her, as if she were his mother, and thought she'd never leave Panagia, or her family. And Petros and Andreas, they had their lives mapped out ahead. I'm the one that doesn't belong anywhere any more.

Chrissi took my hand in hers. She smiled at me and I felt a sudden fear of going ahead on my own, without her, and sank back down again.

That night at the fair, my angel tattoo, although it hurt like hell, and then meeting these lovely new friends, had opened my eyes to a world I had only ever dreamt of. I thought: My life will never be the same again.

I didn't think any more about the gypsy and her threatening words. I knew that whatever was planned in the stars for my future changed after that night.

APHRODITE

'You are running wild, child. You know what the rules are.'

I was up to my elbows in vinegar water, making the pickled vegetables for the winter. My daughter can only run around the village with her arms bare, showing off to anyone who'd stop to see her inky drawing; the one on her arm, MANOLI.

'I told you, Mama, it will come off.'

'And Angel's?'

'Well no, that's a real tattoo. Isn't it brilliant?'

'And when her parents come back? And ask how it happened? They will know who persuaded her. And you listen to me – I will be the one to carry the shame.'

'That's not fair!'

'It may not be fair, but it's true. Andreas's mother told me. And you know what they are saying? That I cannot control my own child, that's what. First dirty underwear for everyone to see, and now this. You disgrace your family, Chrissoula. And you think it's a joke.'

She was trying not to show her giggles and I cuffed her head.

'Wash those carrots there, and those beetroots. Make yourself useful.'

'Oh, Mama, the beetroot dyes my hands red, please, no.'

'Is this the miss who likes colours and names all over her? Beetroots, I said.'

Panagia mou – what next?

'The carving on Angel's arm will be there forever, you

know? Does she know? It is a disgrace, a shameful thing to cut yourself like that. Agatha says—'

'Oh, Mama, you listen too much to the gossips. "Agatha says this, Marina says that . . ." You should tell them all to be quiet! Or should I tell them? Yes, that's it! Angel and I will go down to the spring and—'

'You will do nothing, child. You have said and done enough mischief for a pack of wild animals, you two.'

'You could have been there, Mama, and Papa too. And Manoli. Lots of Panagia families were there altogether. You should have come and seen for yourself what fun it was.'

'Enough, Chrissi. What do you think, that your papa and I should join in all the wild things I heard about? Men running around with pigs on their backs and the like? Who would pay for that, I'd like to know?'

As I added broad beans to the vinegar water, I thought of how they had all talked of this fair at the spring the day after. Never would I say it, but I wish I had been there. Yorgo says I must always be in charge, on top. Always the commander, always the one telling everyone else what to do. And I was only seeking to help. Manoli needs help to try to stand on his own feet and his sister needs help to stop treading on everyone else's.

The baptism of Titi's whatever-relative was to take place on Sunday. Yorgo dithered and mithered around; one minute he would go with Manoli, the next he wouldn't, and so it was no surprise to me that when Sunday came he walked with a stoop in his back and a limp in his leg from first light. The morning had broken all pale gold and orange and before long it had settled into the white light of day.

The wind that had been with us for days left us alone the night before. It happens here in summer. The *meltemi* wind blows in from Africa and covers everything with the fine dust of Libya. We can do nothing; shutters tight, windows closed and still the floor under your feet is thick with the powder. Clothes are gritty when you put them on, and as for fresh washing, best forget it; it's smudged at once.

He is a good groaner, my Yorgo. His weathered and sun-brown face can screw itself into agony in a moment. I always know when he has a chill or a cough coming on – he walks with a limp. He does! So I saw him appear for his coffee that morning, hanging on to the lintel and then a chair back to ease himself slowly to the table. I was at the fire, just lifting the *briki* to pour, and all I could hear was the shuffle, shuffle, limp, pause shuffle.

'You haven't forgotten today is the day for Manoli to play over the mountain, have you?'

Lengthy groan and then another. 'Ah, is it that day already?'

'Yes, it is. No work today, it's Sunday. Remember? And you are to play with him over in Aghios Demetrious.'

More groans. 'I think I had better just see how I am feeling, later. I must tell you that just this minute I feel very bad, very poorly. I am so tired, I barely closed my eyes all night.'

'Oh? So who was the man that shared my bed and made so much noise with his snoring that it set the hens off and woke the dog?'

Yorgo gave me a look of despair. I could see he was going to play up for every bit of sympathy he could get.

'Perhaps you should just go back to bed then, if you are so bad?'

'Good idea,' he said and he shuffled up and off to the door.

'Yes, you have a good rest now, *andras mou*, and then you will be well enough to go with Manoli.'

He paused, mid limp and peered sadly at me. 'You are a hard woman.'

I had to make Manoli smarten himself up for this event, this adventure. He had appeared hobbling like his father.

'Is there something wrong?'

'Must I go, Mama?'

I hugged him to me and I felt the stiff tension in his young body. He was a big lad, tall but not muscled even in his arms. I had hoped the work he did with the lathe and the plane in the workshop would make him fit.

'You will be fine, *giosaki mou* . . .' And I stroked his dark

73

curls back from his forehead. But his eyes were troubled and the dark circles under them told me he must have lain sleepless last night with the worry of what today would bring.

He held his accordion in its case and I hoped that once he started to play the confidence I had seen in him before would come back.

Yorgo shuffled out of his bed and into the kitchen looking as melancholy as his son. I felt a flash of anger.

'Look at the pair of you! You are not going to a funeral today, you know. Ah, *Panagia mou*, you are going across the mountain to a party. The celebration of a birth. Can't you smile! Look a little bit happy please!'

Two wan faces looked back at me and I shrugged. What can I do?

There was little change by the time they left at the end of the afternoon. Yorgo's limp was still bad and the cough was strong. He even managed a hefty sneeze or two. But I ignored this and said to him under my breath, 'You know this is important for Manoli, a big chance. Perhaps there will be others at the baptism that will want him to play for their family occasions.'

I made them a package of some cakes and fruit and a flask of wine and a little jar of raki. Goodness knows why; baptisms are always a time for feasting and there should be refreshments for them aplenty. But it soothed a little of the guilt I was feeling, especially as Yorgo turned to me with a sad droop to his moustache as they left, '*Yassou, yineka mou.*'

'*Sto kalo. Kalo taxidi.*'

Of course I wished them a safe journey. But when I turned back to the house Chrissi said, 'Come on, Mama, they are only going three kilometres round the mountain. Not to Africa, you know.'

They left while the sun was still high. The heat that had been with us all day had hardly changed; the air was heavy. Even the birds were too exhausted to sing and a heavy silence hung like a pall over the village. Most sensible people were in their houses, still dozing. I could almost smell the *pastitsio or moussaka* from the Sunday family gatherings – always dishes that can stretch to feed many.

I sat under the twisted olive tree by the gate and watched them disappear along the track. There had been much debate about whether they would take our donkey with them. But he is so old they would be quicker and more comfortable on foot.

I sighed. More money to find, and it is too soon to tell if this will be a good year for the crops. Yorgo is busy enough with the carpentry, so any more work in the fields will be for me, with perhaps a little help from Chrissi.

I cannot tap the resin from our pine trees alone any more. I must pay for someone to do it. It's man's work, and a strong man too. I've wondered about pushing Manoli towards that. There's good money to be made but Yorgo is reluctant.

'He works well with me. That's enough. He's not as strong as you think. A good boy, willing, but not muscled for that sort of heavy work; maybe in a while.'

It seemed they had hardly gone when I saw in the distance a figure plodding slowly back along our path. But I think I had dozed. Chrissi said she had seen me sleeping under the olive. She swore she said 'goodbye' when she left for the Orfanou-dakis house. I don't remember that.

As the figure got closer I saw it was Yorgo, limping.

I was angry immediately, and then I saw his face. He was clearly unwell. His usually brown cheeks were flushed and his brow was damp with the sweat of a fever. He made it to the tree and sank down beside me, dabbing at his face with a handkerchief that looked far from fresh.

'Where is Manoli?'

'He went on alone. We got to the top of the gorge, you know? Halfway to Saint Demetrious and I could go no further.' He saw my face, saw the questions there. 'He can do well enough alone, Aphrodite. He is nearly a man now. It won't hurt him to go to the Papadakis house on his own. What can happen to him? He will play, they will cheer and dance. He has the package of food you gave us. For the Panagia's sake stop fussing and fretting around him as though he is a china doll.' He broke down into a fit of coughing that racked his body. 'A bit of that care you give your son would go down well for your husband today.'

He looked so sad I knew he was right. I was unfair. I had forced him to go when he was ill. And he was right too, about Manoli. I would wrap my boy in tissue if I could; I am a fool for him.

Later, much later, while Yorgo was sleeping, Chrissi came back.

She was skipping along behind Angel who was carrying a platter draped with muslin.

'Lucy made some *dolmades* for you to try. She wants to know if you think they are good enough. The leaves are from their own vine.'

So it was an afternoon for cooking. I had made jars of *mousmoula* preserved in raki. The sweet orange fruit from our tree and the strong spirit from last year's *kazani*. 'And some *gemista* – tomatoes, peppers stuffed with rice and herbs. These are good.'

I remember so clearly, every mouthful of that *gemisto*. I could never eat it again. Delicious as it is, it would choke in my throat.

'Show me your arm, Angel.'

She held her arm out as if she were proud of it. 'Look and see.'

It had healed, certainly, but it was even clearer now, this angel.

'Lucy is not happy, I know.'

'She'll come round.'

'For your sake I hope so. What of your parents, what news of them?'

'They ring every day just now. No one has heard from Will since he left nearly a week ago.'

'Did you expect to hear from him?'

'He told Lucy he would ring her from the airport. She stayed by the phone all that day.'

'She hardly leaves the house, Mama.'

'She said she's not leaving the village until she has heard from him.'

'So you have added to her worries by doing this to your body?'

Yorgo woke and joined us, already looking better for the sleep and the raki and honey drink I had made him.

Outside, night had come in. It seemed one minute it was the hot sun of the afternoon and the next dark and heavy with the twilight. It happens sometimes here after a windstorm: day swings into night in moments.

It was Angel who said, as she was leaving, 'When will Manoli come back?'

Suddenly I was guilty; I hadn't thought of him for a while.

'He has been away for hours, now.'

And then Yorgo said, 'I hope he hasn't met any of the Saint Demetrious boys on the road around the mountain, little devils they are.'

I was suddenly cold. I had felt ill omens all day. I reached into the neck of my dress for the blue glass eye that hangs there on a thin chain. It is worn to ward off the evil eye. I know the younger generation scorn it; but I know that bad things always happen when I don't wear it. My fingers scrabbled at my neck. There was nothing there. I pulled through my underclothes: nothing. Now I felt a shiver through me. 'Something is wrong,' I said.

Chrissi laughed, 'You've probably got Papa's cold that's all.'

'I will go across to Aghios Demetrious and meet him. He is surely on his way home by now. Yorgo stay here. You rest and get better quick. You have work to do all week, you told me so.'

As I reached for my shawl Chrissi said, 'I will come with you, Mama.'

And then Angel was on her feet and running out the door.

'I'll tell Lucy and join you by the double gate near the top of the gorge. Don't go on without me.'

Yorgo came out as far as the twisted olive and, coughing, said, 'Don't make too much of this. He is not missing, not even late. He will be playing and eating and drinking and flirting with the girls and having a great time. Don't make him afraid to go out alone, Aphrodite. He is a man now. Let him go.'

As I pulled my shawl over my head, I said over my shoulder, 'I think you are living in a different world to the rest of your family. We are not talking of Aristos here. Manoli flirting? What rubbish you talk.'

But as we hurried on in the gathering dark, I thought, If only it could be true. *Panagia mou*, let him be like the rest of the young men, let us meet him on the path with a girl on his arm and wine on his breath and let him greet us with a laugh at our worrying.

So who was being foolish now?

ANGEL

It was me who found him.

The others had gone ahead on the main path to Saint Demetrious, but something made me pause by the cypress trees that shielded the track down to the gorge. There was a sound; a soft scratchy whimper, like an animal caught in a trap. A hoarse, whispery sound, and then again. I had to look, even though I was afraid. It was so dark, the moon hidden in clouds just now, and I tiptoed carefully down through the acacia and thorn bushes, catching my bare arm on the loose bark of a pomegranate tree and then I saw it; a bundle under a lemon tree. It was flat up against the trunk, supported by it as if it had been flung down here.

This was where the sound came from. And then the moon came suddenly out from a cloud and lit the sky like a beacon. And I knew I had found Manoli.

Oh how I wish I hadn't, not like this.

He was so still, I thought he was dead.

There was blood, dark and sticky looking. He was curled all round himself like a baby. But he lifted his head as I approached, just a tiny bit, and I saw that one of his eyes was full of blood, nearly closed.

There was a gash on his head and his hands looked huge, his fingers swollen. And as I called out to bring the others to this place, I saw other things. His shirt was gone and there were little round brown marks down his arms and, as he turned, I saw they were on his chest, too. I realised I had almost bitten through my lip as I pulled my head back.

79

I tasted blood but it didn't matter. The pain I felt was nothing like his. Poor Manoli, who never hurt anything in his life. Once I saw him lift a scorpion so gently in his hands and take it from the house to a tree, so that it could live.

'Chrissi! Aphrodite! Help!'

Only the echo of my words came back to me.

I felt cold; I was shivering. And then hot again with anger.

My hands were shaking and I clenched my fists tight until my nails dug deep into my palms. I had never seen anyone injured like this in my life before.

And then, after what seemed ages, there was a scrambling and a blur of noise and at first I didn't know what it was. I thought it might be whoever had done this come back, and I was really scared. But it was Chrissi and my aunt.

For a moment I wanted to keep this to myself. No mother should see her son like this, no sister her brother. But of course they must, and they were here now and the scream that came from Aphrodite's throat was so terrible it was as if it was torn from her. And then she was down beside him, not a thought for the thorn bush she was kneeling in, and she was cradling him and crooning to him with sobs and tears.

I wanted to say, 'It's all right, he is hurt, badly, probably, but not dead.' But what did I know?

Chrissi was beside her, looking up at me.

'Where is his accordion? Look around please, please.'

I scrambled to my feet thinking, 'What does the accordion matter?' But I began to scour the ground for it. I found it quickly. It wasn't far from Manoli, but it was a broken image of itself.

Someone had thrown it against a tree, stamped on it maybe. It was bent and twisted with slashes in the hide. But it was only an instrument – we would get him another. We couldn't replace Manoli so easily.

It was a long night.

I had run as fast as I could to their house and, sick as he was, Yorgo had come straight away.

'Go to Papa Diamedes, his wife has medical knowledge, bring her here, quick, quick,' he said, and he was gone.

I beat on the door of the priest's house and, perhaps used to emergencies, he leaned out of his upstairs window within a moment.

'Please, please come, Papa. The Babyottis family need you. There has been an accident, near the gorge. Manoli is hurt.'

I didn't wait. The Papa and his wife were fast behind me, and with their mule. Of course, we needed it to carry Manoli home.

The full moon shone down brightly on the gorge now, lighting up this strange little group. Manoli's head lay in Aphrodite's lap. His body was still twisted around itself, and Chrissi was stroking his head and Yorgo knelt at his feet.

The Papa and his wife, Agni, had brought a bag that she opened at once. It had bandages, ointments; things like that.

Nobody spoke and that, with the little movements, was as if it was a scene from a film and not really happening.

I don't know how long we stayed there before, carefully, Yorgo and the Papa lifted Manoli on to the back of the mule. His eyes were open now. Agni and Aphrodite urged Chrissi on as well and I saw she was like a cushion, softening her brother's journey home.

Suddenly I felt awkward, as if I had no right to be here; like an onlooker at a car crash. There was nothing for me to do. I wanted to cry, but they didn't need my tears now. I wanted someone to hold me, but of course there wasn't anyone.

I felt so muddled and guilty, thinking only of myself. I didn't even say goodbye but they didn't notice.

The anger I was feeling stayed with me as I hurried home to Lucy and I was burning up with it by the time I arrived.

The house looked warm and inviting, the lights shining through the open doors and windows. Music was playing from a now very battered record player Will had given me one birthday. A lush, rich sound, from an opera, I think. Part of me wanted to stay outside and be soothed by this and then I could go in as though nothing had happened and Lucy would make me laugh and everything would be all right again. But there was another bit of me that knew that this was one of those moments in your life when time stops and the world stands still. And then, when things slowly start again, everything has changed.

I was sad that it wasn't anything good but something violent and disgusting.

I walked forward, up the heavy stone steps, past the dusty vine. Past the thin red geranium, looking as though it would be dead by the morning, into this house, my home, that always comforted me, even in its shadows.

'Is that you, Angel? Come and taste.'

We sat on the terrace, Lucy and me. She made me a drink of hot cocoa with a bit of brandy or something in it to help me stop shaking.

'You've had a shock, Angel, a bad shock.'

She was angry, like me, when I told her what had happened to Manoli and kept saying over and over again, 'Who would do this? Why would anyone do this?'

She wanted to go to the Babyottis's house at once, but I told her there was nothing she could do there.

I think the worst thing was that this had happened barely yards from the village; my safe place, my home; the place I had dreamed of every night in that school and told myself that everything would be good if I could only get back to it.

Sitting there on our terrace, under the moon that had seen everything that happened tonight, I suddenly thought of poor Manoli's accordion, all broken and smashed up and the beautiful music I had heard him play, and then I began to cry and Lucy, lovely kind Lucy, put her arms around my shoulders and hugged me tightly and rocked me like a baby. I sobbed as though I would never stop.

I did, of course, and I slept and I didn't even have bad dreams because Lucy tucked me up in her big bed and cuddled me all night.

*

The next morning we went early over to the Babyottis's house, but there were lots of people inside all talking and Lucy pulled me away.

'We should come back later,' she said. 'The president of the village is there, I think. Isn't that him in the dark suit and the tie? That little man with the thin moustache who has the look of a weasel?'

I nodded, but I wasn't really sure.

Chrissi had seen us pass by the open door and came out.

'How is Manoli?' Lucy whispered. 'Is he here or has he gone to the clinic in Sitia?'

'He's here. He's sleeping. The doctor came up from Tres Petromas last night and saw to all his wounds and bandaged them and everything. He says there are no broken bones. He had to stitch a big cut on his head and give him an injection. He's coming back again in a few days. He says he doesn't think he needs to go to hospital. But he must have lots of sleep. Mama sat with him all night, and Papa is with him now.'

'What are they doing to find who did this?'

'That's why Stelios Panayiotis is here. Papa went to his house to tell him what had happened and he came back to see for himself. Papa Michaelis is here too. Mama is afraid they won't do anything. They have already said Manoli shouldn't have been out after dark on his own.'

'Shush!' said Lucy pulling us back. 'Angel, I am not staying here now. This is private, for Aphrodite's family only, I think.'

There were raised voices coming from inside now and Chrissi held my hand tightly.

'Don't leave me,' she said.

'You stay,' Lucy whispered. 'I'll see you at home.'

'Come on, come in with me,' Chrissi said and we inched forward, hand in hand, and into her house.

Aphrodite saw us in the doorway and waved us forward.

I have always loved the great strength of my aunt; she is like a rock, I always thought she would protect us from anything bad. So I was shocked to see her just now. A big woman, she suddenly seemed small and helpless.

She stood in the centre of the room and those men sat at the side, and you could see a tired defeat in the way she was standing, her hands in front twisting and turning.

'Of course it is a bad thing to happen, Aphrodite, no one denies that. But what are we expected to do?' This was Stelios, the president.

'You surely don't want us to scour every house in Aghios Demetrious, looking for clues?' said the Papa, and he was sort of laughing, as though it were funny.

Stelios added, also sort of laughing, 'We are not detectives.'

Then Aphrodite spoke, and even though she was breathing heavily, she sounded so cold and angry.

'You are the people who run this village. You are supposed to look after all of us, aren't you?'

'Aphrodite, come now. Do you seriously expect us to run to the assistance of every lad who gets into a fight?'

'This was not a fight! Go and look at him and see for yourselves! Manoli was attacked, his accordion smashed, he was burned all over with lighted cigarettes . . .'

Those marks on his body, of course! Now I knew what they were, I felt sick.

There was a pause but only for a moment. The Papa said, 'It is a pity Vangelis Kostalakis is away just now, at a conference.'

'What use would he be to us here?' This was Aphrodite again.

'Well, he knows your son, doesn't he?'

'He did nothing for him when he was in the school, nothing. That poor boy was the victim of bullies every day and came home in tears. And your Vangelis said he should leave the school – that was his answer. That is always the answer here, now. Get out, look the other way, ask no questions. *Panagia mou*! What do we have to do to get justice?'

This was the Aphrodite I knew! Cold steel in her voice now.

Stelios said slowly, 'Is your boy— What's his name?'

'Manoli, you know well his name is Manoli.'

'Ah yes, Manoli, of course. Is Manoli a man or a boy, would you say?'

'Oh, I see,' she said slowly, and her face turned to us in disgust. 'Make note of this girls, this is their game. You must learn their rules.'

'I wonder if you do see?' said the Papa, and I thought I could see the evil in his eyes.

I agree with Lucy, 'Never trust a man of the cloth.'

'If your Manoli is a man, then he must fight his own battles. Of course, we will expect him to contribute to the community as a man. But I seem to remember, that in this very room such a short while ago, you were quite clear that we should consider your son as still a child; a child to be protected under his mother's apron. Isn't that right? Please do correct me if I am wrong.'

I could see Aphrodite bite down on her lip hard. She was right, this did seem like a game and I didn't know any of the rules.

After a short, icy silence, the president said, 'Of course, as a child, there is no question but that it is an offence for him to be out after seven o'clock without a parent.'

The Papa came in with, 'If Manoli had been with a parent, well, I think we know what difference that would make, don't we? So you see, Aphrodite, you would do well to consider why we make these rules that you consider to be irritating, trifling. They are for your own protection.'

He rocked backwards and forwards, still with a nasty, fat smile on his nasty fat face.

A smile of triumph.

I knew what was going on here and I understood that nothing would be done.

Both men were now on their feet.

'We should just see the lad before we go, I think. Pay our respects to your husband. Upstairs, are they?'

Aphrodite nodded just once, her face rigid, and pointed to the stairs.

We couldn't hear anything after they had clumped, clumped up.

It seemed only a few minutes later that Yorgo came down with them clump, clumping behind him.

He looked exhausted, anxious, dark bruised-looking eyes in his dear familiar face.

'Manoli is sleeping. Best just to leave him for now. But, er, Chrissi . . .'

Chrissi started forward, 'Papa?'

He didn't reply. He had no need.

As the men emerged from the shadow of the stairwell, we could all see what they had in their hands.

Yorgo nodded slowly. 'There appears to be some problem.'

'Are these yours, miss?' said the Papa.

He held up two rather tattered papers. One fell to the floor; it was Chrissi's poster of James Dean.

I knew that it hung over her bed. I had that same picture. I had kept it hidden in my school papers. He was a forbidden rebel at The Oaks. Just like here it seemed, now.

'This?'

'This' was a torn picture of Mick Jagger.

Chrissi jumped forwards, furious, and tried to take the pictures, but they just ripped even more. The president waved his trophies, a smug look of triumph on his face; he held up two LP records. I guessed what they were without even looking. The Rolling Stones was one, of course, and the other was a Greek blues group, Socrates. Will told me they only play in a small underground music club in Athens; their music is forbidden now.

Chrissi clenched her hands into fists at her sides and I instinctively moved forwards and put my arm around her.

'Are these yours, *koritsaki mou*?'

Chrissi looked mutely at her mother and nodded her head stiffly.

'Are there more like this?' asked the priest. 'The truth, please.'

Chrissi shook her head furiously. I could see she wanted to

scream and probably hit them and I knew what it cost her to keep silent.

They didn't speak again but walked to the door, tearing the pictures into pieces as they went. President Stelios turned, almost as an afterthought, saying, 'We do hope your son recovers quickly, Yorgo.'

The priest added, 'Such a trial, boys, aren't they? Always in mischief.'

Later, Chrissi walked with me and we went to my house. Along these familiar and loved old paths through the village, past houses that suddenly seemed now like part of a different world. Faces at windows; voices in the empty air. All the shadows now seemed full of stories, and they were not stories I wanted to hear.

Today, Yorgo and Aphrodite's house seemed cold, as if with the frost of forbidden things. Once, such a short time ago we had danced there and laughed.

Would it ever be the same again?

The phone was ringing as we went up the steps.

For a long time Heavenly had resisted this interruption from another world, but Hugh insisted, saying that he always needed to be in touch when he was in Athens or away somewhere. There aren't many who can afford telephones here. Aphrodite and Yorgo have one – their doctor son in Athens pays for it – but I think Aphrodite is rather afraid of it and Yorgo never answers it, ever. But it meant they could summon the doctor for Manoli last night.

We heard Lucy speaking to whoever it was. I held my finger up for Chrissi to pause as I heard: 'She's not here just now, Hugh.'

It seemed an eternity until we heard the phone bang down again and it was safe to go in.

But I couldn't escape. We'd barely sat down and started to tell Lucy what had happened when the phone rang again and Lucy said I had to answer.

Of course he'd found me another school and I am to start

there in the autumn term. I kept trying to say something, but I hadn't a chance.

'Can I . . . ?' But he wouldn't let me interrupt.

Eventually I managed to say, 'Can I speak to Mother, please?'

'No, I'm afraid you can't. She's taken to her bed. Picked up some virus, the doctor reckons. There are a million out here, as well all the usual malaria, dengue fever sort of stuff.'

And then the line went all crackly and the phone went down three thousand miles away and I was left with my future in bits.

Lucy and Chrissi were out on the terrace and now, as I went out to join them, looked at me questioningly.

'I'm not going!' I burst out. 'I'm not and he can't make me! Now my mother is ill and I can't even speak to her on the phone. And what's this virus she's got? I read all about these things when they first went to Thailand and often they have no cure. It's a really dangerous place.'

'I'm sure she will be fine, Angel,' said Lucy. 'She's such a strong woman, Heavenly. Give her time.'

I knew that despite all my complaining there was, of course, nothing anyone could do.

'Oh, how I hate being sixteen. Why don't they ask me what *I* want for a change? It's my life, isn't it? Does my mother want me to go to this bloody school? I bet not.'

'You'll speak to her soon. She'll ring you when she can, you know that.'

'I know what they'll say. It will be all, "You are still a child. A child cannot decide, cannot know what is best." I thought you were different, you and Will. I thought you really understood. But you don't, do you? You can all shove me off anywhere to suit yourselves, as long as it's away, out of sight. I worked so hard at that horrible school to prove that I could. To show them that whatever they threw at me I wouldn't let it beat me. I could be trusted.'

I paused as I realised Chrissi, obviously hating being part of this, had wriggled out of her chair and was heading for the door. She gave a little wave as she vanished.

88

But that didn't stop me.

'One stupid thing goes wrong and that's me labelled for life – irresponsible. What do any of you know about me any more? I'm pushed around like a thing – a parcel with the wrong address; everyone throwing me into a corner out of the way.'

A shadow, a cloud passed across the sun and for a moment Lucy was out of sight.

A thin, cold blade of fear ran through me. They don't know me. Nobody really knows me. I am completely alone.

On my arm a tiny itch prickled – my angel is healing and as I pressed it gently a memory came of the beautiful, colourful people sitting together under the thousand-year-old olive tree; Raggeh and Anya smiling up at me. I heard their words, 'Why not come and join us?' Now all I can think is, why not? I thought all the good, lovely special things of my life were here. That's what I thought. Now even this is all going wrong.

Chrissi hadn't left, she was just hanging around in the house and then, when she clearly was about to leave, Lucy said, 'Why not go swimming, you two?' We had barely looked at each other and she said, 'I'll come too.'

It was fun, a good thing to do, especially as I had avoided the water because of my angel. It took my mind off things but underneath, of course, everything was the same.

Later that evening I could see worry lines still creased Lucy's face. I knew she was upset about Will but I was sure she didn't need to be.

'There'll be a reason for the silence,' I said. 'It's always something silly like a train breakdown or he was late and missed it.'

'He wasn't catching a train.'

'I know that! I meant there will be a reason, a silly reason. He's so clever and sensible – you know he is. Will is always fine.'

She wasn't convinced. Deep down, nor was I. I couldn't begin to imagine why there was this silence from him. Will was the most reliable person I knew. If he said he'd do something, he always did.

Usually, I only have to look around me, over the village rooftops and away to the mountains and I can feel better, happier to be part of all this – I can feel the strength of these huge heights. But as the days passed and the nights and there was only silence from Will, even the magic of the village seemed to offer little comfort. The sun was high up there now and where it caught a crevasse or even a spike of rock it glittered gold, silver. It dazzled my eyes and I squinted. A great eagle or maybe a falcon flew through. These mountains were one thing that never changed; whatever people did below, they were always the same.

That evening we sat on the bed in her room and Lucy leant forward and gently touched my arm. It didn't hurt any more.

'Hmm, you won't be able to feel anything in a day or so.'

I loved the way Lucy had made this room her own. It smelt gorgeous, a mix of make-up and perfume – just like her. Only usually she's cooking and so there's a bit of cinnamon or vanilla mixed in.

All the bedrooms here are off a corridor running under the big main room. I think it was all part of the animal room in the original house.

Lucy is like Heavenly in so many ways. She isn't tall like her, but then again, she isn't short either. She cooks such lovely stuff that she should be fat, but she isn't. She has the greatest smile; it fills her whole face and it does sort of light up the room she's in. I honestly think that's probably because when she smiles everyone else seems to smile with her.

If I try and smile like that it only looks like a mouthful of teeth.

She has lovely hair too, rich brown, silky and a bit curly. It always seems to be just right. Not like mine which some days seems to belong to someone else, I can't control it. And the awful streaky red bits.

These rooms were all carved out of the side of the hill; none of the walls are straight or the corners square. The stones of the walls have been here for generations and they are full of dreams, full of memories.

The phone rang, and Lucy ran for it. I went out on the terrace. She seemed to be ages and when she came out I said, 'Was it Will?'

She slowly shook her head. She looked awful; her face seemed to have lost all its colour and she looked like a ghost. She sank back down into the old blue chair.

'Lucy?' I said. 'What's wrong? Who was on the phone?'

For a moment she didn't speak. Her lips opened as if words were stuck in there trying to get out.

'That was Hugh. They're on their way to Greece today.'

My face must have lit up with the burning happiness I felt instantly.

'No. No, wait. It's not like that.' She reached for her glass of wine, gulped it down. 'Will has been arrested. He's in prison in Athens.'

Her words fell into the suddenly empty air. She looked at me.

'And Heavenly is ill; your father wants her to see doctors in Athens so he was bringing her home anyway.'

It was after midnight when we went silently to our beds. I slept only a little bit. I heard Lucy moving around the house and once I thought she was crying, but when I went up to see, the terrace was dark and silent. I stood at the edge looking down, down to the empty sea below. As my eyes grew accustomed to the shadowy horizon I saw a million darting fireflies skimming the air. Away over the mountains, far to the side, a fox howled at the stars. I shivered, and for a moment a childhood memory of stories of wolves in these hills skittered into my mind. But thoughts of Will and horrible anxieties about my mother pushed them out, back into distant memories.

After that each day passed by in a haze. We seemed to be marking time until the evening, when, at more or less nine o'clock precisely, the phone would ring. There was hardly ever any news. And I still hadn't spoken to my mother. Hugh hadn't given us a clue as to where Will was or why he was arrested. I heard Lucy ask. I know she felt sick with worry.

And then one evening there was no call; no news and we sat together waiting, waiting.

And the next morning we learnt they were actually in Athens. They still have an apartment there, a huge great mausoleum of a place in Plutarchou Street, right in the centre. It has Hugh stamped on it firmly – all high ceilings with fancy mouldings, heavy furniture and drapes, everything dark, serviceable, not ringing with warmth or family life. Will and I have our own rooms there and when we go for visits we decorate them with posters and stuff, but every time we leave, Soula, the concierge, clears them all away. So each time we have to start again, trying to make our rooms look lived in by *us* not some anonymous grey people who hung oil paintings of ancestors foggily on walls, which peer down miserably at the goings on in these gloomy rooms.

And it seemed in no time at all they were here. All of them. My parents and Will. In fact it was twelve days, and thirteen hours.

We had scrubbed and cleaned and polished and dusted inside and outside the house.

My father rang every day to tell us what was happening. I still hadn't spoken to my mother, not even once. He said she was in the hospital, 'having tests'. But although we talked about it all the time, Lucy and me and Chrissi and Aphrodite, we had no idea at all what was wrong with her, and when I asked him he got cross and said that was precisely why she was there, to find out what was wrong, and I should stop asking questions.

'He's worried,' Lucy said. 'Men aren't good at dealing with women's health problems.'

And nor did we know exactly what had happened to Will except that my father, through the British embassy where he had been quite important for years, had got him out of the prison. We just knew it was something to do with the financing of his film. A lot of the money for it had come from Russia and there would be Russian people working as the crew.

'Why that should have anything to do with the Greeks, I can't imagine,' said Lucy. 'He's making it for the BBC in England.'

And so they were all coming back to the village, even my mother, who had refused to stay in the hospital.

And at five o'clock in the afternoon, on a beautiful sunny day in August, the horn of a car shattered the still quiet air and the word spread like a breeze through the hills.

'Heavenly is home!'

Lucy and I clattered down the steps to the square as a long silver car, hired by the embassy, drew slowly to a halt.

I stopped for a moment as Heavenly climbed oh so slowly out of the back seat.

She was here! I could hardly believe it! We were hugging and hugging like we would never let each other go. Oh, that delicious scent of her I had longed for. Then there was Will. Bloody! He looked older and so tired. We hugged and kissed and created such a rumpus that some of the villagers, Athena and her husband Michaelis and her sister next door and the man who lives with his crippled brother ran out to the square to see and then – oops! They joined in as well.

'*Kalos orisate!*' Welcome! They said again and again. And they stroked the car, unlike anything they had seen in the village before. So we were a great crowd, laughing and hugging and all of us, of course, so pleased to see Heavenly back.

And then my father was out of the car and said in rather a cross voice, '*Poli Fassaria.*'

Too much fuss! The villagers scattered like so many mice. But he hugged me. As always, it was a rather angular, bony hug, not soft and sweet like hers.

Mother smiled at him and said, 'Let's go home. I'm a little tired, but very happy to be here with everyone.'

She squeezed my hand tight as we went towards the house.

'I wanted to be here for your birthday,' she said.

Oh goodness, that was the next day and I'd forgotten all about it.

While I was so glad to see her, I was horrified too; she looked about ninety years old. Her hand in mine felt like a skeleton hand. I was afraid to squeeze her fingers, I might break them they were so fragile. And she was slow, so slow. She paused at every step and I heard her puffing for air, like that kitten I once found almost drowned, all bones sticking out and sad eyes.

Oh, Heavenly, oh my mother, you are so ill.

'Panathanaikos are not the best.'

'So who are the champions, then?'

'AEK – better every time.'

'Wrong! Alpha Ethniki League champions, last season – Panathanaikos!'

'Ah! but not the European champions.'

'So what? Who cares about the European league, when you are the Greek champions! And who has Antonis Antoniadis playing for them? The best scorer in all of Greece.'

Yorgo and his brother-in-law Vassili were at it hammer and tongs. They could never have ten minutes in each other's company without almost coming to blows about football. It was my birthday and my party and I agreed with Yorgo – Panathanaikos every time. Manoli stood with us looking excitedly from one to the other. He said first 'AEK', then 'Panathanaikos', and then to all our surprise 'Olympiakos'. And none of us could quite work out what to say to him next.

'Make way, make way!'

And there was Aphrodite with food, and Chrissi behind her and they were carrying trays of *moussaka* and a whole *anti christo* lamb, like it was Easter and not just my birthday.

They had been cooking all day in Aphrodite's kitchen and the scent of that lamb made my mouth water. Most of the guests – which was most of the village, I thought – were here, bringing the food into our house. It was supposed to be my birthday party, but mostly it was a celebration for Heavenly's homecoming. Name days are much more important than birthdays here, anyway.

I was so happy to be with her, so pleased she was back, but I could see that everyone knew she was very ill. She sat in a corner of the terrace on one of the long chairs with cushions at her back and one of her beautiful throws over her legs. But I could see, we all could see, her hands were blue and lined and her feet in her fine sandals were thin like a mouse's feet. If you could see her legs, they were like the stalks of a flower – no, not so sturdy, more like a twig. But she was still Heavenly, still my mother and nothing could take that away from me.

She had brought me a wonderful piece of blue silk from Thailand to throw over my bed, and two pairs of new jeans. Two! Levi's. Everyone knows they are the best. And a silk shirt, big and loose and amazing! It was black! I loved it. I felt so grown up. And Will and Lucy gave me two bottles of sherry.

Chrissi and Aphrodite and Lucy had vanished, and then they came back with yet more dishes of food.

My father stood up and clapped his hands together and everyone was quiet.

'Welcome to all our friends. Come and eat. Today is my daughter's birthday and she is glad you can all be here.' He sat down. Well that was a big speech for him and I caught Heavenly's eye and she winked just a little bit, but I knew what it meant – good for him.

Everyone was here, Aphrodite's sister Georgia, the wife of Vassili the baker was over there with a group of village women. She is a tall woman, but with Aphrodite's crinkly grey hair and the same lovely smiley face. Loula and her sister Toula and Adriana and Fotini were there with their husbands in the living room – all of them brought me gifts; cakes and sweeties they have made, a jar of jelly and one even a bottle of *mousmoula* raki. Hugh took that one away rather speedily, I saw.

What had Despina done to her hair? Usually it was a tight grey bun but here she was with a curly perm, all short and around her face and she had dyed it that deep red wine colour they love here. It was stiff and shiny with lacquer.

These women were all in their Sunday best; sparkly nylon frocks and one or two sported rather ratty old fur jackets. That accounted for the smell of mothballs that wafted around them as they moved.

They were crowding around Heavenly and my father called over their heads to me in English, 'Give her some air,' and I tried to break up the group a little and move them away.

He said he was angry at first when she said she was coming.

'She should be in the hospital, and that's that. She needs proper care and good doctors.'

We were all sitting on the terrace then, the evening of their arrival. I sat on a little stool at her feet and she was stroking my hair. She always seemed so strong, yet here she was a shadow. Her wild hair was tied back and dull, streaked with more silver than red. But it was her eyes that shocked me most. They were so circled with dark that the pupils had all but disappeared. Her cheeks and brow were lined and drawn and her lips had sunk into her face.

'I am sick and tired of being in bed. This is where I want to be.'

'So you keep saying, Evadne. But you need doctors, nurses, medication.'

'Doctors? They know nothing. I saw doctors in Thailand, doctors that came from New York and Sydney. They none of them knew anything. They all take my blood from here and here,' she waved her arms shakily in the air. 'They sent bits of me off all over the world and the result, every time was "tropical virus – source and nature unknown". They even sent some of my blood to China! Imagine that. But the Chinese didn't have a clue either.'

The effort of talking with such seeming vivacity had clearly exhausted her and she was breathing shallow and fast, gulping air, it seemed, to strengthen herself.

She was still so beautiful, even like this, and stylish too. The fine grey silk of her blouse was rumpled a little after the journey, but tucked into a soft printed lawn skirt and belted there with a man's grey silk tie.

She went to bed after that and Lucy went down with her; came back and said she was asleep at once.

Will said, 'Come on, we're going for a walk.'

I started to jump up, but my father reached his hand out to my arm and said, 'That leaves you and I to have a good chat, Angel.'

I sank down again, defeated. I knew what was coming and I really didn't want to have that conversation.

And of course we had barely heard their laughter fade as they walked up the path before he asked me to tell him about my school. I tried not to exaggerate its horrors, but he did wince when I told him how they had locked me in for the night without any water after the accidental burning of the barn.

'Sounds a bit like prison,' he said. 'That's what they did to Will in Athens.'

And then he told me how he found him and got him out. I was shocked but secretly rather pleased to have left the subject of my education behind.

'Just because of the money for his film coming from Russia?'

He nodded. 'There were too many questions he couldn't, or wouldn't answer. He should have thought of that, bloody idiot. It's dangerous here now. One sniff of Russia and they panic. Everyone must be on their guard all the time. Especially any friend of the Papandreou family. He knew that. Give them the excuse and they'll lock you up for as long as they like. Some never come out; just vanish and no one knows where they are or what they are supposed to have done. Your mother's friend, Amalia Fleming, is in that same prison. Like Will, she won't answer questions, so none of us can do anything to get her out.'

I told him about Manoli and he said he was almost certainly a victim because of Yorgo.

'That's awful,' I said, 'wicked.'

And he told me how the rumours and gossip are handed down from generation to generation.

'The evil is enlarged with the telling. That's how these villages work; as it's passed along it grows. By the time it's stopped, it's changed beyond any recognition.'

He looked way out across the mountains and down, down to the Libyan sea below.

I started to tell him about Chrissi's posters. But he yawned, so I grabbed the opportunity and jumping up, kissed him goodnight and ran down to my room.

I peeped into my mother's as I passed and even though she seemed asleep, she said, 'I love you, Angel. Good night.'

The clatter of plates and the hum of voices fought with the night birds calling and the cicadas. In spite of all my worries, this was my birthday party and everyone was here. Dusk had begun to fall in waves – grey, green and blue jeans' colour. The air had the scent of blossom. And mothballs, of course. I was just thinking how perfect it all was when I felt a tug at my sleeve and Chrissi said, 'Shall we go and have a smoke?'

We ran out through the house and down to the lower terrace outside. It was quieter there and we sat propped up beside an amphora and smoked a whole cigarette each. Chrissi had brought wine with her. We hadn't got any glasses but it didn't matter, we swigged it from the lip of the jug. We had to do it slowly or it dribbled down our chins, but we laughed and slurped it up anyway.

'Heavenly looks so ill,' she said, 'and your father is being nice to everyone.'

'I know. I think it's because he's worried about her. He wants her to go to a hospital in England but they talked about it with Will and Lucy and me last night, and she says she won't go.'

'What do Will and Lucy really think?'

'They said she was quite clear about it, the doctors have tried everything and nothing does any good, so what's the point?'

'Are they going to stay here?'

'No, Will has to go to Afghanistan to make his film. But Lucy and me will stay and look after Heavenly.'

'Aren't you going to some school in England?'

I shook my head furiously.

'Don't talk about it on my birthday! You'll spoil everything.'

'Sorry.'

'I hope my mother can work on him and stop it, anyway.'

'She doesn't look as if she could work on anything at the moment.'

'All right! I've got eyes; I don't need you telling me what I can see for myself.'

She pulled two more cigs from the packet and lit them both, handing one to me. I puffed and coughed. I don't usually smoke more than one at once, usually half a one.

We sat in silence for a while. Upstairs we could hear laughter and talking.

I could hear the low throaty voice of Papa Diamedes.

'The sexy priest is here,' said Chrissi and I looked at her in surprise.

'Do you think he's sexy?' I said. 'Lucy said that, too.'

We heard the beginnings of music wafting through the windows so we went back into the party. Yorgo and Manoli had their instruments out and were starting up a tune and everyone was clearing back and leaving the centre of the room empty for dancing.

Heavenly sat on some cushions by the wine press just looking so beautiful. Hugh was beside her on the floor. I'd never seen him sit on the floor before, anywhere. And then I saw his head was nodding and he was asleep, his head on her shoulder.

Will and Lucy were in each other's arms not far away and they looked so in love and happy that suddenly I felt alone.

Chrissi squeezed my hand and whispered, 'Come on, let's dance.'

And Yorgo and Manoli played and everyone stood around

clapping in time to the music and so we did and like always, we were laughing and I felt loads better. Then Will was dancing with us. He linked arms and dipped and swirled to the music. He'd had lessons, much against his wishes, but like everything he does, if he is going to do it, he will be the best, so he was good at it.

His feet moved like lightning, here and there and up and down in half a second.

The village ladies in their tight perms and thick stockings watched him out of the corners of their eyes, and gave themselves a little thrill imagining they were there with him, not me. He steered me gently, but firmly out to the terrace and we paused, gasping for breath and pretending we weren't.

Night was spreading into the sky; the mountains seemed to grow darker as we watched and the evening cries of the goats broke the near silence.

'What was it like in that prison? Where you scared?' I asked him.

He smiled, but not with his eyes.

'Me? Scared?'

I saw he was going to make a joke of it and I said, 'No, tell me, truly.'

Then he saw my face. His shoulders dropped down and he put his arm around me.

'Of course I was terrified, but only at first. It's the sounds that get to you. In the dark, at night, a scream and then a laugh, again and again; screaming and laughing all together.' He shook his head, 'Wrong, quite wrong.'

And as he fished in the pocket of his jeans and pulled out a cigarette I saw his hands were shaking so he couldn't make the flame from the lighter reach the end of the fag and I took it from him and lit it for him myself. He didn't acknowledge my help, he was back in that other place and I started to say 'sorry', but he shook his head and drew on the cigarette, blowing smoke way off into the distance.

'And the smells,' he said and his voice was hoarse with remembering. 'Bodies too close, unwashed. And you know you stink, and they stand around you, smiling and their uniforms are all clean, freshly pressed. Your face, your body filthy in front of these immaculate officers. Bastards.'

'That's what Aphrodite calls them, all of them – *malakas*.'

'She's right. That's exactly what they are.'

'Did they hurt you? That's what we were worried about most. Lucy said people go into that army interrogation centre and never come out.'

'That happens, but no, I was lucky. Father got me out pretty damn quick. To be honest, Pickle, I don't think they knew what to do with me. The things they accused me of were so ridiculous. That might be enough for other people but Father is a British diplomat, so a load of rubbish about film financing wouldn't hold up for long. I think everyone was relieved when he turned up. They could get rid of me, without losing too much face.'

I didn't say anything, just thought, as I always do, how handsome he is and how lucky I am to have him as my brother.

'What's Father going to do about you?'

That was a raw nerve.

'I've got to persuade him to let me stay and go to school here.'

'I wish you luck.'

'If not,' I started, 'I'm not going back to England to another—'

But I'd lost him, he was already heading back inside saying, 'Hey, come on, Mother's sitting on her own in there.'

We went over and I sprawled down at her feet. I was still out of breath and sweating. Will was talking to Father now. Perhaps trying to persuade him not to send me away?

Heavenly was tugging gently on my sleeve.

'Manoli plays that accordion wonderfully, doesn't he? How long has he been doing that?'

I realised she didn't know what had happened here, so I told her and she was really shocked and angry.

'So who owns that accordion then?'

101

'That belongs to Toula's husband, Michaelis.'

'And Yorgo's lyre?'

'Oh that's his. He's always had it. He just never played it much. Aphrodite says they can't afford a new accordion for Manoli; they cost millions of drachmas I think.'

'I like your tattoo.'

I looked at her, surprised. 'You do? But how did you . . . ? When did you . . . ?'

'I heard a little whisper, so I looked while you were sleeping. I think you are very brave. I wish I had one.'

'Really?' I was astonished. My mother with a tattoo. And then I thought of my father.

'Leave him to me,' she said. She can read my mind!

Being here with her was how I wanted to spend the rest of my life. It was the one thing I could be sure of: the safety of her love. I wanted to tell her about Madame Eftoxia the fortune-teller, ask her what she might have meant, and I was just about to when I saw a great wave of pain pass over her face. Her eyes were closed and she was gritting her teeth.

'Are you all right?'

But I could see she wasn't. She was breathing great deep gulps of breath and trying to swallow. Her face had gone a horrible sort of bluish white, and she was trying to stand. I jumped up and took her hands; those thin, bird-skeleton hands and pulled her upright as gently as I could. She was standing but still clinging on to me and swaying.

'Sorry, Angel. Better lie down, I think.'

'Hang on to me. I'm really strong. I'm OK. Let's walk slowly, slowly.'

And we did. Manoli and Yorgo were oblivious and the music went on. But people had stopped dancing and stood back to let us pass. We walked step by slow step down the middle of the room. I could see from the faces peering at us how shocking she looked – she had aged twenty years in the space of a heartbeat.

Still the music played on and our steps were taken to the

broken rhythm of a lively song. Then Will was on the other side of her, his strong arms around her.

'It's OK, Angel, I've got her now.' But somehow I couldn't let her go, so I walked with them and we stumbled clumsily down the stairs to her room.

Once there she fell on to the bed. All pretence had left her; no more smiles, just the pain that dulled her eyes. Narrow as slits they were, and deep lines I have never seen before creased her dear face.

'Shall I sit with her for a while?' Then I realised Lucy had followed us down.

'No, let me.'

And she knew that I really must do this myself, and taking Will's arm she led him back upstairs.

Manoli and Yorgo had started another dance and over the music I heard Will call out, 'Come on, everyone!' and there was the shuffling sound of feet sliding and gliding and the music got faster and faster and there was laughter filling the evening air.

'Music and laughter, that's all we ever need,' Heavenly whispered and her lips were curved once more into a smile. She was so brave.

I stayed there with her, sitting on the bed. Chrissi appeared down the stairs at some point and I waved her away. We sat for a long time, the party, my party, going on over our heads. Her face was flushed but she was breathing more easily. Her thin hand in mine twitched occasionally and I stroked it gently, as you would a tiny animal or a bird. She smiled.

'I want you to do something for me.' I had to put my head close to hers, she was speaking so faintly.

'Of course I will. Anything. Tell me.'

I thought she was going to ask for fresh water but instead she surprised me.

'I want to give you the money to buy Manoli a new accordion.'

I could only nod.

'You will need to find out, from Sitia probably, how much

they cost, and you must tell me. Or maybe Toula will know.' The little speech had exhausted her and her eyes fluttered closed. But after a moment or two she squeezed my hand and I bent down again to hear her. 'Only me, Angel, no need to tell anyone else.'

I think she meant my father.

'Of course.'

'Or, or if . . .' Her voice trailed away for a moment.

'Yes?'

'Well, if I'm not here, tell Will or Lucy.'

'Of course; but you will be here. Where else would you be?'

Her eyes were closed and she didn't answer. I supposed she meant if Hugh made her go to the hospital. But we'll stop him. She doesn't want to go and she shan't. I thought she might sleep, so I said, 'Shall I leave you to rest now?'

'No, stay for a while, will you? I miss you so when I am away.'

It didn't matter any more about my party. Here was where I wanted to be.

'I'm sorry about the school.'

'Oh that. Don't worry about that, it was nothing important.'

The faint squeeze of my hand again.

'I know you, my darling girl. We are so alike, you can't fool me. You hated it, didn't you?'

'Well . . .' And I thought for a bit. 'You know you told me about when you were a nurse? And how you were always in trouble with the matron or the sister; but you stuck it out, didn't you? And then all those years later you were glad you did because you could be a nurse again here for all the wounded fighters?'

Her head nodded very gently on the pillow.

'Well I thought of that and that helped.'

'Not enough though, did it?'

'Nearly enough. For a while anyway.'

'Always remember, my Angel. I love you, and even when I am not with you, I'll be loving you.'

I thought I might cry, and I so didn't want to. She suddenly gave a little gasp, and I realised I was squeezing her hand too hard.

'Sorry, sorry,' I said, but she had sunk right into the pillows now, her eyes tight closed and I just sat there with her while she slept. I had so much love in my heart for her, I knew it was in danger of bubbling over. I wish my love could take some of her pain away.

Father appeared after a while, his face a mask of worry. No longer the diplomat, the important man who could open prison doors; all I could see was a man, not understanding things over which he had no control.

'Bloody hell! What have you done to yourself? You should be in the hospital. You need doctors, medicine, everything they can do and we can't.'

He had woken her with his loud voice and I thought, This rage of his is just to cover up fear. Oh God, is she really that ill? And suddenly I was frightened too.

'Push off, Angel. I'm here now.'

I stumbled over to the door that leads on to the lower terrace. But I didn't want to go, didn't want to leave her. As I slowly opened the door I nearly knocked Chrissi down; she was sitting outside it.

'Come on, come and sit here,' she whispered. 'Doesn't look like you can do much in there.'

And I sank down beside her. She had already lit a cigarette for me and I gulped down the smoke. I couldn't really think straight, so I said, 'I'll be a chain smoker if I spend much time with you.'

In the inky dark sky we watched the bats circling; the stars were out now like a host of tiny lamps up there.

'See that one? The brightest one, the evening star?'

I nodded.

'My grandfather always said it was the good luck star. If it shone over your house, everything inside would be OK.'

'I wish I could believe that, now. It doesn't feel OK in there.'

Chrissi put her arm around my shoulders.

'Try to remember how strong she is, your mother. She was always the one to make everything come out right, just think about that.'

So I tried, but I couldn't really do it, couldn't believe in the sort of luck that a star is supposed to bring. I could hear the low murmur of voices inside Heavenly's room.

And all I could believe in was there, in what I could hear; and it was voices filled with pain and fear. Not even much hope and I didn't know what it meant, but it wasn't good, and as I sat there, even with Chrissi's strong arm around me, I was afraid.

APHRODITE

'Quick, quick, Aphrodite, come now!'

It was Angel who came for me. I had been waiting. Since Heavenly arrived home, one look was enough to show me how ill she was. No secret. And on the night of the party everyone in the village could see it.

There were days when she forced herself to get out of bed and walk slowly to her terrace, but they were few. She loved that terrace. She'd always sat there alone, day or night. I remember it was where I had taught her to knit, just when the war was starting.

She was good at everything, Heavenly, except knitting. I remember Hugh had come to the village for a few days and after that visit she was pregnant. And later we heard the child had died. We didn't speak of it then or since. It's the way here; one person's trouble is another's bad luck. Not the sort of thing to talk about.

She lived mostly up in a cave in those days, near the little hospital she and Anthi had started in the church on top of the mountain.

The birth was up there, a stillbirth I heard.

The night of the party, Angel's birthday party, my Yorgo and my Manoli had played such music! If there was anyone in the village not at the party they could have heard it echoing round the hills most of the night.

It was a good party in its way, but for that one thing; Heavenly was in all our eyes so ill. The next morning the doctor came up from Tres Petromas and left an hour later looking grave and then he fetched the doctor from Sitia.

I know that one. I don't like him or trust him. My aunt died while in his care – one day getting better, the next dead.

I went over during the morning. If Hugh were to ask, I had come to collect our dishes from the food. He looked like a man in hell. He is a good-looking man, I grant you, but these days his face was the colour of the tomb.

'Is there anything I can—' I started to ask and he grabbed my arm.

'Talk to her, Aphrodite. Make her see she has to go to the hospital. They think she has pneumonia now and she needs to be nursed properly. You tell her, please? She won't listen to us.'

So I went down to her bedroom. She was sleeping, I thought at first. I stood at the end of the bed and her eyes opened. She tried to crack her face into a smile and before I could speak she said, 'I know what you want. I know what you all want, but I'm not going anywhere. There is nothing like a hospital to make you feel worse. I need to live without needles. No more needles. No more tubes and drips.'

Then she started to cough and it seemed to rack right through her. Her body arched up out of the bed and her face seemed like a mask of pain.

I held her in my arms and rocked her gently until the spasms stopped.

Over my shoulder I saw Angel was on the stairs. She looked so frightened I wanted to hug her to me as well. I lowered Heavenly slowly down until her head was resting back on the pillow. She was like a sack of small bones; you could almost hear them crackle together as she moved.

'I saw your mother this ill once before, you know, Angel. It was many, many years ago, but she got better then. She is strong.'

I knew my words were hollow with untruth – yes, that was then, she was perhaps twenty-five years old and she had strength; but this time the sickness came from that foreign place, so far away. How could anyone from here understand it, fight it?

I thought Angel could hear the desperation of the lie in my voice.

'Chrissi is here,' she said, 'we will bring your pots back later.'

What could I do? I shrugged and whispered goodbye to Heavenly.

Oh, *Panagia mou*, look after her for us all.

Heavenly did improve, a little. I heard that she slept for days and woke feeling stronger. Plenty in the village would interfere if they could, but I knew they would fetch me if they wanted me.

But one night I was sleepless and in the heat of midnight I sat outside. Yorgo came with me, sat beside me, fanned me with a branch of the pomegranate tree. We didn't speak. The air was so heavy with the day's sun, the effort of breathing took energy enough, let alone the search for idle words.

He pointed. And away over the roofs and chimneys of the dark, silent village I saw a single light burning. It flickered. It was a lamp on Heavenly's terrace. She must be sitting there, probably alone.

It was too hot for more sleep that night so I stayed where I was; just me and a scops owl wittering low and that great falcon that seemed to live in these hills just now. Its wings beat through the air with a low fury, like the west wind. That light flickered and burned until the first rays of the dawn sun broke the horizon.

I went over early and the house was sleeping. So as silently as I could I took a bundle of soiled linen from the bathroom, and went down to the spring. I was alone there, that early, and the sheets were soon washed. I carried them back and by the time I arrived the household was stirring.

I took the coffee Will offered and went into the cool of the living in room with Lucy.

'What's to do, Aphrodite?' he said. 'How can we make her strong again?'

And Lucy said, 'Have you no old remedies? Isn't there something you can make for her? These pains, headaches cripple her. She said the doctors had examined every bit of her, but there were no answers. They said the virus that attacked her in Thailand destroyed her immune system and that she will just get any infection there is going around the place. The chest pains from the pneumonia are gone now, but she has no strength left to fight. Can you not think of something, anything to help make her strong again?'

'I've got a mixture of calendula, figwort and coneflower. Maybe . . .'

'Will you try?' She sounded so desperate, poor Lucy.

'I made it when Manoli was hurt and it helped his body to heal, I swear it.'

'Can it do anything to hurt her?' Will asked.

'It won't hurt. I have seen these old cures work time and again.'

'Then bring her your mixture, please; anything that might help.'

And it was as I was pounding the dried flowers and seeds in the pestle that Angel ran in.

'Quick, quick, Aphrodite, come now.'

And I knew. Her breathing was hoarse, laboured, and at first I thought the pneumonia was back. But the grey pallor of her face was now tinged with blue round her mouth.

Her eyes were half open and as they fluttered, her long eyelashes almost shadowed her cheek.

The room seemed full of people, but it was only family. Hugh knelt beside the bed, her thin hand twitched in his strong brown one.

Angel had run ahead of me and was now panting, at her mother's other side.

Heavenly smiled, and for a moment her face had all its old beauty restored. She clutched the air with one hand, those thin, twig-like fingers and Angel reached for it and took it.

'Yes, Christo,' Heavenly said, quite clearly.

Angel looked round, puzzled.

'I think it's the name of the doctor,' said Will who was on the stairs.

'Do you think we should call him?' Hugh asked, his voice croaked with anxiety.

'I did,' said Will, 'an hour ago. He should be here by now.'

'I've heard her call for him, before,' said Angel, 'and Constantinos. She was calling Christo and Constantinos in the night. Over and over again. I thought she was asleep.'

'Do we know any of these names?' said Hugh turning away from her.

'Only . . .' I started to say, 'only Yorgo's nephew Christos—'

But Hugh cut across my words. 'Why would she know him? Call for him?'

I didn't answer. What would I say? What would I know?

And then a great look of calm came over Heavenly's face, and she smiled. She seemed transformed as we looked at her, from a frail old woman, back to the girl we had known all those years ago when she first came here to Panagia. The girl who stayed and changed the lives of all who knew her, all who loved her.

Outside there was a sudden great rushing sound, like giant wings beating the air, and then a still, silent calm, broken only by the sweet call of a song bird.

The room darkened for a moment; a cloud passing across the sun and with a long low breath, Heavenly died.

ANGEL

They must have cried an ocean in the village. You would think they were the survivors of some catastrophic disaster.

Everyone looked at me. All the time, all they could do was look at me, watch me. I didn't know what they wanted. They all kept touching me, trying to kiss me, and I hated it. All that grabbing at me, arms going around me, made me feel so grubby, mucky, with their clutching hands holding bits of tear-wet rag all over me. They were Cretans and Cretans were supposed to be proud people.

I wish I knew what I felt. I knew what I was supposed to feel, I could see it in their faces, 'Poor Angel, poor child.'

It was as if it hadn't happened. As if she was still out there in Thailand with Hugh and one day soon she'd come back.

Even though I was there with her, even though I was holding her hand. But it wasn't her hand, I knew that. It was thin, dry and hot in mine. Heavenly's hands were strong, the hands of a worker or a gardener. She helped restore this house, she told me about it. She worked side by side with Aphrodite's Yorgo and his nephew Christo, the same Christo that died over in Sitia the day after. I felt sorry for Aphrodite; having to stay in her black clothes for another funeral.

When we all walked up that mountain, to the little church at the top, you could see the clouds scudding to cover the sun, and Papa Diamedes walking beside me, pointed upwards saying, 'No birds sing today.'

They came from everywhere for the funeral. Everyone and their wives and children, their brothers and sisters, old

Pappouses and Yayas. They wore their best black and even out here on the mountains you could smell the mothballs of their well-stored finery.

There was Andreas; he saw me and looked down, not knowing how to behave. And Petros with his father the ironworker. They were up the front. He turned, saw me and waved.

The sun was low in the west and the few clouds had gone, leaving the evening to drift in slowly over the mountains. A slight breeze whispered up from the sea far below.

Behind us the village was still sunless, silent, no birds; not the scops owl nor that great falcon. Where have they gone, the birds? And the gossip, the chat, the smiles have all been stilled. You could almost touch a grey blanket of sadness hanging over the village.

I did feel different; it felt as if everything that was familiar, comforting in my life had gone. This family, my family broken; nothing fitted any more.

And it seemed everyone was crying; even Hugh and Will and Yorgo. And Manoli and Aphrodite, they were all crying; big fat tears.

Chrissi told me that sometimes they pay people to come to funerals and sob and moan and clutch themselves in pretend grief. Fancy that! I looked around at the crowd of everyone walking slowly up the mountain, all weeping, but I couldn't see anyone I didn't know. They weren't needed here anyway; these Panagians wept enough for an army.

There was a tiny movement of a breeze through the gorse and wild thyme, and it filled the air with the heady scent of late summer, all mixed in with a salty tang from the sea below. But the only sound was of the tears falling.

I was walking behind the coffin. Will and Father carried it.

You could see it weighed almost nothing – a box of feathers.

Heavenly was big, tall like me and she would have weighed a lot.

In the graveyard there were only a few tombstones and those were all broken and bent. It must be years since anyone was buried there. I closed my eyes when they put it down, over a big hole that someone must have dug, I didn't know who.

And over everything that awful doomy bell started; bong, pause, bong, pause, bong.

I hated that. If the sun had tried to come out that day that horrible clang would have sent it away again.

I didn't want to look. Everyone else did. They all crowded around. It was disgusting, their eagerness to peer inside. I thought they should close the lid, seal it up, but nobody wanted to know what I thought.

The coffin was closed eventually; three fat planks, banged down one after the other.

It had been only an hour after she . . . well, anyway, after that Yorgo and Manoli brought the coffin round. They were really proud of it, and it was beautiful – carved with tiny flowers and birds on the edges. Aphrodite said they had been working on it secretly ever since Heavenly came back to the village. So they must have known.

And thinking that and probably preparing the wood and everything, they must have had all those bad, dark thoughts at my birthday party when they played the music for the dancing. So I suppose everyone in the whole village knew.

Except me, I didn't know.

Hugh went straight back to Thailand after. But he's coming back soon. Will went too, to make his film in Afghanistan. I said I would be fine but I didn't want him to go. My father asked Lucy to stay.

'I'm not a baby,' I said, 'I'm seventeen now. I'll be fine on my own.'

But they didn't believe me. I heard them talking the day after.

'I knew it was the end,' Lucy said. 'I knew when you said she wanted to come back here to the village. You knew it too, didn't you?' I didn't hear Will's reply but I guessed he was nodding. 'Yes I knew it.'

Well, thanks a lot then. Because nobody told me. I didn't know it.

He rang, Will did, every night or so. Lucy gave me the phone once and I listened but it was just the echo of his voice, very faint and a lot of crackling over the alien airwaves. I gave it back to her but he had gone, cut off at the whim of the Afghan telephone operator.

I looked for her everywhere: in the village, on the hills.

I walked up on those hills every day. I went out at dawn, leaving Lucy asleep. If I went then, I could mostly avoid the villagers. Sometimes I wondered if I called her name out loud, would she hear and come running and we'd hug each other and laugh like we used to do.

Even at night I couldn't find her. It was so hot those nights and I thought that was why I lay awake. Perhaps if I could sleep I'd dream and she would be there in my dreams. And I tried and tried to whisper myself into sleep, but if it came it was a surprise and there were no dreams.

I held the lapis blue silk cloth she gave me on my birthday, in my hand, under my cheek and I imagined her smiling at me. And I smiled back.

I suppose I must have slept sometimes, but it was an empty, dull, headachy kind of sleep. And when I woke up all I could think was, Where are you?

Lucy watched me the most, and Chrissi; she came round here every day. First in the morning, and sometimes I was here and sometimes I was still out so she waited for me. Lucy didn't know what to do for the best – you could see her hesitating. Each time she went to speak to me, she paused and thought, then spoke. Usually about food.

'Sure,' she always started, in that Irish way. 'Sure, Angel?' and I waited to see what it was each time.

'Is it a Cretan salad I can make for you? Or maybe some *moussaka* or *kleftiko*?'

Did she really think I could sit down in all this heat and eat a great hot dish of lamb bones or rich sauces? And if I did would that make it better?

I didn't want to be rude to her. Poor Lucy, what had she done? Sometimes I thought that she was the only person, grown-up, adult, that I could talk to and I didn't even want to talk to her. What was there to say? I felt as though I was all filled up with the heat from the hills and the sky and if I spoke it would all come out. Like flames, hot.

I sat in random corners of these many rooms; sometimes my room, sometimes hers. Her bed was all straightened out and clean. One of her throws, a silk one with a dragon on it, spread over. But not like she always had it, as though her body was still inside or had just got out or was soon coming back. It was all tidy neat and tucked in. Empty.

And nothing smelled like her, anywhere; not the pillows or the throws. Her clothes in the wardrobe gave off a faint breath of her scent; it was called Fracas, she'd always worn it at special times. But when I buried my face in her dresses, within moments it seemed to have faded, died away and there was no smell left.

Couldn't anyone see I just wanted to be left alone?

Chrissi often walked out on the hillside to find me. She didn't say that's what she was doing, but I knew it was. There are miles and miles and miles of hills and mountains around here and she always seemed to be on the same bit as me.

And then today she was quite deliberately following me. I could see her from the corner of my eye, just a few paces behind.

I carried on and on up, higher and higher along a goat track. I knew where it was leading; I'd been this way before many times.

And then when it seemed I just couldn't get any higher, there we were at the crumbled wall of Saint Kosmas and Damianos church. I climbed over, as I always do, and of course I heard Chrissi a little way behind me. But I forgot her, because there was the new grave, just the one. The fresh dug earth, rich and red, good for growing things.

I climbed over the broken slabs of marble and granite and the bits and pieces of the shrines to other villagers long ago. And then I was there and that was where I wanted to be.

Because if they were right and Heavenly was just here, I wanted to be beside her.

I knew all my life I would keep coming back here. I won't let her stones fall apart and the grass around her wither and die.

There were some bunched up flowers still there, on that fresh dug earth and they were all wilted and dying from the heat of the sun so I grabbed them up and cleared them away and made a pile, rotted and bad smelling by the edge of the wall.

I stopped and sat under a tree and Chrissi came up to me then and, gasping with the heat, flopped down beside me. We sat there together like that for a while and I began to think it was just like the old days, before . . . then. I turned my head towards her, just a tiny bit and she caught my eye and smiled.

It was the same old lovely Chrissi smile, and I found I was smiling back a little bit.

We sat for a while, just being together and then I said, and I don't know what made me think it, 'Do you still bind up your bosom?'

'No, I don't do that any more.'

And I started to laugh. I didn't mean to and she looked puzzled. She couldn't see what was funny. I tried to stop laughing but I couldn't and through it I said, 'I'm sorry. I just had a vision of Petros putting his hand under your T-shirt and . . . and . . .'

And then she laughed too and we neither of us could stop. We were choking with laughs, spluttering and spitting and then my nose started to run and I couldn't stop and then I wasn't laughing I was crying. And I cried and cried and it felt as if my whole face was leaking tears, as though I might never stop. And I thought, I am just like all the others after all.

And then when I did stop, Chrissi put her arms right round me and hugged and hugged me tightly and I could feel this great big hole inside me. It was empty and as I thought about it, it started to fill up with tears. It was a big hole, a Heavenly-sized hole. And then I was crying again and I was so sad, so sad. And Chrissi took my hand in her big strong one, with her bitten down nails and pulled me up to my feet and ever so gently started to walk me down the hill and home. And I cried all the way down. I didn't think I would ever stop. And I had to keep blowing my nose on leaves and I was such a mess. And dear Chrissi pulled her head kerchief out from her pocket and gave it to me to blow my nose on. She hardly ever wore it, but I thought it was Sunday today and she was supposed to wear it to church. When I looked at her, she just smiled and shrugged as if to say, 'Who cares?'

I was still holding Chrissi's hand, still crying when we got back to the house. Lucy ran out to us and said, 'Your father's back.'

Chrissi gave me a hug and said, 'I'm off home now.'

'No, stay,' I started to say, but Lucy said,

'Let her go, just for now. Your father will want to see you, talk to you.'

It was a shock to see him. He looked terrible: gaunt, haggard and suddenly old.

'You look awful, Hugh, have you been feeding yourself properly?' Lucy asked, but he didn't answer. 'Well, your looks don't pity you. I'll get you some dinner.'

And she brought him a plate of the *moussaka* she'd made that morning.

We sat in an awkward silence for about half an hour. It was the middle of the afternoon but he was drinking raki as though it were lemonade. Lucy gave him a tumbler of water but he didn't look at it. I wondered if I could have a little glass of my birthday sherry but thought probably not.

Outside the air hung heavy and dark overhead and in the distance was the faint sound of a soft lazy music that seemed weighted with the melancholy we all felt. It seemed to have been hanging around these mountains forever.

He stood on the edge of the terrace looking out to the mountains, the hills and down, down to the sea below. He looked not just old – I could bear that. But there was something I'd never seen in him before, never expected to see; he looked frightened.

'She didn't just love this house,' he said. 'She loved this village, and all these people here, these villagers, were her friends. More than that, they were her family. She knew them and loved them. She didn't care if they were rich or poor, old or young; she didn't care who they were, she always smiled for them and with them. If they needed help, any help, they would come to her and she never turned them away, never. She gave them everything she had to give, and then more. I tried to understand this of her. But I never did. They are not my people. She preferred them to me, you know.' He turned to face us. 'She chose to stay here, rather than come back with me to Athens.

'It was a lonely war. I tried to tell myself she was safer here, but it wasn't that. It was with these people she was at home. All those years ago, my mother told me she was the woman I should marry.' He gave a sad, croaky sort of humourless laugh. 'She thought she would be a "steadying influence" on me. Ha! Funny, that, when she was the rebel all along. This is where she lived and this is where she came to die.'

He turned to us and there was a resignation in his eyes along with the tears. I put my hand out and he pulled me to him. For a moment we just looked at each other, and then we were hugging.

My thin useless arms clasped round his bony but unexpectedly fragile solidity.

I thought he could see I'd been crying when he held me away from him for a moment.

'She loved you so much, you and Will. Every day she spoke of you. Our house was full of your pictures. All the drawings you did as a child here she kept in a big scrapbook and I would often find her looking through it, turning the pages and smiling. Every day I felt guilty for taking her so far away from you. But I needed her too, you know.' He sighed, a deep sobbing sound from inside his heart, it seemed to me. 'You are her daughter in every way.'

And the sun went down on another Panagia day, and we tried to go on as before.

APHRODITE

It seemed there was to be nothing but sadness in our lives now. They say it goes in threes, so perhaps I waited for it. Barely had we got back into the house after burying Heavenly when the telephone rang. It was Yorgo's sister, over Sitia way; her son had died suddenly of a heart attack. We had known Christo well during the war. Training to be an architect, he had come to Panagia to work side by side with Yorgo restoring the old Orfanoudakis house for Heavenly. He lived in a cave in the hills above the village and had eaten many times at our table. With the coming of peace and then the angers of the civil war here, he had stopped coming and in truth it was years since we had seen him.

I had some raki ready for Yorgo when he came in, Manoli of course at his heels. I knew he would be sad to hear of this passing.

There was no question but that we should all attend the funeral. Getting there might be the problem but Yorgo insisted we could all get into his truck.

'You will clean it first?'

'Manoli and Chrissi will help me.'

Chrissi pulled such a face, I could have slapped her.

'And don't think you can wear those jeans trousers to a family funeral, my girl.'

'Oh, Mama, for goodness sake! If they were good enough for Angel's family, can't I . . . ?'

'You will wear the grey dress. Go and get it from my cupboard.'

'That's your dress; I'm not wearing that, it's an old ladies' dress.'

Such cheek!

It was a strain to get it over her head; and then it was pulling at the seams because she was already so full in the chest. I thought to myself, It is a long time since I wore it, would I have the same problem now?

She flung it across the room and said, 'I'm not wearing it, Mama. You can see I will be bursting out of it before we get there. I wear my jeans or nothing.'

So in the end she stayed behind. I was not happy about this but we could not turn up for a family burial with the mess that she would be.

Manoli cleaned the truck with Yorgo helping him. He was almost his old strong self again – thank the Panagia. Chrissi helped me to make some more sesame biscuits, and a walnut cake to take across, and Yorgo got a flagon of his wine and his raki to offer. He had little to do with his family – they lived too far away, over two mountain ranges – and it would be a long and hard journey.

I was awake before daybreak. For me this was an adventure, although I wouldn't tell anyone. It's sad, of course it is, any life ending is sad. And Christo was not of a dying age. But it was a whole day out for me; a day without stoking the logs for the oven, digging the leeks and potatoes in the *gypo*, no laundry to drag down to the spring, no need to avoid Titi and her poking-in nose. And on our return I will have news to share around the spring, where usually I can only listen to Marina and her family tales. She has seven sisters and they all seem to lead most peculiar lives if she is to be believed; either starving poor, or gold-plated rich. Palaces are their homes and if not they live in hovels or caves. Who knew what words were true that rattled from her lips? Such tales!

I sat with my first coffee of the morning in the dark doorway. Yorgo snored upstairs. He had been restless in the night, thinking of Christo, I expect. They had become good friends during the war. In a village where many were Royalists, like-minded friends are a treasure indeed. I wondered how Christo's family had coped with the regime in their village. I would find out.

Slowly, cautiously, the dawn came into the eastern sky, the sky over the sea. I saw chinks of vague light between the dark clouds. It was four-thirty. I had forgotten the day began so early. But I suspected that what I could see was merely a glimmer, a hint of the beginning of dawn, and there was no change in the sky for some time.

We were in Tres Petromas by second light. Already my bones and body were crying with the pain of rattling down that road. If I said so, Yorgo reminded me we had grown up with nothing better than a goat track.

'You want me to be grateful for this road we have now? Is that it? This road, paid for with our taxes, is already little better than a dirt track and you know with the first rains of winter this will be flooded and most of the surface washed away.'

'So many complainings; would you like me to leave you with your cousin?'

Spend the day with Caliope? Huh. I would rather walk. I didn't answer. My cousin Caliope lived alone in two rooms at the edge of Tres Petromas. She inherited the space from her grandmother, my great-aunt. But more importantly she owned many *stremata* of the land behind it. She had never married and, in my opinion is losing her mind. She walks along the beach muttering to herself by day and night, picking up bits of old wood or stones or any rubbish thrown up by the sea that has a shape she insists is original; 'a work of art', she tells anyone who will listen. These days that is almost no one except one or two villagers who are as strange in the head as she is herself.

The journey took us four, almost five hours. We had to stop many times; Manoli, who drank water enough to drown, must pass this water again every few miles. And no sooner is he settled back, than Yorgo had the need himself.

I told Yorgo we should park outside the village and walk in.

'I will be glad to stretch myself,' I said, but truly I did not

123

want to be seen arriving in this working truck. I need not have troubled; the trucks were two deep even as we approached; barely a car to be seen. Times are hard and we are not alone in not having money to spare for luxuries. We have been here only twice before, both for family funerals and on both occasions without any of the children. The house where Yorgo's sister Maria lived was on the crest of a hill, with a path only of stone slabs and I groaned silently as I realised I must climb yet higher with nothing except my husband's arm to cling to, and the hard place on the ball of my foot was drawing at every step.

There were people spilling out of the doorway and halfway down that hill. Christo was a popular man and the whole village seemed to have gathered for his burial. I was panting for breath and bursting at the seams of my dress with the exertion of the climb. I could already feel the patches of damp all over me.

I pulled on Yorgo's arm.

'Wait, stay back. Give me breath to recover before you go pushing us forward.'

But he ignored me and was already at Maria, his sister's side and she was crossing herself as she greeted him. Her face was puffy with tears and as she hugged my husband I saw they were now both openly weeping.

There is always extra sadness when a mother buries her child. His age is immaterial. He remains her child. Her feelings for him will be the same as they were on the day he was born. Yorgo's niece Sophia sat beside the coffin, crossing herself as anyone approached to offer condolences. Standing behind her was a young man, his hand protectively on her shoulder.

I approached and she said, 'I am glad you are here, Aphrodite. Thank you for coming. This is my son. Christo was his godfather. He has been like a second father to him. He will miss him sorely.'

The young man's lips moved slowly and reluctantly into a greeting. He was clearly deeply distressed and I was struck by his piercing blue eyes. He was a handsome man, for sure, his hair thick and curly, almost raven wing black, and there was something about his face that suddenly seemed familiar to me. I couldn't immediately say what it was, so I asked, 'Have we met before?'

'I don't believe we have, Kyria.'

'At your grandfather's funeral, perhaps?'

But Sophia answered for him.

'My son has been studying medicine in Athens for six years now. This is his first family funeral, I think?' and she turned to him.

Before he could answer, we all heard the bell of the church start to toll and everyone began to move towards the door.

I found Yorgo, Manoli, of course, at his side, and we joined the line of mourners that was slowly set to walk to the church.

There was a shaft of sunlight that suddenly broke through the low clouds and it lit up the group walking quietly, sadly. The young doctor carried one corner of the coffin and his father Petros and two others carried with him.

'Whoever made that coffin threw it together without care,' I whispered to Yorgo.

But he waved me away and I realised he was weeping. I regretted my words. My Yorgo was truly grieving and I should have understood the depth of his feelings.

It was not an easy last journey for Christo; the coffin lurched as the men walked unevenly. He seemed a fine up-standing fellow, the godson, but his father was a squat man with arms so thick you could hardly see the elbows. In spite of the heat he should have worn a jacket, in my opinion. And because of the difference in height and strength of the bearers the box swerved raggedly, carelessly, from side to side.

All the men stood to one side of the church for the incantations and blessings and I looked at him, and his father beside him. They were so different. I could not be alone in thinking it was hard to believe they were father and son. I was still puzzling over who he seemed most to resemble with those

125

looks. A sudden flash of insight brought Heavenly's son Will into my mind. But I dismissed that as foolishness; the same head of ragged curls, yes, and the height is the same but I told myself there were many young men all over Crete with those piercing all-seeing blue eyes: 'Minoan eyes' they called them. The other one I had known like this was, of course, his godfather Christo as we had known him all those years ago.

Sometime later, after we had taken the special funeral sweetmeat, *kolya*, and some other well chosen refreshments including my own walnut cake (I was gratified to overhear the compliments it received), I realised I had sipped through three glasses of *metaxa*. Yorgo was standing against a wall, his face animated with the conversation he was having and as I approached I realised he and three others were speaking of football teams. What else?

I paid our final respects to Sophia and her son. He still stood quietly, sad and alone with a dignity rare in my opinion, in young men of his age.

I complimented Sophia on her son and she smiled, slowly proudly.

'He is good,' she said. 'He came immediately from the hospital in Athens when I told him what had happened here. Such a shock it was to us all. Christo had returned from the fishing, hauled his catch up the beach with Petros at his side and Petros said suddenly he looked up at the sky, called out something about heaven and dropped to the ground.'

She crossed herself three times and fresh tears wet her sun-reddened cheeks. In my heart I wept with her, her grief filling the air between us.

She looked up at her son; she was herself a tiny neat woman; he must have been a big baby she carried.

'He has taken a leave of absence from his hospital and will work in,' and she named a town nearby, 'for a year so that he can be with his family. He is our only child and he was so close to his godfather. It was Christo who worked as a fisherman with Petros to pay for our boy to go through medical school.'

'And now,' said the doctor, turning towards us as he heard

her words, 'I can never really thank him, for what he did for me.'

'Oh, son, never doubt he knew how much you loved him. He knew how hard you worked to pass your exams. Every letter you wrote to him, he kept and read them over and over. Sometimes he read them to us at night as well. He knew, he always knew.'

I didn't find it hard to leave that house of mourning. We walked slowly up the road. Manoli had gone on ahead an hour ago. He is never easy in crowds, fights for words and sits in unlit corners. When we reached the truck the sun was already low in the sky and Manoli was asleep in the truck bed. His head was resting on a big old sheepdog that had somehow found its way in beside him. I smiled – Manoli and animals are an easier pairing than Manoli and people.

We had to push the dog away or it would have come home with us, I believe.

'Did you meet Sophia's son?'

'The tall young man, the coffin bearer?'

'Did he remind you of anyone, I wonder?'

'Don't think so, why?'

'The eyes, just like Christo's.'

'Plenty with those eyes in Crete.'

And that was the extent of our conversation as we rumbled, tumbled, lurched and jolted our way home until I thought every bone in my body was shaken out of sorts.

Grief had hung in the air of that village, just as it did in Panagia these days.

ANGEL

Life slowly went on as before. Days fell into nights and more days and the gentle rhythm of life here carried me along with it. But however hard Lucy tried, and she did, the chatter and odd bursts of laughter that filtered through the house were unreal.

The centre had gone; we were like a ship without a sail.

I thought you could feel it, grief as you came in through the door. It hung in the air like a cobweb, hiding in corners. Each room echoed quietly with the loss of my mother. It was heartbreaking.

Athena brought cakes, Aphrodite called and drank coffee, Papa Diamedes came and took a whisky. Sometimes Hugh walked up to the Piperia and sat with the card players.

He seemed always to be in a world of his own. Whisky became his best friend, his only friend. Every day he tried, but he didn't know how to be with us. He was awkward, loving but uncomfortable, unable to express his feelings. He had little to do with Lucy or me. He sat on the terrace hour after hour gazing out to sea. Lucy tried and I tried to talk to him but he only muttered in reply – what he said we often couldn't tell. He turned up for meals, picked at all Lucy's deliciousness, ate almost nothing and went away again.

In all my dreams, here in Panagia is where I should be. So why can't I settle?

I began to think what my mother left for me was a sense of restlessness, of not belonging. I felt as though I was waiting for something, but I didn't know what.

Every night, every morning, I looked at my angel and remembered my mother's words, 'I wish I had one.' When I turned out my light at night I thought of the gypsy and her words to me and wished, how I wished I had talked to Heavenly about that, asked her help in what it meant. I did try to talk to Lucy but I had hardly started when she was telling me how unlucky it was to cross a gypsy. Not the words I wanted to hear.

I felt old, too. Well, older than before. I felt as though my childhood was buried with her. It's gone now, I thought, and it'll never come back.

Things will change, move on, time will pass and summer will turn into autumn and then winter.

I love winter here: it is dark by four. We bolt the shutters tight; the fire will be crackling and snapping from the sweet scented logs of olive and cypress we have scavenged. Chestnuts and potatoes will roast slowly in the ashes, and sometimes eggs. We will huddle under blankets, our breath warming us through to our toes. I wonder if this year there will be snow? And then winter will come into spring and then the best time of all: Easter. With red painted eggs and flowers in the streets. And I tell myself I will see all these things as if for the first time because I am seeing them for her, Heavenly, she taught me how to see. That's what she would want me to do, wouldn't she?

But then, oh then my father shattered all those dreams.

Like finding a scorpion under my pillow in the dark; he spoke and my cosy, safe but fragile world fell apart.

The day had started much like any other. I had told Chrissi of Heavenly's wish for Manoli to have a new accordion and we went out of the village and into the hills, not the ones that were now so familiar, but the craggy rough paths down to Tres Petromas. There we found Toula's Michaelis, under a crooked pine while his goats roamed freely. They skittered around like mad as we approached and one instantly started munching on the hem of my old shorts. Michaelis was happy to tell us about accordions. There is a music place in Palea

Chorio run by his friend Kotsifos, who would give us a good price.

We climbed back up to the village, pleased with our morning's work.

Chrissi went home and I helped Lucy in the kitchen. She said she would give me the money for the accordion, Will had asked her to, and not to ask Hugh. It was steamy hot in there because she was making a *kleftiko*.

All day the house smelled sweetly of the slow roasting lamb. Outside the air grew gradually heavier and still in the coming night.

I set the table and Hugh came in slowly from the terrace. He didn't speak, but picked at the lamb on his plate and I saw Lucy was really fed up. She'd spent ages in that hot kitchen – he could at least eat it or say something nice.

He mumbled something like, 'Thank you for this,' and that would have to do.

Outside the sounds of night in the deserted mountains broke through our silence; a hawk nearby shrieked and on the edge of the village a dog barked loudly, incessantly and disturbed some cats out on the prowl looking for a fight. They screamed and mewed back at him.

'From Saturday you'll have to look after yourselves, I'm afraid.' Lucy's tone was sharp in spite of the softness of her Irish accent, and those were hard words.

What did she mean?

'Why, Lucy, what's happening?'

'I must go back to London, to my home. I would love to stay but it's simply not possible. I have work to do, a book to write, money to earn.'

My father carefully, slowly put his fork down, his dinner mostly uneaten. I looked from him to Lucy, what about me?

Father cleared his throat, took a sip of wine and reaching deep into a pocket pulled out a slightly bent cigar and, straightening it, said, 'Time now for us all to move on.'

I could scarcely breathe and waited to see what would come next. But deep inside I knew.

'I'm so sorry, my dear. I am evil company these days. I find it hard to think of anything except how to continue my life without . . . Well, I must do everything alone. Not your problem, Lucy. Of course you must leave us and continue your life. It was kind of you to stay this long; we shall manage well enough here.'

He lit the cigar and its thick pungent smoke drifted immediately across the table.

He seemed to speak round it.

'Something must be done about that mess, that hair.' He was pointing at me. 'Perhaps you could take Angel off somewhere, find a hairdresser, get it cut? I don't know much about these things. Has she got clothes and stuff like that?'

Lucy barely glanced in my direction as she said, 'The uniform is more or less the same as The Oaks, just basic grey skirts and blouses for the winter. We can worry about summer later on.'

I wanted to shout, 'Excuse me, I am here, right here. Can't you see me?' I pinched myself, am I invisible?

I said, 'I can go on the bus, get my own hair cut.'

He laughed, he actually laughed.

'Goodness knows what you will come back with if you go on your own. Another sculpture on your arm or your hair dyed green, I suppose.' So he had seen my tattoo then, knew what it was. 'Whatever they taught you at that school it certainly wasn't neatness, tidiness, or indeed much by the way of common sense. Let's hope this one is better.'

He cleared his throat, again. 'I have to go back to Thailand soon and before that I must take Angel to her new school in England.' He filled his glass again and drank the dark liquid deeply down. 'Unless, of course, you feel like taking Angel with you, Lucy, and dropping her off at the school. I'm sure she would like that?'

I wondered if there was any way I could go back to this afternoon and stop this happening? In the silence that followed I knew I was being silly. I heard what he said.

I can't push back time.

There will be no cosy winter dreams here; no crackling fires, no olive picking, no laughing with Aphrodite as I help her plant her leeks. No watching Manoli brushing the few flakes of snow off the parsley and rosemary.

It will all happen, of course, just as it always does. But it will happen without me, just as it will happen without her, Heavenly.

I don't know where I shall be, but it won't be at some bloody school in England, I know that now for sure.

It was two days before I made a plan. And I made it with Chrissi.

APHRODITE

Angel stood in our doorway. She was breathless from running. Her face was stone-like.

'Sit down, child. You want some *pastitsio*? Salad?' Whatever happens I can only think to offer food.

She shook her head and then, as an afterthought, 'I'm sorry, can Chrissi come out for a while?'

Chrissi was on her feet in an instant. She patted the pocket in her jeans. She thinks I don't know that she is checking for cigarettes. Why do children always think mothers are blind, stupid?

'Sit, Angel. Sit, Chrissoula, and finish your meal.'

Only seconds and with a clatter of plates, forks, my daughter was out of the door.

When she came back she had changed. How or in what way I don't know, but there was a buzz about her after those couple of hours with Angel that hadn't been there before. She hugged me.

'I love you, Mama,' she says.

Now I know something is happening.

And over the next days I am sure of it. The Orfanoudakis house is being cleaned, and swept and all that is needed to be done to put the house away for the winter.

The family will go their separate ways; that much I learn from Chrissi.

As is always the way here with arrivals or departures, the village gathers.

Gifts are brought, mostly food but also wine, oil, raki. We

expect to see the family move on with great helpings of provisions.

I went over to the house late one afternoon.

Maybe I will cook a meal to say goodbye. We have shared many happy meals together; but they were before. All good things were before.

I walked out on to the terrace, their house as familiar to me as my own. It was still catching the dying rays of the sun. There was no sign of Angel, but Hugh was standing at the edge, looking down. I stood awkwardly for a moment.

I was shocked to see his shoulders were shaking. He had no idea I was there and he was weeping. I was about to creep away but he heard me and turned and his eyes were wet with tears. He grunted and rubbed them with a none-too-clean handkerchief.

I have no knowledge of the language of grief, but before I could mumble anything he patted my shoulder and was gone. Within moments I heard his steps leave the house and guessed he was going up to the Piperia to drown his sorrows once more.

I thought of his life in Thailand. Heavenly had told me that he seemed always surrounded by friends, never alone. Perhaps those friends would prop him up, fill his life with the easy humour of like minds? Would he meet another woman? He was a good-looking man for an Englishman and it seemed hard to believe his bed would be empty for long.

And Angel? With luck this school wouldn't be as bad as she imagined and a year, two, would pass and she would – what? I sighed.

And suddenly it was the day. For the last time the windows were closed, the shutters bolted tight across, every door locked. At noon sharp they went down to the square where Vassili the taxi driver was waiting. They climbed in and the big old car pulled slowly through and away until they were out of sight of the village and the lingering well-wishers. Many of us stood waving as they left.

Of Chrissi there was no sign. It was hard to believe she didn't want to say goodbye.

I walked through their house one last time, locking the door behind me with the big old key, ready for the winter, and went home.

When I got there Titi was there ahead of me. I had noticed she had not been in the square; no goodbyes for her. I made her coffee of course and tried to make conversation but to be honest her company wearies me these days. I don't trust her as a friend, she seems to live on the other side of darkness and we have little in common.

After an hour or even more she placed her cup on the table, wiped her thin mouth and sat with her hands in her lap. I offered more coffee, a *koulouria sesame*. She has a sweet tooth I know but she waved her hand in refusal, her brow frowning.

'Under my plate – the seeds get under my plate.'

I tried to nod sympathetically but I was only offering in the hope that it would be a hint for her to go. But oh, *Panagia mou*, she had taken her teeth out and was rubbing them on her underskirt; none too clean it was either. Titi is one here who still wears traditional clothes. You would think a dressmaker would allow herself a little change now and then? But no, that same old dark thick skirt day after day. And oh, save me, *Panagia*, I could see her woollen drawers as well.

I have cleaned the pots over and again and set the *briki* upside down to dry. Signs enough surely that it was time to go?

'What is your Chrissi up to with Heavenly's girl?'

Ah, so that was why she was here. She wanted gossip to spread around the village.

'I don't think they are up to anything. Angel has left now to go to school in England.'

'Not if what I heard her planning with your Chrissi is anything like true.'

'What do you mean? Tell me what you mean.'

Her smile was tight, miserly but triumphant; she knew something I didn't.

'They were in your *gypo*, under the orange tree. They didn't see me digging potatoes in my sister's patch, but,' and she paused dramatically, teasing, 'it's not for me to say. Ask your daughter.'

I was not going to beg her, of all people but something was going on for sure.

'Lucy seems the only sensible one in that family, except for all those questions she has about food; "how many this, how much of that?"' And she clicked her teeth back and forth in that thin, mean mouth. 'She's a wild one for sure, just like her mother before her.'

'Lucy?' What was she talking about? Trying to follow her conversation was like following a rat in a maze.

'Angel, of course. And I was not the only one who found your blessed Heavenly crazy wild herself.'

'Why are you saying this? What are you talking about?'

She laughed, an evil cackle sort of sound.

'You do leap to their defence, don't you? I was not the only one here who thought the English woman strange. Mind you, I was no age myself at the time.'

Now I know for sure she is mad. She is younger than me by some years, so how come she speaks of herself as a child during the war? There is a streak of viciousness in her too, in all her family, I remember, although most of them are dead now. She married a swarthy man from over Aghios Demetrious. A gypsy from Turkey it was said at the time and their only child was stillborn. Like Heavenly's, I was about to say, but something made me hold my tongue.

'Chrissi not here just now?'

'She'll be back any time now.'

Another laugh. 'Unless she's gone to get her arm carved up like her friend. You must admit, Aphrodite, you are relieved they have left? Such a bad influence on your Chrissi. Underwear on the flagpole, tsk, tsk.'

'Not at all. And I prefer not to speak ill words of the recently dead in my house.'

She could wound with her spiteful ignorance, this woman. What can I do to make her go?

'I merely referred to your dear friend Heavenly behaving strangely. Read into that what you like, but I was not alone in wondering—'

'Well?'

'She didn't behave like a proper married woman, did she? Sent her husband packing and worked all hours of the day and night with village men in the Orfanoudakis house. Up ladders, sawing wood, what have you.'

'My Yorgo, you mean, and his nephew. And they did a good job. Look at that house today. I remember what it was like before – even if you were barely out of your mother's womb yourself. Falling down, it was.'

She was on her feet now, at last.

'Better ask your Chrissi where her English friend is running away to. Maybe she will want to run too, eh? They seem to be joined at the hip. Well, I can't stay here all day gossiping and chatting. So goodbye and thank you for your hospitality. Shame about the *koulouria sesame*. Nowadays some here make them without the sesame seeds so that others like me can enjoy them.'

Finally she peered out of the doorway and then was gone and she left me more out of sorts than even I was before.

I watched after her and saw just around the corner she had met up with the one with the red wart on her nose. What does she have to do with her? Always when there is trouble she is there, it seems to me; all hunched over, her teeth gleaming yellow from a mouth bordered by a strong black moustache on a sharp lined face. And Titi was now walking beside her. As I watched they turned to look at me and I pulled back inside my door.

I seized on Chrissi when she came back later, but she would say nothing. Not of Angel nor Lucy nor any of them. Nothing.

'Running away, Titi said. She heard you up at the *gypo*. Who is running where?'

But she just sat, her mouth closed firmly and shook her head.

Something is planned, I know it. I found a pile of food; cakes, biscuits, fruit and tomatoes and even a bottle of oil in Chrissi's room.

'What is this?' I demanded. 'These are things we gave to Lucy. These were some of my best cookies.'

Still she said nothing.

Whatever was going on I shall be the last to hear of it, I think.

ANGEL

The boy raced across the sand screaming with joy. Legs and arms flying wild, in that way of children. Behind him Chrissi, arms spread wide, bearing down on him like a plane, zooming and wheeling, her face a mask of delight, a child herself again. She reached him, caught him, which was, of course, what he wanted and whirled him around in the air. Panting and gasping she lifted him high and then down, down, beside me where I sat on this endless, gilded beach.

'Enough,' she gasped and fell in a heap at my side.

The boy, Rufus, beat his little fists on her leg, his wild, woolly black hair falling across his eyes.

'More! More!' he yelled.

In all my life I have never known Chrissi as happy as she is here. As a matter of fact, I'm pretty cheery myself. It's not just because of the children, but it helps.

It seemed luck was with us from the start. Chrissi hesitated at first.

'It will kill my mother.'

'Aristos and Zambia left; she still loves them.'

I let her think about it for a little, but then she thought back to the fair, and the beauty and simplicity of the people we met there; their ease in living and the pleasure, shining out of their eyes.

And she didn't need long to make up her mind. She said the thing that finally decided her was seeing the empty space on her wall where James Dean had hung.

We made a plan of how and where we would meet and I would phone her when I was free. She had stowed all the food given to us by the villagers under her bed; that would keep us going until we were settled with the hippies. That was the plan.

The day we left Panagia, all three of us, Father, Lucy and me, was one of the saddest days of my life.

In the years before, at the end of every summer, it was bad enough having to say goodbye to my mother. But nothing like that last, lonely day. Lucy and I went early to the church on the hill and said farewell. The wind was blowing strongly and her grave seemed nothing but the loneliest saddest place in the world. We held each other and wept, and then blew back down to where my father waited impatiently. I don't know if he had said his own goodbye to her, I wasn't asking. And if he had, he had gone alone.

The wind in the churchyard stayed there and we drove the rest of the way in brilliant sunshine. Every corner down the mountain to Tres Petromas, and there were many, it seemed to me I was going in the wrong direction – away. Away from the village, away from my home, away from everything I had loved for all the years of my life and into a future that held only questions. There were no more certainties. For most of that ride I was sad and afraid and then I thought the worst thing in the whole world has already happened to me. And a small flicker of something inside me said, 'So there can be no more worst things.'

At the beginning the plan was simple: Vassili's taxi to Heraklion, then Father would take a plane to Berlin and from there fly on to Bangkok while Lucy and I would travel to Athens together and then on to Heathrow. I had persuaded them that I could travel onwards from there alone to the god-forsaken place in Herefordshire, to the school they had found.

Cattle country – famous for cows. I naively imagined hundreds of girls (no boys of course) with straw in their hair and brothers called Seth and Reuben and nasty goings-on in their woodsheds. *Cold Comfort Farm* crossed with Hardy's

Tess. My set books at The Oaks had served my imagination well.

Worryingly for them, and perfect for me, was Lucy's last minute change. We were just leaving the house when the phone rang. Always thinking it might be Will, Lucy dropped her bags and ran indoors. Not Will but her agent in London – who had found a Greek publishing company interested in her book of Greek food and she had to spend the day in Athens with them and go on to London the following morning.

Therefore I must fly to London alone or miss the first day of term.

'I couldn't miss the first day,' I said.

It was agreed that I was to phone Lucy after a few days and tell her all was well and she would pass that on to Hugh. I had made her promise not to try and ring me.

'It will make me too homesick,' I said, 'waiting for your call. I must try and settle in properly.'

It was only a very small lie, I told myself, and I kept my fingers crossed. Hugh had grave doubts about this arrangement at first, but it was Lucy who persuaded him, not me.

'She's seventeen now, we can trust her to do the right thing,' she said.

I am doing the right thing, I thought, but it's the right thing for me, not quite the same as the right thing for them.

Anyway, I had the huge bonus of not having to fly to England and then all the way back again.

My father hugged me to him at the airport. Awkwardly, his bony arms clasped tightly around me, and as I looked up I saw there were tears in his eyes. I wasn't sure about that.

'You'll be all right, old girl,' he said. 'It can't possibly be as bad as you imagine. I'll send you a postcard or something.'

And then with a rather sad attempt at a cheery wave over his shoulder, he was gone through gate seven.

All I could think was, 'That's what he called my mother, "old girl".'

Lucy stood in the taxi queue at Athens airport and panicked.

'Do I look all right? Do I look serious enough to write a

book? Do I look as though I deserve to be paid lots of drachmas? Does my hair smell of chips?'

'Yes, yes, yes and absolutely not,' I said.

'Omonia Square please,' she said to the driver and she was gone.

And then I stood there, on my own at last and for just a moment or two felt cold and frightened, so I thought I should start. I approached the airline desk clerk at check-in. Putting on what I hoped was a pathetic, needy face, I said, 'Can you help me, please?'

'If I can. What is it?'

He was older than me but not much and had swept back hair and a thin, pointy nose, but a friendly-looking smile.

'I have to change my arrangements and go back to Crete rather urgently.' I crossed my fingers behind my back. I'll have totally cramped hands if I tell many more fibs. 'My aunt has been taken ill and can't have me to stay in London, so I must go home, do you see? I can't stay in a foreign city alone, can I?'

'There's a plane in forty minutes to Crete. Is that what you want?'

'Will you change this ticket to Heathrow for one to Heraklion, then?'

This was a bit of risky, wild card playing but I thought it worth a chance.

'I don't know about that. Hang on, I'll have to speak to my supervisor.' And he made not one but three phone calls while I looked hopeless and helpless and counted the minutes passing. Eventually he was back with me again. 'I can do that for you, but I'm not allowed to refund the difference, so I can give you a voucher for another flight with our airline for some other time. Is that OK?' I nodded.

'The gate has closed now for that flight, I'm sorry. Two hours to wait. Maybe get yourself something to eat?'

'I haven't any money.' Flying fingers again.

He grinned. 'Not your day, is it? I can give you another voucher we give to passengers when flights are delayed; you can get a sandwich and some coffee, would that help? Or,' and he turned pink, 'I'm off in twenty minutes, perhaps I could buy you a drink?'

Not what I wanted!

'Thank you so much, but perhaps another time?'

He knew and I knew this was never going to happen, so I smiled over my shoulder as I walked away, trying to work out what animal it was he reminded me of.

I rang Panagia from Heraklion and managed to persuade Aphrodite to let me speak to Chrissi.

'I'm set to go,' I said, 'are you?'

'Now?' she said.

'I'll tell you later, but Aghios bus station, yes? Soon as you can?'

I could feel her mother hovering behind her and knew she could say little. But we had planned well and we knew exactly what to do.

I had one more call to make before I got the bus across the island. I bought another phone card from the kiosk and dialled through to England, to a number I had learned by heart. The phone was answered by a clipped, deep female voice,

'Meadowhurst School.'

'Can I speak to Miss Norrish please?'

'May I ask who is calling?'

'My name is Evadne Timberlake. My daughter Angeliki is due to start in the sixth form with you.'

'I am so sorry, Mrs Timberlake, Miss Norrish has another parent with her just now. Can I take a message?'

'I have some rather bad news, I'm afraid. Her father has been taken gravely ill and she must stay here with us for the foreseeable future.'

I put the phone down quickly. I could hear planes overhead and announcements on the tannoy. She might wonder just a little bit why my mother would need to use a public telephone.

Poor Chrissi did her best but I had to hang around the bus station in Aghios for a day and a night, avoiding women,

145

gangs of children and even worse – persistent old men who all wanted to chat about when, why and how I was going anywhere. At one point I was almost asleep; it was the morning of the next day, I was starving and really didn't want to break into the accordion fund. I hoped that Chrissi had managed to smuggle the food we had been given into her bag.

She had managed to persuade her parents that she could miss a term at school and stay with her sister Zambia in Chania and help her with the children.

'I'm thinking about becoming a teacher,' she had said, 'so some practice like that would be really useful to me.' Probably lots of crossed fingers going round her back, I thought.

Yorgo had said yes straight away, delighted to think of another of his children having a professional life. Aphrodite took longer, but realised that her life would be simpler if she had one less child to watch, curfew and defend from the *malakas*. Chrissi would write to her sister who would of course notice that her new babysitter hadn't arrived, and tell her she had been delayed.

'Some time they'll discover we are missing,' I said, 'but we'll deal with that when it happens.'

What I hadn't expected was the sight of Aphrodite and Manoli arriving at the bus station. Bloody!

I stood behind a pillar and hoped I didn't look too suspicious. I then saw Chrissi trailing behind them. If Aphrodite was going with her all the way to where she was supposed to be going, then I hadn't a clue what would happen. I would have to go on my own, I supposed, and I didn't fancy that much.

Chrissi was walking now in my direction. I felt like a spy in a bad comedy film as I whispered, 'Here, psss!'

She jumped and looked at me.

'What's happening?'

'I'm supposed to be going to the ladies' room.'

So we darted in there together.

'They're only coming this far to see me off,' Chrissi said. 'You were much earlier than I expected. You know how suspicious she can be. Wanted to know where you were when you rang me and why were you ringing and all sorts of stuff.'

So I watched while Chrissi got on a bus which, with a roar, disappeared out of sight and out through the town, leaving Aphrodite and Manoli barely ten yards away from me waving and waving and dabbing their eyes.

They finally got on another bus. Back to Tres Petromas, I suppose, and I wondered how far Chrissi would have to go before she could get off and catch another bus back here and together we could start this adventure – being grown-ups in our future life, on our own.

As it happened she was back with me within twenty minutes, her bus appearing as Aphrodite's disappeared.

It took us two whole days to find the right caves on the right beach and in the end it was the music that drew us there.

In spite of being completely exhausted I had managed to keep going until we were well out of Aghios and on the coast road to the end of the island.

We had to break into the accordion fund to buy bus tickets to Sitia, but Chrissi said Manoli would completely understand.

'And after that, we must walk.'

And we walked and walked through the fag ends of the town. Places we'd known all our lives, the electricity company, the tax office, Hugh's bank and the high building with OTE on the front where the telephone company lived; all modern scars on a landscape as old as the mountains around.

There were the crumbly old bits of the fortress wall from the occupation by the Venetians. My father brought me here when I was ten and we saw *Madame Butterfly* in the open-air theatre and I fell asleep.

The town is set high on a hilltop and seems to tumble down to the shore below.

I made Chrissi stop when all the buildings had given way to the long beach. I thought it must be midday; the sun was high and I was starving.

We sat down on the shingles.

'Let's swim,' I said, pulling off my jeans and T-shirt.

I was halfway to the water's edge before I realised Chrissi wasn't with me.

'Come on, I'm filthy and hot, I need this water.'

Slowly and with obvious reluctance she came after me.

'Are you OK?' I said, rubbing my face and treading water.

She didn't answer just shook the water off her head and swam away, out, out to sea.

'Hey, wait for me!'

And I was after her and caught her feet in my hands.

'Tell me what's wrong?'

'Manoli,' she muttered and looked as though she might cry, 'he'll miss me.'

'Of course he will. But you know it might not be all a bad thing for him. With you out of the way he might start to, oh I don't know, get a proper life of his own.'

But I didn't even convince myself and she shook her head.

'Nice try, Angel, but I don't think so.'

And for a moment I thought my dream was over and that if I wanted to go, I must go alone. But she smiled, a wise Aphrodite smile, and at that moment a wave of homesickness ran through me too. I missed Aphrodite, Yorgo and dear innocent Manoli. I had no one else to regret; in Panagia there was no one for me now.

'Mama was so worried about the goats' feet when I left. Titi told her of a new infection, a foot rot going around.'

'And now you think you will never know?'

She nodded.

'Come on, I'm hungry.'

And turning, we swam strongly back to the shore. I flung myself down flat on my back for a moment and then – bloody it was sore! Chips of flint and granite were digging hard into my bum. I turned over carefully and Chrissi pulled them out.

'Ouch,' I said.

'Look at this one.' She was holding up a minute shard. 'It's the end of an ammonite.'

'How on earth do you know that?'

'Manoli,' she said. 'He knows a lot about fossils. One of the only things he learned in school.'

We had our first picnic, sitting there on that rough beach that seemed to be miles from anywhere. There wasn't much to eat, Aphrodite had found the stash of goodies and taken them herself.

'She grumbled like anything, saying I'd bring rats into the house if I kept food under my bed and then she told me how ungrateful Lucy was to reject all the lovely things from her *gypo*.'

We were both laughing by the time we'd had our meagre lunch.

'We'll have to break into the accordion fund again, and find a shop.'

Then we swam. The sparkling clear blue water revived me for a while but the warmth from the sun sent me to sleep as I lay drying myself on the beach.

Chrissi woke me by rubbing my arm.

'Supposing they don't want us to stay with them, then what will we do?'

'I'm sure they will,' I said. 'They asked us, remember?'

'But supposing there are too many of them and not enough caves, what then?'

'Then we'll find our own cave somewhere and live there, the two of us.' I sounded confident but actually Chrissi had rattled me with her worry.

'I hope you brought your yellow dress?'

She started to giggle.

'It'll look good hanging on the wall of a cave.'

And the mood had changed in a heartbeat.

We had to move on all the time. With only a bit of money and barely a clue to where we were going there was a temptation to pause, linger. So many birds we didn't know. We saw blue rock thrushes and crag martins; Will had told me about them, but until today I had only seen pictures of them in books.

We walked along a beach that seemed endless, our only companions the most vivid and beautiful butterflies: scarlet and emerald and turquoise wings dipped and swirled around us.

As the sun fell lower in the sky we walked on as far as we could on the sand, until at the moment darkness began to fall through the soft air of twilight we held hands and paddled along at the water's edge.

We settled that night in the shelter of a great rock. Chrissi slept at once, her head in my lap. I stayed awake for ages under the great curtain of the midnight sky. Sounds of seabirds calling in a kind of rhythm lulled me into sleep. And I awoke at dawn, just as the first hints of the coming day crept into the sky. We had no more food, not even a mouldy crust was left, and we started the day aching and moaning. Both of us I know longing to turn around and go home.

But we saw a long stone wall running along the back of the beach and a sign on its open gate said it was a monastery.

'Monks,' I said. 'They're kind and generous, aren't they? Help travellers on their pilgrimages. Isn't that what they do?'

'As long as they're not like Papa Michaelis,' she said, 'maybe.'

There was a blue wooden door just inside the gate; it was locked. I banged on it loudly.

They were indeed kind to travellers and sent us on our way several hours later, full after a rich and delicious meal of roasted kid, potatoes and wild greens.

'I thought monks were supposed to live on bread and water,' said Chrissi, patting her full and distinctly rounded tummy.

'Let's be grateful these monks didn't. That was very good wine, I think. What's in the bag?'

'Cold roast goat and potatoes. Tomatoes, a whole cheese and two more bottles of the wine.'

We trudged along at the edge of the sea. I felt the warmth of the sun and the soothing of the gentle blue waves at our feet. 'Is it much further?'

'Just a while yet,' I took her hand, 'I expect. We're miles past Kato Zakros already.'

We took turns to carry Chrissi's bag. I just had a small backpack. My battered old trunk would be sitting in Heathrow airport now. I had sneaked any labels off when I checked it in at Heraklion so it couldn't be identified.

'We'll have to share your knickers,' I said, and we giggled.

And then, just when we thought we couldn't go any further I heard it; the clear, sweet sound of a penny whistle singing like a late bird through the evening sky.

We stood still and listened. It was an old Greek melody Chrissi and I had learned as children. Heavenly used to sing it to us. A violent pang of homesickness swept through me and I felt Chrissi grip my hand tight; she felt it too. A guitar picked up the refrain and then slowly a voice, a girl's voice clear and sweet joined in and then other voices and we rounded a corner of the beach and there they were; a group in shadows in the moonlight. The flames of a bonfire leapt high and we counted six or eight people, maybe even ten and three or four children.

It was the children who saw us first. One turned and then the others and as the parents saw us too, the children jumped up and raced across the sand towards us.

'It's them!' they called. 'From the fair. You said they'd come.'

And their small hands were grabbing us and they pulled us over towards the fire. We didn't need urging, we were laughing, both of us, as we felt their pleasure. We sat with them while they played and sang far into the night. And then as the children were one by one falling asleep, they led us around the bay and there along the back of the beach were caves spreading as far as the next cove.

The cliff face there was high and some caves were higher than others, some bigger, some little more than holes in the darkness. But they didn't look scary: they looked fun and welcoming. Bright cloths, pinned down by stones waved cheerily as the small breeze lifted the corners.

I don't know how but Chrissi and I found ourselves wrapped in bright striped rugs and we were taken to a cave lined with what I later saw were sleeping bags. Somehow mugs of hot chocolate, dark and sweet, were in our hands and before I could even start to say thank you, we lay down and were asleep I think, in the middle of a sentence.

The next morning I awoke slowly and although the cave we were in was darkish, I could see outside the sun was high. I shook Chrissi awake and we stretched and went outside to the sandy beach. The children sat in a row outside and jumped up when they saw us and called and one, the boy with a mass of black curls, whistled loud and clearly and from around a corner their parents came across to us, smiling. Just as at the fair, they all wore brightly coloured clothes, and some of the men wore sarong skirts just like the women. Some wore jeans.

There were three children. Two belonged to Anya and Raggeh; Tink (that's short for Tinkerbell from Peter Pan), she was twelve, and Rolly. He was about ten and had been born with a twisted foot and there was no money to pay for the medical treatment he would need to set it right. Despite that, he was a wanderer, Rolly, and unless he was watched day and night he'd slowly and quietly vanish; turning up in another group or another cave or even at the edge of the sea. He would even sometimes walk off in his sleep. They were good-natured, sweet children and we loved them, Chrissi and I. Then there was Rufus. He was Libby's son. She doesn't have a man: not a husband or a boyfriend. I try not to have favourites because they are all three of them with us all the time, but Rufus would be, if I did. Probably because his hair was rather like mine: wild and with lots of red bits. But from the start he was adoring only of Chrissi. It was a love affair that had begun that night at the fair.

There were more children and more people all living along this stretch of cave-lined beach. But these, the first group we met, became our friends. They accepted us immediately; and they were our 'family'.

Raggeh disappeared for days at a time and came back with

loads of stuff – books, and tins of food, fruit, hard Cretan rusks, bread and eggs. Everyone ate like kings then for a few days, including me and Chrissi. Then after a while someone else went off with the empty sacks and returned with them bulging. But it was Raggeh most often and he always brought the best stuff. I don't know what happened for money. We tried to give Raggeh a good stash of the accordion fund to spend, but he wouldn't take much.

So we earned our keep by babysitting children or doing someone's washing for them. That seemed to be fine. As far as I could see, we were the only ones our age, so we were popular as helpers.

It took us no time at all to get used to sleeping here. There were no normal rules so sometimes people chose to sleep during the day, but not many, not often. We slept on mats of woven straw with a bit of old carpet underneath. At first I woke every morning so stiff I could barely move, but Libby said 'You'll get used to it' and I did. But there was always some times when I pretended I was fine and I wasn't.

There was a line of tamarisk trees at the back of this beach. Their frondy greenery draped down like curtains. Chrissi and I went behind them and they were our bathroom. When we'd finished we dug it in with a little spade Libby had and ran straight into the sea to get clean. We peed in the sea of course. That took getting used to but no knickers helped. Natural, I told myself.

I thought of Heavenly every day and when I did she was always in Panagia, smiling at me. I missed the village, too. I thought of Petros and Andreas in the senior class at school there. I wondered if they missed us. Probably not.

Life in the village would all be going on without us; the fish truck coming to the square and the cheese man with his big knife. I missed the cries of '*Fresco, fresco! Poli fresco!*'

And the watermelon man who made you take two for the price of one and how guilty we all were because they were so huge you had to throw lots to the chickens.

Some days I tried to talk to Chrissi about these feelings, but she seemed to be far too busy with the new life to waste time thinking about the old. Some days I hardly saw her; if she'd been fishing at night she might sleep during the day.

We swam every day; sometimes twice or three times. Always naked – a wonderful feeling! It took some getting used to at first. I don't have a bra, my breasts are too small to need holding up. But here nobody wore anything, not even men, so after only a few days I was totally used to it.

Chrissi didn't, for ages. That was a surprise. Always so much bolder than me, she didn't swim, saying it was too rough, too cold. That was rubbish, it was the closest thing to paradise I'd ever found. At the end of summer, the sea is always at its warmest. It had absorbed months and months of sunshine. Then, I made her so she had to; there were no baths or showers here, just the sea and she started to smell rather sweaty and I told her. Then she did; tearing her things off and racing in so fast I was always miles behind.

That was mainly because of the children alongside grabbing at any available hand, our feet all splashing together through the blue green water. Then one of them would see a tiny fish and we'd stop and search for more, laughing as we would feel them tickle against our feet.

Chrissi, once she got used to swimming without her clothes in front of everyone, became really good at fishing. She went way out and using the nets that we found at the end of the beach one night, brought back all sorts; rock lobsters, some-times, and loads of *barbounia*, the red mullet that swim near the shore. We didn't steal the nets. They were full of holes and had been abandoned. We sat up nearly all one night and sewed them until they were proper again.

I'm not exactly sure how long we'd been here. No one had watches or calendars. The tides changed with the moon and I knew the days were shorter and the nights longer. I thought it was forty-six days, which meant it must be November. I only knew that because I counted the days since Heavenly died and that was 21st September 1971.

Sometimes winds blew right across the beaches and filled

the air with the whistling of the breeze, a sort of music. And it could be cold. Every night we had a fire on the beach and anyone who wanted could come and sit beside it. The kids loved it. And we sat under blankets all snuggled up together and I made up stories for them about mermen and sea queens. They usually fell asleep long before I'd finished. It didn't matter, we all slept like that. We kept each other warm.

There was a group around the bay who earned money by selling blankets they made. There were about six of them, some quite old. They went to the market to sell them but any people living in the caves could buy them for a special price. They gave Chrissi and me two each because we got the blankets ready for them to sell. We washed them in pure clean spring water. It took ages to get them dry and smoothly soft with special brushes and combs. It was like washing my hair when it was all tangled up.

We were good at it, Chrissi and me; we'd learnt from our mothers at the spring in Panagia. We squeezed them gently in the icy cold water and then laid them out neatly, flatly on a clean patch of beach weighted down at the corners with smooth stones.

After that first night we slept on the beach. People gave us blankets and rugs so we weren't cold. Everyone shared; food, clothes, books, covers. What you had you shared. My jeans, my best ones that Heavenly gave me, disappeared for a few weeks and a sarong wrap came in their place. I minded at first, but then I got to quite enjoy wrapping myself around each morning with the bright patterned cloth. Then one morning I woke up and the jeans were back, all washed and folded neatly. I still had the sarong, though.

After a while we shared a cave with Libby and Rufus. It was quite small and, for ages, was lived in by only one old man. He disappeared one day and Anya said he had probably gone away to finish his life somewhere else. No one asked why or where but I thought he had gone away to die, like cats do. They know the time is ready; they've done everything they want to do and they go off privately and just, well die. That's it: the end.

When we went into his cave there was almost nothing there, but what there was he had left stacked in a tidy neat pile beside the entrance, with his sandals lying side by side on the top. That night Raggeh lit a great fire from driftwood and brought his things down to the edge and we all gathered around and each took something and threw it into the flames. Tink held a striped shirt we had seen him in lots and she kissed it before throwing it in and I heard her whisper, 'Goodbye, sweet dreams.' Then we all held hands in a circle round the fire and no one quite knew what to do next so I started to sing:

'If you're happy and you know it, clap your hands.
If you're happy and you know it, clap your hands.
If you're happy and you know it,
And you really want to show it,
If you're happy and you know it, clap your hands!'

Heavenly had taught me that and lots of other children's songs as well.

Soon we were all laughing and dancing around the fire together. I hope, wherever he was, the old man knew.

We didn't know everyone, just some that we became close to. Like Raggeh, Anya and Libby. Anya says one of the great things about this place is respect. You respect everyone else here and they will respect you, even the children. Especially the children.

She said that most of the problems in the world were caused by people not showing respect for each other. Heavenly always said that too, and she said you don't drop bombs on people or start wars if you respect them. I told Anya that and she said Heavenly must have been a very wise and special person.

And so we settled in there and we were both happy, I thought. And the days grew shorter and the nights longer and the chill winter breezes seemed not to trouble us too much; well most of the time. I was really glad when we got the cave.

I think it's very hard having just about no privacy. One day I woke up after a sleepless night and I was in a ratty old mood and Rufus, who seemed never to sleep, was sitting there looking at me. That morning I just wanted to be left alone. I went down the beach and huddled up in a corner under a big rock to keep warm. It was cold then in the early mornings – winter chill. When I had slept I'd dreamed about Heavenly and every time I woke up, which was about every hour, I was crying. All I could think was what would she feel if she saw me here? Would she be pleased we were doing this? I didn't really think she would be but I thought she might understand. She just might.

There were two brothers who lived at the far end of the next beach. They would wander along the seashore, their feet always just in the water. They came close but never right up to us. I could see the first one who walked in front was short, but very, very short like a child and he walked with a bad limp. One day I had been swimming, was rubbing myself dry with an old striped towel Libby had. It was a *hammam* towel, she told me. She had been given it in a Turkish bath in Morocco. I was cold so I wrapped it around myself and ran up and down in the sand. And slowly they came along and stopped when they came to me.

'Hello,' I said, and for want of anything else to do, stuck my hand out. The little one grabbed it and kissed it. It was a sweet gesture and I smiled. 'Thank you.'

The big one said, 'My brother doesn't speak so well. I hope he hasn't offended you?'

'Offended me? No I'm honoured. My name is Angel, what are yours?'

The little one opened his mouth and grunted, over and over but smiling at the same time.

'He is called Ligo,' his brother said, 'and I am called Mago. Like sort of little and big.'

'Very appropriate names,' I said. 'But although I am called Angel, I'm not at all an angel.'

'Perhaps it's because you look like an angel.'

I might have blushed. Ligo was already running ahead splashing in and out of the waves and laughing and grunting.

'He's very happy,' I said.

Mago sighed.

'That's how it seems to you. I'm pleased you can say that. He lives in a lot of pain almost all the time.'

We were walking along the edge of the sea together as we spoke and I learnt a lot about this strange pair in just that first half hour.

Mago told me their mother had died a while ago in a hospital in Italy. Their father had died years before, so now they had no one and nothing. No Pappous, no Yaya, no aunts or uncles or cousins. No money, no clothes, no house to live in so they lived on the road. Or more like off the road. They caught lifts when they wanted to go further and had no idea how long they had been travelling when they arrived in this place.

Mago did odd jobs for women in houses they passed in return for a little money or a meal or occasionally a bed for the night, which they shared.

They had found a very small cave and Mago explained that if he curled over double and held Ligo to him, they slept.

They shied away when I suggested they come and meet my friends.

Mago said, 'We don't make friends with people, if you don't mind. Ligo gets attached very quickly and then it's too painful for him when we must move on.'

I offered him food; he turned away saying, 'We manage well enough, thank you.'

'Don't I count as a friend?' I asked.

'Not really,' he said. 'You are an angel, that's different.'

Ligo was very excited by my tattoo and every day liked to touch it, stroke it. One day he held my hand tightly and reaching forward licked it; it tickled and I laughed.

We walked along the beach every afternoon and talked about all sorts of things;

I learnt that Ligo had always been crippled.

'An accident of birth,' Mago described it, as though it was a phrase he had used many times. 'The night he was born was dark and cold. It was that time of year that is always dark and cold.'

'You mean winter?'

'That's it, winter it's called. There was a thunderstorm. Big thunder filled the air and lightning crawled across the sky – flash and crash.' Ligo giggled now and jumped up and down; he knew we were speaking about him. 'My father had not come home from the fields and my mother's pains had already started but she said she must find him. She said he could be in trouble. So we went out there. Cold. Wet.' Mago was shivering now, as if this was that moment. 'We didn't find him, but my mother had to crouch down under a tree and I held her. She made some noises and then I saw that there was something there, on the ground. It was a baby. It was Ligo. He was so small and all twisted up like he is now. He never untwisted. Just got a bit bigger.'

'And your father?'

'I never saw him again. My mother said he came home, looked at Ligo, left the house and never came back. "Who cares?" my mother said. But I did. I cared. He promised to teach me how to fish. And he could kick a good ball. I wanted him back.'

It was a sad story to me but Mago told it as though things like that happened every day to people.

We talked about the stars, the moon, the sea. Mago was fascinated to hear about my school. Somehow his mother had let them slip through the system and they had never been to any school and he found it hard to understand why my parents had sent me away to school.

'Did they have to do that? Was your father on the run?'

I tried to explain but the idea of Hugh as a fugitive only made me laugh and I realised that to some the behaviour of rich people only seemed very strange indeed.

Mago had taught himself to read and write very crudely.

But it was so basic that he could barely tell me the names of places they had been to before here.

They had become so much a part of my life that I never questioned they would be there each day in the afternoon. I told Chrissi about them, but she didn't seem interested in meeting them. In the last couple of weeks she had been living more and more inside herself, disappearing for hours at a time, and when I asked how she was, she just shook her head. Some days she was happy and smiling, her usual old self, but there were days when she closed her face not just to me but to Rufus, who didn't understand. I began to worry: was this all a terrible mistake for her? It was my fault if it was.

Then one day I went down to the sea in the afternoon and waited and waited for my new friends. They didn't come. I did that for two or three days and then suddenly they were there again. Smiling, I ran to meet them. Ligo hugged my leg and hung on there, his little face turned up to me. I stroked the dark curling hair of this little person and realised he was crying; fat tears ran down his sun-browned face.

Mago said, 'We came to say goodbye.'

'Is there something wrong? Can I help?'

Looking away, his long rangy body seemed to be moving away already. He shook his head.

'This is why we must go,' he said and pointed to Ligo who was now sobbing and trying to speak, his grunts getting softer as he paused for breath. 'He is telling you he loves you,' he said gruffly. I was stricken. 'We must go, move on. It's always best we don't get too close to people. I told you when we met. I just brought him here now to say goodbye.'

And he pulled his brother's arms away from where they hung so hard to my leg.

I thought how useless words are at times like this. Surely goodbye is the saddest word? But it had to be enough – there was nothing else.

'Goodbye,' I said and, turning away from them, ran up the beach. My own tears were falling now, as I realised I had started to love that funny little chap myself. Where would they go? What would happen to them?

I turned round once. The beach was empty; the waves trickled unevenly on the white sand. I would never know.

After we'd been there a while I did what I had dreaded doing for ages; I wrote a letter.

Darling Will,

I hope you can forgive me. I hope you and Lucy understand I just couldn't carry on being treated like a child. Our father could never see that. He thought we should all go on after Mother died as though nothing had changed.

The most important thing is that you know that I am not just all right, I am really happier than I've been for a long, long while. I was always happy in the village when it was just me and Heavenly or when Lucy and you were there with us. I suppose I thought it could go on forever like that. That was when I was still a child, before Chrissi and I came here and had to grow up quickly in order to look after ourselves.

I've made her promise to write to Aphrodite and Yorgo.

I'm really sorry about this but I'm not going to tell you where here is. I know you would feel honour-bound to come and find me.

Dear Will, I do miss you but I feel I have to do this for myself. I don't know how you did it – grow up, I mean, and grow away but this seems so right to me.

Please tell Father I love him and I am happy and I am not giving up now, whatever he says.

I hope your film about Afghanistan was brilliant. I know one day I shall see it. I hope you stayed safe.

I'm sorry I took all the money; the accordion money. One day we will buy it for Manoli, I promise.

I will write again another time.

I love you and Lucy.

Angel xx

I ran along the sand to find Chrissi. She was playing football with the children and I sat down under the shade of an over-hanging rock in the cliff face. There was a man standing alone, watching. I could see it was a man because he was tall with bulging muscles; his hair was long and not tied back like Raggeh's, just hanging down, greasy. The way he was looking at Chrissi, he might as well have had his tongue out. He was old too, probably at least thirty. I didn't like the look of him at all.

I stuffed the letter into my pocket and sat down. Chrissi and the kids carried on playing. I wanted to go to her, tell her to take care. Her breasts were moving under her T-shirt. It wasn't that it had a low neck but rather that her high, round bosoms gave her a film star sort of cleavage.

The game ground to a halt when Anya came and called the kids to eat. I waited, and then I saw that instead of coming over to join me she had gone over to this bloke. He held his hand out to her and as she took it I realised that she hadn't seen me.

It wasn't hard to see that this was certainly not a stranger to her, so why didn't I know about him? They were laughing now, and as I got up and Chrissi saw me, she froze.

But I walked over to them anyway and as they stood there I could see that now, with his arm around her shoulders, she had already moved into a different place; a place where a stranger could hold her like that, as if he owned her.

I tried to stay cool, calm, not to show my feelings.

'Hi, Chrissi,' I said, like it happened every day. 'I wrote a letter to Will. Raggeh is going to post it.'

'Oh yeah?'

'I'll tell you later what I put.'

I waited, looking at her, expectant. She moved from foot to foot, awkward. I stuck my hand out to him.

'Hi, I'm Angel.'

He looked at my hand, frowned slightly and gave a funny sort of giggle and then ignored it. He squeezed her around the shoulders, pulling her even closer and whispered loudly, 'Off you go, babe, the guardian angel calls.'

I never thought to see Chrissi blush. My Chrissi would never go pink like that because some goon nuzzled her ear. My Chrissi wouldn't say, in a horrible pleading sort of voice, 'See you later?'

He dropped his arm, turned his back to us and walked away, saying over his shoulder, 'Catch you around, babe.'

I watched as his bottom swayed from side to side in his tight jeans. Jeans that hung too low, just showing the crack in his bum, I thought deliberately.

Chrissi watched him and then turned, doing a cartwheel in the sand.

Coming upright she grinned, as though nothing had happened.

I turned and walked away across the beach. She followed, singing under her breath,

'. . . three to get ready, now go, cat, go . . .'

'Who the bloody was that?'

'That's Simeon,' she said. 'Isn't he gorgeous? And, you know, it's time you learned to swear properly. You should say, "who the bloody hell was that" or "who the fuck was that". Just saying "bloody" all the time, on its own, is very childish.'

'Thanks,' I muttered. 'OK, who the fuck was that?'

'You know who it is, I just told you, that's Simeon. He's my friend.'

'Oh sure he is, I could see that: very friendly with you. He ignored me. Did you find him under some weed when you were out fishing?'

'I did meet him when I was out fishing, funnily enough. He's only just come here. He hitch-hiked from Israel. He got out of the army and came all this way. He says war is bad and he wants only to live in peace.'

'I bet he does.'

Suddenly war seemed a very attractive thought to me.

'Why are you being like this? All sniffy and nose in the air. Are you jealous I've got a friend and you haven't?'

I could only laugh. 'If you think I want a friend like that –
think again, *babe*.'

'We sat up most of last night when we came back. He
knows the names of all the stars, *and* their constellations.'

'So does Raggeh. And Rufus, come to that.'

'Oh Raggeh and Rufus! There are more people to know
than Raggeh and Rufus. He's with a really interesting group;
they live in a couple of tents, they don't need caves, they say.'

I knew of this group. They'd been here a couple of weeks.
They played cards, which was all they seemed to do. It was a
way of life to them. I wandered over with Tink one afternoon
shortly after they arrived, said hello. They ignored us. They
weren't like everyone else here; they seemed not to want to
talk to anyone who didn't play cards with them. They had
funny names; Brig, O'Hare and The Dope and another one
called Klinex. They played twelve-hour marathon games of
poker and drank whisky out of the bottle.

Raggeh knew about them; he said they had been here the
year before.

'They come and go, they are wanderers.' He said they kept
themselves awake with Peruvian Flake. I didn't let him see I
had no idea what that was. 'If they sleep they can't win,' he
said.

I think Chrissi was more interested in them than me and
our first run-in with them had come a week or so before.

Chrissi had been with a group of children, beachcombing;
looking for small driftwood for the evening fire. One came
back to us just ahead of the rest. I couldn't see who it was at
first but then the limp gave him away; it was Rolly.

'Guess what? Guess what?'

Anya beside me laughed.

'Well I expect you'll tell us.'

She and I were sorting balls of sheep and goats' wool found
in bushes further along the cliffs. The blanket makers would
dye them with plant dyes they made by boiling different herbs
into glorious, subtle colours: saffron yellow, sage green and
blue like the deepest night sky.

If he hadn't had a limp, Rolly would have been jumping up and down. He did try but fell straight down. Instead he was so excited he waved his arms frantically in the air. The other children were close behind him and we saw instantly the stranger who was with them. I heard Anya beside me draw in her breath.

'Oh no,' she said. 'The Ratman. He was here last year.'

The stranger was tall and skinny, much taller than me for sure. He looked like a scarecrow; his hair stuck out around his head like a brush; it was the colour of wild straw. He wore a brown furry coat even though the day was warm. It hung to the ground and as he moved it gave off a hideous aroma of dead animal.

'Now,' said Rolly. 'Do it now.'

He was echoed by some of the others, but I saw a small breakaway group who huddled together and looked frightened.

'No,' said Anya loudly, firmly, 'we don't want you here.'

He ignored her and said loudly, 'Got any raki?'

'Yes, loads and loads, haven't we, Anya?'

'Not for him, Rolly, we haven't.'

The stranger reached into the battered canvas bag he wore over his shoulder and pulled out a grey-brown wriggling thing. It was the size of . . . bloody, no! It was a live rat. Holding it by the tail he swung it in the air.

'I'll bite its head off for a swig of raki.'

Anya was on her feet in a second and pushed him away. I jumped up beside her and seeing the two of us meant what we said, he stepped back and turning on his heels walked away, calling over his shoulder, 'I'll be back and you'll be sorry.'

'They're a strange lot,' said Libby later, and Chrissi added,

'There's one man there who won his wife in a card game with a straight flush.'

I realised now that Chrissi must have spent more time with them than I had realised.

'Your friend, this Simeon; the way he looked at you. He was

undressing you, I saw him. You were running about with the kids and he was drooling.'

'He told me he thinks I'm gorgeous. A real woman, he said.'

'He just wants to get inside your knickers.'

She ran off then, right away from me, over the sand banks and the rocks and out of sight. I swear as she disappeared I heard her call back to me, 'Perhaps he already has.'

This had just become one of the most horrible days since I left. I had thought at last I was happy and now . . . I kicked a stone, hard, only hurting my toe. Oh bloody! And then out loud and deliberately, '*Oh bloody!* I'll swear how I bloody well bloody like!'

We went back to the cave, not quite together. Chrissi was walking ahead of me, arms swinging, and I thought she was swaying herself from side to side as if she was Marilyn Monroe or someone.

Rufus came tearing up to us.

'Hey, Chrissi, come and play.'

He was bouncing the football up and down beside him.

'Later, hon,' she said. 'Gotta sleep right now.'

Hon? Babe?

She was asleep within seconds of lying down and I sat and watched her.

I realised that when I woke up this morning and thought she was already away it was likely that she hadn't been back all night. She had been out there with what's-his-face, Simeon. As she slept, like a sweet baby, her face a mask of innocence, I thought back to some of the other nights lately. She had been out late, sure, very late. But that's when she goes fishing. And the last few mornings she was already gone. Or perhaps not. Was she with him? And she's become really moody.

How could this have happened? I thought I knew all there was to know about her, yet now I see how little I know of anything.

I sat, resting my back against the rough wall of the cave and tried to think. A slow chill crept through me. I felt so alone. For ages I had got used to my life being Chrissi and me and now . . . ? And then I knew what an idiot I'd been; thinking myself so grown up, so independent and all the time I was just a stupid child, needing its mother and when the mother went away forever, replacing her with a friend. I was just as needy as I'd always been. I put my head between my knees and wept silently, lonely, a child, longing for a cuddle.

Funnily enough, I slept. I never do that, sleep in the morning, but this morning wasn't like any others. Chrissi was sitting beside me with a beaker in her hands. As I opened my eyes, she held it out to me.

'I got you some lemonade. And I did what you said I should.' And she handed me a piece of paper.

'Thanks.'

APHRODITE

Things have not been good here since Chrissi left. For me especially they have been bad. I waved to her goodbye on the bus when she went to Chania. She told us she wanted to help her sister Zambia with the children. I didn't think she even knew their names. She didn't want to go back to school straight away. She wanted to be a teacher.

I worried, but she told me she would surely come back and then go to school later. She was, she said, still so unhappy after Heavenly died.

'We are all unhappy,' I told her. 'But Heavenly would want us all to go on with our lives.'

But at last she wore me out with her arguing and Yorgo and even Manoli said to let her go. So I did. She promised me she would write me a postcard to tell me she had arrived safe; none came.

Of course it was noticed here that she had gone. I told that stick insect, Vangelis the schoolteacher, she was away for a while.

But somehow, those *malakas*, they knew she was not just away – she was missing. They came here and questioned Yorgo and me, but what could we say? At first I told them she was with her sister in Chania but they went away and 'made enquiries'. When they came back they knew she was not in Chania. By then we knew that already. The week before, Aristos had been to see his sister; he was at a big doctors' meeting there and of course went to her house for dinner.

He rang us, and even though he was very careful what he

said on the telephone, he told us that Zambia had not seen Chrissi since her visit here at Easter. Two children gone away and now a third. She has run away with Angel, I'm sure.

Then daily they came, the *malakas*. Sometimes one, other times all three:

'Where is your daughter? Where is your child? Is she alive or dead? What do you know of her whereabouts?'

When I went about the village, eyes always followed me.

They all knew and Yorgo said the men talk every night in the Piperia. So he stopped going. Poor Yorgo, his nightly game of *prefa* had been for years his daily treat. Work all day and in the evening an hour or so with a card game and a raki with his friends – all gone. And Manoli? He had started going for the occasional game with his papa – now stays at home looking always sad, just sad. I said to Yorgo, 'Since she left, not one smile.'

Titi came, the last person I wanted to see, and she was cackling with delight.

'I told you so, didn't I? I warned you. That Heavenly's child took over her mind.' Her friend, the warty one was hovering by my door. She caught my eye and spat on the ground. 'Thank you, Titi –' I curse myself for my politeness – 'I have much to do, goodbye.' And they were gone.

At the fish truck one day Toula said, 'They think you have done away with her, your Chrissi.'

That is what they think; my own child? Has this world gone mad?

She could be anywhere. And then I thought with a shiver, anywhere in the world. It's not a good feeling not to know where your child is.

What if she is dead? You hear of terrible things happening to girls. Last year there was someone who killed young women, lonely girls, and buried their bodies under rocks.

So I lay next to snoring Yorgo, and imagined my girl under rocks and then I fell asleep with tears on my face and a cold fear inside.

For many nights I sat up all the hours thinking and

wondering where she could be. At last I was so tired I could hardly see and Yorgo made me go to bed and I slept for eighteen hours without waking.

I am nothing without my family. I never do anything but go to and from the *gypo*, grow a few vegetables, even more weeds. I am already old, each day older.

When I think of my Chrissi she is a baby in my arms. That's the first thought. A chubby happy infant who suckled eagerly from my breast: always hungry, always smiling. The other day I had a memory of her when she was about six years old. She idolised her papa. She followed him everywhere. When he was out she would stand at the window waiting for his return. Then she would run up and jump into his arms.

I know here in the village there are women who have no parents – orphans. Others who are widows and I will be the mother of a dead child: for which there is no special word, it's such a dreadful thing.

Then Lucy rang. All the way from London in England, and she told me Angel was also missing; she had run away from her school. So those girls *must* be together. We couldn't speak for more than a moment; Aristos says all conversations are heard, dangerous. I did feel a little better; but not for long; two dead girls perhaps.

And then today:

Dear Mama and Papa and Manoli
I am quite all right. I am with nice people. I am happy. I miss you but I don't want to go back to school and I don't want to get married for a long time. I am sorry if you worry about me.
Love from your daughter, Chrissi. x

My hand was shaking so much I thought I should drop the paper on the ground. Nothing but silence – and now there were just three lines. Five, if you count the top and bottom. I sat down heavily, clumsily and the thick old wood of the table, so lovingly made by my Yorgo when we were first married steadied me and I read the words over and over again. Nice people? Who are these nice people? People she would rather be with than her father, her brother and me, for sure.

I ran to Yorgo's workshop, calling, 'Yorgo, Manoli, come quick.'

And they did and I read the letter to them. Yorgo has a few words, Manoli another few but I am the only reader in our family here. Well, me and Chrissi, that is, before she ran away to 'nice people'.

Yorgo said, 'She doesn't say where she is, does she?'

I just looked at him. There are times when I know for sure that Manoli gets his lack of brain from his father. Just to be sure I read the letter out loud again.

Yorgo said, 'What shall we do, do you think?'

I closed my eyes in exasperation.

'There is nothing we can do, is there? We can't write back to her, because we don't know where she is. Go back to your workshop; let me think.'

So they did.

And I went to the *gypo*, where else?

ANGEL

We sat awkwardly for a moment or two and then, 'I'm not telling them where I am, or that I'm with you.' There was a funny silence for a moment and we both scratched the sandy floor of the cave. She broke the awkwardness, saying, 'Just because I've got Simeon doesn't mean I'm not your friend any more.'

I wanted to say, 'But he's vile! How could you let him even touch you?'

Then I thought better of it, and said, 'Why did you keep him secret? Why didn't you tell me about him?'

'I don't have to tell you everything.'

'Not if you don't want to, but it was quite a surprise, him suddenly being there and touching you, knowing you that well.' I thought I should stop there, say no more.

She jumped up but you can't do that in here, it's too small and she banged her head on the rock, said '*Skata!*' and sat down again.

'I knew you would be like that; there's no point in my even trying to tell you.'

And she was beginning to crawl out of the cave very fast.

'Wait, Chrissi, please wait.'

She did, but she didn't turn around, didn't look at me.

'Why don't you tell me about him; tell me what's special?'

I crawled after her and then I thought how completely ridiculous this all was, and I started to laugh.

'Funny?' she said. 'What's so funny?'

'Us! Look at us crawling around like a couple of toddlers in a playpen.'

She turned her head, looked at me for a moment, and then was laughing too.

'You're cross I've got a new toy and you haven't.'

I took her hand and we sat there on the floor of the cave looking at each other.

'If you really care about this bloke, I'll just have to get used to it, won't I?'

Then she told me how wonderful he was, how interesting, how different to any other boys she'd known. How mature he was, how he really understood her and how kind too.

'He thinks I'm beautiful.' And she laughed, 'No one's ever thought I was beautiful. I think I'm really falling in love with him and he loves me too.'

'Is that what he told you?'

'Not exactly, no. But when we were lying together under his blanket he made me feel so different, so special. He looks at me and keeps his eyes open when we, well when . . . all the time.'

This was worse than I'd thought, much worse.

'Have you – you know, had sex with him?'

'Well, sort of, nearly. Not exactly I think, but I really want to. Now you are going to be like my mother.'

It was hard to believe she had ever had a conversation with Aphrodite about lying under blankets with boys. No, not boys; men.

After that we somehow managed to rescue the day. We played football with the kids; Raggeh showed me how to make bolognaise sauce for spaghetti without any meat and we sat around the fire late with them, talking in low voices about the world in general and the Vietnam war in particular.

Every few minutes Chrissi jumped up, looked around and once even ran off, into the darkness, only to reappear looking miserable.

'Are you looking for a bogeyman?' That was Tink; her fair

hair hanging down almost covering her sweet face. 'Because they don't exist.'

The fire was in front of our caves, which were around a corner rock near the end of this beach. The moon was full tonight and the stars danced in and out of the clouds.

The gentle drift of smoke from other fires, the murmur of people, a far distant music, all filled us with a soft, welcome calm. Bats circled in an inky sky and over all the soft rhythmic lapping of the waves gave a peace at the end of a day spent in uneasy anxiety.

Rufus was fast asleep, his head in my lap. Gently I stroked his hair, felt its warmth through my fingers. It was soothing, bringing a stillness I hadn't felt all day. Chrissi seemed at last to relax and she sat, my bare foot in her hand, her strong fingers roughened from gutting the fish, gave me comfort. My head drooped and a drowsy heaviness closed my eyes.

Suddenly her hand clutched my ankle sharply, she was rigid, and I heard the whistle which had alerted her, again, shrill.

And without a word, she was up and away.

She was gone for three days. None of us saw her. I'm sure the others could tell how upset I was, lost; yet trying to pretend nothing was wrong.

The kids kept me busy. Each morning I took them down to the third rock from the end of our beach. It was flat like a table. And there I became like a teacher for Rufus, Tink and Rolly. We all walked slowly along because Rolly couldn't walk fast and we took a pile of books. Raggeh and Anya had taught their two to read and write really well.

But Libby seemed only concerned that Rufus kept quiet when she wanted to sleep and if that meant he had his head in a book; that was fine.

He seemed to love books anyway. He was a fast learner and I was really proud that I got him to follow the lines of words on the page and then say them aloud back to me.

'*And the rat said, "You can buy me for only one penny."*' And

175

his finger pointed to each word in turn and Tink and Rolly gazed in rapt attention at the picture of the chirpy rat.

We had to watch Rolly every moment or he was off, and twice we had to bring him back from wandering at the water's edge. He seemed mostly in another world. I thought it was hard for Tink who felt she was responsible for him.

'Put him on a lead,' was Rufus's solution. But the thought of that golden curly head and angelic smile tied up was unthinkable.

Rufus was not the same happy child since Chrissi left. He looked for her everywhere, many times a day. He was sad too, not smiling.

Raggeh always brought books, children's books, back with him when he went off on his trips to get food.

'Where do they come from?' I asked.

'Bookshops, of course,' and he laughed.

Anya said, 'Don't ask too many questions, Angel.'

It was ages before I realised he probably stole them. 'How do you get them out of the shop without anyone seeing you?'

Standing in front of me, his hair tied neatly back in a ponytail and his feet bare, he swung open the front of the long black, patchwork coat he always wore on his foraging trips.

It was lined from top to bottom inside with pockets, each the right size to hold a couple of books or a packet or two of rice.

'Little trick I learned from my great-uncle when I was a kid. He was known as Will Waistcoat.'

'What about the other food, fresh food?'

'That's a different story.' He tapped the side of his nose and winked. 'That's all quite legit. Back sides of tavernas, packed with good things nobody wants.'

'You mean garbage from dustbins?'

'I prefer to think of it as going round again. Nothing wasted. It's shocking the good stuff that's chucked out each night, criminal.'

I felt a bit squeamish but I couldn't really complain.

Just as Rufus had done in the beginning with Chrissi, now

Tink took to following me around, a slender shadow. She asked those questions I think all twelve-year-old girls do; why do men grow hair on their faces? And one day she confided in me what was obviously a great secret fear; 'I'm growing a chest, you know, but only on one side. Do you think I'll ever grow another one?'

Of course I answered her seriously; 'I'm sure you will; probably quite soon.'

Moments like that I felt as old as the sand.

And then Chrissi was back. And it was clear to me that she was changing, growing. The caterpillar had hatched into a moth, a silky rounded creature now – sleek and pampered, albeit with a tacky leather thong round her ankle and a silver ring on her thumb; big, with a bull's head on it, heavy and clumsy: a man's ring. I needn't ask whose.

I felt I had to pretend it was cool; act like it didn't matter.

I said, casually, 'Hey! Perhaps you could tell us when you're going to vanish?'

She looked puzzled, didn't answer, so of course, I blundered on, 'It's just you know, something might have happened to you.'

'Like?'

'Oh, I don't know; you might get ill, have an accident or something.'

'I promise, if I fall off the cliff I'll shout for help really loudly, OK?'

That night, Raggeh and Anya hitched into a nearby town to a music club and we stayed with Libby and the kids. She had made a big fish stew with Chrissi's catch the night before; mussels, shrimps and a giant crab. We pulled the fish apart with our hands and sucked on the lemons it was flavoured with, picked from a tree on the edge of the beach; a feast.

And then I heard that whistle; sharp, clear, piercing the night.

Libby heard it too and laughed, 'Here's your old man of the sea, Chrissi. You'll be off, then?' And she was. And I sat on, trying not to mind and thinking with a sudden horror – am I turning into my father? All this need I had to be in charge, expecting Chrissi to behave as I want her to? Well it certainly wasn't how Heavenly would be, that was for sure.

And then what I had secretly been dreading, a few days later.

'Simeon and I are going away – get some money. I can't keep living off you and the others.'

'We've got plenty. We've hardly used any of the accordion stash.'

But that wasn't really the point, I could see.

'Where will you go? What will you do?' I sounded so unconcerned; I was plaiting Tink's hair and she squealed, 'Ouch!'

'Sorry, little one, I'll be more careful.'

'He's got this great idea to get some cash. He's done it before; says it's easy.'

'Oh yes?'

'We're going to the hospital in Heraklion to sell our blood.'

'Your blood?'

'Yep. They pay quite a lot, Simeon says. Up to four hundred drachmas. And skin, too.'

'Could I sell my hair?' said Tink, flinching away from my plaiting hands.

'Probably. But they mightn't want that in a hospital.'

'What do they do with skin?'

'Oh I don't know, I'll tell you when we're back.' I was annoying her so I didn't say anything else.

Raggeh said he knew people who had done this, hippies. He said it was certainly one way to make money; blood group A, he said, fetched most.

But 'Be careful,' he warned Chrissi that night. 'The risk of infection is high; you have to keep really clean and that's not so easy when you're on the road.'

She laughed; at Raggeh and his warning; she laughed at me. That night Simeon came and joined us all for supper. He sauntered up carrying a guitar on his shoulder and sat down by the fire. The kids were all fascinated by him, sitting at his feet. I tried not to mind, even when Rolly put his hand out and fingered the ring he wore on his toe.

He didn't say much, except to Chrissi who sat beside him gazing up into his face adoringly.

'Play something,' she said.

Raggeh seemed to know the music he played; he said it was Santana and another was a Led Zeppelin song.

'You've been to The Odyssey?'

'Athens? You mean the club in the Plaka, The Trip?'

'That's the one.'

'Yeah. Oh man – a great place to hang out. I slept on the roof there when John's was full.' Chrissi was nodding wisely through this, but I was pretty sure she didn't know any more than I did what all these places were.

'Better watch out in Heraklion; no long hair,' Anya said. 'And you,' she nodded at Chrissi, 'no miniskirts, remember.'

'It's not so bad here as in Athens,' said Simeon. 'We'll be cool.'

He rolled a cigarette. As soon as he lit it I could smell it was marijuana. He drew deeply on it and passed it round. When it came to Chrissi she took it and smoked it just like she had done it many times before. Perhaps she had. She offered it to me and I took it and thought, what the hell, and puffed on it; throwing my head back and pursing my lips, blowing out a long drag of smoke.

I saw she was watching me, her eyes screwed up. She knew I'd never done it before.

I held my breath hoping she wouldn't say – and she didn't. So I passed it straight on to Libby beside me. But it was too late; I collapsed, coughing and gasping.

I took it again and again, thinking, 'I bet Heavenly would have a go at this.'

I know everyone here smokes dope so I shouldn't be surprised or shocked at my friend drawing the smoke down into her lungs and throwing her head back, her eyes closed as if in ecstasy. That night I staggered back to the cave, alone; my head spinning and when I lay down I felt so woozy and ill I had to get up fast, run out of the cave and was sick round the back of the rocks.

Chrissi's ability to look so cool was all part of the growing away from me that I saw every day now. Even if I ran I couldn't keep up with her.

And then she was gone. Early one morning a few days later I woke with a thick buzzy feeling in my head, looked around and there was only Libby lying on her back. Even Rufus wasn't there. In Chrissi's space there was just her blanket, folded. And her yellow dress was still hanging on the wall, just as it had done from the beginning.

'She's gone kiddo. Better get used to it.'

'She'll be back.'

'Maybe. Maybe not. She seems pretty smitten with the old man from the sea.'

'He's disgusting. He's old and horrible. Why is he interested in someone so much younger than himself?'

She laughed. 'He's not so bad. Reminds me of Rufus's dad, same old thing. One day she'll wake up just like I did and find him gone. If she's lucky he'll leave a note on the pillow. What's that worth when you're up the duff with a baby on the way? Sweet fuck all.'

I was horrified. 'But he loves her.'

'Oh, sweetheart, you've got a lot of growing up to do. And so has she if she believes that.'

I sat trying to absorb this. 'Why didn't you try and stop her?'

'You think we didn't? I tried and so did Anya. Raggeh pointed out the difference in their ages, but she didn't want to know. Get used to it, girl. This is the real world out here.'

'But you all—'

'We all what? Look cool and hip? Is that so? You think we are all the beautiful people, flowers in our hair and peace and love for all mankind?'

And then Rufus ran in, howling, 'Tink and Rolly hit me. Punched me in the head and said I took their ball.'

'And did you?'

He didn't answer but howled some more and kicking me on the leg he ran out again.

I stopped then, as if there were no more breath inside me. I came to a stop from emptiness, as if there was nothing to say any more, ever.

Over the next days I had a strong sense of loss. I wanted to cling on to Chrissi even as her presence inside me faded; to be replaced only by the odd word or thought remembered for no good reason. There was over all a savage disappointment in this loss and a fear that there was nothing to replace it.

The days here had their own rhythm. Just as in the village the sun or the wind, the moon or even the rain, led us. I liked it when it rained; I ran into the sea and swam furiously as far as I could. And then I lay in the water, the sea below and the crashing thunder of a storm above drenching me as I turned and twisted and then I swam back and ran through the downpour trying to stay as wet as I could.

I tried not to count the days but I knew anyway it was day twenty-five when I decided I must make a plan for my life without Chrissi. I was alone. So was Libby, alone except for Rufus. She managed and so will I.

With Chrissi gone, no one was using the fishing nets. Everyone missed the fresh fish she had brought back for us. Oh, Chrissi, I wish you had shown me how to do this; I wish I had asked. I talked to myself sometimes those days. Tink caught me chatting as I untangled the last of the nets.

'Are you talking to her, to Chrissi?'

'I think I probably am.'

'You could talk to me instead, if you like.'

'That's very kind of you, Tink.'

'I could be your friend.'

I reached over and hugged her. 'You are already, little one, and a very special friend too.'

'Could we go fishing together?'

'Why not?' But the next morning we awoke and the wind had come again and kept us inside the caves. Even swimming

181

was dangerous. The waves splashed high, tipped with white foam, and crashed down on the beach. When it blows you stay under cover. It lasted three days and nights. It's measured each time by what it can transport: 'a chair's worth' or 'a table's worth'. Once, I knew, a 'tree's worth'.

Everything was covered in a fine reddish yellowish dust that I remembered attacking the village. There it came every July, sometimes more often, bringing the sands of Africa across the Libyan sea into our houses.

Raggeh had been to town for supplies the day before it came so we just huddled in the caves. Even tucked inside with the others I felt sad and alone. Tink came and asked me to judge a painting and drawing competition organised by a travelling artist in a cave around the bay. But my heart wasn't in it.

And then it was the third and last day and the sky gradually calmed during the night and I woke to a stillness over every-thing. I sat on the beach and watched the sun rise in the mountains in the east. The shafts of light that glided across the far sands were that golden colour I loved and when they reached where I was sitting they warmed my face, my out-stretched legs, all of me, right through. And I knew I would survive; more than survive, I would live and enjoy my living.

I stroked my arm, gilded by the sun, my angel.

And then there was Christmas. Just one day: there is no Boxing Day in Greece.

It was a beautiful morning; the air crisp and clear in the sharp sunlight so that every rock and crevice glittered. Birds called and sang to each other and in the distance the mountains glistened as if covered in ice.

That day I missed Chrissi more than ever. We had been together at Christmas for many years. Sitting on the sand at the edge of the sea splashing my fingers in a pool of blue water, I shed tears. I hugged myself and wished those were my mother's arms around me. Today my loneliness was a pain so severe it was like the very worst stomach ache ever.

Behind me the children had just woken and I heard the

distant screams and yelps of joy as they found the few gifts we had gathered for them. Anya had gone with Raggeh into Monostiraki and I had given her a few drachmas from the dwindling accordion fund.

'Please buy some small things from Chrissi and me.'

Tink had a length of blue-green stuff for a sarong like mine. I knew she wanted one. I had asked Raggeh to buy books for the others.

'Strange feeling,' he said, 'buying them.'

'Old habits,' said Anya. 'He refused a carrier bag and put them inside, in his pockets.'

Over the fire we cooked a chicken, a cockerel that Raggeh had found 'wandering and lonely, near a farm'.

'An orphan, I suppose.'

'Exactly so; it was just asking to be eaten by a caring family.'

The succulent juices dribbled down our chins and we mopped them up with some bread.

'Only two days old,' said Anya. 'Quite fresh, really.'

As the sun sank slowly that afternoon we sat around the fire singing carols. Raggeh and Anya smiled at each other. I thought they were like two pieces of a jigsaw that locked together effortlessly.

And like always, barely was Christmas gone and it was New Year. We danced around the fire holding hands and singing once again, 'If you're happy and you know it, clap your hands.' And when it was about midnight the beach rang with cheers and from around the corner we heard the blanket makers start up a chant. It was 'Auld Lang Syne'.

'Happy nineteen seventy-two!' we all wished each other, and gripping Libby's hand I thought of Chrissi and tried not to cry.

And then the *malakas* came. Not the same ones from Panagia, of course, but united by the same philosophy. They couldn't preach to us about the wonders of electricity although I'm sure they'd like to.

There were four priests and two policemen with guns. Assorted shapes and sizes but the priests all had little ponytails of hair they had scraped back and those long black frocks and I'm sure a unity of thought about how we live. Raggeh had vanished at dawn. Anya said he'd heard they were coming and he'd gone off to hide his dope. That's why they are here, apparently; believing we have great stashes of marijuana; maybe other stuff, too. They searched each cave savagely, throwing everything they found outside in untidy heaps on the sand. Anya and Libby said the penalties for drug use are high.

If you are busted, Anya said, unless you are very well connected you can get ten years or longer in prison.

I watched our sad little pile of belongings soar into the air and land in a heap looking like nothing more than rejects from a jumble sale. The blue silk throw that was Heavenly's last gift caught on a rock and I ran to release it. It ripped a little as I pulled. Down at the water's edge two children, girls from around the bay, were playing tug of war with Chrissi's yellow dress. I'd babysat them a couple of times so I ran up to them calling, 'Hey, hey you!'

Oh bloody, I couldn't remember their names. They looked, dropped the dress and ran away. It was certainly the worse for soaking in a rock pool and bits of flying seaweed, brown and shrivelled clung to the hem. It was hideous, even more so now but I carried it back to the cave as though it was the most precious thing I owned.

I approached the youngest-looking priest with a suety face and a squashed-up nose and I asked what they wanted, what were we doing wrong.

He held out a rather grey and sweaty hand for me to kiss his ring, but I ignored that.

He explained to me that these caves are holy shrines and it is necessary to see that they are kept so.

'You mean no harm, child, I can see that. Do you have documentation?'

I showed him my passport and with a wave of his hand he crossed himself three times and was away to join his friends, leaving me wondering what kind of world I am in where I have to show a priest my ID.

They were there all day and it was as I was coming out of the cave again into the fast-growing evening that Raggeh appeared.

'Angel, something strange one of those priests said. I think you and me, we should go up to the road by the beach, take a look.'

'What kind of thing? Look at what?'

'He said there was a girl wandering there. Young, he said, alone. He thought she was ill or drugged.'

'You think it might be . . . ?'

'I don't know what I think, but let's go; sounds like some-one needs help anyway.'

As we climbed up the steep rocks that lined the road, Raggeh told me that last year three teenagers were arrested here for carrying one small piece of hashish. In the papers and on the radio news they became 'a notorious gang of drug pushers'.

When we got there, to the edge of the road, there was just a little figure, all hunched over. And even from a distance I knew it was Chrissi. We ran the last few yards and crouched down to her. Dusty cars and trucks raced past, horns bursting the air with the grotesque screams of over-used klaxons.

Raggeh pulled his T-shirt off and made a sort of shade over her and I knelt and took her hands. The day was one of the hottest but those fingers were like ice in mine. It seemed too much of an effort to raise her head, but her eyes flickered open and I swear she tried to smile at us.

My arms were around her.

'Chrissi, oh my Chrissi,' I said, 'what has happened to you?'

Her shoulders under the thin torn shirt were scrawny. She used to be plump. She shrugged minutely, and a long sigh whispered out.

'Pain, head,' she said, and leaving her one hand to trail on the verge I put my free hand up to her forehead. It was burning hot. The touch seemed too much for her to bear, for her head instantly drooped forward and I felt her body slide

185

away from me. She would have fallen, if Raggeh hadn't put his knee quickly across as a prop and there she rested. Her whole body was like a limp cloth and when Raggeh asked if I could help to lift her I was only surprised that he should think I couldn't do it alone. In the end I did take his help, for frail as she now was, her bones were heavy.

Tink and Bill ran across the dunes to meet us and behind I could see Rufus. His face was puzzled and frowning, close to tears and I realised in that moment that much as I had missed my friend, Rufus and probably the others too had their own loss.

We made a strange caravan; a small pilgrimage to what was now home.

The day was almost finished, the sun gone in that curious, hazy yellow-grey that are the evenings here.

Inside our cave the air was still thick and hot – too hot for Chrissi, I thought, and much as I wanted her to be back with me, Raggeh only made sense when he said we should put her on a makeshift mattress in an empty space in front of the cave.

'There's no rain up there.' He pointed to the sky; where across the distant horizon, at the edge of the sea the moon was already rising.

I sat beside her but she didn't move; just the occasional flicker of her eyelids. I held her hand, still icy in mine. Once I think I felt the small pressure of a squeeze.

She was so thin, even her breasts seemed diminished under the rag that had once been a T-shirt. The children solemnly brought bowls of fresh seawater every few minutes, to bathe her fevered forehead, until I stopped them and whispered that we had plenty. Dear Tink cleverly plucked three giant leaves from a nearby palm and wrinkled and dry as they were, they made good fans, and she, Bill and Rufus sat around in a circle waving them rhythmically over the little body lying there. They were called off to eat a while later and I took over as it did seem to offer some help.

Libby came and joined me and while I was still so worried, I felt a great comforting safety in this group, friends who had become our family.

The evening turned into night and little happened to change.

Libby had brought aspirin, the soluble kind, and Chrissi managed to drink down the milky water if I held her propped firmly in my hands.

Raggeh came then. His tall, lanky body created shadows on the sand and he crouched down like a cat. I lowered Chrissi down gently on to the folded covers that were now her mattress. As she sipped, I saw that around her mouth were sores, red and scabby like cold sores and one was open and pus seeped out.

Raggeh said, 'She needs more help than we can give her, Angel. What do you think of doing?'

I realised that here, now, I was the grown-up; the one who made the decisions, who, when it was needed, became the nurse, the carer.

'We'll have to get a doctor here, won't we? We can't carry her in to Monostiraki on our own.' He paused and then said, 'You know the night Anya and I went into the music club there?' I nodded. 'We got talking to a guy there, my age. He was a doctor. Most nights, he said, he went to the club to take a beer or two and listen to the music.'

'Would he be better, do you think, than getting one of the general doctors?'

'I guess, much better, if he's still around. Well, certainly easier. He might just do it for a friend, rather than the official ones. All they'd want to do is fill in forms.'

I knew that Raggeh has a particular hatred of anything that smacks of official; even so I thought his idea was worth a try.

'I should go now then, shouldn't I? Music clubs won't be very lively in the morning?'

'You'll pick up a lift easily at this time.'

I glanced at an imaginary watch on my wrist. Raggeh smiled; one or other of us is always doing it – old habits.

None of us knew exactly what the time was – but it was evening, night, whatever, it would have to do.

It seemed to take forever to catch a lift. The main road into the nearest town, Monostiraki, usually crammed during the summer with cars and lorries, was almost deserted at this hour and I guess it took three-quarters of an hour before a jeep pulled into the side ahead of me and I ran to catch it up.

The old guy driving was rather seedy and smelly and gulped down something from a paper-wrapped bottle clasped between his knees. He looked at me out of the side of his eyes rather too often and I curled myself into the passenger door well away from him.

'The Gauloise, eh? You go often?'

I shrugged my shoulders, hoped he thought that an answer.

'You go alone?' Coughing on the yellowing fag hanging out of the side of his mouth, he gave a dirty, throaty laugh.

'I'm meeting my friends there,' I said primly.

He said he'd heard of the club, although he wasn't exactly sure of the street.

'How old are you?' he asked.

'Why do you want to know?'

'Kids around your age don't usually go to clubs playing jazz, that's all,' he said, with a sneer.

'I told you I'm meeting my boyfriend there.' And the lie seemed to shut him up.

The air inside the Gauloise was hot and heavy and thick with cigarette smoke. I had to stand for a minute at the top of some stairs as my eyes stung. The place was only lit by candles or oil lamps. Gradually, as I got used to the haze I could see there were some bodies moving, dancing in the small space below. There was a strong mix of heady smells; cigarettes mostly but a boozy wine smell and over all the cloying scent of patchouli that I knew so well now from the caves. The music pounded, throbbing through the air.

I made my way down the stairs, clinging on to a thick rope

on the wall. There was a small bar, with a few people around it. I ignored it. I wouldn't have known what to ask for in such a place. I would have loved a sherry but I didn't think that was a good idea here. There was a stage at one end of this dingy room and that's where the musicians were playing. It was an easy, rhythmic piece.

I'd no idea what it was but I liked it and I thought if Chrissi were here we'd probably be bopping about to it. Around the room there were crammed little groups of tables and chairs, most of them full of bodies, but at the back, behind a pillar, I found one with a couple of empty chairs. So I sat there wondering what to do next. Look for someone who looks like a doctor, I thought, wondering what a doctor might look like here.

My eyes had totally adjusted to the smoke and greyness now so I started to enjoy the music. After a while I knew I had to pee and I got to my feet and peered around again. There was a couple a little way away gazing into each other's eyes, so I asked the girl where the loo was and she pointed. I struggled through the people and went in through a door with a picture of two hats on it; a sombrero and a lady's bonnet, so I guess it was meant for men and women. It was very smelly inside and dark with light only from a guttering candle on a shelf high on the wall. There was a hole in the floor with foot places either side. So this was it then. I crouched to pee, clutching my knickers in one hand. I was just about to look for any paper when the door swung open and a tall bloke was standing there.

'Excuse me,' I said loudly, firmly, and when he didn't move I said, in English, 'Bugger off.'

He laughed, and replied, 'Sorry, madame, but you need to lock the door if you want to be alone.'

He spoke in English! But bugger off he did and the draught from the closing door blew the candle out. Thanks to him I was left standing over a pee hole with my knickers in my hand and no chance of finding any paper. I stumbled into my underwear, hopping about trying to guess where the hole was but I found it by stepping into it, of course. Now I had a smelly wet foot on top of everything else.

He was standing waiting when I came out and smiled.

'I apologise for so rudely interrupting you.' Again he spoke perfect English.

'It's OK,' I muttered and then, just to be awkward, shot out a sentence in Greek, which translated means, 'If you are truly sorry you can buy me a drink.'

'Wait for me here,' he said back in faultless Greek, and disappeared behind the hats.

When he came out, he said, 'Let's find somewhere to sit and I'll get us a drink.' As we moved away, he said over his shoulder, 'I take it you're on your own?'

I tried to say that I was but he was fast disappearing into the dancers and couldn't hear anything. I pushed through after him and then he put his hand out and took mine into it and pulled me along. I didn't need to tell him, he had found his way to the tables behind the pillar and I sat down.

'What will you drink?'

I didn't know many drinks – only sherry and wine and whisky of course.

'Can I have a wine?'

'I'm sure you can. Red or white?'

'Oh, red, please.'

I don't know why I said that, I've hardly even tasted red wine but I thought it sounded more sophisticated.

It seemed to take ages and I felt a bit of a lemon, sitting by myself, especially as people – well, men – kept trying to sit with me and I had to wave them away saying I was waiting for a friend. The band stopped playing for a while and there was even more of a crush around the bar. And then he was back carrying a beer and a quite large tumbler of wine.

'I'm afraid it was cheap so it'll probably be pretty bad.'

He passed me the wine and sat down and I took a gulp. It was strong and sour and I nearly choked on that first mouthful.

'I don't think I've seen you here before?' he said.

'You haven't. I've never been here.'

'If you don't mind my asking, how come you are here on your own?'

'You're on your own, aren't you?'

He nodded, taking a great swig of beer.

'Well then.'

I thought that was enough of an answer for now. He sat just looking at me so I thought fair enough, and I looked back. I suppose he was quite good looking and he had hair rather like Rufus, dark and rather wildly curly. And then I thought, Oh, that's like mine as well. And it was. He had what I suppose you might call a strong face.

'Good bones,' Lucy would say.

Light suddenly shone across the room, the beam of a torch, and it was met with a great whoop, a cheer and then more torches flashed and shone for the band to come back on the stage again.

'It's a kind of tradition here, when the audience want the music back they flash torches; they bring them with them.'

Interesting, but of even more interest to me were this man's eyes, now astonishingly clear and blue in the flashes of light. They crinkled at the corners and I remember thinking that he must smile or laugh a lot. But more than that, the blue was so deep, so piercing and fine, I thought, He will not lie with these eyes. This is a truthful man.

'I'm looking for a doctor.'

He put his head back and laughed.

'It's not funny is it? Why is it funny?'

'I think if I asked every single person in this room, "why are you here?" I would get, "for the music" from about ninety per cent and "to pick up girls" – or boys of course – from the rest. I don't think anyone else is here to find a doctor, or a dentist, perhaps.'

I felt stupid, and didn't say anything for a moment. I sipped my wine and tried not to choke on it.

'You didn't come here by mistake thinking it was a hospital, did you?'

'Oh stop it! You are making me feel very silly.'

And he did, so we sat for a moment in silence. Then he held his hand out to me.

'I am Constantinos, usually Costas, Dukakis.'

'My name is Angel Timberlake.' I took his hand. It was not just brown from the sun, but with long fingers, smooth and oh how strong and firm was that grip.

'That's an interesting name. Now, Angel, why are you here in a jazz club looking for a doctor?' And I saw he was trying not to laugh again. 'Why don't you go to a hospital, or to a doctor's office – there are plenty around here?'

'Because I don't want an ordinary doctor.'

'An extraordinary doctor then?'

'If you stop making fun of me I'll try and tell you.'

He bowed his head low over my hand.

'I apologise. Tell me.'

'I need a doctor who won't ask too many awkward questions, and want to fill in forms and things and would help someone who lives in a cave.'

He sat unmoving; just those blue eyes still locked into mine.

'You worry me now, Angel. If you are looking for someone who will work illegally, I begin to get an idea of what is your problem.'

I didn't answer; just kept trying to get away from those eyes. He reminded me of someone; someone I knew well. It was a strong face; warm, friendly.

He continued, 'Is it you that needs the help? Tell me. But if what I am thinking is true, then I'm afraid I can't help. Actually, I *won't* help. I know there are doctors who will offer assistance to young women in your sort of trouble, but I'm not one of them.'

Suddenly I knew what he was talking about. How dare he? I jumped up and then realised exactly what he had said.

'You are a doctor, aren't you?'

'Yes, I am.'

'And you think I am looking for a doctor to help me lose a baby?'

'Aren't you?'

'No, I'm bloody not!'

So then I told him about Chrissi. How ill she was, where she had been and why and all about us living in the cave and how we worried that form-filling doctors would report us to the authorities even though we weren't doing anything wrong. And I told him about Raggeh and Anya coming to this club and talking to a doctor. He was nodding.

'Yes, I think I remember your friends. They struck me as too middle class, too in love and too ready to show me pictures of their children, to be what I think of as "hippies".'

'So it was you.' He nodded. 'And I found you straight away?' He nodded again. 'Will you come? Please? Don't make me go and find a doctor in an office. He'll be stern and grey and like my father and spend time filling in forms. We don't have the money to pay some doctor like that. Although I have got some money and I can pay you,' I finished hastily.

He was already on his feet.

'I don't want your money. I'll come and see your Chrissi. Let's go.'

And before I could think of anything at all, we were outside, and I was climbing on the back of a big Harley Davidson bike and roaring off into the night clutching this Doctor Costas around his waist and thinking, 'I will probably die now without a crash helmet, and who will tell Will and Father?' But I lived and we were back at the beach fast. In spite of being worried about Chrissi, I thrilled at the terrible, wicked speed and power of this great black machine. I remember thinking, 'Another time I would love this.'

'Temperature one-oh-two, heart rate one-fifty, BP one-fifteen over forty.' He was murmuring these figures aloud as he used the instruments from the black bag he had taken from one of the panniers on his bike. I crouched down beside him and mouthed the words as he said them. I guessed he did all this in the hospital when he was surrounded by nurses and other doctors. He lifted her head and cradled it gently in his arms.

She was barely conscious, a dead weight with her eyes just flickering. The sores around her mouth looked terrible in the light of his torch. He looked to me. 'Angel, can you and what's-his-name get some more light out here.'

Raggeh said, 'On my way.'

He was back almost before he'd gone with a large flashlight and held it up high.

Costas reached into his bag several times, bringing out cotton swabs and bottles of pale and dark liquid. He asked for my help in undressing Chrissi. That was when I discovered that the T-shirt was stuck to a place on her stomach and at first, before I realised and pulled at it, she gave an awful moaning sort of noise and her face screwed up in pain.

'Cut it off,' Costas said and passed me a pair of scissors from that bag. I did and that was when we saw there was a large patch of raw skin, jagged around the edges as if it had been ripped off. I flinched and Raggeh, holding the lamp, shut his eyes and looked away.

'This,' said Costas. 'Here is where skin was taken, and this is the cause of the trouble now. See, it is infected.'

And he gently dabbed and swabbed at the hideous wound from a bottle of clear fluid. I tried to stay steady, looking at my friend, but it was hard. I felt her pain. And with eyes closed, there were fat tears rolling down her cheek.

Without thinking, my arm rubbed my angel, now of course completely healed.

'You say she has taken aspirin?' Costas asked.

'Yes.'

'She kept it down? Didn't vomit?'

I shook my head.

'Then we must keep up the intake of fluids. If she rejects them she must go to hospital, be put on a drip.'

I shook my head violently.

'No, she would hate that, we must keep her here, please.'

Sensible Raggeh said, 'What do you think, Costas?'

'I think that, apart from being very ill, she will be in serious trouble. You see what they have done? No reputable hospital should have released her in this condition. So I suspect that she probably left without being authorised. This practice is very much frowned on by the authorities – selling skin. But blood? Plasma?' He shrugged. 'Not so bad, not so dangerous.'

'And these?' I pointed to her mouth as he carefully, tenderly bandaged her middle.

He shrugged.

'My guess is that she got a bite, something like that, picked at it, and because her body is weak from fighting this bigger infection, it wouldn't heal. I would guess it's a long time since she bathed.'

He picked up her hand and held it, blackened, scabby and tiny in his big strong one. How odd! A sudden longing to change places with her swept through me. A moment only and the feeling passed. It had surprised me.

'She will be all right, won't she?' Raggeh asked.

And because Costas paused before answering, I held my breath.

'I think so. She's young; that helps. Another day or so and I think it would have been . . . How long since she took the aspirin?'

Raggeh and I looked at each other; of course we hadn't a clue.

'About three, three and a half hours, but that's a guess,' Raggeh said.

'Then we can give her something else now, something stronger.' And again he was into that bag of tricks. He crushed a couple of tablets between a piece of paper and his scissors and dropped them into her cup of water. I watched as he pulled her up so gently into his arms and, although her head lolled back helplessly, managed to persuade the liquid through her lips.

He laid her back down and her head fell to one side, her eyes still closed.

He sank back on to his heels.

'This will all help to bring her temperature down. But she must have antibiotics, and soon, to fight the infection. I'll go now, but I'll come back in the morning.' He looked from Raggeh to me and back again. 'You two: one of you should sit with her tonight.'

'I will, of course, I will,' I said.

He glanced at his wrist. He did have a watch there. 'It's three-thirty now. I'll be back by eight at the latest. OK?'

He climbed back over the rocks and I scrambled after him. He turned as he reached the bike. Climbing on, he said, 'You're a good friend to have, Angel. You really care for her, don't you?'

'I do, I really do. She's like a sister.'

He looked puzzled.

'Is she English or Greek?'

'Greek, of course.'

'And you?'

I paused, then, 'I'm both.'

He reached out and down towards my face and for a moment he cupped my chin in his hand. Through the darkness I felt the strength, the kindness of those hands.

'She's lucky to have you. Until the morning, then.'

And I nodded furiously.

'And sometime you can tell me about you and Chrissi. Why you girls are here, living on the beach. What are you running away from?'

Before I could even think of an answer, he had kicked the engine into life and roared off into the gradually fading dark.

I stood watching the red light wink until it was a tiny dot and then nothing. An owl hooted into the silence, a moth brushed my face. Far out at sea the horn blew on a passing liner. I needed Chrissi or Lucy to explain to me what I was feeling. Whatever it was, it was something I'd never felt before. Worry, I suppose and gratitude as well.

Chrissi barely moved for the rest of the night; she lay, curled round herself, protecting that horrible wound. I felt her forehead from time to time and it still seemed hot to me, but her face was less flushed. Once, her hand reached out in her sleep, towards her mouth but before she could scratch or touch there I took it gently and her fingers curled around in mine and held on.

Nobody sleeps late here, but the sun had yet to rise and Libby was beside me.

'Get some sleep, kid,' she said, 'you look done in.' She was already sitting and reaching into the bright patchwork bag she keeps her crochet work in. I stood and hesitated for a moment. 'Off,' she said.

'When Costas, the doctor, comes back, will you fetch me?'

'Give yourself a break, I can handle him.'

'No! No, please, promise you'll get me?'

'OK. By the way, Rufe won't disturb you, he's gone fishing with Anya.'

It was the roar of the motorbike that woke me. I heard it turn and with a final roar stop dead. I finger-raked my hair and knew it was hopeless; it was standing up all over the place, just as it always did; today it was itchy as well. I'll wash it in the sea later, I decided.

I'd noticed that Chrissi's hair was now chopped short, ragged. Filthy as it was, it kind of suited her. Perhaps I should do the same?

I ran along the sand and waited to catch Costas as he came down over the rocks. He smiled as he saw me and we walked together.

'How is the patient this morning? Did she sleep?'

'A bit, I think.'

'Did you?'

'Oh yes.'

Libby slowly stood up as we approached, looking Costas up and down. She flicked her glorious long, silky hair over her shoulders and smiled, more at him than me, I thought.

We heard Raggeh call, 'Hey Libby, give me a hand.'

I could see her reluctance but she shrugged, gave Costas a last lingering look and sashayed away.

Costas did all the checks he had done in the night and it sounded to me as if all the figures were the same.

He took the bandage off and carefully peeled back the dressing. It still looked bad, yellow at the edges and almost shining in the sunlight.

'Is she taking fluids?'

I nodded; the water bottle was almost empty.

'We've got a spring that comes down the mountain and out back along the beach.'

'Fill this one up then, will you? She needs water, lots of it – as much as you can get into her.'

I did, and while I was gone, only a moment or two, he prepared a syringe and I helped him turn her gently over and he pushed it into her bottom.

All the movements had caused Chrissi to stir and blink open her eyes.

I ran my hand through her stubbly hair and she almost cracked her face into a smile.

'Heavenly?'

Before I could answer, her eyes had closed and she drifted off again.

Costas looked up, questioning. I shrugged; didn't want to go into that now.

'After medication and water, sleep is the best thing for her for a while. I'll come back tonight and give her another injection.' He handed me an envelope. 'Codeine; she can have one every six hours. They'll keep her temperature down. And help with the pain.'

I walked with him back to his bike. I didn't know what to say, felt awkward, gawky and clumsy.

'Thank you,' I managed finally.

'You do understand that if she doesn't improve quickly I must admit her to the hospital?'

I nodded.

'You're a funny one, aren't you?'

'Me?'

'English and Greek, living in a cave, not at school.' I glared at him and he said quickly, 'Or university.'

I think I would have told him my life story, but he was already on the bike and starting the engine.

'Tonight,' he said. 'I'll be back and you can tell me about you and Miss Chrissi.' He wheeled it around and as he left, said, 'And Heavenly?'

Then he was gone.

He came in the morning and the evening, every day. Each time giving Chrissi an injection of antibiotic, but he always left quickly. We could see her getting better every day; her temperature slowly came down to normal, and the mouth sores were beginning to heal. The patch on her abdomen was still pretty nasty and she slept a lot of each day and all night through. Costas said that was a good thing.

We moved her back into the cave on that third night. Still she couldn't stand without help, so Costas and I carried her in and as she lay down she curled into a shell with her eyes closed. It's how she lies most of the time now. I've tried asking her what happened, but except to whisper 'thank you' she hasn't spoken.

As we walked out to get the bottle of water and some shells the kids had collected for her, Costas said, 'She's so much better, but she's hiding inside herself. Do you know what she's afraid of?'

I shook my head.

'That Simeon bloke, I would think, the one she went off with. He can't have looked after her at all to let her come back to us like that.'

'Did you think he would look after her? Expect him to?'

I thought for a bit, then, 'I suppose I did. But no one else seemed bothered. You mean she should be able to look after herself?'

The expression on his face was answer enough.

The water bottle was beside her with the shells in a ring. She didn't stir, even as I said, 'Chrissi, you must drink as much as you can.'

Rufus was sleeping with Tink and Rolly as Libby had taken up with a group in some caves around the beach: musicians.

I looked forward to Costas coming; found myself thinking about him during the day, wondered how old he was: he was certainly a man and not a boy. I tried to tidy myself up, even. Apart from my wretched hair, I'd never even thought about how I looked before.

Waiting by the road to catch the first sight of the big black bike, I would rake my fingers through the ratty, itchy tangles and think, I'm going to chop it off, like Chrissi.

On the fourth night, as I waited, I watched the ragged clouds scudding across the sky like balloons waiting for the party to begin.

When he arrived, Costas said, 'The club is closed. The police and the military came yesterday, late, and closed it down, for "investigation".'

'Investigation of what?'

He laughed and shrugged. 'They don't need to give a reason. Surely you know the times we are living in?'

We walked along the beach away from the caves.

'Does that mean that you can stay a while tonight?'

'Why not? I'm not on duty until Thursday.'

'When's that?'

'Two days away. How do you all manage without watches or clocks or calendars?'

'Why would we need them?'

His stride was long and firm; he was used to walking. I hopped along to keep up. He was tall and slim, rangy; Will's build. As he turned to me he slowed down a little, smiled, and his eyes flashed clear and bright. I felt a butterfly in my stomach quiver; no, it was just my heart that I could feel beating, rather fast; how peculiar. In the distance we heard music; mysterious, beautiful, spiralling upward through the twilight and we walked towards it.

There was a fire, way down on the beach, and mixed with the scent of wood smoke were the fragrant scents of thyme and sage. In the dusky light we saw people sitting around. One or two had instruments; a guitar and a lyre, I think, and yes, a chord or two played on an accordion, and suddenly, in my head, I was back in Chrissi's house and the herb scents were from Aphrodite's lamb . . .

On the beach, out of the smoke and over the crackle of the rising flames a woman's voice pierced the air, clear and beautiful. 'Where have all the flowers gone? Long time passing . . .'

'Do you want to . . . ?' he whispered, but I shook my head and, taking my hand he pulled me down to sit beside him, a way away. We listened to those heartbreaking words and I thought of Heavenly; she had loved this song, had a whole Pete Seeger album she would play to me when I was little on Will's record player. I always laughed at it, this machine, which I think was called a Dancette. Then, oh bloody! I was crying.

He didn't notice at first and then I scrubbed at my face with the back of my wrist. He didn't speak; just put a hand out and gently rubbed my back. That was nice. But soothing as it was, it made it worse and I was now really weeping. When you cry like that, you get tears all over the place, and my nose started to run as well. I gave a huge, snotty sniff and found Costas had pushed a handkerchief into my hand, so I blew my nose, hard, and hoped that would put a stop to all these leaks.

His hand was still on my back. I didn't move.

'Want to tell me?'

I shook my head, for I didn't trust myself to speak and he took his hand away, so I said, 'You can put it back if you like.' So he did; but only to give me a quick rub across the shoulders. 'A bit before we came here, my mother died. She loved that song.'

'I'm sorry. I, too, had someone very close to me who died, a while ago.'

'Not your mother, though?'

'Not my mother.' And there was a pause and he continued, 'My godfather.'

'Were you close to him, as close, say, as to your mother?'

'Even closer; so I know how it feels to have an empty hole inside. Look around and he's not there, turn to tell him something and you're alone. He was always a big part of my life. It was because of him I became a doctor; because of him I learned to speak English; he loved the English. He wanted me to make something of myself, not just be a fisherman like my father. He had once wanted a career himself, but then the war came and he led a resistance group all around here, in these hills. He was a very brave man.'

Tears all gone now, I had a sudden thought: 'Perhaps my mother knew him! She was a nurse; she and her friend looked after lots of the resistance workers, the *andartes.*'

He nodded. 'My family may have known them, but I was only a baby at the time.'

As he spoke he was building a castle with stones; little over big, square and round, and I watched his fingers move delicately as he piled them one atop another.

'If I tried to do that, they'd fall down straight away; I'm so clumsy.'

'You don't have a very high opinion of yourself, do you, Angel?'

'No. I'm hopeless. My mother was like it too when she was a girl. But she grew out of it; probably by marrying my father.'

His face asked the question, so I told him all about Hugh and the embassy; the schools, everything.

'Your mother sounds very special. Was she the Heavenly Chrissi spoke of?'

I nodded furiously. 'She was special; oh she was.'

'What would she think of you running away?'

'She was a real rebel herself.'

'A rebel, maybe, but it sounds like she did something very important with her life.'

I thought about this a while.

'I didn't become anything; there wasn't time.'

He laughed. 'You've got plenty of time; your whole life is ahead of you.'

'Why are you always laughing at me?'

'I'm not laughing at you; I don't *mean* to laugh at you. Tell me more about you, about your mother.'

So I did, and I realised that except for one occasion I'd never talked about her to anyone, ever. Everyone close to me knew her and I couldn't bear to talk about her to people at school. I tried once and they'd laughed at her name and made fun of me and said I must think she was a saint or something. Now, on the beach, the tears had dried on my face and I lifted it to look at him. Those eyes! I felt they could see into my soul.

'You're your mother's daughter, I can see that. She stopped running, didn't she? So must you.'

We sat in silence, partly because I didn't know what to say to him. I wasn't ready for complicated thoughts.

The flames had died down and soft red embers glowed; occasionally sending sharp sparks into the sky like sparklers, fireworks. Images of chestnuts filled my mind, and I was suddenly hungry. The singer, I now saw, was Libby, and she was coming over the sand towards us.

She was wearing a sarong made of some silky material, the colour of the sea, and it clung to her body. It was split at the sides and as she moved you caught glimpses of her long tanned legs. Her hips swayed as she walked.

My legs are as brown as hers, I thought and glanced to my dirty jeans. It's just that I don't show them off.

'Want something to eat?' she said.

'Have you enough?' Costas asked.

'For you, doctor, always plenty.'

I didn't speak, sat with my head down, playing with my fingers.

'And Angel?'

'Sure, if she wants.'

My face was burning with embarrassment, humiliation. I longed to have the strength to say no. But the smells, the delicious roasting, herby smells were sending my stomach into a merry-go-round and so I muttered, 'OK.'

'Just "OK", Angel?' Libby asked, eyebrows raised.

'Yes, please,' I said through gritted teeth.

Libby's laugh trilled into the night. I'd never noticed before how irritating it was.

'Sweet child,' she said.

She turned as Costas rose and put her hand out to him. He had little option but to take it. She led him over to the fire, her hair swinging down, gleaming in the light of the last flames. I struggled along behind. My foot had gone to sleep and now dragged behind me like a lead weight. There were welcoming cries from the group around the fire. I knew some of them and a couple beckoned me into a space. I looked across and old would-be Joan Baez had Costas still firmly in tow.

I liked the couple who were there; Marty and Steve. They had a roly-poly pink sausage of a baby, Jango, who wriggled and held his arms out to me. I minded him sometimes, and he was always laughing, like now; chortle, chortle. I couldn't help but smile as I cuddled him to me. You can't be depressed with a baby. On the other side of the fire I watched Libby flirt with Costas. She seemed good at that; I hadn't seen it before. He was smiling now and saying something that had her giggling and hiding her face behind her hair.

And then she put her hand up and touched his face. A fly, a fly I told myself, she's brushing off a fly – yuk!

Marty was getting me some food, wooden skewers of sweet meat, and a potato from the embers and Steve was asking me about Chrissi. Everyone knew what had happened.

'She was unlucky,' he said. 'Guys I know sold their skin and they're fine.'

Costas waved to me from the other side of the fire; was he beckoning me over? I was on my feet in a jiffy and handed Jango back to his mum.

Libby smiled up at me, but her eyes were cold. Costas made a space and I sat down to attack my kebab. The stick it was on snapped as I bit into the first piece of meat. I was almost dribbling it was so succulent and juicy, surely the most delicious thing I had ever eaten.

Libby was called to sing again. Her voice was full of meaning as she sang:

'When somebody waits for me,
Sugar's sweet, so is he,
Bye bye, blackbird!'

And she was looking at Costas. '*No one here can love and understand me . . .*'

The guitarist clearly adored her, he was gazing with eyes full of love, and she did have a wonderful voice; now low and husky, slow.

The song finished and she gave a little wave in our direction. People were drifting away now, the fire was dying and soon we were the last still there.

I reached out and touched Costas's hand with my grubby fingers. He turned them over, took my hand and held it; smiled.

'You have good hands, Angel. Strong, it's a shame not to use them for something. Come on.'

And he was on his feet, pulling me up.

I was breathing very quickly as we walked slowly away. I didn't want him to let go of my hand. There was something safe in his grip; at the same time it stirred me up inside, but of course, he let go, and the moment was broken.

Above us now, the still night sky was full of stars with the skinny crescent of a new moon just breaking through the clouds, the air clear and fresh. I lifted my hand and my fingers raked through the tangles of my hair. I scratched an itch and Costas reached out, took my hand away and held it again. I wanted him to hold it forever.

He started to say, 'Your hair, I think—'

'Oh don't look at my hair! I hate it.' I scratched through it. 'It won't stay in one place and it itches. I'm going to cut it all off!'

'Angel, there is something I think I must say to you.'

I gazed into those blue eyes. I knew what I wanted him to say; longed for him to say.

His other hand reached out and touched my head; I could hardly breathe, closed my eyes.

'I think I have to tell you that the reason it is itching is because you have lice in your hair.'

I pulled my hand away in horror.

'I'm so sorry to tell you this.'

Suddenly my head was on fire with itching and I was jumping around tearing at it, as if that would make some difference.

'How disgusting! Where have they come from? What can I do?'

And then I realised he was laughing! He was laughing at me again, and I hit him around the shoulders, saying over and over. 'Stop laughing! Stop!'

And then I sat down again on the hard sand, put my head between my knees and wished I could die. Right there, right then.

He had his arms around me now, saying, 'I'm sorry. I'm so sorry. It's just that you looked so wild and very beautiful leaping around like that. It's all right, don't worry, I'll bring you some shampoo from the hospital and a special comb and I'll help you get rid of them. I promise.'

So these nights when I had lain awake or asleep dreaming of him, were as nothing? I was just another patient needing his help. Had he thought nothing of me? But then, had he really said, I looked so beautiful? Wild and beautiful?

I said, 'I must be dirty, filthy; that's why I've got them haven't I? I try so hard not to be, I do truly . . .'

He was still holding me.

'Angel, dear Angel, no. It's because you are clean. They live on clean hair, you are not dirty at all, you must believe me. You have caught them from one of the children, or even Chrissi.'

We were standing beside a rock pool and I plunged my hands in the cool sea water and splashed my face. I had never felt more miserable in my life, thinking: Everything has gone. Chrissi will never be the same, I'm sure. Heavenly has gone forever, Will and Lucy are a million miles away and all I've got are lice and foul creatures burrowing into my horrible hair.

And this lovely man, this doctor isn't going to kiss me or love me – he's going to bring me stuff to get my head clean.

I ran off then; didn't say goodbye. I ran back to the caves and that night I put my rug outside, but I hardly slept. Was it that my head was itching? Or was it that he had said I was beautiful and called me 'dear Angel'?

Did anything mean what it seemed?

I lay there on the sand watching clouds chase the moon, and I hated everything; but most of all I hated myself for being so stupid.

And that night I decided things had to change. Costas was right; I must stop running away. Chrissi had only come with me because I made her.

And now look what a mess she was in: ill and sad and frightened.

And I had caused nothing but worry and trouble to the people I love.

I must make a proper plan for the future. But first, oh God, first I had to get rid of these parasites in my hair.

Chrissi was sitting up in the morning and even said she was hungry. Her eyes were ringed with dark shadows, haunted puddles of darkness in her thin face.

Where once she was so solid, chunky, dependable, her mother's daughter, now Aphrodite wouldn't know her. I saw that her hand, still grimed with dirt, shook if she moved it from her lap. How had all this happened? I should have stopped her. I forgot her insistence, her determination to go and only felt the raw pain of guilt.

I said, 'What happened to you, when you went off?'

I tore the crusts off a piece of stale bread and soaked it in some milk and sugar Anya had given us. Chrissi ate it as if she hadn't touched food for weeks. And perhaps she hadn't.

'Some other time; not now. Now all I want to do is eat. Have you anything else?'

And I remembered an old apple I had. It was in a box we keep to store food in. It was usually empty; when food came we ate it. But this, wrinkled and brown as it was, was still an apple. It had sat in that box for weeks probably. I held it up after polishing it on my T-shirt and said, 'Does this remind you of anyone?' She didn't answer, just smiled. 'It's the image of Titi, isn't it?' I said, and then we were both giggling.

It was good to hear her laugh again. But I knew she thought suddenly, as I did, 'I wish I was there now.'

And then I heard the sound of Costas's motorbike. And I made myself stay, not go running to find it. I had made no plan with him. But when he reappeared, carrying as always his big bag, he smiled, and of course he had come to give Chrissi an injection.

She smiled cautiously, said she was starting to feel better and looked a little surprised to see the needle. She had no memory of the last few days and he had barely finished when she was lying down again and was asleep within moments.

I couldn't look at him. I knew those blue, blue eyes were fixed on me but I didn't care. He put his hand out and touched my knee; it was as if an electric bolt went through me.

He spoke quietly: 'I haven't forgotten. I'll go into the hospital today, get what I need and then come back here later. OK?'

I was so embarrassed and shrugged. 'If you like.'

'I do like; so I'll be here at about nine. Well, for people with no clocks that's when it starts to get dark.' That made me smile and I felt a bit better straight away – only a bit, though.

Chrissi spent the day between sleeping and waking. Rufus helped bring jugs of cool sea water and bathed her face and as I gently pulled her head down I peered into her hair for any sign of the creatures; nothing there.

Later I said to her, as jauntily as I could manage, 'I'm going to cut my hair, like yours. In fact I'm going to do it right now.'

'I'll do it for you.'

We sat outside and I tried desperately hard not to scratch.

'All off?'

'All off.'

I watched as my hair fell in clumps on the sand around me.

The children stood in a row in front of us, chanting, 'All off! All off!'

Tink said, 'Me next.'

But Anya appeared at that moment and clapping her hands in horror said, 'No way, Miss Tinkerbell,' and led her away.

Afterwards, Chrissi said, 'That's finished me for the day, I think. I'm going to lie down again, but hey, you look great.'

I sat by the edge of the sea at sundown. I'd swum several times that afternoon even though so early in the spring it was very cold. Every time I put my head under for ages, rubbing this new hair. Well, no. I wished it *was* new hair, clean, lice-free hair like other people's.

I thought: I'm going to like it really short. Already I could feel there were no tangles. One less problem to worry about.

The only sound was the soft lapping of the waves and the wailing call of a hungry seabird swooping after a fish. Then over this gentleness came the distant roar of the bike. My heart started to beat faster and I tried to talk myself into calmness.

I didn't look up, or turn and even though his footsteps were unheard on the sand, I knew he was near. And then he was sitting beside me.

He smelled so good, so clean. He smelled like the sea and as I thought this he reached out a hand and rumpled my hair.

'It's good; it suits you. I like it. Do you?'

'How can you bear to touch it? Aren't you afraid you'll catch them?'

'I've said I'll help you and I will. I've brought the shampoo and the special comb. If it helps, think of me as a doctor treating a patient.'

But that was exactly it. I didn't want to think of him as a doctor and me just one of his useless patients. But I didn't say it.

To my surprise, he started to take his clothes off, down to his whatever underneath. 'Come on,' he said, 'I think the best way to do this is if we go in the sea and I'll put the shampoo in your hair and leave it on for a bit.'

I tried not to look at his body. That was hard, it was beautiful; no spare fat, nothing but lean muscle.

I don't know how old he is, I thought, but probably a bit older than Will.

He was brown from the sun and there was a sprouting of hair on his chest and down his belly, which was dark and a little bit red.

I realised he was ready and waiting for me to undress. So I tore everything off quickly, even my knickers. Well, I always swim like that.

I paused for a moment, realising that my whiskery bits were the same colour as his, and I ran fast into the sea. He was behind me. The first cold splash of the water made me gasp, but only for a moment.

'Do you want to swim first?' he asked.

I didn't answer, just threw myself into going as fast as I could, straight out towards the horizon. But he was quicker and with strong strokes he passed me in moments.

'It's glorious!' he called. 'I wish I could do this every day, it feels so good.'

He was treading water then and I caught up with him.

I knew that he looked at me. I felt him seeing my tiny breasts. Now I wasn't afraid to meet his eyes and for a moment we were poised there, unmoving.

'You are very beautiful,' he said.

And just for that one moment I believed him and smiled.

'What's this?' He was pointing at my angel.

'It's a tattoo,' I said. 'Last year at the fair.'

'It's you, isn't it? Angel, I like it. Did it hurt?'

'Not really,' I shrugged, lying.

Then he lifted his hand and I saw he had a small jar in it.

'Here,' he said, 'I'll put some of this on. Then you can swim for a while but keep your head out of the water. OK? It needs to do its work before we rinse it off.'

I shrugged. 'I just hope it's easy to get rid of the creatures like this. And no,' and I looked up into that dear face, that had just told me I was beautiful, 'no, I don't want to think of you as a doctor.'

There was a sandbank here, so I stood in the cool, clear water as the tiny fish swam around my toes. And Costas gently lifted my stubbly and infested hair, strand by short strand and, with such care, threaded his magic cream through it.

'Sorry about the smell.'

I was holding my nose not to inhale it. But it still made me cough and my eyes water. And then, 'Ow! It's burning me!'

'Try and bear it. It should stop in a moment.'

'Is that what it does? Burn them to death on my head?'

'Something like that.'

I stood there under the darkening sky, my head on fire. All I wanted to do was duck it in the cool water, ease this pain. But at least he was holding my hand.

It seemed like hours but it was probably only a few minutes before he said, 'OK, now you can wash it off' and I was under the water scrabbling and scratching through my hair until every last scrap was clean, squeaking clean.

We swam then, side by side. I watched the muscles of his strong arms cleave the water with barely a splash.

On the shore I stood with him. 'What now?'

'Now, we comb very, very carefully each little bit and you will see what has been the problem.'

The metal comb looked like an instrument of torture.

He sat on the sand and he pulled me down so that I sat between his legs with my back to him.

The combing was agony but the sitting there, so close I could feel his breath on my back, was heaven.

'Yes,' he said, 'all gone. Look here.' And on the palm of his hand there were a cluster of small, black ant-like things.

'Are they dead?'

'Oh, sure. And look here, we have killed off all the eggs, as well.' And there were tiny white pearly dots lying there.

'They were breeding in my hair?' I was sickened.

He shook his hand out on to the sand and then put it on my shoulder, leaving it there. So I leaned back a tiny little bit and we were touching and he didn't move away and there was just his hand moving gently on my back. His body felt both deliciously warm and cool from the water. I thought, I could stay here forever. The tufts of that dark hair on his chest tickled sweetly.

I could almost hear the movement of the stars it was so still and quiet. I gradually pressed myself against him. My eyes were closed and I was in his arms. I knew that I knew nothing, had never even been kissed by a man, but I knew that he felt something, for I heard his breathing quicken and under those damp shorts he was hard and I knew that was what happened when a man wanted a woman.

I didn't breathe, wanting nothing to change, ever, but he pushed me away from him, a bit roughly even, and was on his feet, his back to me and pulling on his clothes.

I stood up, and of course I was still naked. I wasn't even shy, now, so I stood there and didn't move as he dressed.

Where were those blue eyes now, those deep searching eyes? For sure, not looking at me. He patted me on the shoulder, as he might a friendly dog, muttered a fast goodbye and was gone.

I stayed there long after I heard the starting roar of the bike. Even as it faded into the distance and other traffic on that road took its place, I stayed.

And then, gathering my things, my soggy, grubby T-shirt, my old faded, patched jeans that smelt faintly of food, I walked back to what I'd thought of as home but which was in reality a small, airless cave; and I felt very confused.

Two more nights he came and both times we went to swim. He always kept his undershorts on and I always didn't.

I was learning so much about myself. I knew that what I felt for him was something I'd never felt for anyone in my life before.

At night, however tired I was, I just lay looking up at the sky and thought about this. I understand about Will and Lucy but it was hard to think of others: Chrissi and Simeon? No! My mother and Hugh? I suppose so.

He came again the next night – Chrissi was getting so much better she didn't need the injection in the morning. The old, dear Chrissi was almost back with us. I think Rufus was more pleased than anyone; he barely left her side.

Libby still spent most of her time with the guitarist.

And Costas and I walked on the beach and talked. Every minute I seemed to feel not just closer, but that he was really becoming a friend; a wise friend. I could talk with him, just as I could in the old days with Lucy or Will.

When I was with him, I knew anything was possible. I felt joyous and excited – thought what a wonderful place the world was!

After a while we sat, our backs to an abandoned wreck of a boat, a fishing boat, and he told me how lucky Chrissi had been.

'Another few hours and I think blood poisoning would have set in. We took a risk, she should have been in hospital; I was worried.'

'But she really is OK now, isn't she?'

'She's good – thanks to you.'

I loved it when he said 'we' – it meant we were partners.

He told me more about his family. His godfather, the one who worked in the resistance and might, just might, have known Heavenly. I said, 'There was a Christo who helped restore our house.' But I could see he wasn't really listening. He was miles away in his own thoughts.

He said, 'Sometimes I wonder if he was really my father.'

'Why do you think that? Surely your mother would have told you, or your father?'

'My father is a difficult man, very distant, locked inside himself.'

'You said that about Chrissi.'

'I've seen it often in patients. It usually means there is a history of depression. Sometimes, carrying so many burdens of life, they fear they will explode if they open just a crack.' He picked up a stone and threw it towards the sea. It flew high in the air leaving behind a family of crabs that must have lived under it. They scuttled in all directions, whizzing and whirring the sand around their backs.

'Tell me more; I want to know everything about you.'

He laughed and ruffled my hair, my new short, empty, uninhabited hair.

'I think most of it is pretty dull. I came back from Athens and took any locum work I could find. The death of my godfather was so unexpected. It seemed for a while the family would fall apart. We all loved him so much, but more than that; he was the centre of our lives.'

He paused and looked into the distance. 'The centre of my life then suddenly one day, he was . . . gone.'

The waves cooled our feet, a small whisper of a breeze was on our faces and we sat so close together if I moved my arm just the smallest bit, I was touching him.

'I feel I have known you forever,' I said. He jumped up, pulling me up with him and we walked side by side in silence for a while. Our hands sometimes brushed against each other and every time it made me tingle. 'I've been thinking about what you said and I know you are right. I must stop running away. I worked hard when I was at that school; passed all the exams, everything. I was determined to show my father I wasn't the idiot he thought I was. But I can't bear the thought of going back to England. Apart from Will and Lucy I have no one there, nothing. Greece is my home. I did think I could be a nurse, like Heavenly.'

A shaft of moonlight broke through a cloud and lit up the twisted trunk of an ancient tree. Its roots spread under the sand, beneath the rocks, and as we passed, the screech of a night bird in its branches startled us both and I stumbled. It seemed automatic that he should put his arm around me as I fell against him. But I straightened up and his arm stayed there. I could hardly breathe.

'Or maybe I could even think of becoming a doctor, like you,' I managed to go on.

He turned me to face him; looked straight into my eyes.

'You could become anything, do you know that? Anything. You could be a surgeon, or an engineer; you are a very special woman.' And then, 'Hey,' and his arm dropped, 'let's swim.'

On the next night, I deliberately dressed up a bit before he came.

Chrissi helped and put some olive oil in my hair, which made it shiny, and Tink brought her mother's patchouli scent and dabbed some on my ears. I loved my new hair, so short now I could just shake it dry. I wore the sarong and let my legs show a bit as I walked, and the black silk shirt my mother bought me for my birthday. It was rather crumpled but you don't iron clothes when you live in a cave.

I didn't need to tell Chrissi, she just knew and squeezed my hand and whispered 'good luck' as I left.

When we'd swum, we walked along the shore and his hand brushed my leg. I took it in mine and after what seemed an age he took it to his face and held it there. We were standing at the edge of the water and the beams of the moon slanted across the sea. My heart was beating so fast and I turned towards him and as he looked at me, still holding my hand, I reached up and kissed his lips. A moment only and then his arms were around me and his mouth opened under mine. I tasted his cool salty tang, and I thought, Never in my life will a kiss be as sweet and magic as this.

We stayed like that for an age; his hands were stroking my back, my breasts were tight against him and even though they were tiny, the nipples were tingling.

I didn't want him to stop, ever. There was something so familiar, comforting in him as if I'd known him all my life and this was where I belonged.

But he pulled away, and looking at me, held my head in both his hands.

'Sit down, for a moment.' So I did and leaned against his damp cool shoulder. 'I will be leaving soon, Angel.' His hand took mine.

The only thing wrong with this precious moment was not

being able to see into his eyes. I could barely trust myself to speak, but I said, 'Can you stay a little while? I have been thinking such a lot after our talks together and I think I know what I am going to do.'

'Angel, I—'

'No, hush, let me tell you what I thought. I am definitely going to ask my father to help me. If he thinks I am going to behave properly and go on with my education, he may well be prepared to pay for it. I'll get Lucy and Will to talk to him for me. He's bound to listen to them. And this is what I have decided I am going to do; I'm going to ask him to let me go to a gymnasio in Greece, to take the exams here to go to the university or the *polytechnio*. There. What do you think of that?'

'Wonderful, yes, very good; but I don't mean that.' I felt his fingers now move on my shoulder and across the back of my neck. I wanted this moment to last forever, this stroking. His breath was flickering as his fingers touched me. His voice was hoarse now. Surely he was feeling the same as me? And then he said, 'I must go back to Athens next week.'

'So soon?'

'My job is waiting in the hospital there and I am needed. My family here can manage without me now.'

'Then I must hurry up, so that I can come to Athens too! That's even better; the gymnasio in Athens will surely be the best.'

'There is something else I have to tell you, dear Angel. I am not free. I'm engaged to be married. My fiancée is there.'

I don't remember much of the night after that. Slowly we walked side by side back to the cave.

'I'm sorry, Angel, I—'

'There's nothing to be sorry for.' I tried to laugh. 'I shall always be grateful to you for saving Chrissi's life. That's what's important.' I managed to say, 'Hey, you've really straightened me out, haven't you? That's great.'

'I'll see you in Athens, then? You'll come, won't you?'

'Oh sure I will.'

'Maybe I can help you there, somehow?'

'Oh, you'll be busy with your hospital and your . . .' I thought I might choke on this. 'Your fiancée. She's a lucky woman. By the way, how old is she?'

'She's twenty-seven.'

'Well, there you are then; you'll suit each other very well.'

'Glykeria. She's a nurse.' He paused. 'Like Heavenly, your mother.'

As if that suddenly made it all right. And then my voice just stopped, as if there were no more breath inside; as if it came to a stop from emptiness – as if there was nothing to say any more, ever. He gave me a quick hug as he left me at the cave. He took my hand in his, looked into my eyes, and before he could say more I squeezed his hand and pushed him away.

'Good night,' I croaked. 'Thanks again – for everything.'

Chrissi was sleeping and Rufus was dead to the world beside her. I managed to turn and wave, even smile as Costas left the beach.

After what seemed like hours, I heard the engine of his bike give a dull roar into life and gradually disappear into the lonely night.

I looked at the remnants of my life here; some scraps of grubby clothing, the piece of blue cloth that was Heavenly's last gift to me; a small pile of pretty stones, all the little bits and pieces of nothing. Is this all we had, Chrissi and me? Is this what we had run away to find? Is this what we had broken our hearts for? I swallowed, tasting the bitter-sweet tang of loss.

I know now that my childhood ended that night. Not when my mother died, after all. But here, now. All my shabby hopes and dreams seemed like phantoms flying away from me up into that deceitful starry sky.

Around me the air was scented with the sharpness of the sea. I sat on the sand, alone and empty. I thought, That's enough; no more running. I wanted nothing now but to go home to everything that is Panagia Sta Perivolia. There would be no Heavenly there. No Hugh. But I wanted to see the old

Orfanoudakis house; the scarlet geraniums in the tubs outside, the tired old gnarly trunk of the vine. I wanted to hear the rustle of the bats as they fly out of the eaves at night and the whistling crack of the cicadas. I even wanted that wretched old scops owl to parp nightly at the moon and the irritating clang of the church bells in the morning causing me to bury my head under the pillow. All those things that I had run away from, I wanted them all back.

'That's where I live,' I told myself. 'That's where I belong. And that's where I will make the next important decisions about my life.'

I arranged my sad old bits of rubbish, lay down on the faded yellow carpet I called bed, closed my eyes and listened to my own heartbeat.

APHRODITE

I was in the *gypo* when they came home; every day the same; dig, weed, water, sweat and pain. Today the *vleeta* and courgettes. I'll add them to yesterday's potatoes and with lemon fresh from the tree squeezed over, that will be dinner. I made myself think like this all the time – lists of what I do filled my brain: dig, wipe and into the trug. Any other thoughts were dangerous. Like my dreams at night they would be full of death and cold horror.

I walked through the door and there were those two girls. Seven months and twenty-two days since they left us.

The basket dropped to the floor, the *vleeta* shed its leaves and the courgettes bounced and rolled into the corner. My hand was gripping the back of Yorgo's chair to save me from a fall as my legs jellied beneath me, and 'Oh, *Panagia mou, Panagia mou,*' I gasped and my hands flew across my chest in the treble cross. I had to make myself breathe as my Chrissi leapt from the chair and hugged me so tight I thought there would be no breath left in my body.

I looked at them as if I would print their faces on my memory.

'Oh, *Panagia*, you are so thin! Never, never did I see you look like this. Have you lived without food for all these months? And your hair? And that smell – what is that smell, like a house of sin?'

'It's called patchouli, Mama – all the hippy girls wear it.'

And then of course, I knew. They have been in the caves

with the Americans. Everyone knows the Americans take drugs all the time.

'Are you taking drugs? What are you taking?'

And she laughed.

'Oh, Mama, please. We have no drugs.'

Angel just sat there. She hadn't spoken and I took her face in my hands and looked into her eyes. *Panagia mou*: it is her mother come back to us; she left us a child, this one and has returned a woman. She smiled slowly but with her mouth only; those eyes didn't smile. They are full of sadness.

I turned back to my child. 'What have you seen, what have you done that has turned you into old women? Chrissi, you look like a ghost, a skeleton. Are you ill? Tell me the truth.'

And then Angel spoke, she told me a few things, I thought none of them were good. The 'nice people' they had lived with; some were children it seemed. I said I thought it not the way to bring up a child – in a cave, on a beach.

And then Yorgo and Manoli came in and it was like a party suddenly; all laughing and chattering. I sat then and let them all jump around me, shouting as though something amazing had happened.

'This is wonderful!' Yorgo said, holding Chrissi around the waist, and even Angel was smiling at last as he waved her hand in the air. 'Our girls are back with us!' But I could only feel sour as I prepared the spinach-like leaves of the *vleeta* and courgettes.

So much noise they made, chatter, chatter, laughing and tears – everything. People from the village were gathering in my doorway. Yes, of course, Titi was there and just behind her the warty-faced one. So bold are they now they walk around the village together always. But not in my house, never.

I stood in the doorway facing them; these are not days for our famous goodwill and hospitality; they are gone. Keep to yourself, lock your doors and beware of strangers. Already Titi and the wart were whispering and pointing at the girls, so I shooed them away like stray cats.

Of course those girls ate every scrap of food I put before

them, and then hard bread and cheese and four apples, cut into pieces and dusted with cinnamon sugar; like they loved when they were children.

'Have you spoken to Will? To your father? What did they say?'

She shook her head.

'My father is in Thailand. But I would like to telephone Will and Lucy if I may?'

Of course I said she could. And we left the room so she could be private.

She called us in and gave me the phone so I could speak to Lucy myself.

Lucy was crying. She kept saying over and over, 'Oh I'm so pleased they are safe and well, so happy.'

I said nothing.

'Aphrodite? Aphrodite? Are you there?'

'I am here.'

'Isn't this good? Aren't you so pleased they are home again safely?'

'If you saw them—'

'Why? What's wrong with them?'

'They have been living in caves with foreigners – Americans and children. Taking drugs. They look as if they haven't eaten in weeks and Chrissi, I think, has been ill. No one has told me anything. You know how we live now, Lucy. We will all be in trouble, you will see.'

'Aphrodite, you are worrying me!'

'I can't speak any more, too much said already.'

Bang! I put the phone down. I have come to hate this thing in my house. Might as well have someone writing down everything we say. I was sorry I was hasty with Lucy, but too late now.

As I turned back into the room, the pain I have felt in my lower belly for weeks was there again. I held it, pushed into myself with my fist, and breathed slow and deep. At first, I thought it was the anxiety I felt when my child disappeared, all gathered together there in a lump. It was bad, and as I gripped the arm of Yorgo's chair, trying to breathe slow and steady, I felt giddy and thought I might fall. Chrissi saw me.

'Mama, Mama? You look so pale suddenly, what is it?'

Yorgo said, 'The happiness at seeing you back here, makes her pain bad.'

'What pain, Papa?'

And Angel, 'What pain, Uncle?'

I didn't need to speak, Yorgo answered.

'It's nothing, is it, Aphrodite? Nothing at all, really. Tell them. Just a little pinch in the gut, wind probably, or something like that. Yes, wind, I expect.'

Let him tell them what they want to hear. He is my voice these days. But I had forgotten how young people are – questions, questions.

Chrissi said straight away, 'Have you talked to Aristos? What does he say?'

And Angel: 'He would tell you to go to the doctor at once. How long have you had the pain?'

I sat in the chair then. I gave in.

'A while, is all.'

And Chrissi was on the floor at my feet, crying and saying, 'Oh, Mama, Mama, I am so sorry. It's because of me, isn't it? I worried you and made you ill. I'm so sorry.'

'Stupid child – you can't get pain from worry, everyone knows that. It will go away. It usually does after a few hours.'

'And comes back again, and then again.' This from Manoli; what does he know?

Before I could even speak, I saw Vangelis the schoolteacher coming into my house. His moustache gleamed with oil and his hair too, although that was about a dozen hairs stretched and glued across his head. An old man trying to impress with his looks – what a fraud!

Oh, *Panagia mou*! There behind him were the police, two of them with guns. They waited outside of course; so the whole village saw them.

The stick insect didn't wait a moment to greet us, just said: 'Yorgo. You will be pleased your daughter has decided to come home. But there are some things we need to know. Where has she been, things like that.'

Yorgo was simply confused and stumbled through a few words none of us could hear. He looked to me in bewilderment.

'What do you want with her?'

'Surely I don't have to spell out to you what is wrong?'

'So, she has been away for a little while—'

'More than a little while, Yorgo, seven, eight months, I believe? And living with people in caves, taking drugs, all sorts. You will come with me, Chrissoula. There are questions we need to ask you.'

I saw my girl did not know how to deal with this and looked to Angel for help.

'I'll come with you,' she said, but the *malaka* shook his head.

'We may need to speak with you later, but for now it is the Greek girl only.'

Of course Angel was enraged by this.

'I am just as Greek as she is!'

He laughed.

'I don't think so; your parents were both English.' He had a smug little smile. 'Speaking Greek is not the same as being born a Greek.'

And that sly smile turned into a sneer of a laugh.

And that was that. Home for an hour, maybe two and then taken, arrested. That is what it is. And I want to weep with all the unshed tears at our helplessness. Chrissi went with him, what choice did she have?

The pain in my belly gripped me then and I knew I must take some of the mixture the doctor gave me. Of course I saw the doctor. I'm not a fool. The Sitia one has a clinic in Tres Petromas once a week. He examined me and shrugged; looked sourly at my aging body, grasped my breasts which once stood proud and caused Yorgo spasms of delight; now flabby, ignored. And wiping his hands on a none-too-clean towel, he said words which no normal woman would understand, urithea this and uterine that and as he saw my look of ignorance, despair, said dismissively, 'Women's problems.'

I did not believe my Aristos treated his patients with so little respect. I did not believe that if Yorgo were sitting in my place the doctor would say, 'Man's trouble.'

He searched in the cardboard box which until a while ago had contained packets of Papagalos Coffee, or so it said, and discarding several bottles of evil-coloured liquid and boxes of rattling tablets, he settled on a brown jar of powder, handed it to me and said, 'Mix a spoonful in water, take when needed.'

I stood up and he was already calling, 'Next patient!' before I was out of the door.

Women's trouble, huh! All women get them; why bother my family? They would just worry and nag. For now, what is happening to my girl is worry enough. They let her come home, and then they came again and took her away and then she was home with us again. Not Angel, just my Chrissi.

And then the two of them told us they want to go to Athens. Athens! *Panagia mou*, what were we to say? In Athens she would at least be away from the *malakas*, but that is a city with all its own dangers. I tried to telephone to Aristos but they were away, so no one could help. Maybe Lucy? I must think. I looked to Yorgo; but he just smiled, shrugged and walked away. What does he know? I must think. I must do this on my own. At least she is alive; yes, at least she is alive.

ANGEL

And so we came to Athens, a city that seems never to sleep, a hot, smoky ashtray of a city, a city that I loved and hated at the same time. Loved, because it's so beautiful, hated because it was the city that always seemed to take my mother away from me. The best thing of all was that Chrissi came too. We had persuaded Aphrodite that it was a good idea; a few days at home, her mother's cooking and a laugh or two from her father, and the old Chrissi was soon restored and, having tasted freedom once, couldn't wait for more.

'Well, if we survived living in a cave, Hugh's apartment in the centre of Athens must be better,' Chrissi said.

Aphrodite made us promise to keep in touch and so far, having been here four hours, she has rung three times and Will said he thought that one of them should be there to settle us in, and that he was between films at the moment and he would come. I was really pleased to see him.

Chrissi's brother Aristos's wife, Irini, has a cousin here who is the hosiery buyer at Magnion – a big department store near the centre and she arranged an interview in the store for Chrissi, so this morning, early, we all set off and were determined not to be frightened by the great imposing gilded windows, the escalators to hidden heights, the wafting fragrances from the perfume department. I wanted to try on hats while Chrissi was interviewed, but Will wanted coffee instead. Eventually Chrissi came back to us with a great smile on her face – she's going to work in a department on the ground floor selling ribbons and bows, lace and buttons, for a six-week trial. You'd have thought she'd won the lotto. It was the first time since we came back that I saw her really looking happy. I laughed as she told us what she was to wear: a black dress to the knee or a white blouse and navy or black skirt.

'What shall I do? I told them, no problem!'

'Soula,' I said, 'the housekeeper, that's all she ever wears. I'm sure she'll come up with something.'

That was Chrissi sorted; now me next. Today was Thursday, Chrissi was to start the following Monday so the next morning we all went to the gymnasio that was just ten minutes' walk from the apartment.

I liked it the minute we walked in through the arched gates.

It was an old building. It must have survived the war somehow. It had a beguiling air of warmth and serenity. As we walked down the long corridor that divided the ground floor, the first thing we saw ahead was a huge glass window that gave on to a park or gardens and out there a tennis court and a playing field with a whole lot of girls running about.

'Are there boys here?' Chrissi asked in a loud whisper.

'If there aren't, I'm not coming.'

A man was coming towards us – tall, imposing, even though he had a limp. He had a pile of books under his arm.

'Can I help you?' he said and smiled.

'I'd like to register as a student, please, to study here.'

He showed us the principal's room and I knocked. A voice from inside called and I opened the big door with a shove.

I was in there for nearly an hour. Will and Chrissi sat on a bench outside and waited.

I had rung Will to tell him we were home and Aphrodite spoke to Lucy and said, 'Safe, but tired; Chrissi looks like death. She's been ill. Angel is well, but now they talk of heading off again, this time to Athens.'

Hugh was in Thailand so Will thought he'd better see for himself what was going on.

I was waiting in the square when he arrived back in Panagia. And we had a great hug.

'My God, you've grown,' he said. 'You're tall and beautiful now; the image of our mother.' He ruffled my hair and said, 'What do you call this? A gamine cut, is that it? What do you brush it with, a toothbrush? And are those my shorts you're wearing?'

We hugged again and walked hand in hand up to the house. The doors and shutters were wide open.

'I cleaned it for you; can you tell?'

'Of course I can.'

We walked around the house together. There was a delicate sweet smell from the wild flowers I had cut and put into tall jugs in the living room.

And there at the end by the old wine press were Heavenly's cushions and – my addition this – woven baskets and old wine demijohns on the floor around the walls. Some filled with stones, some with shells, and some with lollipops. I give them to village children if they visit, which of course they do, and then hurry away afterwards to fetch little brothers and sisters for a treat.

Will had looked at me.

'Well, you're certainly growing into the woman our mother would have been proud of. But I'm sorry you chose to run away to do it. We were so worried, Angel. Father was on the point of coming back and getting the police involved.'

I was on the brink of tears.

'Oh Will, I'm sorry. I just couldn't face being sent away again to another bloody English school, can you understand that?'

He was nodding slowly, but still looked angry and disapproving.

'I needed to make my own decisions. Be in charge of my own life. That's something I learnt at The Oaks – independence.'

'You could have told us, couldn't you? Lucy and me? Or doesn't being independent include a bit of thought for others?'

227

I walked out on to the terrace to hide the tears now falling fast.

'I couldn't imagine you would approve or help.' I rubbed my eyes and turned to face him. 'After you'd gone, it seemed that I didn't really matter any more. Pack me off to school, get me out of the way, that was what it felt like. Perhaps Lucy thought I didn't really mind, but I did, Will, I minded desperately. I felt I had to do it alone – well, all right, with Chrissi, but I *had* to go right away and try and be independent. I'm truly sorry, Will. At the time it seemed the only possible thing to do.'

He looked at me, and I thought: He doesn't understand, and then he was giving me a great big Will hug, just what I had been missing, and he said, 'You do seem a whole lot more grown up, I will say that. You even look more mature, more confident and I reckon you've got something Heavenly had in bucket loads but always denied: grace. Style and grace. I suppose if running away was what did it for you, then maybe . . .'

Later, he even complimented me on the supper I had made, Raggeh's special spaghetti bolognaise without meat. After we ate, we walked and we talked even more. There was a slight chill in the air now; the warmth of the sun faded quickly. It was dusk as we walked through to the very far edge of the village – Kato Panagia.

As the path divided by the crooked pomegranate tree, we took the upper level and stumbled along. We know most of the villagers by name and as we passed through we were greeted cheerfully,

'*Yassou, Panos, ti kanis.*'

'*Mia hara.*'

'*Na sekala!*'

Will said, 'You remember all the names, don't you? I'm ashamed to say I've forgotten most of them but I remember Panos – didn't his wife die a while ago?'

I nodded. 'Even his moustache seems to have lost its bloom

228

since then. He's getting very vague. Did you see he was wearing two jackets?'

'And two shirts by the look of it.'

'He would never have done that when Rania was alive.'

'Lucy has to give *me* the once-over most days. I never notice holes in shirts or buttons off.'

A woman who looked about a hundred came by slowly. She smiled with pleasure to see Will but declined his offer to help carry the huge armfuls of straw she had.

'They're all as proud as ever,' he said.

The village was coming home at the end of a day spent planting, herding, shepherding. The pace, as always, slow. Why hurry? There was something so comforting and ever-lasting about these lives. The air was ringing with the sound of goat bells, the cicadas and occasionally the piercing song of an unseen bird. Will breathed in deeply, coughing the last of London out of his lungs.

'It's good to be back.'

I steered us on to the path that leads up and up. Without words we were headed to the church of Saint Kosmas and Damianos – Heavenly's church.

It was only when we were there and cleared a bramble from the top of her grave that we sat. There was none of the usual paraphernalia that Greeks decorate graves with; oil, photo-graphs and stuff that turns a grave into a shrine. Aphrodite comes here, I bet.

I began to tell him some of the things that had happened to us.

'There is little I can say except to tell you that we've all been there; fallen in love for the first time with the wrong person. He seems to have done some good, this Costas, although frankly I could murder the bugger. Him, a man of what, how old?'

'Thirtyish, I suppose.'

'And you, not yet eighteen.'

I changed the subject and told him I was determined to

finish my education, make up for the time I've lost and I wanted to do it in Athens.

'Do you have any idea how dangerous that city is right now?' he asked.

'Only if you antagonise the authorities; I'll be a student; I will work hard and stay out of trouble, I promise. And . . . Costas will be there.'

'And his fiancée?'

'Yes. And his fiancée. But he has promised to help me. I've got his address, his telephone number and I know the hospital he works in.'

'Where his fiancée works as well, probably, her being a nurse.'

'Yes! Oh, Will, you are exasperating. He is a friend, a good friend. He really cares; he said he will help me, be there for me.' I looked away, down and down into the far distant sea and a falcon flew suddenly over our heads, startling us.

'Yes, in the beginning I did feel, well, probably a bit more than I should. But that was *me*, not him and he kept coming to the caves to check up on Chrissi. He did save her life, you know; he's a wonderful doctor.'

'Don't you think if he was that good he'd have had her in the hospital? Not left her lying on the stone floor of a damp old cave?'

I scrambled to my feet at that.

'You're completely determined to think only bad things about him, aren't you?'

'Angel, I'm sorry. You know I love you. Everything I do or say is only because I really care.'

And I had to live with that. He was pleased, of course, with my decision to settle and do something with my life. That night it was he who telephoned Hugh and got him to agree to finance my plan.

'She's thought of everything, Father, even arranging for copies of her exam results to be forwarded from The Oaks. They'll be in the apartment when we arrive.'

'I'll speak to her when you're in Athens,' Hugh said. 'I'm still too damn mad at her for letting me down like that.'

And he'd put the phone down.

Eventually I was out of the head teacher's room, still clutching my papers. Behind me was the head; a short, squat, determined-looking woman; steel grey hair in a tight perm, and a face that looked as though it got a good scrub with a brush each morning and evening. No nonsense there.

As we all walked off down the corridor, she called, 'Eight o'clock sharp tomorrow morning.'

I spun round.

'Excuse me, Kyria Katzakis, but I have a medical appointment, so I'll come on Monday. Yes?'

Will looked surprised as we headed out of there.

On the steps outside he said, 'She's from Crete.'

'Yes,' I said. He'd known because Cretan names end in 'akis'. A parting gift from the Turks in one or other of the occupations; it means 'little people'.

'And this medical appointment?'

'I couldn't miss Chrissi's last day of freedom, could I? And I do have a hospital appointment, well, sort of. I'll tell you later. But she did think my exam papers were excellent. Couldn't find a single fault, and boy, did she scour them. I told her I hadn't yet decided what I was going to do with my life and she said "with results like these, Angel, you can do anything you like. Arts and Sciences, I see. You could consider being an assistant to a scientist or even a researcher for an arts professor".'

'Really? That's brilliant,' said Chrissi.

'And what did you say?' Will said.

'I said, or an actual scientist or an arts professor, myself.'

'And?'

'She laughed. She did! She said, "I can see someone who's a little bit big for their booties." Why does everyone laugh at me?'

'Do you still want to go on with all this?'

231

I faced them, as we reached the street outside.

'You bet I do! I'll show them – all these teachers, professors. Besides, I can't give up now, can I? Chrissi's got a job.'

Chrissi beamed, and said, 'Good for you! Come on, let's go and swim.'

We collected our costumes and walked down Makriyannis Street and got the bus to Lake Vouliagmeni.

The water was cool and welcoming and hardly anyone else was swimming because it was a working day. But around the edge of the lake you couldn't miss the soldiers patrolling with their guns swinging along at their sides.

As we sat giggling and eating ice creams Will asked me about the 'hospital appointment'.

'Is it what I think it is?'

'Well, I'm not a mind reader, but probably, yes.'

'We've only been here five minutes and already you're chasing after him.'

He lit a cigarette, the last in the packet.

Chrissi said, 'I think the thing is that Angel thinks it's important you meet him. He is lovely, truly. And anyway, then he can see for himself that I'm better.'

'I might just tell him what I think of him, this Doctor Costas.'

'Oh Will, please! Just remember he saved Chrissi's life.'

He grunted, and didn't answer.

We stayed there lazing for the rest of the day and went home tired but— no, not happy, but I could see there was a possibility of happiness ahead.

Next day I noticed that people on the streets walked quickly, heads down. There was a tension here in the very air.

The hospital was, as they all seem to be, a cold, grey establishment. There were armed soldiers patrolling outside.

We were directed to Costas's ward, passing x-ray, out-patients, psychotherapy and a place that could only be a canteen of sorts and, pausing, Will said, 'I'm going to get a coffee.'

Another few wards and then we saw him, Costas. He was sitting on the bed of an elderly woman, holding her hand and smiling gently. He didn't see us at first, but was saying something to a nurse at his side. She nodded and scribbled quickly on the clipboard she carried. I had never understood when people said 'my heart was in my mouth' but in that moment I did. It was jumping about so fast in my chest that I thought: If I swallow, I'll lose it.

We just stood in the doorway, Chrissi and me, and I found I was gripping her hand tight.

'It's OK,' she whispered, 'don't panic.'

And a very senior-looking nurse, grey hair scraped back in a tight bun, saw us, got up from the desk where she sat and came over.

'Do you want something?' she asked in an icy voice.

There was a lump in her cheek she kept moving around with her tongue; I think she was eating a sweet, a big one. Probably she hoped we wouldn't notice.

'We would like to see Doctor Dukakis,' I said firmly.

'Do you have an appointment?'

'No.'

'But I am a patient of his.' Bold Chrissi!

The nurse led us then to a room off the end of the ward. It was empty and stuffy, with greasy-looking grey paint and smeared dirty windows that refused to open. We sat on hard, upright chairs with wobbly legs and waited. Chrissi dived immediately into a pile of magazines and grabbing one with a garish, grinning blonde on the cover, settled down with it. 'Enlarge your breasts!' it screamed across the front.

'Two cup sizes in two weeks,' I read over her shoulder.

'You need this more than me,' she said.

I sat back to wait and thought then, just as I do every day, every night, of the last time I had seen Costas . . .

It wasn't that long lonely night when I had decided to go home. It was two days later. He came back at sundown. Our two sad little backpacks stood in the entrance to the cave and we were trying to explain to Rufus why we were leaving him. It was Chrissi who mattered most to him; he'd always adored her. His eyes were wide and staring in his little brown face and he kept gulping and trying hard not to cry.

We'd thought to leave very early the next morning, hitch a lift to Sitia or Monastiraki and get the early bus from there to Tres Petromas. It would take most of the day and several changes of bus but we should be home by nightfall and Chrissi said she would ring home then and get Yorgo to come down to meet us.

'I promise I'll send you postcards,' she said to Rufus.

'Are you better enough to go now?' he asked. 'Will that man look after you?'

We knew he meant Simeon.

'No, not him,' Chrissi said. 'I'm going home to my mummy.'

'Do you have a daddy?'

Dangerous ground, this. 'Yes I do.'

'Will he be pleased to see you?'

Before she could answer he went on, 'They took my daddy away in the thunderstorm.'

It was at that moment that a shadow fell across the entrance and, expecting Libby or Raggeh, I looked around.

It was Costas. I hadn't heard the bike.

We walked on the beach as the last rays of the dying sun fell through the sky.

Around us the sand leached into dry salty earth and sharp twigs of broom had sprung up; if you caught them with your foot they either snapped off or dug into you.

It was that moment in the day when it feels like another ending, another chapter closing. And I suppose that's exactly what it was.

'I wanted to see you again before I leave tomorrow. Wanted to make sure you were OK.'

'And Chrissi?'

'Of course, Chrissi. But I watched her in there with that child and she seems pretty well. Is that right?'

'Yes. Thanks to you.'

'And you, little one. Angel, what of you? What are you going to do?'

So I told him all about our plans: first Panagia and then we hoped on to Athens.

'Where will you stay there?'

'My father has an apartment, Plutarchou Street.' And I pulled a face.

'You are very lucky. Here, I wrote this down for you.' And he gave me a piece of paper torn roughly from a notebook. 'My address, phone number and the hospital where I work.'

'But you won't want me bothering you, will you?'

'To hear from you won't be a bother, I promise.'

'Don't play with me, Costas.'

I had shocked him. 'Play with you? What does that mean, play with you?'

Now I wasn't sure how to go on. 'I don't know how to think of you. That worries me.'

He took my hand, turned me to face him. 'I like you very much. I think you are very special, a once-only person. I'm glad I met you and I want you to stay in my life. There, is that an answer?'

I said nothing at first.

Then he said, 'Can we be friends? How is that?'

'If you like. But what about Glykeria?'

'I will tell her about you. I'd like you to meet her. I think you would like each other.'

I suppose that was the price I must pay. To have Costas in my life, I must become his fiancée's friend too. I would decide later that anything was worth it: just to see him. I looked into those deep blue eyes. His hair was shorter, but still swept wildly across his head, lifting and falling in the little wind there was here off the sea. He lifted his hand and ruffled mine.

'No more problems? No more itches?'

Why did he have to remind me of that, now?

'No,' I said as though it were a question about the weather, 'nothing at all.'

'When do you leave?'

'Tomorrow, early, very early.'

'Shall we have one last swim?'

My heart was beating so fast, so hard he must surely hear it. And I fought to stay calm. 'Why not?'

As I knew he would, he pulled off his clothes, scattering them here and there as they fell. His body was still the most beautiful I had ever seen. Even in art galleries, museums. I kept my hands busy taking my own things off; my foul old jeans and a T-shirt that Raggeh had discarded, screaming *Santa Fe Animal Park* across my non-existent breasts.

My hands were shaking and I thought, If he stands there much longer I am going to touch him. And as if he heard me, he turned and ran into the sea. He yelled immediately when he felt the cold water.

We talked more, later, when we were dressed, and then the moment came when he left and, in a way, I was relieved. I felt I hadn't drawn breath since he arrived.

I walked with him up to the road. '*Kalo taxidi,*' he said and 'Safe journey,' I said in reply.

And then once again he had gone; moved out of my life as easily as he had moved in . . .

I think Will could see that I have such passionate feelings for him. I can't pretend enough to deceive someone who knows me as well as he does. I don't care. I will meet Glykeria. I will smile and be so sweet to her; anything just to keep this lovely man in my life forever and ever.

And now we were in the hospital where he worked. In a minute he would come through that door and he would smile, I knew he would. I knew he'd be pleased to see me; I told myself that's why he came back to give me his address.

And suddenly he was there and smiling. Chrissi grunted but otherwise ignored him. I learned later that she was terrified of showing her scars to anyone – even herself; and carried on learning how to enlarge her breasts.

I didn't run across and hold him. I just stood there, doing

my best to look cool and calm. He came to me first and kissed me on both cheeks.

I remembered the salty tang of his mouth, open under mine. Now there was no sea smell, just a smooth shaven cheek and a faint aroma of some men's stuff; aftershave? Probably a gift from Glykeria; grudgingly I admitted she'd chosen well.

He turned straight to Chrissi and she looked up as he said her name.

'You look better,' he said, and sitting down beside her he kissed her on both cheeks as well. He'd never done that before.

His hand was on her wrist. I hoped he was taking her pulse.

'All good so far; now I'd like to check that wound.' She was wearing an old shirt, probably one of Yorgo's, hanging loose over her jeans. But as she started to unbutton it, 'No no,' he said, 'not here. We must do it properly, come with me.' And he took her by the hand and led her out of that room. I wasn't staying there on my own, so I followed them back into the ward.

He pointed to one of the empty beds, said, 'Jump up on there and I'll get a nurse.'

Chrissi sat on the edge of the bed. 'You won't leave me, will you?' she said to me.

'Of course not.'

And then he was back with a woman in a nurse's uniform; a very beautiful, slim, young, blonde. Her hair was short like mine, but sleek and shiny. Automatically I ran my fingers through my crop, catching my reflection in the glass of the window, and realised that, as usual, it was standing up all over my head like a hedgehog. She had baby blue eyes, but they were hard as buttons. The way she was looking at him, I thought she must be Glykeria.

She fluttered about us like some rather pathetic moth caught in the light and pulled the curtain round the bed indicating that I should wait on the other side of it.

'No. My friend would like me to stay, wouldn't you, Chrissi?'

Vigorous nodding of head from the bed.

Glykeria shrugged.

'Shall I help you undress?'

Vigorous shaking of head and Chrissi quickly unbuttoned the shirt. Well, there were only two buttons left on it, and as she slipped it off her shoulders I saw she was not wearing a bra and her full breasts, brown from the sun, stood there proudly tipped with rosy nipples like ripe raspberries. She looked wonderful, stunning. I stared in amazement, Glykeria blushed, and grabbing the sheet from the end of the bed tried to cover Chrissi.

Costas seemed to barely notice, checked his watch and asked Chrissi to lie back, discarding the sheet at once.

Since we left the caves I hadn't seen this wound. It had healed, but what remained was a hideous, puckered, shiny red ugliness about eight inches across. My poor, beloved friend. I felt tears prickling the back of my eyes. Chrissi looked at me and I knew she was thinking as I was: I will have to live with this for the rest of my life.

Costas peered at it closely, then gently pressed the skin around the edges.

'No pain here?' She shook her head. 'Or here? Or here?' And as he touched the skin all around she shook her head.

Straightening up, he said, 'Well, you were lucky in one way – we got to you just in time but sadly you will be badly scarred, I think possibly forever.'

I could see Glykeria was longing to ask how this had happened. I thought, He'll tell her when they are alone, perhaps tonight.

I guessed he hadn't yet told her about me because he hadn't said who we were. So I decided to introduce myself.

'Hello, Glykeria,' I said and held out my hand. She looked at me, then at him. 'I'm Angel,' I said, 'Angeliki. It's a pleasure to meet you. Costas told us about you when we were all in Crete.' I paused. 'Together.'

Her astonished silence told me at once I had made a mistake. His roar of laughter confirmed it.

'This is Nurse Djaferis.' He peered at the name badge on the upward swell of her breasts. 'Victoria. Glykeria works in the maternity hospital in Glyfada, not here.'

So poor old Victoria, who I'm glad to say didn't join in this hilarious mockery, simply nodded her head and said, 'I'll go back to the medicine trolley now, doctor, if that is all?'

'Thank you for your time, nurse.'

And trying to stifle a giggle, she hurried away. That'll be round the nurses' home by the end of the day, I thought.

'I'm sorry, Costas, I feel so—'

'Don't worry; it was a mistake. Come, I'll walk you down the corridor. Are you well? Settled in Athens?'

Chrissi had done up her two buttons and covered herself rather more modestly and, squeezing my hand, said, 'Thanks for all your help, Costas.'

By that time we were back at the canteen place and we stopped in the doorway. Will sat at a small table and his head was down reading a newspaper.

I called his name and he looked across to us.

'This is Costas,' I said as we walked to him. 'I'm not sure if I told you he was such a help to Chrissi in Crete.'

'Costas? Yes, you have been mentioned. I'm not myself this morning, forgive me. I find this city a hard place to live these days.'

'You are not alone. You can only survive here now by keeping your head down and moving on. Are you staying long?'

Will was examining him closely. I wished he wouldn't. His eyes brushed him from head to toe. Was he going to give him marks out of ten?

'As short a time as possible. I'll settle these girls in and then be away.'

'I'll keep an eye on them for you.' There was a blue-eyed smile in his voice.

'You will? I thought you were busy elsewhere?'

'Not too busy for friends. But forgive me, I must go back to the ward now.'

He had got to the door when Will suddenly said, 'Costas,

can you join us for dinner tonight? I would like to get to know you a little before I go to London. And your fiancée, of course.'

So we will get to meet her, this Glykeria . . .

It took a while for me to understand what is different about this city. And then it came to me. In the tensions that I can feel everywhere, this is a city of loss, of suffering; there was no feeling of happiness anywhere, just hurry, rush and fear.

The main avenues, the ones on show, were clean, almost too shining to be real. But wander down side streets and alleys, which we did to get into the Plaka that night, and the gutters were thick with rubbish; forgotten things; a bicycle wheel, a headless doll, a broken toy truck, used condoms, a cracked and broken boot; the debris of people who owned little worth remembering so the loss was hardly noticed.

Costas had told us of a café he liked, in the Plaka, and as we approached there was the haunting sound of Greek music.

I had spent nearly an hour getting myself ready, changing from one pair of jeans to another identical pair; finally settling on the sarong I made from the piece of cloth Heavenly had brought me from Thailand. I squeezed myself into a white T-shirt and when Will pointed out it was filthy, I whipped it off, washed it, and tried to dry it with the hairdryer. It was very damp still, but I pulled it over my head anyway and as we were leaving realised my hair needed washing too and persuaded Chrissi to give it an extra trim.

'Angel, you look terrific, can we be on our way please!' Will said.

Will hates being late anywhere and was not in the best of moods by the time we got to the café. We were shown to a table by a girl who was about my age; a pretty, dark thing with green eyes. She could have been Irish. On the walls there were posters of the singer Melina Mercouri and a woman I didn't recognise.

'That's Sofia Vembo, the singer,' Will said. 'Mercouri is in exile, but Sofia Vembo does what she can to oppose the regime.'

The café was about half full, but there was no sign of Costas. He had told us he would be there when he could get away from the hospital.

The girl brought us small glasses of ouzo on ice, 'From the house,' she said and we toasted her and each other, '*Stin y a mas.*'

In the course of the next half-hour or so, three separate groups of soldiers walked past the open door, peering in before going on. They weren't laughing or smiling.

Will said, 'They are everywhere!'

Chrissi looked up. 'Who? Where?'

I answered, '*Malakas.*'

Will looked around. 'This is what worries me. You two just aren't aware of threats. You have to watch out for it.'

I had just started to say, 'Evil is in the eye of—' when the door opened again and I felt a blush; Costas had arrived. He was alone.

He came straight to us saying, 'I'm sorry, so sorry, there was an emergency at the hospital and everyone was needed at once.' As he sat down he said, 'Glykeria will hopefully join us later.'

He barely glanced at the menu. 'I know this place well; I usually leave the choice to Vassili. Is that OK with you?'

The girl brought him an ouzo and smiled at him rather flirtatiously, I thought.

There was a loud crash and the place suddenly seemed full of soldiers with guns raised, though there were just four of them. We were all of us, everyone, having a quiet dinner and now, horribly, we were aware that we mustn't speak or move. The smell of fear mixed with sweat is a pungent reminder that guns contain bullets that can misfire or hit an innocent passer-by. I flicked my eyes around the other tables; no one was eating and not a sip of wine or water was taken. The sound of breathing, the odd gasp, cut through the eerie silence; the only proof of life here.

The music had stopped abruptly as they came through the door. The owner came out from the back kitchen wiping his hands on his apron. A thick-muscled man, bearded and swarthy. A match, I thought, for any troublemaker.

'What do you want?' he said.

'Show me the cover of the music you are playing.'

'Cover? I haven't got a cover. It was lost years ago. Why?'

'You know the law. Give me that disc.'

And the chef turned slowly and from behind the counter took the LP from the player and handed it over. They didn't even look at it. The one who took it raised his knee, pushed the record hard on it and snapped it in two. The others snatched the pictures from the wall and ripped them across; the pieces drifted to the floor.

Away to the right, someone shouted, a moment of protest and then tried to stifle it. Two of the soldiers had swung round, pointing at the elderly man who had dared to let himself be heard. One uniform nodded at the other and he went across to the man, bent down and said something in his ear that caused him to frantically empty his pockets on to the table; a packet of cigarettes, a silver lighter. He raised his hands; they trembled and he said something to his wife. She ransacked her handbag, finally producing some papers.

The old man snatched them up and waved them at the soldiers.

'Here you are; my papers, my identity card.'

Slowly, ponderously, the soldier read each word on each page.

You could hear every breath in this place. Costas looked at me and shook his head slightly. When the soldier got to the last page he brought it up to the tip of his nose and appeared to be sniffing it. He waved his colleague across and they both peered at the paper with squinty eyes.

Then aloud, 'Manodopoulou Manolis? Is that you?'

'Yes yes,' the man answered in a panicky whisper.

The soldier called something I couldn't understand to the man guarding the door and he shouted back.

He bent again to the old man and whispered something in his ear. The man looked to his wife and back to the soldier. Again the soldier spoke and this time the other soldier came across and roughly grasping him by the arm, pulled him to his feet and across to the door. He barely protested.

'Manoli, Manoli!' called his wife, running to the door after them. A chair clattered to the floor as she passed. Still no one moved. 'What's happening? He's done nothing. He's eighty years old, he fought in the war; he got medals.'

The soldiers laughed. 'Then he can show us how brave he is, can't he?' And they were gone as quickly as they had arrived.

The door swung on its hinges. It creaked, needed oil. We could see outside. The soldiers at first surrounded the old man. Voice out here shouted something, and then one last time it opened and we saw the street was empty. But inside the atmosphere was imprinted with their casual brutality.

His wife stood helpless. She looked around her and the chef hurried to her side.

'Where?' she started. 'Why?'

'His papers,' he said, 'they were in order?'

She looked bleakly back at him.

'We thought so. But nowadays . . . ?' She fumbled in her bag. 'The bill,' she said, 'I must—'

'No charge, no charge tonight. I'll get you a taxi. Go home now, wait for him there.'

'But what if . . . ?'

The chef shook his head.

'They won't bring him back here.'

He took her arm gently and led her outside. A few moments and he was back, alone. He looked around his restaurant. There was silence; no one spoke. He whispered something to the waitress and then, 'Ladies and gentlemen, friends; I apologise for the intrusion. I offer you all a *metaxa* on the house.'

Within no time music was heard again, a selection of undemanding melodies, and conversation gradually resumed.

'Why?' I said. 'What for?'

'Theodorakis,' said Costas. 'The music.'

'That's forbidden, isn't it?' Chrissi spoke.

The chef was beside us now.

'I know, I know,' he said. 'But sometimes, you can't let them take everything away from you: your freedom, your books, even your music. If they could see inside our heads they'd lock us up for our thoughts.'

'Who was the man, Vassili? Do you know him?' Costas asked.

He nodded. 'He was a trade union official, a senior one, years ago now. Of course they assume he is a communist. I am sorry you were here to see this.'

He turned away to visit other tables, explain to other diners.

Costas spoke first. 'You must try not to worry too much about this. You have witnessed an unpleasant incident. But that is what it is, an incident. I know of your experience, Will. But there is absolutely no reason why a student and a shop assistant going about their normal life should have any problems at all. I promise you.'

Before I could ask or even think of any questions he had broken off, jumped up and moved to the door, smiling, and the girl he had taken in his arms there looked across to us; this must be Glykeria.

She was tiny, and the soft, indistinct light in the doorway made her look roundish, and as she approached, smiling, it seemed she was made of ice cream; but that was just the play of light and shade. She was stunningly pretty with very dark curls mostly tied back, but leaving a few whispers framing her face. And the smile she gave us was so warm and welcoming, and the way that Costas kept his arm around her and the way he looked at her and the quick little twitch of a smile she sent to him told everyone in the room, probably everyone in the Plaka, and possibly everyone in Athens, that here were two people who were so completely in love with each other that not even a war or an earthquake could take them apart.

And I had to tell myself to smile as she took my hand and

said, 'Angeliki? You must be Angeliki. Costas described you to me so well and you are just as beautiful as he said.'

'Angel, I am called Angel,' I said in a thick, dull voice that even I could hear sounded like an ungracious pig.

'Then I shall call you Angel too.' She sat down beside me and said to Costas, 'Have you asked Vassili for some food? I am starving! I hope he's made *stifado* tonight?'

And Will said immediately, 'I like *stifado* too. Lucy, my girlfriend is a good cook and she makes it at home.'

'Does she put in lots of cinnamon?'

'Yes, and juniper.'

'Here Vassili puts in juniper as well. He says it's the secret of a good *stifado*.'

Of course, on top of being the prettiest girl anywhere and the most adored and adoring woman, she would of course be a good cook. Fancy someone who looks like that knowing what you put in a stew!

Chrissi looked across at me and I realised the stupid fixed wooden grin I had was still stuck there, so I forced the ends of my lips down and Chrissi gave a mocking grimace and crossed her eyes so I couldn't help but start to smile.

Costas, who was still gazing at Glykeria, said, 'What happened to the woman with the cervical problem?'

'Well, she survived in spite of everything and has the most wonderful baby girl.'

And they were off into a world of their own. A world of patients and clinics and operations and babies; a world they shared while the rest of us just watched and blinked. Thank God at that moment Vassili appeared with dishes of glorious-smelling food and the world opened up again to include us all. I hadn't thought, after the awfulness earlier, that I could eat a thing but we ate up everything; the meat and the juices and the dish of roast potatoes and the *vleeta* (which I'd always thought Aphrodite alone in the world grew in her *gypo*) and the salad and the beetroot and the *fava* and the *tsatsiki* and then the entire huge dish of green beans cooked in stock like the village women made it. It was all so delicious I had some of everything.

I was happy to see that Glykeria enjoyed it just like we did and dripped gravy down her chin, like me, and on to her white silk T-shirt and even on to the grey linen trousers that snaked over her perfect hips.

'Well, what did you expect?' Chrissi said to me later that night. 'A little team of fairies would come tripping in and feed her with silver spoons?'

And when we were all stuffed full Glykeria asked me about the school I had chosen. She had friends who had been there and they had liked it and done well. I couldn't help but notice that Will barely ate a morsel, just picked with his fork.

And then we were leaving and Costas insisted on paying for all of us and they went one way through the Plaka, their arms around each other, and we went the opposite, and Costas made me promise to call after the weekend and Glykeria said she had a day off and would take us to the airport to see Will off. She was really nice – damn!

We walked slowly home through the dusty streets, and the apartment felt alien in its emptiness. Tonight its austerity made it feel even more like an office, a posh waiting room.

Chrissi moved towards the kitchen.

'I'll make hot chocolate,' she said. 'That's what we need, comfort.'

But Will was suddenly angry.

'Now do you understand? Now do you see what it's like here? It's like living under a microscope. Nobody here is free to live their own lives any more.'

The kettle began to sing as it boiled and Chrissi ran to turn it off.

'Thousands are imprisoned, often tortured until they confess to whatever it is the soldiers want to hear. Why do you think Yorgo and Aphrodite never come to visit Aristos and Irini?'

There was no answer.

'Maybe it could have been them in that café tonight? Eh?

Why do you think Aphrodite rang three times yesterday? To check on Chrissi's underwear?'

Chrissi said, 'If they think it's so dangerous, why did they let us come?'

I sank back down into the vast squashed brown cushions of the horrible sofa.

'I guess because they know they can't keep us under lock and key. Not any more,' I said. 'And we know what it is like, Will. We live with it in the village too. Remember the curfews? Armed police to question Chrissi? But perhaps they think we are sensible enough not to do anything stupid? Why can't you trust us like they do?'

I was defeated, exhausted now, and he said, 'Because they don't really understand what it's like in this city. I do. I know what is going on here.'

After that we sat slumped and silent until Chrissi said, 'Hot chocolate', and she made some and we drank it down and went to bed.

Chrissi slept at once but I lay for ages trying to think about Costas without Glykeria, but that was impossible now, and anyway, gnawing away at the back of my mind, was that poor old man and his wife.

I can't let Will see any of my fears, I thought. He'd have us straight back to Panagia. Only another two days and he will go back to Lucy in London. I've never wished him away from me before, but while he is here I must pretend we're fine. And we are, aren't we? And we will be. Comforting myself with that thought I turned my pillow over to the cool side and slept.

But at two o'clock I woke suddenly. I lay there hot and stuffy in the dark city night. Through the open window a siren broke the air, a plane overhead droned past, and the steady throb of passing cars. All city noises – no birds, no cicadas, not a lone bullfrog. And inside I felt the first stirrings of an anger; the bitter juice of the world, my world, not at peace any more. The justice I had grown up with, gone. And why? Why were the streets full of soldiers? Why did we sit there, in silence and simply watch them terrify that old man? Costas too. Couldn't he, a doctor, have intervened?

Glykeria came in the evening to collect us all and drive us to the airport. She looked so beautiful and she was so kind and nice it was impossible to dislike her. And of course the moment we had waved Will goodbye and we were back in the apartment Chrissi and I both wept. We hugged and said we'd be fine. But I know we both felt suddenly alone. I searched in Hugh's horrible cocktail cabinet and found a bottle of Spanish sherry. A glass or two of that, a couple of cigs, as we sat on the floor of the little balcony overlooking the street, and we felt better.

Chrissi was still wearing her uniform. I thought she looked great in Soula's skirt and blouse – really sexy, but she ran in and pulled them off and came back in her knickers and bra.

She was full of stories about life in the big store; in the staff canteen they have two teaspoons to stir your coffee – on chains, imagine!

I envied her actually earning money, but she said we should share it; put it together with the allowance Hugh had arranged for me. We didn't have rent to pay, so we could afford to live pretty well if we wanted to.

'Lots for ciggies,' she said, 'and lots more for sherry.'

Even though the apartment was spacious we stuck together in the same bedroom and our late-night talks soon became one of the most important parts of our day. Chrissi was being romanced by a bloke in the furniture department.

'Haris in sheets,' she called him, and I promised to go and look him over.

I became more and more aware of soldiers everywhere; always carrying their guns, but Chrissi said apart from once or twice in the streets, she hadn't noticed them. There were always several in the few streets on my way to the gymnasio and if I looked at them curiously, as I had done once or twice early on, they met my gaze with frowns and I always put my head down and hurried straight past.

I think I liked the school. It was very different to The Oaks.

The gymnasio was a state school, so it was home to a mixture of all sorts. Here there were Orthodox, Muslims and in my group, one Roman Catholic. Some students were clearly much poorer than others, with threadbare clothes, worn down shoes. Several were chic and city slick. Like most, I stuck to my jeans – any age, any time, any place, classless.

Above all, there was a feeling of purpose. This was not a dumping ground for rich girls to be groomed for marriage. You could feel the teachers wanted to share knowledge and the students wanted to learn.

When I first arrived I was aware of being older than most of the students. Not a lot, but I worried at first it would make me an oddity. That drop-out time in the caves meant this was the price I must pay. But no one seemed to notice, so I quickly forgot it myself.

Some students were in partnerships, walking through the corridors entwined or sometimes passionately kissing in corners. I avoided closeness with anyone. I was a curiosity. I was English.

But mostly no one bothered me – they were too busy with work. And there was plenty of that. Within a week I realised that with luck and hard work I should be fine. The maths I understood and started getting top marks; Greek literature I had mostly learned at Heavenly's knee, and history I had always loved, wherever I was.

It was at school I learnt the full extent of the ruling Junta's powers of censorship. It wasn't just the musicians – Theodorakis, the Rolling Stones or the rock band Socrates and many, many others. It was also classical philosophers and writers like Nikos Kazantzakis, and a poet whose work Heavenly had admired, Kostis Palamos. Even Dionysios Solomos, the poet who had written the words of the Greek national anthem!

All were considered to be subversive and dangerous, no longer allowed to be taught. Their books were snatched from the libraries, along with Russian writers we took for granted like Dostoyevsky and Tolstoy, and the French writer, Emile Zola. If they really looked at the books in our house in Panagia they would burn the lot but I guess the ones Aphrodite called the *malakas* in the village weren't sufficiently well educated to spot them from a distance.

There was to be a concert one day, for all the junior musicians to show off their skills to adoring parents. We'd had this sort of thing at The Oaks – brain numbingly boring. But here, only one parent was allowed to come for each child. Special tickets were issued and had to be returned, signed.

'Why the restrictions?' I asked Fanis, a sort of friend.

He laughed. 'Can't let them all in – they might start a riot.'

'What? Your playing is that bad, is it?'

'Probably! But more likely they think there may be some parents who are considered dangerous now. My dad, for instance.' He lowered his voice. 'His father worked for Papandreou. He still thinks he's lucky every day he's not taken.'

'So?' I said, feeling stupid now. 'What do they think your dad will do if he comes to hear you play the lyre?'

He didn't answer, just looked around and turned the collar of his denim jacket over. Underneath there was a badge which had only one word on it, *ELEFTHERIA* – Freedom. The collar flipped down and it was gone.

One of the classes I liked best was art. It was taught by a young, attractive woman, Kyria Tropoulou, from Thessaloniki. I liked her because she always wore different coloured tights – yellow or scarlet – and she was tall, like me, and thin, with a beaky face and cropped dyed-blonde hair and bright shocking pink lipstick.

And as the days passed and turned into weeks, and then slowly into months, that feeling of anger that started with the old man in the café gradually grew stronger and stronger. I thought of him a lot; how was he? All those armed soldiers patrolling the streets like the Gestapo. Was that what they did? Searched out anyone who might have vaguely left-wing views and call them communists and throw them in prison? I thought about Heavenly too. No wonder she had stayed in Thailand, and feeling as she must have done, of course, she would want me out of the country; and sending me to school in England was the obvious answer. I had always blamed my father for that decision but of course it was her, as well, thinking of my safety.

I knew that groups of students were protesting, demonstrating, but I didn't know how to get involved or show support. As everything was secret, covered up, how could the word be spread? Public meetings were banned, and if there was the occasional one, it was broken up immediately. There was never anything in any newspaper or television or even on the radio.

Many students, like Fanis, wore freedom badges under collars, never to be seen in public. If I could see them so could any patrolling police or army.

On my eighteenth birthday, Chrissi and I went for a meal in a taverna near Omonia Square and talked about my mother. I missed her desperately that day. Glykeria rang to wish me a happy day; she said Costas was on duty, 'but sends his good wishes'.

Christmas came and went and the New Year stretched ahead, seemingly unchanging. Sundays we would walk or go for bus rides and there was a feeling of tension in the atmosphere. No one in the streets ever smiled, or caught your eye. Everyone rushed along, head down.

We often walked down Amalias Avenue towards Zappeion, passing Hadrian's Arch and the statue of Byron cradled by Hellas. I love that statue; I always want to cry when I see it. What would he think of what was happening here now? He would mourn, I'm sure, for the loss of that most Greek of all states, democracy.

At the National Gardens one day we bought a carnet of tickets from the tidy little piles weighted down with coins; then decided not to take a bus but walk through the Plaka and down Vironas Street, passing the sunken monument to Lysistrata. Slouching against her green painted railings, a couple of soldiers tossed their guns around in their fingers.

'Now she was a woman who would have fought back against this government, surely?' I whispered to Chrissi. 'And of course we are not allowed to read this or anything of Aristophanes' work. He's considered subversive.'

'Can't say that upsets me,' Chrissi said carelessly.

'It's the principle that matters.'

I was constantly angered by the sights and sounds of occupation; that's what it felt like. We were occupied by the army; only shockingly, it was the Greek army and not the Germans spitting on our liberty.

But that particular day there were fewer people everywhere and the wind was chill.

'Let's go home, please,' Chrissi begged.

Poor Chrissi; I constantly organised our lives to suit myself. I must be careful of her. I didn't want her disappearing again with another Simeon.

I'd been in the store and had a look at her Haris. He was as different from Simeon as it was possible to be. Small, square and round, he was stocky like a wrestler. His wide-apart deep brown eyes were full of humour, and when I mentioned Chrissi, his face lit up with an unreserved delight – he clearly adored her. I was happy for her, and I urged her to invite him to the apartment. But he never came.

One day as we were walking home through the fading light, she told me why. He lived with his mother, an invalid. Every day before and after working was devoted to her care. Greek men at the best of times worship Mother. All their love songs are about the sanctity of Mother, so this one had got poor Haris exactly where she felt he should be.

But it would hurt Chrissi too much to say that, so I said he was gorgeous and a marvellous man for his devotion. They met every day for coffee and shared their lunch together and I couldn't imagine them ever having more than that.

Late one Sunday afternoon Costas rang. He was finished for the day at the hospital and asked if he and Glykeria could call to see us.

Sometimes I managed to see Costas alone, but only on days

when I got some free time between classes, and then I hung around the hospital. I didn't tell Chrissi; it seemed so pathetic.

I had learnt his shifts and could often find him just to walk along the road with. That would have been enough, but twice he had suggested coffee and of course I said yes.

Soula hadn't been to clean for a couple of days, so we ran around the apartment hiding away knickers, socks, old jeans, T-shirts and sweaters; drawers were stuffed full and cupboards crammed.

It was as though they brought the sunshine inside with them; they radiated this wondrous aura – is that what love does? How would I know? Although they sat on opposite sides of the room their eyes constantly flickered to each other and it seemed their lips were smiling almost all the time.

They laughed at our offer of sherry and accepted some wine.

'Have you seen Angel's poster?' Chrissi asked.

I hadn't made it at school but I pinched some paper and bought crayons and coloured it here. It hung proudly over my bed.

'No, no!' I said.

My bed was unmade and we hadn't let Soula even change the sheets, but Chrissi laughed and led them to the door, opening it with a flourish saying, 'Ta Da!' and there it was, covering half of one wall; *ELEFTHERIA*. Scarlet on white, each letter outlined in black.

They were silent.

'What's wrong?' I asked. 'Surely you approve?'

'It's not that.'

They closed the door of the bedroom and sat down. There was a sudden chill in the room, in the air, inside me.

'What's the matter?' I said again.

'Angel, you know that this is a proscribed movement. Forbidden.'

'Yes, of course I know that – that's why it's there. There wouldn't be much point otherwise, would there?'

'Do you realise if this were to be seen, you would be in

253

trouble immediately? You could be arrested. Chrissi too, more than likely.'

'Oh thanks, Costas,' I said. 'Do you think I open my bedroom to any old passer-by?'

I felt sudden rage upon my rage, anger toppling over anger.

'What was it your friend Vassili said that night in the café? "They cannot control our thoughts?" Something like that? Well, my bedroom . . .' I swung round to face Chrissi. '. . . *our* bedroom, is only for our thoughts. Nobody else, nothing else, do you see? Do you understand that?'

'And Soula? Is she happy with that?' Costas asked.

I was deflated. I had assumed she was sympathetic but I didn't know.

Costas shook his head.

'Dearest Angel,' he said. 'Dear, dear girl, I – *we* – promised Will to take care of you. Of course you will not have visitors in your bedroom. We know that. But you must realise, if for any reason whatsoever they choose to go in there – and they could, any time, any day, any night, for whatever imagined reason they like, *demand* to go in – you would be in serious trouble immediately. And Chrissi and Soula too. Unless it was Soula that had informed them. Will was taken because of your parents' relationship with the Papandreous. They may well feel the same about you – if you give them cause.'

He stood and walked across the room to the window. Outside the fading light was luminous with the artificial glow of the street lamps.

Glykeria said, 'Chrissi, you told us how your posters of – James Dean, was it? Mick Jagger? – were taken in the village. You must know it is ten times, twenty times, worse here in Athens.'

Costas turned.

'Your father is well connected. You told us how he got your brother freed from the EAT/ESA, the army special interrogation centre?'

'I know. I know.'

And I walked into our room and, jumping on my bed, I tore the poster down and ripped it across again and again and the pieces fell and flew around the room landing here and there and everywhere.

We all sat in silence; the sounds of the Sunday streets drifted in through the shimmering curtain; laughter, a happiness of sorts, I suppose. And then over everything, the ubiquitous police siren telling us of another disturbance, another arrest. My first thought was no longer of an accident, a fire, or harmless drunks.

Costas said, 'Oh Angel, what can I say to you? I don't mean to anger you, upset you. Believe me, I know the worst feeling is the helplessness. You think I just sat there in Vassili's café and didn't open my mouth because I didn't care? Eh? Is that what you thought? Let them terrify that old man, the Union official, not my business to interfere? Is that what you thought? Tell me!'

I couldn't answer, just shook my head.

Glykeria looked at him, frowning, a question in her eyes. He hadn't told her.

He was pacing up and down in his own angry world.

'I've seen that happen again and again and I know that anyone who tries to stop them is in trouble themselves. I've seen them brought into the hospital, battered, beaten up, as good as dead. My job is to try the best I can to mend them. I can't do that if I'm lying there beaten up myself, can I?'

He didn't need an answer to his question but I shook my head anyway.

'You girls thought you knew all about it in your village, didn't you? The petty rules, the inspections, all that. Well, we have lived with the military in charge of our streets, our schools, our libraries, our lives, for *years* now and believe me, it destroys us that we can do nothing.'

This anger that shot out from him like sparks from a burning fire . . . I had never seen this before.

Glykeria stroked his arm, tried to persuade him to sit down, saying quietly, 'Costas, it's OK, Costas, we all know.'

He spun round to face her. 'No, it's not OK. We *don't* all know. Most of the world doesn't know, doesn't want to know – isn't allowed to know.'

He sank back down now on to the sofa. He had the air of a desperate man.

I know he was mourning, as I was, the lost Greece of our childhood. The Greece that had taught the world about peace and love and, above all, freedom; the Greece Heavenly had struggled for through one devastating war. And as if he read my mind, Costas said, 'I do believe that the Greece my godfather fought for will be ours again one day, but for now I can't see how.'

'And, until then?'

'Until then, we will think our thoughts and dream our dreams and no one can take those away from us.'

'But we can't put posters on the wall to advertise our dreams?'

He shook his head slowly.

'We must keep our thoughts to ourselves just for now. And I pray it is only just for now.' He paused, looked across to me and smiled. 'It's young people like you, Angel, who care so passionately that will bring about change, I'm sure of it.'

I suppose that was a little sop to my ambitions but it didn't satisfy for long. I wanted change; I was full of ideas, plans these days, big plans to change everything. But when it came to bringing these dreams to life, they narrowed down to such small things as reading Tolstoy under the sheets at night with a torch so as not to wake Chrissi.

I went to a mosque to see how the Muslims worshipped and a Roman Catholic church on a Sunday morning during mass. I was restless and dissatisfied with everything around me.

And then it was Easter and Glykeria had told us she and Costas were going to his village for the celebrations. Will rang and told me he and Lucy were going to open the Orfanou- dakis house in Panagia and that was enough for me. I said to Chrissi, 'Let's do that. Let's go home to Panagia. Will and

Lucy will be there and Aphrodite and Yorgo will be happy to see you.'

So that's what we did.

On the Saturday before Easter we went shopping and bought ourselves new dresses and shoes. Chrissi laughed as I bought a black skirt, short, and some black tights.

'I wear that all week,' she said. 'You could have borrowed mine.'

I didn't tell her that it was an exact copy of a skirt that Glykeria wore; and she wore it with black tights. I bought a T-shirt with a red poppy design on the front; again, a replica of one Glykeria had told me Costas had bought her. I had seen her in it many times.

Chrissi picked out a short dress herself, in grey cotton with stripes. She looked good.

We bought shoes; Chrissi's had stiletto heels which made her legs look slimmer. I bought flat pumps, like ballet slippers. My big feet can't fit into any shoes that Athenian girls would wear. For a moment I thought of Glykeria with her tiny feet, and felt, as usual, a pang of envy. Any man would fall in love with her.

We went to the best chocolate shop and bought a box of almond truffles for Aphrodite.

'What a waste of good money,' she said. 'That's what my mama will say, I bet you.'

I could only think how good it was to be going to see Will and Lucy and my beloved home again.

APHRODITE

People had been coming and going to the church all evening. The paths and squares were crowded. Everyone came home to their village from all over for the special Easter services and processions. It is a time for families to be together.

Chrissi was home and that made me happy; but thin, she was a whisper of herself, I thought. I've seen more meat on a butcher's apron.

And Angel? As skinny as six o'clock. What food do they eat in Athens? Nothing fresh-grown, for sure. Once I asked my smart lawyer daughter-in-law if they had a *gypo* and she laughed.

'Perhaps they could grow vegetables on the Parthenon hill, do you think?'

People here say that before Easter, during the Lenten fast, city people drink only vinegar water and eat spiders' webs.

'Did you obey the holy Lenten diet?'

'Of course,' said Chrissi.

'Sometimes,' said Angel.

'Just be pleased she is here,' Yorgo said. 'She will feast with us and you can stop worrying for her.'

She had bought us a big box of chocolates from some fancy shop. Even the letters on the box were gold.

'A waste of good money,' I said; but secretly I was pleased she had thought to bring us such a gift and brought it out when anyone called to visit; and being Easter that was often. I will cook the Easter lamb, of course, and have asked Will and Lucy and Angel to join us for it on Sunday. Chrissi took Yorgo and Manoli to the Orfanoudakis house on Friday evening, but of course I went to the church with most of the village women – those still young enough to see and walk.

I had been sewing the orange blossom into garlands all week. There was no sign of Titi and the warty one and I was glad I did not have to pretend to give them my Easter blessings. It seems no time ago that I would welcome her with only a little reluctance and she made the yellow dress for Chrissi. That came back a rag from those caves; I noticed that.

At the last minute Chrissi came up to the church and found me in the crowd.

'I decided I'd like to walk with you, Mama,' she said.

'Please yourself,' I said, but inside I was happy, and as we walked slowly through the village, I wanted to point her out to everyone, 'This is my daughter, she works in the biggest department store in Athens. See how smart she is in her city dress and shoes.'

'I could let the hem down for you, then that dress might be decent to wear,' I said, but of course she laughed.

'What about my shoes, Mama, do you like them? Shall I get you a pair and send them to you?'

'Huh. I'd fall over if I had to totter around in things like that.'

She is full of laughter these days, my daughter. I suppose city life must suit her.

After the service we slowly all began the walk through the village streets. Not in twos or even threes, but whole families together. In our midst Papa Diamedes and the elders of the church carried on high the flower-decked bier of Christ and the Panagia. From every garden in the village the flowers had been picked and piled high and wide. As the line wound through the little streets, we stopped at each house, which was then blessed by the priest and flowers were strewn in its doorway. From the back of the cortège the sound of a gentle melody drifted over everyone; some of the village children were playing lyres and recorders. It was sweet music indeed on this night before Easter.

Later we went and sat with Will, Lucy and Angel on their terrace. Will poured us all some local wine and Lucy had made *kalitsounia Pasqua*. I had taught her my recipe for these sweet cakes and she had made them well.

I was glad to sit for a while. The pain inside me still causes me gripes and I try not to let it show on my face. I breathe slow and steady as the doctor showed me. Only Yorgo looked at me, a question in his eyes.

This countryside has seen many battles, big and small; many lives, many deaths and seems to resist the changes and survives. Tonight I know in the moment's silence we all thought of Heavenly, and as we sat there in some sadness, the telephone shrieked through the air. It was Hugh, wishing us all *Kalo Pascha*.

Both Will and Angel spoke to him in that strange foreign place where he lives now and when they came back on to the terrace, both of them were wiping tears from their eyes.

On Easter Saturday there was great excitement in the air; you could almost touch it.

Such a day this was. It celebrated the resurrection of Jesus. All day people had been coming and going; there was laughter and music. Yorgo had prepared the thorn bush, which he burnt outside our door, bringing us good luck for all the year. And at half past eleven, after Lucy had cooked us all dinner of pork meat in wine with coriander seeds, we all walked up the hill to the church where we heard the cantor intoning the words of the service. We squeezed in through the door; it seemed the whole village was there. We were each given a candle, even the children. The words are special – a recital of love and hope. As midnight approached, the lights in the church dimmed and slowly went out. Papa Diamedes's candle was the only illumination in the darkness.

Then, one by one, his light lit the wicks of all the other candles. From mother to child, father to son, neighbour to friend, the flame was passed on until the interior of the church was a blaze of glory.

We all turned and slowly moved through the doorway to the courtyard and each of us lit the candles of the others in the crowd waiting outside.

I stood next to Will and Lucy and as each torch was lit '*Theos essai apporeios*' was said by the one lighting the torch and '*Enai elektrina*' by the person receiving the light.

And Will explained to Lucy: 'Christ is risen', and the response, 'He is truly'.

Within moments no one was without a flickering light and the sky seemed to glow.

Toula's Michaelis was on top of a sort of scaffold. His face shining, he set fire to the first rocket. It leapt into the sky and the crackling flames of the bonfire began to splutter as they caught and spread through the huge pyre of dry branches.

Everyone was smiling and happy and there were kisses and hugs all round.

Rockets, wheels and golden showers caused everyone to whoop with excitement as the life-sized effigy of Judas Iscariot began to burn on top of the bonfire.

It was late before we slept that night, gone three o'clock. I did not rest easily – meat cooked in wine eaten late does not agree with me.

I was awake before six. A far-off dog was barking and a solitary firework lit the sky for a moment. From the Piperia all was quiet and somewhere a baby was crying. A last shooting star flashed across the lightening sky.

I turned in my bed for a final moment or two and then I found the sheets on that side were cool to the touch; the pillow plump and smooth. Where was my husband? He had gone with Toula's Michaelis late to the Piperia last night.

They were to play a game of *prefa* and then collect one of Michaelis's lambs, already slaughtered, for our feast. So why had he not come home?

I went down and opened the outer door and saw that he had built the *souvla*, the special mounted grill for roasting the lamb on the spit. But no Yorgo, no lamb and without the lamb I cannot make the special feast day *kokoretsi* and this is every Greek's special treat for Easter: the tripe and intestines rolled tight in the lining of the stomach and cooked with the lamb.

And then I saw him stumbling along from the end of the garden, bent almost double under the weight of the carcass he carried. I ran down to him.

'Where were you all night?'

Groaning, he straightened up. 'It took time to kill this animal. Then I had to sit and have a little rest, of course, didn't I?'

'And a little raki, I suppose?'

'Well, just a little. But you know Toula's Michaelis's raki is very good, but very strong, so it went to my head, I think.'

'And you passed out and couldn't get home?' I answered for him. 'Always the same old story. Give me that lamb. I thought Michaelis and Toula were to skin it, prepare it? The sun is already getting high and nothing is done.'

I took the lamb from him and together we tied it on to the hanging straight.

'I will do it myself,' I said, getting the skinning knife.

'Here, let me . . .' His was the feeblest voice I have ever heard.

Manoli appeared from his bed a moment or two later and, taking the knife from me, slit down the belly as I held the creature steady. I grabbed the slippery intestines as they started to fall. My hands were full and, clutching the liver, lights and all, I went into my house to start on the day's work. I cursed my husband's easiness with his friends; his inability to think for himself, or to say no.

Manoli pulled me outside later as he and Yorgo were starting the fire under the spit. We had collected kindling wood for weeks past to be ready for this day; it was dry and ready and as Yorgo struck the match it roared into life.

Sparks flew into the air and the sweet scent of olive, pine and branches of dry sage, rosemary and thyme filled the air. I may despair of Yorgo sometimes, but every year at Easter it is from his workshop that we have the sweetest wood in the village. We survive the Lenten fast with the thought of this coming meal to sustain us.

Will, Lucy and Angel came later, bringing some good wine from Hugh's stocks, and the feasting and celebrations began. Neighbours and friends came by to wish us well, and shouts of 'Xronia Polla' filled the air. Happy returns of this special day.

It was as Yorgo started to cut slices of the soft fragrant meat from the roasting beast that the *malaka* arrived.

Just the one I thought at first, Stelios, the village president. My husband, of course, called a greeting to him and said, 'Come and join us!'

I turned, furious, to stop him. Why Stelios is here is more important than a greeting of welcome and then I saw, we all saw, that he had not entered over the threshold, but stood in the doorway. And beside him was a policeman from Stavrochori, in his uniform too. Their faces bore only ill will: nothing of celebration there. This was not a happy visit.

'Whose animal is this?' asked Stelios, his weaselly face full of misery.

'What do you mean?' I stepped forward. 'It is ours, of course. Paid for with good money.'

'And exactly where did it come from?'

'From Toula's Michaelis, the shepherd.'

'Show us the pelt.'

I crossed myself furiously three times. 'Why do you want to see this? What is wrong that you come and disturb a peaceful family on this day?'

Behind me Yorgo had stopped carving, his long knife poised in mid-air, bewilderment on his face.

The two of them still stood in the doorway and behind them the sun tried to break through and send some rays to warm this frosty, mean atmosphere that had come in with them.

'Papa Diamedes is already in the police station. He needs to answer some questions, also.'

'You have arrested the priest?' The words almost froze my lips.

President Stelios stepped forward. 'We will take for questioning anyone who handles stolen goods, Kyria Babyottis.'

'Stolen goods? What is this, stolen goods?'

'I repeat,' said the weasel. 'Show us the pelt of this animal here – the hide, the fleece. Do you understand what I am saying?'

'Yorgo, show them what they ask for.'

Will, Lucy and Angel had been sitting quietly watching with curiosity this nonsense. Now Will stood up. He is an impressive figure and I saw these men could only look up to him with some respect. At least that's what I thought at first. They shuffled from foot to foot, unable to meet his eyes.

Yorgo had come back inside with the fleece of our lamb over his shoulder.

Will said, 'The simplest way to get this over quickly is to give them what they want.' And he took the pelt from Yorgo and handed it to the policeman, a small rather rat-faced man. I knew his cousin once; I went to a dance with her one time in Stavrachori town hall. She left with the lyre player without me and I had to walk home alone across the mountain. I remember that family.

As the policeman held the greasy fur I could see it still dripped with animal secretions and globules of white fat glistened on the underside. The policeman – Vassili was his name, I remembered – swung the skin over and peered at the wool. His thick fingers pulled and tweaked and paddled in it, then he held it high, a look of triumph on his face.

'Here, look right here.' And Yorgo stepped close and tried to peer between them, a look of fear on his face.

'Aphrodite,' he said, 'help me here. What have they found? What is wrong?'

I could see that there was some bright blue dye on a small piece of the hide.

'Can you please explain to this family what all this is about?' Will spoke; his voice strong and clear. I knew as I opened *my* mouth, nothing good would come out, so I shut it again firmly.

'Yorgo Babyottis, please come with us. There are questions we need to ask you about this animal.'

Yorgo's eyes flickered wildly from side to side; the sweat on his brow ran in tiny rivulets down his dear face. For a moment, more, I wanted to hold him close to me. No man should be so humiliated in front of his family and friends.

'Why? What? Questions? What questions,' I started to ask.

Will stepped forward now. 'I will come with you, Yorgo. You won't be alone. I am sure there is a mistake in all this and we shall find out what's going on.' He turned, his arm around Yorgo's shoulders. 'I presume you have no problem with that?'

And I saw that the expressions on their faces showed they had many problems with that, but I knew they had no way to stop Will. I breathed deeply.

'Thank you, Will. If you would. I believe you both will be home almost as soon as you have left.'

Yorgo still looked frightened. I got his good jacket.

'Wash your hands, quick,' I whispered. 'You will get grease on your sleeves.' And even softer, I said, 'Stand up, walk tall. You have nothing to fear.'

But as they left, with a last lingering glance from Yorgo, I crossed myself and sent up a quick prayer to the Panagia. If they chose, these people could keep Yorgo in a cell in the police station for as long as they wanted.

And what were the blue marks on the sheepskin, and what has Toula's Michaelis been doing to get us all in trouble?

ANGEL

Yorgo Babyottis was gone for three days and three nights and Chrissi never left her mother's side. I rang the department store and told them she had been taken ill and would be away for a few days. Well, it was a sort of truth. After that horrible day we were all sick. Sick with worry.

It seemed that Toula's Michaelis had been slaughtering lambs, six of them altogether, without something called 'a proper licence'. No one seemed to know what that was. Toula swore he had been selling his lambs for the Easter feast for years.

'In past years they mostly went to Aghios Demetrious,' she told Aphrodite. 'We never had trouble from there.'

Aphrodite took this as a slight on families from Panagia.

'We never bought one of his lambs before. No matter where they are supposed to come from or what licence he had.' She paused, crossed herself three times and said, 'And I don't think we will buy any of them in future.'

She was full of apologies to Lucy and me and almost on her knees with gratitude to Will. My dear brother had stayed with Yorgo in the police station over in Stavrachori for the whole of Easter Sunday and had gone over there again when we were told he could bring Yorgo home. There were to be no charges, apparently. Will said it was a trumped-up excuse and how odd that it was only Yorgo, Papa Diamedes, and two of their friends, who had been known supporters of the left for many years who had been taken and questioned. Aphrodite's scorn when she heard this was something to see. She marched up and down in her living room, raging against the colonels of the right wing who 'have our country in their grip like the claws of mad wild animals'. She said it again and again.

I had a few more days of the Easter vacation left before classes started so I stayed in Panagia too. I tried and failed to persuade Chrissi to travel with me over the mountain and find Costas's village.

'I can't go anywhere; I am here for Mama,' she said.

Of course she was right and I felt instantly mean for trying to persuade her to leave.

'We don't even know when he was going back to Athens,' she said.

'I know. But we could meet his mother, his family. I could ask them about Heavenly. I'd love to know more of what she did in the war, if they knew her.'

I could see her wavering, but at that moment Aphrodite came back into the house from her *gypo* and she was in tears as she told us how Titi had abused her as she was pulling leeks and artichokes and wanted to go on and on about the lamb.

'Why should I have to defend myself, my Yorgo, from women like her?' she asked, dabbing her eyes. It was so unlike Aphrodite to cry in front of anyone. In fact, I had never seen her do this before.

Chrissi said, 'Do you think, Mama, it could have been Titi who reported Toula's Michaelis to the police?'

You could have heard a dead man breathe as Aphrodite thought about this. It was an age before she spoke. 'Her and that ratty, warty-faced one I should think, of course.'

That set her off for ages running through the women in the village and deciding who would side with whom.

'It is bickering like this that brought the colonels into power in the first place,' I said to Chrissi when we finally left.

Will drove us to Heraklion, although we offered to hitchhike. He and Lucy were staying a further week and then he would go home and start to prepare a film about the Hasidic

268

Jewish community in Stamford Hill in London. Lucy was delighted.

'He'll come home every night,' she said, 'just like a normal man.'

In Athens nothing had changed in our absence. The soldiers and the police seemed to be everywhere. We saw a man arrested at the airport. He was led away, clutching his documents in his hand, protesting his innocence. Around him everyone hurried and scurried past, heads lowered. I nudged Chrissi.

'They've almost got signs on their heads, saying *NOT ME, NOT ME.*'

Soon after we got back I had coffee with Costas. Because I knew his shifts, if I could escape the gymnasio at the right time and hang around near his hospital, I didn't find it hard to appear to be walking by, and more times than not he would suggest we stop by a coffee bar in the next street. We spoke of Easter and he told me his father has difficulties with Glykeria.

'He insists she comes from a family richer than ours. The truth is that they are city people. They don't earn their living on the land or the sea. And that's all he really understands.'

'Did your godfather like her?'

'He never got to meet her. That's my great sadness. I know he would have loved her. Everyone does.'

And it was true. I really liked and admired her. I just wish she'd chosen another bloke.

Back at school I tried to lose myself in work. We were coming up to exams, important ones, and I so wanted to do well to show Costas I could do it. And my father, of course, and Will.

But at the bottom of it all, not to be denied, were my continuing feelings for Costas. I could think or do nothing that would hurt Glykeria, but I yearned every day for a sight of him. I trembled in his presence and would do anything just to be near him. My nerves were tight; blood rushed to my cheeks at the slightest provocation. Everything he did was of the first importance, and when I learned he was to take part in a swimming competition at the hospital, for charity, I had to go, see him among his friends. Just to watch him. I felt embarrassed and guilty, but I went. And I found a seat right at the back, to one side, to see but not be seen. There was that curious hollow echo you get only in swimming pools and the light through the high windows was green with the reflection of water as it met the sun.

Glykeria was on duty that Saturday afternoon so I knew she wouldn't be there. And Chrissi's Haris had arranged for his aunt to visit his mother so he could escape for a couple of hours and they were going to the cinema.

Costas looked just as he had done when we were together on the beach. His swimming shorts were tight and his body was still tanned from the Cretan sun.

That beautiful body, his speed and strength excited me. He seemed to dwarf his opponents, and when he won, as it seemed to me inevitable, he laughed and smiled with his friends as he towelled his hair. I longed to jump up and cheer, but everyone around merely clapped politely, so I shrank down in my seat and left with everyone else with my head down and my mother's old sunglasses my disguise.

Fanis had a cousin at the Law School, Pavlos. I'd met him once or twice for coffee. He had a tattoo on the back of his arm done by a friend. It said, *Eleftheria H Thanatos*. Freedom or Death. Oh how I envied him this tattoo! My angel seemed trivial beside it. I showed it to him and he seemed impressed, but I think that was only because girls mostly don't get tattoos.

Everyone knew by now that the law school was where the students had been protesting the loudest, and a couple of times the students from there and other colleges had gathered on the roof and occupied it for days. All students had lost the right to elect their own committees and then a law was rushed through which denied them the right to postpone National Service. We had all been watching on the television news a protest of students in Thailand, which had forced a change of regime. It could be done!

Pavlos, Fanis and I planned to get up on to the roof of the Law School on the day we heard there was to be a major demonstration there.

I didn't tell Chrissi, she might just have got all sensible and tried to stop me. And to be fair, she also had big worries of her own.

She had seemed troubled for days, just not her usual happy self. I had been taken up with revising for a maths exam – and guiltily I realised I had hoped her problem would go away, whatever it was. But that night I was packing up my books when she came in and sat down. She was so clearly troubled I couldn't ignore it.

'Last ciggie before bed?'

She nodded. I lit two and passed her one.

'Want to tell me?'

There was a long silence while I puffed away and she sat holding hers as though it were an alien object.

'Shall I just guess what's wrong?'

She shook her head and at last looked up, met my eyes and said, 'I'm in real trouble at work.'

Work? Well it could be worse.

'Why, Chrissi, what's happened? Been caught pinching a bit of lace edging for your underwear?'

And that sent her into a flood of tears. I went round the table and hugged her tightly.

'Dear friend, tell me what's happened,' I said, really concerned now.

And out it came. It seemed she had got so hopelessly confused trying to work out all the sums, such as: 'How much for three-quarters of a metre of seventeen centimetres wide edging ribbon' that for ages she had just been making up the prices each time she sold some.

'I never overcharged anyone,' she said, 'I promise.'

'Of course you didn't, but what happened?'

'You know the senior man? Hector?'

271

'Is that the one with tight trousers and a comb-over?'

She nodded. 'He'd been watching me, and noticed that apparently, while I had the most customers each day, I cashed up less than anyone else. So he got Kyrios Salamos, the haberdashery buyer, to come on the counter and observe me.'

'Sneaky!'

And she started crying again. I hugged her tighter. 'And now I've to go to the personnel department on Monday morning. I know I'll get sacked and then I'll never get another job in Athens and I'll have to go back to Panagia and everyone will know I'm disgraced and . . . and . . .'

'Stop! It might not be that bad. Have you told Haris?'

She nodded again, blowing her nose hard.

'He laughed. Well, only at first, then he said he'd come with me, and they'd have to sack him as well.'

'That's true love, Chrissi,' I said. And I felt a sudden sharp pang of envy.

The next day the streets were full of protesters and the air was ablaze with the sounds of sirens. A helicopter circled the city all day and most of the night. I skipped the last class and went straight to the law school. I had to push and shove to get through; it seemed half of Athens was there. I met Pavlos in a café and as we walked through the streets near the college there were crowds of people with banners saying, BREAD EDUCATION FREEDOM, and, NATO – GET OUT OF GREECE. There were songs, cheers and great waves of clamour and fury. Pavlos told me that many of the students had stayed there all night. There had been a big demonstration outside the Ministry of Public Order and stories were coming through that hundreds had been arrested and many wounded and injured. Everyone else came to the Law School and as many as could get up there brought their banners and singing with them.

As we got near the Law School it was impossible to ignore the chanting, shouting and singing that was coming from the roof. When I looked up I saw that ELEFTHERIA H THANATOS was painted all around the edge in huge white letters. How amazing! How brave! That was where I wanted to be.

It was cold on the roof, but I didn't care; I was alive with a fire inside – I was actually part of it now! The wind whipped through chimney stacks and whined around the TV aerials. The city below us was a constant moving hybrid of noise and space, everything in black and white, zigzagging around streets and squares. There was Omonia square with dots and dashes of people rushing here and there; cars and bicycles, trucks and vans all jumbled in a giant traffic circus. Eleftheria was the word on everyone's lips up here and down there: Freedom!

'Can I have one of those?' I asked a girl who seemed to have several of the badges Fanis wore under his collar.

'Sure,' she said and she gave me two.

There were lots of us up there on the roof; I couldn't count how many, but we were crammed in shoulder to shoulder. There was constant movement as students came and went. A new banner was carried up, huge, saying, *USA – GET OUT*. The Americans wanted bases in Greece – the easier to attack Russia, just as Costas said.

If I stood on the side of the roof, Pavlos told me, I could see the bus station below. I squeezed through.

'Look, look there,' he said and he pointed downwards. 'See the commuters?'

And I looked and I saw. People: men, women, old and young, crippled and active, even children, all waving up to us and cheering voices shouting, 'Yes! Yes! Yes!' and '*Efharisto!*'

They were thanking us for taking a stand on their behalf.

The strength of feeling, support, that came up was overwhelming. This was the first time I was aware that it wasn't just angry students who felt so strongly.

Pavlos said the city was like a bonfire waiting for a match and it would explode. When I told him about the old couple in the café in the Plaka he said every family had at least one relative missing, 'usually more'.

It was exhilarating and I joined in the songs and found myself at one point holding up a sheet painted with the words,

FASCISM WILL PERISH. I saw that the other end was held by my art teacher, Kyria Tropoulou, with her orange tights. She grinned at me now.

'Surprised?' she asked, and I shook my head.

'No, pleased,' I replied.

Then there was an increase in the sound everyone here knew so well and hated; police sirens wailing through the night, coming closer and closer.

From the edge we saw what seemed like hundreds of armed police, a great tide of them surrounding this building. I didn't feel the least bit afraid, just excited. But Pavlos pushed his way through to me, grabbed my hand and led me to the fire door, saying, 'You are no good to anyone in prison.'

We got through and down the iron stairs in a great crush of people with the same idea. It would have been impossible to do anything except go with them and try and keep my feet on the steps and my hand in Pavlos's.

I remember calling to him, as we came out into the street, 'good night for burglars eh?' before he was swept off in one direction and me in the other. It was chaos out there, a living mass of heaving bodies, police vehicles, vans and cars and fire engines and ambulances.

To my horror, in front of me a policeman raised his baton and brought it down viciously on the shoulders of a woman who staggered and fell. I saw it was my art teacher; if it had hit her head, I thought, she would be dead. I tried to reach down to help her, but it was impossible; I was being pressed along and I had no choices.

Eventually I was pushed so far that I was at the edge of the crowd, and by stepping to one side and shoving with my elbows I broke free. I had never seen so many uniformed police in one place and they were laying about them with metal bars, batons and truncheons. Anyone who was near was in danger, serious danger. I was struggling to catch my breath when a man with a microphone appeared beside me. He spoke rapidly in Greek but his accent gave him away – he was English.

I pulled on his sleeve. 'Are you a journalist?'

'Yes,' he said, surprised. 'BBC. London. Have you been in there?' and he was pointing up to the roof of the Law School. 'Very dangerous. Yes?'

'The only danger is here and now,' I said, 'from the police. Have you seen what they are doing?'

'I was told anarchists are in charge up there.'

We were being pushed to one side by the great crowd trying to leave the building. I managed to say, 'I have seen only students and teachers.'

'You're English?' he asked, and before I could do more than nod, he held the microphone in front of my face and said, 'Tell me who you are, what you are doing here and what you have seen.'

I only had time to say, 'My name doesn't matter. I live here, and this was a peaceful demonstration about student rights. They are being grabbed away from us by the regime. They say anyone with an opinion is an anarchist and anyone slightly to the left of centre is a communist. You must tell people that. It's really important. You must make people in England know the truth.'

And then I was aware that if I didn't move away I was at risk of fresh abuse from four or five policemen pouring out of a newly arrived car. I dodged through a rain of sticks and batons and running like hell I was out of there at last.

It was two in the morning before I got home. Everywhere, it seemed, the city was rising against the bloody colonels. Chrissi was waiting for me, and she hugged me as I walked in, cold, hungry and very, very tired.

And more determined than ever to continue to fight.

APHRODITE

Lucy has rung twice now. She saw Angel on the television news programme.

'And Chrissi?'

'Just Angel.'

So that means she is in trouble, I suppose. Again. I sent Yorgo to the Piperia to watch the news programmes but he only found football games, of course.

Then Will rang; said he had spoken to someone in Athens, some friend who says the city is boiling with rage. I rang Aristos at once but he had little to say as usual. He laughed when I asked if he saw this television.

'If you think I have time to watch TV, think again,' he said. 'The hospitals have cancelled all leave; there are riots all over the city. Must go.'

And the telephone clicked once and died. Silence. I rang again, but he didn't answer, just some machine talking.

I know they have seen Chrissi twice since the girls have been there. Just for dinner, nothing else. Why don't families live like they used to? Close together. Nowadays they are all over the world, it seems to me. Doing nothing to protect and care for each other.

As for me, I had to tell Yorgo about the doctor eventually. I'd finished his medicine (for all the good it did me) so I went back to the doctor from Sitia. He poked and prodded more and asked a lot of questions about private things, periods and all that.

'Periods? They stopped years ago,' I said.

'And yet you still lose some blood?'

'Sometimes. A little.'

'Intercourse? Does that cause you pain?'

I had never spoken of such things before and this doctor was a man! Why did he want to know this?

He smiled. 'If there is pain, then it is possible there is an obstruction of some kind; a polyp perhaps.'

I don't know what that is. I didn't like the sound of it and wasn't going to ask. I didn't think he should smile while asking me these things.

I was just beginning to wish I hadn't come, when he said, 'I would like you to see a specialist, a surgeon. In Athens.'

'And if I don't?'

'Then I would think you are a foolish woman and I know you are not, Kyria Babyottis.'

He said I should talk it over with Yorgo and come to see him again the following week. He said maybe Yorgo would come with me next time. No! Bad enough to discuss my body with a man, without having Yorgo listening to all these things as well.

So I told Yorgo. Not the part about him coming too, but all the rest of it. At first he said nothing. We had finished our meal and Manoli had gone back to the workshop to put another layer of veneer on a chair he is making. It is a beautiful thing, this chair, made of olive wood with a pattern of leaves across the back. He is making it for his own pleasure – no one has asked for it. Which means no one will pay for it.

'Then we must go to Athens,' Yorgo said at once.

He didn't laugh and make jokes; to my surprise he came around the table and put his arms about me. He squeezed me quite hard and said, 'You are the world to me, Aphrodite. I will do anything to make you well. I hate seeing you in pain, so of course we must go.'

I brushed him away, just gently, mind, and saw he had a tear or two in his eyes. It was November. It would be cold in the city. It was even cold some days here, now, so we must pack warm clothes. More than that: we must take good clothes. We couldn't disgrace our family by looking like a couple of Cretan peasants. Even if that is exactly what we are. So it had to be suits for Yorgo and Manoli and a new dress for me or perhaps a skirt and jacket. Serviceable material, of course; then it can come in to be useful if we have the need. You never know.

ANGEL

He was waiting for me when I came out of school. He had never done that before.

I pushed Fanis aside calling 'See you later' and ran down to where he stood. He looked very tired, with exhausted lines around his eyes, but he was there.

The collar of his grey overcoat was turned up and his hands were deep in his pockets. For the first time I saw there were some grey hairs in the crinkly black: not grey, silver. I wanted to touch them.

'Your friend is saying something,' he said.

I turned, impatient, and Fanis said, 'Don't forget the meeting.'

I waved him off.

'Do you have time for a coffee?'

For you, Constantinos, I have all the time in the world, I thought, but I said, 'Oh, I think so.'

And putting my hand inside his in his pocket I walked us down the road, away from Fanis and away from school.

'What meeting?' he asked.

I pushed open the door of the café and a rush of steamy heat came out.

'Is this OK?'

'It's fine. What meeting, Angel?'

'The owner's wife is Italian and she makes really good espresso. Or cappuccino if you . . . look, here's a table,' I said and I pulled him to sit down.

'Angel, I am asking you; what meeting?'

Liliana came over, so I couldn't answer. She is a big voluptuous mama of a woman; her hair dyed that burgundy wine colour beloved of ladies of a certain age. Five children and a happy husband. She wiped a cloth over the already clean table.

'You see the crowds?' she asked.

'Yes! Thousands of people all over the centre of the city.'

'You know why today? I don' know why today. What's today?'

I was about to speak but Costas said, 'It's the anniversary of Papandreou's funeral.'

'Is he important man? I don' know who he is.'

'He was the last democratically elected Prime Minister,' I said. 'Double espresso for me, Liliana, please.'

Costas ordered a cappuccino and she went to the counter to make them.

'I'm sure you could give her a rundown of all the ministers of the Junta, if you wanted to, Angel. Do the crowds today have anything to do with your meeting?'

'I guess so.'

'Do you know what you are getting yourself into?'

'It's just a chance to *do* something, that's all. Surely that's better than doing nothing?'

Coffee arrived steaming hot and Liliana said, 'I close when you finish – it's gonna get nasty out there. People are shouting, singing, and many, many police have guns and big batons. Best to stay in home.'

She needn't have told us. It was impossible to ignore now. I was torn; I wanted to get out there and be part of it and I wanted to be here with him.

'Do you know how worried your family are for your safety? Glykeria has spoken to Will several times. They have seen you on the television, BBC television.'

'I know, that's fantastic! It's so important to tell the world what is happening here.'

He sipped his cooling coffee and told me something I didn't want to hear, didn't want to know.

'My parents are in Athens just now,' he said.

'Can we meet them? Will you bring them to the apartment?'

'I don't think so. They are here for our wedding; Glykeria and I will be married on . . .' and he named a date which disappeared from my mind even as I heard it.

'I told you we were to be married.'

'Oh yes. She's very lovely and I'm sure you will be happy.' I tried to make it sound as though I meant it, but it was hard.

We drank the coffee down, fast, and left. Costas shepherded me through the crowds as best he could.

'I'll take you home.'

'No, Costas. I am going to meet some friends. And I will take care. I won't do anything silly, I promise, promise, cross my heart and hope to die.'

We were facing each other on the edge of the pavement; the crowds were spilling through now from the main street ahead. Our eyes met and he took me in his arms and pulled me into him, a great bear hug. I melted – if I could only stay here.

His hand was on my back, the tips of his fingers so sensual as they brushed my face in passing. My stomach ached with tension; I was hungry for him.

But he pushed me away and I had to get on with being, pretending to be normal.

And, so soon, he would be a married man.

'If you won't go home I don't know what to say to you. I've promised Will to look after you. But if you insist in joining in all this,' and he waved down the street, 'I can promise him nothing. I must go now.'

I looked up at the sky, grey in the wintry gloom, the colour of a dirty bandage.

'I know you feel as I feel. Can you not imagine being me? Now? Would *you* have gone home, and watched from the window as everyone else fought for your freedom?'

His sigh was tired and heavy. 'I do what I can for this revolution of yours by stitching up the wounded. That's how I help.' And he was gone.

I watched him walk away, his collar up, his back straight and tall, hair ruffling in a wind that blew in from somewhere else, smelling of wet chalk. There was about him a weariness that I've only seen since coming to the city. This was not my Constantinos of the jazz club, the beach. When did his dreams grow up, get old and die?

Then he was lost to me in the crowd and I turned and ran back to my school; looking for a sight of Fanis, Pavlos or any of our friends who were planning to join the protest.

Later I learned thirty-seven people were arrested that day, seventeen of them sent for trial. But they were the lucky ones. There was no record of any that died or any that were beaten so severely they would never walk straight again. They joined the nameless crowds of ordinary people who had no special political allegiances, nor fanatical beliefs, not communists, nor anarchists.

I stayed for an hour or so, but today my heart and my mind were elsewhere and I pushed my way through the crowd outside the Ministry of Public Order and went home.

'We came to look for you at your school but that was closed. We went to Liliana's coffee shop but that was locked up.'

Chrissi was home. She had been there for hours; they had closed the store early because of the demonstrations. Haris was with her and they jumped up from the brown sofa when they heard me. Nice to think the love they shared had enriched that bit of old furniture, given it new life, but I doubted it.

Haris said, 'There's a lot of anger out there.'

'Most of it for the police with their iron bars, sticks and guns. They are so scary,' I said.

I threw my things down on the floor and was walking through to the kitchen when Chrissi said, 'I didn't get sacked.'

Of course! It was today, her meeting with personnel. How could I have forgotten?

'I'm so glad.' And I hugged her guiltily. Our eyes met, and I could see she knew. 'I'm so, so sorry. Please don't think I don't care.'

'You're OK,' she said and smiled. 'Other things on your mind.'

Haris added, 'Like changing the world.'

We all had cigs and Haris said, 'Chrissi did well. In fact, they are so impressed with her system of keeping customers loyal, they're going to adopt it in all departments.'

Now we were all laughing.

'Yes, madam, what do you think these towels are worth? Forty drachmas? No problem – give me thirty if you like.'

Every day I went to the gymnasio, I attended my classes, I did my homework, I was a model student. They would all have been proud of me, Costas, Lucy, Will, Hugh. But my heart was in the streets. There was an occasional quiet day but most days more and more people were gathering in forbidden crowds, chanting, meeting together in the Law School, the Department of Medicine, the School of Engineering in the polytechnio. And every day the police grew more and more violent, intolerant.

Rumours spread like a plague; yes, there was a concession to be granted allowing students the freedom to elect their own councils, but within hours this was denied again. Another day we heard about some secret document circulating telling of plans the Authority had to bring in the army to squash the protests. For a long time now the meetings had been about more issues than student rights.

The crowds were so big all the time, and everywhere it seemed they could not be peacefully moved on.

Everywhere there was a terrible sense of hopelessness. The days were cloudy and still with the sort of winter warmth you get in a city with little hope of sunshine. Everyone walked with heads down, hurrying, scurrying.

We were struggling home, Chrissi and I, a few days later. Pushing and jostling our way through another march that was filling and spilling over the pavements and roads around the Ministry of Public Order.

Aphrodite, Yorgo and Manoli were coming on the ferry today and we had arranged to meet to collect Manoli's accordion. Although we had long ago spent the money Heavenly had left for us to buy it, we had set aside something from my allowance each month. That, topped up with some of Chrissi's earnings meant we had enough at last.

'He's probably forgotten how to play,' said Chrissi, 'or taken up the lyre instead.'

The streets were crowded as always now; shoppers, house-wives mingled with people carrying banners. Over everything, as always, the sounds of sirens among shouts and screams – a monstrous cacophony of sound.

'When did they last come to Athens?' I asked.

'Years and years ago, when Aristos and Irini got married.'

'They are going to be in for a surprise then.'

APHRODITE

Aristos was waiting for us at Piraeus. His face was drawn and tight: no smile of welcome. We struggled through with our bags and he loaded them quickly into the boot of his car.

'New car,' I said, looking at the gleaming chrome and the spotless cream body. 'Expensive.'

'Alfa Romeo,' said Yorgo rubbing at a tiny speck of dirt on a window. 'Very nice.'

'We've had it for some years now. Listen, get in and I'll take you to the Timberlakes' apartment. I have to get back to the hospital straight away; we are in a constant state of emergency these days.'

The car slid soundlessly forward along the quays and finally through the gates at the end of the docks. That was the last we had of peace and quiet, until the day we left this city. It took two hours to get to Plutarchou Street and it was already dark. I have never seen so many people in my life. You couldn't hear yourself think for the screams of the sirens and all the time the constant drone of a helicopter circling over our heads.

It was not a hot day, but Aristos was sweating and tense at the wheel. He had the window open as he inched forward through the crowds.

'He'll give himself a heart attack,' I whispered to Yorgo beside me. But he wasn't listening, he was too busy reading out loud the words that were being carried through the streets: *FASCISM WILL PERISH* and *DOWN WITH PAPA-DOPOULOS*.

'That's a good one, look, "WORKERS PEASANTS" and

"STUDENTS UNITE". It's all happening here, Aphrodite. The revolution is here and now. We are lucky to be part of it. Look, Manoli, see all the people with the placards? Peaceful protest. Very good.'

But Manoli said, 'Will we see AEK Athens' stadium if we go this way, Aristos? I want to get a T-shirt.'

Aristos ignored us all. You couldn't blame him.

Chrissi and Angel were waiting for us and Chrissi made coffee – it was good. She behaved as if she owned this apartment, I thought, as she opened the big fridge and passed Yorgo a beer.

Manoli was too excited to drink anything as he was holding his gift from the girls, an accordion. Well, they told me it was really from Heavenly. He stroked every part of it lovingly.

'Is it for me to keep?' he asked over and over as he sat tenderly fingering the keys with his rough woodworker's hands. However many times they told him it was his, he still kept asking the question.

They liked our new clothes.

'I have never seen you in a suit before, Papa,' said Chrissi, and he puffed up with pride and tugged on his tie. He was very impressed that Angel took such a part in these demonstrations.

'Bof to that!' I said. 'Does Will know what you do each day?'

'I work at the gymnasio each day, Aunt, and when I come home I do the homework, don't I, Chrissi? You tell them.'

Chrissi was working in a new department in the store. I suppose they thought she was too clever to stay with ribbons and trimmings forever; so now she sells ladies' underwear.

'You must see them, Mama. I can get you some with a staff discount, lovely lace and silk.'

Before I could say 'Rubbish, what do I want with lace and silk?' Yorgo had answered her for me.

'Please get her some; I will pay,' he said. 'Do you have different sizes? Because she is a big lady.' And he was indicating how big – as if he were holding a couple of melons in his hands.

'Stop it, Yorgo! Take no notice of him. He is an embarrassment,' I said.

'No, Mama, you will have some, you can wear them when you see the specialist doctor.'

'I certainly will not do anything like that! Bad enough I will have to take my clothes off.'

Angel said goodbye and went out very quickly.

'Where does she go now?' I asked and Yorgo said longingly, 'She has gone to the demonstration – I wish I could go with her.'

'Don't talk such rubbish, you are far too old for such nonsense.'

I was in the kitchen then preparing our meal. As I expected, the fridge was empty of anything except beer. Thank the Panagia I have brought food from home; *horta*, cheeses, Cretan bread, tomatoes, yoghourt and a rabbit Yorgo shot, along with some potatoes. Cretan potatoes are the very best; even if the girls had some already they would be city-grown rubbish. There will be a big *stifado* for everyone tonight.

We got to the hospital early. In all these crowds how did I know we could get through at all? But the streets were emptier. I put Yorgo and Manoli in a café nearby and told them to wait. Manoli had not left the accordion for a moment. I think he is afraid someone will take it away from him if he lets it out of his sight.

I awoke early. I don't sleep well in the city. There is so much noise here. And even though I listened all night I didn't hear Angel return. Yorgo drank a lot of their beer and slept like the dead. When I woke him at seven he told me I had snored all night and kept him awake!

I made coffee for everyone and put out some *kalitsounia* to dip in, but Chrissi ran out of the door after one mouthful and there was still no sign of Angel. Yorgo said perhaps she has a boyfriend. But if that is true and she is staying with him, I think that is not good for Chrissi. Maybe she will think she can do the same.

The doctor was late. I sat in a thin grey gown a nurse thrust at me. My clothes had to go in a locker, all screwed up and I pulled at the wrapper, too small for my size.

And the nurse called me and I stood and shivered in this too-thin, too-small gown, and followed her along a corridor and into a room. There was a schoolboy sitting there. He looked up.

'Please sit down, Kyria Babyottis.'

And I did. And then the door opened again and a swarm of young people in white coats with notebooks and pens flocked in and stood behind me in half a circle.

He read from a paper which seemed to be all about me then said, 'Please lie down, Kyria Babyottis.'

And I had no choice but to lie on his couch, pulling fast at my wrapper. I shut my eyes tight and wished this whole time was over and I was at home in Panagia again.

Yorgo and Manoli had gone from the café when I got there. At first I thought they might be in the toilet, so I sat where I had left them and waited. Nothing. Ten minutes, eleven minutes, nothing. They had gone.

The woman making the coffee said they had left a couple of hours ago. I think I left them too long. The schoolboy doctor had been so slow that most of the morning had gone. He only told me there was nothing for him to do that a doctor in the hospital in Heraklion couldn't do as well. A small operation, remove something inside me as big as an orange, and Poof! I would be fine again. All this fuss and expense to be told that! And now I have lost my husband and sons well. I hate this city.

There was the sound of sirens screeching through the thick, steel-coloured air. No sun shone. There was shouting, then screams and the sound of a drum, or something like a drum. I would get in a taxi if there were one. I would get on a bus if I knew where and how; or go on the under-the-ground train, but I didn't know where I would go to.

Everyone seemed to be walking in the opposite direction, away from me. And all of them looked as if they knew where they were going.

I am a strong woman who has run her family for years. I am their rock. I tend our *gypo*, harvest our crops in our fields, care for our olives and our grapes, look after our chickens and goats. And here I am with a schoolboy's orange inside my belly; somewhere in the middle of our capital city, and I am lost and alone and afraid. If I was a woman who knew how to weep, that is what I would do.

I somehow got myself back to the apartment by the end of the day. I was alone there.

So I sat. And I waited.

I had some coffee and a *kalitsounia* and a piece of my cheese. And waited more. I looked through the window; the curtains needed a good wash. The streets outside looked cold, dark and angry. I got out of my good new clothes, no point in wearing them out, and put on an old dress I had brought. I rinsed through my underwear and my stockings, and then thought that I might as well do the curtains as well. Then I saw there was nowhere to dry them except over the bath. So that had to do.

One by one they all returned; thank you, *Panagia mou*. Yorgo didn't want to tell me, at first, but I guessed. He had taken Manoli and the accordion and joined the demonstration outside the Ministry of Public Order.

'It was such an experience, Aphrodite, you should have been there too. There were many women but the police were brutes; hitting out left and right, anyone who was in their way. People were shot, even. I saw three people fall, wounded, and then they disappeared. I heard one policeman shout "slug the flesh". There was a man beside me, he said, "that means shoot".'

' "Why?" I asked. "This is a peaceful protest, isn't it? The only weapons are in the hands of the police." But he just laughed at me. "Clearly you are from out-of-town," he said.'

Earlier, when I needed a policeman to tell me the way, to help me, there was not one to be seen.

'Where is your new tie, Yorgo?' I asked.

His hand went to his neck.

'Aah, I'm not sure. I think someone pulled it off.'

'They did, they did, Papa, the man with the red hair and nose. You said he was drunk.' It was Manoli speaking now. 'Look, Mama, see how much money I got.' And he showed me a handful of silver coins. 'I played my accordion outside a café, and people were very kind and gave me money.'

'So you took our son to beg on the streets?' I said.

'It wasn't begging, Mama. They paid me for playing for them, that's all.'

Yorgo shrugged. He turned to go to the fridge, another beer. Then I saw the back of his new suit; there was blood and it was torn.

'Ah, *Panagia mou*, look at that!' I said and as he turned I saw he had a bruise down the side of his face. It was partly hidden by his big moustache, but it was there.

Finally Chrissi came back and all she could say to me was, 'We have a washing machine, Mama. You didn't need to do this.'

At last Angel came back.

'I saw you, Uncle,' she said. 'I was on the other side of the street. My friend Pavlos had a banner that said "DOWN WITH NATO". Did you see us? I waved.'

They sat together, Yorgo, Angel and my Manoli, as if they had been at a party; a wedding perhaps or a baptism; certainly a celebration.

'They were using tear gas when I left, did you see that, Uncle?'

Chrissi said, 'Tear gas? Oh, *Panagia*. That is very bad.'

And then my heart nearly stopped beating as Angel said, 'Tomorrow is going to be the big one. All of us are going in groups to the polytechnio, and we are going to stay there until the end.'

'What does that mean, what is the end?'

'We will win, Aunt. I am sure of it. Just think what it will mean; no more *malakas* in the villages. No more of those beasts running your lives, telling you how to live. Telling you your children must only go out after seven if they are with you. Making you cut the olives for the church, not for yourselves. Oh, you know! Making Manoli mend the road. Things like that.'

I looked at her, this child I had watched growing into a woman, all the passion of her mother alight in her eyes. I knew she believed what she was saying.

'But it is so dangerous,' I said. 'The police are out there with guns, shooting with tear gas and who knows what else. It is too dangerous.'

'No, no, we have to make it stop somehow. And if we don't it will go on forever.'

She was like a child again now. I thought she would stamp her foot in a moment.

And all I could see, looking at her, was her mother.

The babble of their voices surrounded me, happy, laughing. Manoli was quietly fingering the keys of the accordion. Outside, the noises of the night slithered into this room, and they were not happy sounds.

ANGEL

First Glykeria had rung me, then Will. All I knew was they wanted to stop me being part of all this.

Will said, 'The city is a keg of gunpowder waiting to explode.'

I listened but I said, 'I'm sorry. I *have* listened to all of you, including Chrissi and all her family. And you know, I'm tired of everyone telling me what to do. It's just like when you all wanted me to go to school in England. I didn't do that and I did what I wanted, and I'm here now and you all know I am doing well at school, working hard, getting good grades. And I am going to this one last demonstration. All my friends will be there; they said Sofia Vembo the singer will be there. Everyone! And that must include me.'

I hated all this battling. I'm worn out with telling them over and over I can make my own decisions. Perhaps after this they really will realise I know what I'm doing and just let me live my own life.

Aphrodite had made a rabbit stew, and although I was so excited I thought I couldn't eat a thing, I managed two platefuls. It was delicious and I thought, Who knows? Maybe there will be no food for me tomorrow.

At midnight the phone rang yet again. Everyone was asleep and snoring, even Aphrodite.

It was Costas.

'Do you insist on going through with this?' he asked.

'Yes. Come with me. See for yourself. I am going to do this and I won't stop because you ask me to. OK?'

There was a pause and then he said, 'Come to the hospital first, in the evening. I can't say a time, its non-stop there. I am allowed a couple of hours' break. Maybe there will be a need for a doctor in the polytechnio. I will go with you.'

And the phone went down and he'd gone.

The next day the streets in the centre were either totally deserted or crammed with people. There seemed nothing in between. Banners, some shredded already, littered the pavements. There were rags in gutters that could have been flags once or even, I shuddered, the remains of a person. In one avenue two men were propped against a tree waving a bottle.

I had been to the polytechnio several times during the day. People were coming and going all the time; there were songs, cheers, laments. It was heavy with noise and feelings. As daylight faded more and more were staying and it was getting crowded.

Darkness was falling when I arrived at the hospital. As I went in through the big old doors I remembered visiting Costas in this hospital, a million years ago from here and now. Quiet, almost deserted it was then. This place was screaming with activity.

Trolleys were rushed through with arms dangling from seemingly lifeless bodies. Nurses ran alongside holding those drip stands that they always have on the TV medical shows. Old doctors, young doctors and orderlies, all mixed up with old ladies clutching bandaged limbs; a man on crutches, a bloody wrapped leg in front of him. A child in its mother's arms crying fit to burst with blood running down a tiny face and matting into black, plaited hair. So much blood is shocking. I felt I wanted to shut my eyes, make it go away. I did briefly, but when I opened them I think it was worse.

Outside the scream of sirens was non-stop. I was still near the entrance so the noise was mixed with the squeal of thick rubber tyres. It was bedlam here.

I managed to find a desk and a nurse – or someone who looked like a nurse – and asked her to page Costas. She waved me to a seat and I sat next to an exotically dressed girl who must have come from a party. She was sitting over a pool of urine on the floor. The hem of her silk dress trailed in it and I pointed to it, but she merely looked at me through dead eyes and didn't move.

The nurse at the desk called to me, 'He will come when he can. Will you wait?'

'Yes,' I said. 'Of course.'

I don't know how long it took, but when I looked up Costas was standing over me.

I stood up and he gave me a quick hug, but he didn't smile. His eyes were glazed with exhaustion.

'I can take two hours,' he said, 'no more. Let's go.'

I raced along beside him trying to keep up with his long strides. Tired as he clearly was, he still walked like an athlete.

Outside he strode across the car park and stopped by his old, rather battered, silver Mercedes. He opened my door and then he was in and we were off on our way out of the hospital. He said, 'Everyone knows the students are staging a sit-in tonight.'

He drove slowly through the streets. I had never seen so many police, and said so.

'There are rumours they are bringing in the army now tonight as well. I hope that's not true.'

But we saw armoured vehicles and troops with machine guns walking in formation on the street. There were no traffic signals working, but it hardly mattered: we could only crawl along through the people. As we got closer I could see through the crowds that the gates were open and there was a constant stream of people moving in and out. People were climbing all over the gates and sitting on top of the pillars.

We could see people everywhere carrying bags of food and drink and handing them through the bars and throwing them over the heads of others.

Half a dozen armed police saw Costas's car, the medical pass on his windscreen and roughly cleared the way for us to go ahead.

Once we were through the gates, more police appeared.

They were everywhere, and they told him to leave his car inside the gates and go forward on foot.

The atmosphere was electric.

The crowds were cheering and singing; it really was possible to believe you were in the middle of a revolution. And that you would win! I held on to Costas's sleeve and even he smiled for a moment.

Then he was grabbed by an elderly man, wiry grey hair standing on end, his glasses slightly askew, who said in a low voice, 'Someone said you're a doctor, is that right?'

Costas nodded and the man pulled us through towards one of the buildings of the polytechnicnio in front of us.

'Stay with me for the time being,' Costas said, but I had no intention of going anywhere without him. We walked briskly through a door and up a flight of institutional grey stairs; then along a corridor with people running to and fro, pushing past us.

We were hustled in through a door and into what I guessed in more normal times was a lecture room. The ceilings were high; metal beams strutted across, and some chairs were lying on their sides on a stage.

There was a deathly quiet suddenly in here. In the corner, a woman kneeling on the floor next to some shrouded thing, was silently praying, crossing herself again and again; beside her, an older woman stood as if to attention, her hand on the kneeling woman's head. Over everything was a smell, a strong coppery smell, and I knew it was blood. There were bodies lying on makeshift beds and, as Costas moved among them, I realised this was a war hospital.

The groans here were muted, the living mingled among the dead. It was hard to tell which was which at first, but as my eyes grew accustomed to what I was seeing and my brain opened for me to take it all in, I could soon tell the difference.

The living looked at us. The faces of the dead, three, four I counted, were covered. This was not the place for a casual onlooker.

Costas was saying something to the man with the glasses, then he turned to me and said, 'Can you help?'

'Of course! What shall I do?'

'Here,' and from his bag he produced a couple of packs of cotton wool and said to the man, 'Do you have water, anything?'

The man climbed over the bodies back to the stage and from underneath produced a large bottle of clear liquid. Costas looked at the label.

'Vodka,' he said. 'It'll do.' He passed everything to me and said, 'Wash the wounds.'

He was arguing now with the man. As I knelt beside a young man and pulled the stained sheet from his body, I heard him say, 'We can certify the dead later. For God's sake, let's try and help those still living.'

For an hour, I guess, I worked alongside Costas, feebly doing what I could, what I was told to do. There were two bodies, their shoulders ripped open with gunshot wounds. I soon learned to tell the difference between the ragged exit holes and the cleaner entry wounds. It didn't take long to see that these people had been shot in the back.

'What about the bullets?' I asked.

Costas shrugged and said, 'Later, later.'

Three young men, barely out of their teens, had badly bruised faces; one girl, her T-shirt ripped across her back, had a slash across her forehead that would need stitches.

A man in a once-white coat came in, and Costas called to him. 'Can you take over here?' He stood up, stretched his clearly aching back, and said to me, 'Let's get out now. I have to get back to the hospital; you saw what it was like there tonight.'

All the time more and more were pressing in through the door. I had a quick flash of memory; the infirmary in The Oaks; a good place to bunk off with a headache. Only there the smell was of TCP and lavender water, the clean, good smells of healing. This felt more like a slaughterhouse.

Outside the building the almost impossible had happened

and yet more had come in. We pressed and twisted our way through the crowds. I could see steps ahead leading to the main building. That's where I had been earlier with my friends. That's where I wanted to go now.

Costas was behind me, his hand on my back. Students were three deep at least, up there.

'Every young Greek in the country must be here tonight,' I tried calling to Costas over my shoulder, but my words were swept away in the whirlwind of noise; laughter, screams, cries, cheers and a rhythmic chant of 'Victory! Victory over the Junta tonight!' There was Fanis on top of a pillar, Pavlos beside him, hanging on. They were laughing.

A girl beside me, a crimson flower pinned in her hair, said, 'They've negotiated a truce. Everyone's leaving now. It's over we've won!'

Two o'clock in the morning. The sky was dark above, not a single star, not a hint of moon, just a black mass of silent clouds. I could feel a movement backwards, heavy shifting bodies en masse towards the gates.

I reached the top of the steps. Costas was still being pushed behind me and from here I could see the gates. They were closed. Surely that was wrong? As I turned, puzzled, Costas said, 'Look what's there.'

And I saw the tanks outside, three of them. I also saw Costas's car, trapped inside. How would he get to the hospital?

I gripped the collar of his coat.

'I'm so glad you're here,' I said.

Five minutes past two in the morning. The crowd was still heaving as a single entity towards those gates. I thought again, Why are they closed? How will we all get out?

Costas was still behind me.

Ten minutes past two in the morning. The crowd was jubilant, excited, chanting and singing, 'Junta out!' and 'Goodbye, Papadopoulos, goodbye!' I could sense the thrill of their victory shiver through my bones – a great feeling. A woman next to me in a headscarf clutched a carrier bag with half a dozen loaves of bread sticking out, as if she had just been to the shops instead of being part of this.

She said, 'Perhaps I'll get my sister back now . . .'

All around, everyone was waving, cheering and I cheered too.

'The war is over!' A man, no more than twenty, with startlingly deep brown eyes said, 'They've given us half an hour to get out. But everyone knows we've won. The whole of Athens is with us tonight.'

I felt his joy, his release and for a moment I shared his triumph. I too had lived through it all.

Fifteen minutes past two in the morning. And the movement now came from the other direction, from the gates.

They're opening them, I thought, but they must hurry if we've only got another fifteen minutes to get everyone here out to safety.

And then, terribly, horribly, a sound I will never forget until I die: the great grinding motion of those tanks coming crashing onwards; metal grinding over metal.

And the beginnings of the first screams.

But the gates are closed, I thought, how can they . . .

But then it was all too clear, and the tanks ploughed through those seemingly immovable iron gates, grinding and crushing them like twigs. I saw people fall off the pillars into the forecourt and go under those rolling chunks of metal. I saw Costas's car, in which I had sat a short lifetime ago, crushed now beneath a tank.

The songs of jubilation were finished; replaced by screams of pain, terror, panic. This crowd now was mad with horror and fear. Armed men in khaki uniforms were jumping from the top of the tanks and, guns blazing, were clearing away everyone in their sight. I saw, we all saw, young men fall, girls drop like flies; the air was thick with pain and desperation, we would all surely die . . .

And still they kept on rolling forwards.

'Costas!' I screamed it aloud.

The crowd was scattering; some to safety but many underfoot or shot or beaten down. Those soldiers had guns, but the police were there too, and those that weren't armed carried heavy wooden staves or metal bars and beat around them, knocking everyone away.

I was still in front of Costas and he was lifting me high up and back to the steps and, hopefully, safety. He looked back over his shoulder. Did he see what I saw? A swarthy, thick-bodied soldier, raising his rifle to his shoulder, taking aim. My mouth was open in a scream. I called 'Costas!' just once and he held me close, tight.

The soldier fired and we fell together.

I have tried and tried to keep my thoughts, my memories, of every moment of that night truthful. It is important to be honest, to be clear, because somewhere there is a mother who will want to know; somewhere a lover who will never be a bride, never be a wife. There are dreams that will never be shared and lives that will never be lived.

Always, now, there is a taste of guilt at the back of my throat, trickling down like a vile poison. If I had never . . . if I had only . . . But these are only my pathetic attempts to explain the unexplainable.

That week I knew everything was building towards that night. We all did. All of us who were in this city. We had seen the violence escalating all that month.

And I think back, with shame, to the thrill at being part of it. As if that mattered? As if I was of any importance? The movement had been growing slowly for years and years without me.

I am horrified to remember some of that last week. I lived with death, violent death, and if I am truthful with myself, dare I admit I had even been a little excited by it?

And Costas? He was there for me, because of me, no other reason.

I heard that on 14th November 1973, a man, an ordinary man of thirty-seven, a clerk in the Ministry of the Interior, took his two children for a walk.

The air was crisp, fresh, cold but sunny. His wife was making lunch, *pastitsio*, for his parents. He crossed the road; the children, a boy of seven and a girl of five held his hands. He crossed to avoid a march, a demonstration, alongside them. The police poured into the street, guns waving, a dozen or more of them, and as they fired randomly to disperse the crowd, one of their bullets hit the man and he fell, taking his screaming children down with him. I don't know what happened to him.

I heard about an old lady of seventy-six, on the same day, at four o'clock in the afternoon, walking slowly because she had arthritis, to meet her sister in the Botanic Gardens. She was shot in the street. Many saw her fall, no one saw her rise.

I heard that on Thursday 15th November at eleven twenty in the morning an electrician working on a building jumped down to get some coffee and see what the noise was all about, and was shot as he fell. He was twenty-three.

On Friday 16th November I heard of a man who left work early to collect his two daughters from school, twins of nearly eight. Because there was another demonstration outside the Ministry of Public Order that afternoon, he walked them quickly around the block to safety. Not safe enough; he was caught in crossfire and fell. He lay there, bleeding to death, while the two little girls screamed and cried for help – none came.

During those days twenty-six people, *ordinary* people, died a violent death. They were going about their lawful business, and they were randomly killed.

That last day, the last time when Costas came to my school, he warned me, and I said, 'I'll take care.'

Who wouldn't say that? But what did it mean? Did it stop me taking part in every single demonstration, every march I could find? No of course not. And on that last, fatal night, inside the gates of the polytechnio, which everyone knew later was the moment the reign of the colonels ended, we were there together and I only felt excitement and love. What harm was there to come? How could we know?

At two o'clock in the morning of 17th November a truce was negotiated – a peaceful withdrawal. Thirty minutes to evacuate the polytechnio. But when it came we were given less than ten.

Then the tanks came rolling through, crushing the gates and everyone before them. I opened my arms for Costas and he was there.

I saw the soldier. I saw his gun, I saw him see me, raise it, and take aim.

Then I only saw Costas; reaching up to me, and I fell into his arms. Giddy with the excitement of the moment. We had won! We were there together and victory was ours.

He held me so tightly in those great, strong swimmer's arms. I smelt the clean sweetness of his skin, the slight antiseptic tinge of his hands and his hair. And flickering rapidly through my mind were all the images of him that I store in secret compartments of my brain; never to be revealed.

And, my face against his, I kissed his cheek.

I heard the sharp crack of a shot, followed by another. But there were many of those, all around us. I felt his body spasm, once, and then again. He was suddenly heavy in my arms.

I held him as tightly as I could, but it was not tight enough and he sank to his knees, his hands shaking, trembling, his face turned up to the dark sky, his special smell now gone, replaced by the choking thickness of gunshot and petrol bombs. Only those scents of violence remained and as he sank to the ground, his face turned up to me, his eyes slowly misted.

304

I still held him in my arms and clumsily went down with him.

'Costas?' I whispered into his pale face. 'Costas? Costas?'

He didn't answer, of course he didn't answer. How could he? And the tears that were gathering in my eyes and my throat trickled slowly down and I gasped, 'No, Costas, no, oh please . . .' Then slowly my tears ran down on to his face, his dear beloved face. And I kissed him. At first his cheek and then I pressed my lips to his lips, and I thought of that sweet salty kiss on the beach.

When I raised my head and looked, I saw those lips were now blue.

I buried my face in his shoulder and sobbed as though my heart would break.

I whispered, 'I love you. Please don't . . . please don't . . .'

What had I done? He was there now, where I have always longed for him to be, in my arms. But not like this, oh please, not like this.

We stayed like that. I don't know how long. I didn't care any more. The air, still heavy with the sounds of guns and pain, was thick and hard to breathe.

It was only then that I found my hands were red with his blood, and the front of my coat, my old school coat, which had been pressed tight to him, was drenched and sodden with his blood.

I knew then, that the love I had for this man would be with me for the rest of my life. This moment when he died, saving my life, would be with me, waking and sleeping, forever. I knew I could never, *would* never, love like this again.

APHRODITE

It fell to me to pick up the pieces of that terrible night. Angel was hopeless; no, she was without hope, you could see it. And Will tried, but could offer only small comfort, it seemed. He had flown in, somehow knowing we would all need his strength.

I knew all the pieces of the big picture – the whole world did, I think, knew that night was the beginning of the end for the *malakas*, although the demonstrations continued for days. The State of Emergency lasted for a week. The police and the soldiers patrolled the streets and anyone who disobeyed the curfew knew their life was in danger.

My Yorgo did not know how to understand all that was going on. He was pleased, happy to have been part of this moment of history. Yet everywhere there was grief, emptiness, and nowhere more so than in that apartment.

There was a funeral. Well, there were a thousand funerals, but this was one we all had to attend, it seemed. A doctor, young he was, had been a friend of Will and apparently of Chrissi and Angel, too. Was it for him that Angel wept her heart out? Or another friend, a victim of the violence? I didn't ask.

But this young man, this Constantinos, was to have been married on the day we buried him. Now that *is* sad.

We could not bury him the day after he died, as is usual. His death was violent. It takes longer.

But no matter, it was winter. We left the apartment on

Plutarchou Street, and Angel could barely stand unless she was supported by Will and Chrissi on either side.

She seemed, that day, a thin creature dwarfed by her grief. I said to her, 'Why go, if it distresses you so much. No one will mind.'

But she gave me such a look. I kept my thinking to myself after that.

It wasn't far to the church; we walked there. It was only when we were there and waiting for the coffin to arrive, that Yorgo started nudging me. At first I ignored him but he poked harder as the coffin came around the corner.

'Aphrodite, look, look! This is family, *our* family.'

At first I didn't know what he was talking about, and then I saw.

The young woman in the veil, the fiancée, was holding tight on to an older woman.

This woman, her head was lowered, but then she raised it, and, ravaged by grief as it was, I saw it was Sophia, niece to Yorgo. Her husband, there he was, beside her, was the fisherman, Petros Dukakis. He had carried the coffin at the last funeral we attended, of Yorgo's nephew, Christo. No, oh no! Please, no. But I knew. This young doctor who had died, had been killed, was Christo's godson. I remembered him so well, Sophia's golden boy.

Of course we filed slowly past the coffin and I glanced inside, crossing myself.

Panagia mou, his young face, too young to die. His hair; curly and wild with streaks of red among the black and silver. I know this hair, oh, *Panagia mou* – who is it who has hair like this? I thought it before, and death has not changed him. This Constantinos's eyes were closed of course, but I knew they were blue, clear bright blue, I recall. Minoan eyes.

I didn't linger; you don't on these occasions, but I sat throughout the ceremony trying to pull that face into my living memory.

Later, at the home of the fiancée, Glykeria, we ate the

funeral *kollyva* and drank *metaxa* or raki and I spoke with
Sophia. And through her tears she told me about the boy.

'I didn't tell you before, Aphrodite, he was not truly my
son. But we raised him from infancy, and you should know I
loved him as my own. We were not blessed, as you were, with
children. I had thought my life would dry up as my womb had
done. But my brother, Christo . . .'

Sophia was scrubbing at her eyes now, as though she could
wipe the grief away. We were standing alone, she and I. And in
the garden of this house, under a wintry sky the iron colour of
old wool, she told me that Christo had rescued an orphan
child and brought him to her to nurture.

'He told me the parents were dead at the hands of the
Germans. There were no papers, of course. So many of these
babies, children, were the nameless victims of the war.'

My mind was busy as I listened; picking and scrambling
through small memories of my own; unknitting one thread
and stitching random pieces together; trying to make one
whole piece that made sense to me.

Sophia looked around her. I knew she was checking on
the whereabouts of her husband who was inside the house
standing with the jug of raki in his hand.

'Christo was godfather to my boy, my Constantinos. But,'
she paused, 'you know, Aphrodite, I often wondered, often
thought, but only to myself, I never said; he gave so much love
to the boy that I wondered if perhaps he could be Christo's
own son? His eyes, you see, that same deep blue.'

'Minoan eyes,' I said almost under my breath.

'Precisely so.'

I nodded slowly; she didn't need more comment from me.

'Maybe Christo had loved a woman and perhaps she died,
something like that? And so he stayed with the child, brought
him to us knowing we would love him as our own. We will
never know. Excuse me now, I must speak with Glykeria's
Yaya – she is on her own.' And she moved away.

I stood alone for a while. Chrissi was over there, by a walnut
tree, its branches bare now of fruit. With her stood a young

man, stocky, handsome. I had seen him waiting outside the church. She was laughing at him with her eyes. I must watch this, for sure. There will be no Panagia wedding for her if she gives away her love in the city.

And standing all alone was Angel, just over there by the wooden gate to the flower garden. A sudden ray of unexpected sunshine spilled on to her face. It was afternoon, that time around three o'clock when the day pauses.

She looked so like her mother. So smooth and innocent on the surface, with no cracks through which her inner feelings showed through. And as I thought of Heavenly, I pictured her as I first saw her with her wild hair, streaked with red, that resisted her every effort to tame it.

Then I remembered her big with child and her voice, low like music as she said, 'Teach me to knit, Aphrodite.'

We never saw that child, a boy. We were told he died at birth.

None of us questioned, we were too busy with our own grief; the grief that war always brings.

And with that memory, I think the last small piece of the puzzle slowly fell into place.

Angel saw me looking at her and came towards me.

'Is something wrong, Aunt?'

I didn't answer at once. Then I smiled, patted her arm, and said, 'Nothing, Angel, nothing at all. Just thinking of your mother.'

And she smiled then, her first smile for days, but a sad half smile and said, 'I was thinking of her too. I wish she had met Constantinos. I always thought they would like each other. I knew he was to be married – he always made that clear to me – and I like Glykeria so much. But . . .' and she lowered her voice, 'I liked him, you know. More than liked.' I could see her eyes filling with tears, and she said, 'There was a gypsy once, told me I would not be lucky in love.'

Oh, *Panagia mou*! I crossed myself three times.

'I think she was right, child.' I patted her arm awkwardly.

'Just for now, anyway. This young doctor belonged to another; he was not right for you.'

The faint yellow sunshine flickered through the branches of an old tree near the garden; the sun had finally found us.

Hamilton